Mistakes Were Made

Lucy Score is an instant #1 *New York Times* and *Sunday Times* bestselling author of contemporary romance. She grew up in a literary family, who insisted that the dinner table was for reading, and earned a degree in journalism. Her books have been translated into thirty languages and her international bestseller *Things We Never Got Over* has been optioned for television.

She writes full-time from the Pennsylvania home she and Mr. Lucy share with their opinionated cat, Cleo. When not spending hours crafting unforgettable characters, Lucy can be found reading books other people wrote, snacking and sometimes even working out.

Also by Lucy Score

KNOCKEMOUT SERIES
Things We Never Got Over
Things We Hide From the Light
Things We Left Behind

RILEY THORN SERIES
The Dead Guy Next Door
The Corpse in the Closet
The Blast from the Past
The Body in the Backyard

BENEVOLENCE SERIES
Pretend You're Mine
Finally Mine
Protecting What's Mine

SINNER AND SAINT SERIES
Crossing the Line
Breaking the Rules

WELCOME HOME SERIES
Mr. Fixer Upper
The Christmas Fix

STORY LAKE SERIES
Story of My Life

BLUE MOON SERIES
No More Secrets
Fall into Temptation
The Last Second Chance
Not Part of the Plan
Holding on to Chaos
The Fine Art of Faking It
Where It All Began
The Mistletoe Kisser

BOOTLEG SPRINGS SERIES
Whiskey Chaser
Sidecar Crush
Moonshine Kiss
Bourbon Bliss
Gin Fling
Highball Rush

STANDALONES
By a Thread
Forever Never
Rock Bottom Girl
The Worst Best Man
The Price of Scandal
Undercover Love
Heart of Hope
Maggie Moves On

Mistakes Were Made

LUCY SCORE

HODDER &
STOUGHTON

First published in the United States by BloomBooks,
an imprint of Source Books, in 2026
First published in Great Britain in 2026 by Hodder & Stoughton Limited
An Hachette UK company

The authorised representative in the EEA is Hachette Ireland,
8 Castlecourt Centre, Dublin 15, D15 XTP3, Ireland (email: info@hbgi.ie)

1

Copyright © Lucy Score 2026

The right of Lucy Score to be identified as the Author of the Work has been
asserted by her in accordance with the Copyright, Designs and Patents Act 1988.

Map art by Camila Gray
Internal design © 2026 by Sourcebooks
Internal spot art by Ellis Jones/Sourcebooks
Zoey chapter header image © Olena Zagoruyko/Getty Images, Chaiwate Chat-uthai
Gage chapter header image © oknebulog/Getty Images, procurator/Getty Images

All rights reserved. No part of this publication may be reproduced, stored
in a retrieval system, or transmitted, in any form or by any means without
the prior written permission of the publisher, nor be otherwise circulated
in any form of binding or cover other than that in which it is published and
without a similar condition being imposed on the subsequent purchaser.

All characters in this publication are fictitious and any resemblance to real persons,
living or dead, is purely coincidental.

A CIP catalogue record for this title is available from the British Library

Paperback ISBN 9781399726979
ebook ISBN 9781399726986

Typeset in Adobe Garamond Pro

Printed and bound in Great Britain by Clays Ltd, Elcograf S.p.A.

Hodder & Stoughton policy is to use papers that are natural, renewable
and recyclable products and made from wood grown in sustainable forests.
The logging and manufacturing processes are expected to conform
to the environmental regulations of the country of origin.

Hodder & Stoughton Limited
Carmelite House
50 Victoria Embankment
London EC4Y 0DZ

www.hodder.co.uk

To everyone who has ever been too much and not enough.

1

A snake to the face
Zoey

My cousin was lucky she was an entire state away and that murder was illegal.

"Inez," I said with the last of my patience. "I need you to take the hysteria down about eight notches. I can't help you when you're incoherently wailing."

"Why do you sound like you're in a cave?" Inez demanded, temporarily forgetting whatever drama had caused her to call me in a panic. "Holy shit, Zoey! Are you trapped in an *actual* cave?"

I would have rolled my eyes, but seeing as how I was belly down exploring the nether region under my bed, the effort would have been wasted. "Yes, Inez," I said dryly. "I'm trapped in a cave but I'm so selfless I didn't want to bother you with my life-threatening situation when you called."

"Oh my God!" My gullible cousin's screech through the speaker made my ears want to bleed. "Okay, drop me a pin, and I'll send the Mounties or whoever climbs into caves to rescue people."

"For the love of God. I'm not spelunking. I'm under my bed

looking for a boot. Call off the Mounties, who are Canadian by the way. I'm in Pennsylvania." I continued to scan the dark abyss beneath the lodge's king-size bed with my phone's flashlight.

So that's where my fuzzy knee socks went.

"You're sure you're not trapped in a cave about to be eaten by bats?"

"Positive." *Aha!* I spotted the missing Stuart Weitzman boot wedged between the rustic nightstand and bed leg. It cost me a strained neck muscle and a bump on the head to wrestle it free.

"Good. So back to me then. Where am I going to *liiive*?"

We Moodys were a dramatic people.

"Here's a thought," I said as I inched my way out from under the bed. "Why don't you keep staying in my apartment? You know. The one-bedroom, third-floor walk-up that I generously sublet to you while I temporarily moved to Teeny Hallmarkville. Are you giving up on your modeling-slash-catering career already?"

Inez had moved to Manhattan with dreams of launching a topless catering company. But as she put it, *like an* artsy *topless catering company.* The last I'd heard, she was only serving cold passed appetizers after an unfortunate incident with hot tomato soup.

Out of breath and massaging my sore neck, I threw myself onto the mattress and surveyed the disaster masquerading as my hotel room. Piles of clean and dirty laundry vied for floor space. My "work stuff"—a.k.a. my laptop and several small paperwork explosions—spilled across the bed and occupied the tiny two-person table under the room's expansive lake-view window. The small closet had experienced a clothing apocalypse, and now the doors no longer closed.

Living and working in a hotel room for an extended period of time wasn't nearly as glamorous as I'd hoped. And even with the generous discount the lodge had given me, it was still expensive as hell. Something I was freshly and painfully aware of.

I'd been a few weeks late on my monthly peek at my finances only to realize I'd reached the bottom of my savings account.

Drastic measures were called for to survive until my agent percentage of my only client's advance came through on publication of her book...in seven weeks.

"That's just it, Zoey. You don't *have* an apartment anymore," Inez whined as I held my leg aloft and shoved my foot into the boot.

"You didn't accept any edibles from the baker on the seventh floor and gamble my apartment away in the building poker game, did you? I warned you. Madame Reneski is a card shark. She's been banned from four casinos in Las Vegas."

"What? No! I only lost your Chanel sweater to her."

"You better not mean my red Chanel sweater, or I will murder you at the family reunion."

"Zoey, will you please focus? I'm trying to tell you our apartment isn't an apartment anymore. It's a condo."

I sprang into a seated position like a curly-haired jack-in-the-box. "What did you say?"

"The building is going condo. They said you have thirty days to buy your place or get our stuff out."

"Who said, *Inez*?" I demanded.

"I *don't know, Zoey*. The people who sent all the notices and spoke at the building meeting a couple weeks ago."

I slapped a hand to my forehead. "Why didn't you tell me about this earlier?"

"I thought I did. Didn't I?"

As someone who had endured being labeled as "flighty" for most of my life, I'd always found the romance novel industry's label "too stupid to live" a little harsh. Until this moment.

"No," I countered. "You told me when that hairy guy you met at Pilates clogged my shower drain and when you thought you saw the winner of *RuPaul's Drag Race* buying hot dogs at Quick Stop."

"Oh. Yeah no. This was *way* before that. Maybe I told a different cousin?"

"You know what, Inez? I'm going to call you back." I disconnected before I could give in to the raging impulse to insult her.

The alarm on my phone jangled irritably with my two-minute warning of my appointment with Hazel.

"Damn it," I muttered, snatching a reasonably clean blazer off one of the chairs by the window and dialing another number.

"Zoey! So nice to hear from you. What did your dumbass cousin do now?" Mrs. Newville was an eighty-something-year-old retired Broadway star turned amateur food critic who lived across the hall from me in Manhattan.

"She didn't tell me the building was going condo."

There was a weighty pause. "Well, shit."

"How can this happen?" I demanded, shoving my arm through the sleeve of the blazer.

"Building owner got his hand caught in some pyramid-real-estate-scheme cookie jar and went to prison. The new owner decided she didn't want to deal with rentals and went the condo route. You know you've only got thirty days, right?"

"Thirty days to decide whether I'm going to buy my place?" I asked hopefully as I slicked on a coat of my second favorite lip gloss. I'd misplaced my first favorite a week ago and hadn't remembered to order a new tube. Which I wouldn't be doing now due to the aforementioned financial shit fest.

"Thirty days to close or get the hell out," Mrs. Newville corrected.

"Well, shit," I muttered. There was a cheery knock at my door. I vaulted over last night's dinner tray and flung it open.

Hazel, my best friend and only client, stood there looking all smug, glowy, and in love. Her long chestnut hair was pulled back in a swingy ponytail, her thick fringe of bangs accenting her glasses. The scruffy dog at her feet gave me what I considered to be a judgmental look. Meetcute was a medium-size black-and-white ball of wiry floof that had been part of last summer's grand gesture apology-proposal from Campbell Bishop, Hazel's soon-to-be-husband.

The dog pawed at my boots like they were a rawhide chew. I waved them in and tried to keep some distance between my prized boots and Meetcute's mouth full of tiny razor-sharp teeth.

It wasn't that I didn't *like* animals. I just preferred to appreciate them from a respectful distance. Away from their teeth, claws, fur, and slobber.

"I'm texting you the link," Mrs. Newville said. "Be warned, the asking price ain't for the faint of heart."

"Thanks for the heads-up. Are you staying?" I couldn't imagine the building or New York without her.

She snorted. "At that price? Fuck no. I'm moving to Portugal with my new boyfriend. Listen, I gotta go. I'm meeting a VP of finance and two nuns for karaoke. Ta-ta, kid!"

I could live to be two hundred and still wouldn't have a life as interesting as hers.

"Bye, Mrs. Newville," I said morosely.

This couldn't be happening. This wasn't part of the triumphant comeback I'd been working toward since my unceremonious firing last year. This was a monumental setback.

"How is our favorite broad of Broadway?" Hazel asked, letting Meetcute off the leash when I disconnected the call.

The adorable terror immediately nosedived into my dirty laundry with an ecstatic groan.

"Moving to Portugal. Which might be my next destination depending on the cost of living." I clicked on the text link from Mrs. Newville, violently scrolled, then fervently wished I could reverse the clock to a happier, less homeless time in my life. Even at my previous Literary Agent with a Stable of High-Earning Clients Zoey peak, I couldn't have afforded to buy my own apartment. Down to One Client and Living on Dwindling Savings Zoey was fucked…and not in the good way. "Damn it!"

"What's wrong?" Hazel asked, clearing the stack of mail off one of the dining chairs and sitting.

"My cousin—"

"Topless caterer, hippie innkeeper, or biochemist that raises alpacas?" she cut in.

"The bucket-of-hair-for-brains caterer subletting my apartment just informed me that the building is going condo and I have thirty days to buy or get out."

Hazel did her best not to look gleeful. It wasn't fooling me one bit.

I pointed an accusing finger at her. "Stop it."

"Stop what?" she asked, brown eyes going wide with feigned innocence.

"Stop gloating."

"I'm not gloating. Meetcute, am I gloating?"

The dog looked up from the sock he was mauling and cocked his head thoughtfully.

"I have options," I insisted.

"Of course you do."

"I could buy the place." If I robbed several banks or discovered a wealthy deceased relative I didn't know existed who had left me everything in their will. But that would probably take more than thirty days. "Or I could find a new place in the city. Maybe move to the Village. Or New Jersey. Or maybe I'll find a place with…roommates." I congratulated myself on not choking on the words.

"Sure," she said as she organized my untidy paperwork into piles.

"Don't get comfortable. I'm ready to go," I warned.

"You sure about that?" Hazel asked innocently as she paged through my research on the table and held up a printout. The craggy, irritated face of author Earl Wiggens, my white whale, stared back at me. He was more of a dick than Moby Dick, but if I could land him as a client, my financial woes would turn into whees.

I snatched the paper out of her hand and stuffed it into my oversize tote. "Positive. Do I need a coat?"

Early spring in eastern Pennsylvania was mercurial at best, and it was impossible to gauge the early April temperature and wind speed through my room's window.

Hazel remained seated and looked pointedly at my tote bag. "Earl Wiggens is an old-school misogynist asshole. He once told me at a cocktail party that romance novels are 'unrealistic drivel' because women can't have multiple orgasms. He's never had a female agent because he believes they're genetically inferior. You'll need a coat. And you could move here."

I shot her a dirty look.

The second Hazel had officially gotten engaged to broody contractor Cam, she'd become hell-bent on convincing me that Story Lake was the perfect place to rebuild my literary agent empire.

"Haze, I'm glad you've embraced small-town, 'everybody knows your name' life. Love that for you, blah blah blah. But I can't poach *New York Times* bestselling shitheads from narcissistic buffoons like your ex-husband and the rest of my former colleagues if I'm living hours away in a tiny town that voted for the slogan *Towny McLake Face*. Agents have to live places where book things happen."

She scoffed. "Please. Ninety-five percent of your job can be done from home these days. Most agents don't even commute to an office anymore. Think of how much money you'd save moving here for just a year." She rose and placed her hands on my shoulders. "Think of the closet space you could have here."

This was the problem with best friends. They knew exactly which buttons to push. As a proud and devoted clothes whore, most of my fantasies involved spacious closets. One of the only things New York could not provide in my price range.

"I'll weigh my options," I promised.

Yes, an extended stay in Story Lake was an option. But it felt like accepting failure. I wasn't made for small-town life. I was a busy, successful Manhattanite…or at least I had been. And I would claw my way back if necessary. I just needed to survive the next few months, launch Hazel's book into the stratosphere, and land the moderately gross Earl Wiggens as a client. Easy-peasy.

"Now can we please leave?" I asked. "You have paperback orders to sign, and we need to strategize preorder details."

"Sure. But you do know you're not wearing pants, don't you?"

"Shit!"

After I remedied the pants situation with a pair of cute tailored shorts over patterned tights and wrestled my favorite bra out of Meetcute's jaws, we headed downstairs. Story Lake Lodge sat on the quiet tree-lined eastern shore of the lake. It was a rustic three-story building outfitted with black board and batten siding and green metal roofs. Two wings angled out on each side toward the rocky shoreline.

When I'd first set up camp here, there had been entire weeks when I was the lodge's only tenant. But thanks in large part to the public's interest in Hazel's real-life happily ever after, both the lodge and town were seeing a boost in book-loving tourists. There were even a handful of readers who had inexplicably decided to make Story Lake their new permanent home.

We exited the elevator into the chaos of the sunny lobby.

"Whoa," I said, dodging the end of a roll of shimmery tulle that innkeeper and head chef Hana carried over her tattooed shoulder.

"Sorry, Zo. Wedding prep," she called as her long legs carried her past us.

Two burly men jogged after her, pushing carts stacked with trays of jingling glassware.

Billie, Hana's wife and business partner, waved to us with her elbow from the front desk, where she had two phones to her ears and was using aggressive head nodding to point a delivery guy toward the lobby bar.

I waved back and nearly fell on my ass when a woman with flushed cheeks and manic happiness in her eyes cut in front of me. She was wearing an oversize sweatshirt that said *BRIDE #2*.

"Ohmygod," she said in a starry-eyed rush. "It's really you. I mean, I knew you *lived* here. That's why we—me and my almost wife, yay!—decided to get married here. We came up from Maryland for Winter Fest and the Ultimate Bingo Championship to basically stalk you and ended up falling in love with the town, so we booked the lodge for our wedding, which is this weekend. You should totally come! We love you!"

Bride #2 said all this in one breath over my head to my significantly taller, more famous best friend.

I took an agent-y beat to make sure the bubbly bride posed no physical threat to Hazel before reluctantly taking the dog's leash and stepping out of the way.

"You're getting married here? Me too! Congratulations," Hazel squealed.

"OMG I'm getting married in the *same venue as Hazel Freaking Hart?*"

The octave change had Meetcute whimpering pathetically. I took pity on him and headed out the front doors into the sunny but chilly spring day.

The dog sniffled and snuffled his way down the sidewalk as if he had important business to attend to. "Oh God. Please don't poop. Please don't poop," I chanted to the gods of animal defecation until Hazel joined us a minute later. "That's one excited bride," I said, gratefully hurling the leash at her.

"Adorable, right? Fair warning. I'm going to be totally insufferable for my wedding," she said dreamily.

Meetcute executed a tight circle on the grass and squatted.

Ha. Thank you, poop gods! At least one thing went my way today. "I have no doubt. I'd be disappointed if you weren't. How is Cam handling the wedding planning?"

She unfurled a doggy poop bag out of the fancy dispenser clipped to the leash. "He's surprisingly opinionated on the food, the flowers, and the invitations."

"What's he say about the dress?"

Hazel's smile was sly despite the fact that she was cleaning up crap. Love did strange things to people. "He said it has to be easy to remove."

I sighed. "If I didn't love you so much, I'd probably hate you."

"I get that," she said smugly.

"How's writing going?"

She winced. "I'm still feeling out the characters."

That was code for doing more online shopping than actual writing.

"You know the only thing better for a comeback than a bestselling book is—"

"I know. I know. *Two* bestselling books."

"What are you hung up on?"

"I don't know. I guess I just don't know who they are yet. Which means I don't know why they can't be together."

"Tell Cam you need him to step up the inspiration," I suggested.

"Oh, he did. This morning. In the kitchen," Hazel said with the creepy self-satisfied smile of a woman who had orgasmed on her kitchen countertop.

"Love is so unhygienic."

We decided to walk to the bookstore. It gave Meetcute a chance to pee on every tree we passed. And it gave *me* the chance not to break all my fingernails gripping the door handle while Hazel navigated the half-mile trip in the used Suburban Cam had bought her. Her driving was improving. Slowly. The sheer size of the SUV ensured her safety behind the wheel, but the same couldn't be said for the town's curbs and the neighbors' recycling bins.

The sun was bright in the cloudless blue sky and sparkled off the last vestiges of snow lining Lake Drive. Green spears of daffodils and crocus plants poked their heads up, promising beauty and warmth soon. New beginnings. Fresh starts.

Yep. Everyone was enjoying a new chapter. Mine was just a bit less triumphant than everyone else's. Losing my apartment was the latest metaphorical squirt of lemon juice in the eyeballs of a downward spiral of failures.

"So guess who was sitting on the breakfast table this morning eating cat food when Cam and I got up?" Hazel said, adjusting the leash she had clipped to her belt because she was the type of person who had dog leashes that clipped to her belt now.

"I'm going to guess DeWalt." DeWalt was Hazel's pudgy orange cat that kept her company on her desk while she wrote. And by *kept her company*, I meant spread his girthy body across her keyboard, inserting meaningless characters into her manuscript.

"DeWalt and *Bertha*," she announced as Meetcute trotted into the woods in search of the perfect stick to carry to town.

Hazel had purchased her pink monstrosity of a house in a moment of panic from a less-than-accurate online auction only to discover that it was in a serious state of disrepair…and home to a large kinda-sorta-domesticated raccoon. I liked to think of Bertha as a combination of Liam Neeson and reverse Houdini. She had a special set of skills that allowed her to get back inside the house no matter how many raccoon-proofing measures Cam took.

"This is going to send Cam back down the rabbit hole again, isn't it?" I teased.

"I believe you mean the raccoon hole. And he was already on the phone with his brothers, discussing some surveillance tactics."

"That sounds like inspiration for book two."

"Ugh. We'll see. Writing's hard, but I really don't want to get a real job."

"You wrote a whole book inspired by you and Cam. Maybe you just need to find a new couple to inspire you?" I suggested.

"That's not a terrible idea. No wonder I keep you around."

Meetcute bounced out of the woods with a medium-size tree limb clamped in his teeth. He proudly smacked me in the shins with it.

"Aww! Cutie! What a good job," Hazel crooned.

"Ouch. Yes, very athletic of you. This won't impede our walk *at all*," I said, giving him a grudging pat on the head. He dissolved in joyful full-body wriggles without dropping the stick.

We continued on in the direction of town. As we approached, Hazel gestured toward the nondescript mailbox with a wooden placard that read BISHOP. "Levi's making progress on his manuscript. He's taking it pretty seriously. He's only let me read a few chapters, but they're good. If you're interested, I could get you a copy once his first draft is done."

"If I haven't worn down Earl Wiggens by the time Levi's ready, I'll take a look," I promised.

Hazel wrinkled her nose. "Seriously, what do you want with that old-school, 'back in my day men were men and women made dinner' geezer?"

"That *bestselling* geezer hasn't missed the *New York Times* hardback list in his last fifteen releases," I pointed out. "Besides, once we launch your book to the top of the charts *and* I poach another bestseller from my old firm, I'll have officially won at life."

"Thirsty for Vengeance Zoey is one of my favorite Zoeys. But you know what I'd say if you were my heroine."

"I'm nobody's heroine," I insisted.

Hazel brought her hand to her heart. "I'd be the gorgeous and talented best friend who would point out to the gorgeous and talented heroine that vengeance isn't the most rewarding quest in life."

"Oh really? What is?"

"Love," she said dramatically.

"Well then, it's a good thing this is real life and not one of your books so I don't have to listen to you."

Just then, a shadow fell over us. Meetcute's googly eyes went even wider, and he dropped the stick to bark ferociously at what lurked above us.

"Damn it, Goose," Hazel said, glaring up at the bald eagle that had landed on a bare tree branch over our heads. I still wasn't used to the fact that this town just happened to have its own bald eagle. In New York, all we had were pigeons. This bird was huge and maybe just the slightest bit majestic. He was also an absolute menace. If one could have an animal nemesis, Goose was mine. He'd greeted us on our arrival to Story Lake by hitting Hazel in the head and dumping a giant dead fish in my lap. I was still emotionally scarred.

"Do *not* shit on us," I ordered in my best authoritative voice.

"Do *not* eat my dog," Hazel said.

"Yeah, don't do that either," I added quickly.

"Is that something in his talons?" Hazel asked, cocking her head.

Meetcute paused his barking for a beat and mimicked her head tilt.

I squinted up. There was definitely *something* moving against the knobby gray bark of the oak tree. Something long and thin.

I swear to God, the bird looked me dead in the eye as he spread his massive wings.

"Is that a…?" Hazel's voice trailed off in horror.

"Don't you do it, Goose," I warned in a hoarse whisper.

But it was too late. The bird opened his talons and sent his prey plummeting toward me.

The snake—an actual goddamn live snake—hit me in the forehead and slithered off my shoulder.

"What. The. Fuuuuuuuck? You feathery jackass!" I screamed. Survival instinct kicked in, and I sprinted down the road, brushing vigorously at my hair and shoulders. "Get it off! Get it off!"

I ran a panicked zigzag pattern across the asphalt as I tried to put as much distance as possible between me and that damn eagle and his damn snake. But the fear and adrenaline had narrowed my field of vision. By the time Hazel yelled my name, I was already blinded by the glint of sunlight on glass and metal.

2

A truck to the boobs
Gage

It was the kind of spring day that made the long, gray Pennsylvania winter worth tolerating.

My truck windows were down, my coffee was hot, and the April sun flashed through still-skeletal trees as I steered north on Lake Drive. For the first time in a long time, I felt like I was back on track, and the goals I'd had to set aside a few years ago suddenly seemed attainable again. And I was ready to take aim.

"I'll see you in my office at three, Mrs. Babcock," I promised my client through the truck's speaker.

I was in the middle of my favorite kind of day: busy. A full morning spent with my brothers on contracting jobs would lead right into a neatly stacked afternoon of appointments at my law office.

"I'll bring my famous banana muffins *and* my granddaughter. The single straight one, not the married lesbian," she clarified.

Since Story Lake's population had experienced an oversixty-five bump with the opening of the new assisted living facility, I'd had a string of clients trying to set me up with their single relatives. It didn't matter if I was swinging a hammer or preparing a will. To the retiree crowd, apparently I was a hot commodity as a bachelor.

I didn't mind it, seeing as how the dating apps I'd recently joined hadn't exactly been delivering what I was looking for. Was it really this hard to meet someone who was ready to get serious? My brother Cam—one of the grumpiest people in the universe—had managed to do it just driving around town. I was one hundred percent more charming and in a better mood most of the time. It should have been even easier for me.

"Looking forward to it," I said before disconnecting the call and glancing over at my passenger.

She had her head out the window and was busy painting the side of the vehicle with a steady stream of slobber.

Nana—short for Banana Stand, thanks to my niece and nephews' recent binge watch of *Arrested Development*—was a high-maintenance, low-IQ golden retriever rescued by my mother from a puppy mill. Mom had billed Nana as a "temporary foster" when she dumped the four-legged roommate on me a few months ago. But no one had gotten around to trying to get her adopted, and Nana and I had gotten used to each other.

So now I had a dog.

"Text message from Cammy," my truck's text-to-voice announced flatly. "'Hey, dumbass. Don't bother showing up if you forgot the spray foam.' Would you like to reply?"

"Yeah. I'm going to spray-foam your face shut, dick," I said.

"Text message from Livvy," the truck announced. "'Bring me a sandwich, Gigi. I'll eat it while you suffocate, dickface.'"

My brothers were assholes. Lovable, sometimes even entertaining, assholes. I often wondered how our parents hadn't murdered us during our teen years.

Nana flashed me a look of pure joy like she was having the best day of her life. I ruffled her reddish-gold ears and turned my attention back to the road, where another reddish-gold flash in the road caught my eye.

"Shit!"

I spun the wheel hard to the right while arm-barring Nana against the seat. The truck slid to a hard stop halfway into the ditch a split second before I heard rather than felt a faint *thunk*.

I released my seat belt and jumped out from behind the wheel. My heart stopped doing its job when I spotted her.

"Zoey!"

Behind me, Nana whimpered in the truck.

The woman I'd spent the last several months trying to forget about was lying on the road, having run into and bounced off my fender. Her curls were spread out above her like a fiery halo, and those mossy green eyes were squeezed shut.

Christ. I'd taken my eyes off the road for a split second. She'd come out of nowhere, and now she wasn't moving. I knelt next to her and grabbed her wrist to check for a pulse. "Zoey!" I barked again, dread icing my entire body.

Her chest rose as she sucked in a breath and moaned. My heart restarted.

She let out a groan. "I hit your stupid truck with my body."

Fucking hell.

"Yeah, you did," I said grimly as I ran my hands over her limbs, checking for injuries. "The fuck, Zo? You could have gotten yourself killed. What the hell were you doing running into the middle of the damn road?"

This was exactly why I'd argued myself out of any attraction since she'd come to town. The woman was a natural disaster who failed to take anything seriously. She was impulsive and careless, too busy having a good time to bother with things like safety and responsibility.

"Yeah. Yelling at me is *exactly* what I need right now," she grumbled.

My heart was still trying to pound its way out of my chest as my brain raced through every way this could have been catastrophic. And Zoey was cracking jokes.

"Shut up and tell me if you can move," I ordered.

She had a scrape on her forearm and smudges of dirt everywhere, but nothing else seemed to be bleeding or broken.

She cracked open her eyes. They flashed green fire at me. Much as I tried not to notice them, she had the prettiest eyes I'd ever seen. "Which is it, smartass? Shut up or tell you if I can move?"

I leaned over her and gripped her chin in my hand to check her pupils. The panic receded by a few more degrees, but the adrenaline remained. "Your mouth appears to be working."

"If I didn't have the wind knocked out of me right now, I'd show you just how well it's working…and not in the sexy way," she amended quickly.

"Lucky me."

My truck horn gave a long, aggressive blare, startling us both.

I turned around to find Nana in the driver's seat, front paws on the wheel. It was a trick she'd learned in the Wawa parking lot. Every time she thought I'd been inside too long, she blew the horn like a complete asshole. Cam thought it was hilarious. I was 90 percent sure he'd been the one to teach her the trick.

The dog leaned on the horn again, tongue lolling with joy.

"Nana! Get over here," I ordered.

She hopped out of the truck, dragging her leash behind her, and nudged me nervously in the back. I put an arm around the dog's neck to hold her back from the still-prone Zoey.

"Oh my God, Zoey! Are you okay?" Hazel sprinted up out of breath, dragging the scraggly, overexcited Meetcute. The little dog decided to add insult to injury and dropped the stick he was carrying on Zoey's forehead.

Zoey shrugged off the stick and sat up. "Ow! That better not be another snake."

"Snake? Did you hit your head when you threw yourself into my truck?" I asked, gripping her shoulder with one hand and trying to control the increasingly frantic Nana with the other. Humans at her eye level usually only meant one thing: playtime.

"A snake hit me in the head. You know, slithery, hissy,

reptilian thing? And I didn't *throw myself* into your truck. My boobs smashed into it. Why are you so pissed, by the way? Everyone always says you're the nice brother, but you've been nothing but snarly for the past six months," Zoey said.

"I believe I already pointed out the fact that you could have been killed playing around in the road. You need to be more fucking careful." There was a bite of anger to my words that I couldn't quite control. My family knew all too well what carelessness behind the wheel could lead to. How quickly everything could change.

"Now you're yelling? Great bedside manner, Dr. Asshole."

"That's Attorney Asshole," I corrected snidely. There was something about this woman that kept pushing me off-kilter over and over again until I didn't know which way was up, which was why I avoided her like a kid with lice.

"She wasn't playing around, Gage," Hazel insisted loyally. "Goose dropped a live snake on her back there, and she panicked."

"I wasn't panicking," Zoey insisted as she brushed her hair out of her face, making the overall aesthetic worse without damaging the general punch-in-the-gut beauty.

I didn't enjoy admitting it, but she certainly put the *hot* in *hot mess*.

"I was running and flailing in a perfectly controlled and appropriate manner," Zoey continued.

"Like a fucking tornado," I added.

"Why are you always arguing with me?" she demanded.

"He's a lawyer. He can't help being argumentative," Hazel said.

"I'm *not* argumentative," I argued.

Hazel and Zoey both pinned me with twin "you poor, stupid man" looks.

I started an internal countdown from ten. I was halfway through when I noticed a small scrape on Zoey's jawline and was just reaching out to examine it when Nana slipped out of my grip and joyfully slammed Zoey back to the ground. The damn dog finished her attack with a swipe of long pink tongue to the face.

"*Oooph*!" Zoey screeched as she fought off Nana's aggressive affection and sat back up. "Seriously? Animals are such jerks."

Heaving a sigh, I wrestled the dog off her and shoved the leash in Hazel's direction before reaching for Zoey again. "Give me your hands."

"Why? So you can yell at them separately from the rest of my body?" Zoey asked.

That smart mouth was another prime reason why I had no interest in exploring any potential physical attraction. I wanted a reasonable, responsible partner, not a woman who drove me nuts thirty seconds into every conversation.

Irritated, I slid my hands under her arms and pulled her to her feet. She was short and curvy. Everything about her, from the wild green of her eyes to the riotous red curls, seemed like it was designed specifically to catch my eye. Like some kind of personal purgatory. I held her forearms to keep her steady and credited the electric feeling that coursed through me to the leftover adrenaline and the permanent annoyance she inspired in me.

"You okay?" I asked.

Turns out this was a stupid question.

"No, I am *not* okay! A freaking bald eagle attacks me with a snake. Then I get hit by a truck *and* a stick before being wrestled to the ground by a dog. And *you*!" Zoey pointed at Hazel. "You want me to move here permanently! Birds throw snakes at you here!"

"Sounds like a new town slogan." A hatchback came to a stop next to our roadside spectacle. "Everybody all right?" Garland Russell asked through his open passenger window. He looked more excited than concerned. That could have to do with the fact that the wannabe journalist who reported town gossip on the neighborhood busybody app was recording us on his phone.

"Goose dropped a snake on Zoey's head, and she ran into Gage's truck, and now everyone's mad," Hazel summarized.

Garland chuckled. "Classic Goose. Classic Zoey."

The woman in question wrenched free of my grip and threw her hands in the air. "I'd like to live somewhere where that is *not* classic Zoey."

"Maybe you should move," I suggested.

"That we agree on," Zoey announced.

"Want me to call Chief Bishop?" Garland offered hopefully.

"No," all three of us said in unison.

Last year, my brother Levi had been elected chief of police against his will—with the help of me and the rest of our siblings. A fact that was still entertaining to the entire family. Levi was reluctantly performing his duties, but I knew it was only a matter of time before he wielded them to get some kind of well-deserved revenge on each of us. He'd already gotten to arrest Cam last summer. And I wasn't about to give him an opportunity to take aim at me.

"All righty then. I'll just post my story and be on my way." With an unnecessary flourish, Garland clicked a button on his phone screen and drove off.

I turned my attention back to Zoey. "You sure you're not hurt?" I asked, this time managing not to bite her head off. Barely.

"Only my boobs, my tailbone, my pride, and my emotional well-being," she grumbled, brushing at the dirty paw prints on the lapels of her wool coat. She was always dressed twice as nice as anyone else in the room. Today she had on a blazer and a fitted top with the kind of neckline that could keep a man up all night. She wore tailored shorts over torn black tights and suede knee-high boots caked with dirt.

"Text from Cammy," my truck's sound system announced to everyone within earshot. "'Why did Garland just report you're feeling up my wife's best friend in the middle of the road? And where the fuck is my fucking spray foam?' Would you like to reply?"

"Aww! He called you his wife," Zoey crooned to Hazel.

The woman was acting like nearly getting hit by a car was an everyday event. Another reason to stay far, far away from her.

"Text from Livvy. 'More importantly where's my fucking sandwich?' Would you like to reply?"

"Yeah. 'I'm busy. Fuck you both.'"

"And that's just a delightful slice of the family life I'm marrying into," Hazel said cheerfully, juggling both dogs and their leashes. "Are you able to soldier on to the bookstore, Zo? Or do you want to go back to the lodge and pretend this day never happened?"

"Bookstore," Zoey said with bitter determination as she brushed at the dead leaves and dirt stuck to her tights.

"I'll drive you," I said. I'd like nothing more than to leave her there in the middle of the road, but knowing Zoey, she'd find a way to get crushed by a falling tree or cause a multivehicle accident on the quietest road in the county.

"You know, that's how Cam and I met. Goose brought us together," Hazel reminded us. My brother had witnessed the eagle dive-bombing Hazel and Zoey in their convertible, causing them to make a memorable first impression by crashing into Story Lake's welcome sign. "Now here we are with another eagle-related catastrophe, and another Bishop brother rides to the rescue. It's like we're starting a new tradition."

"No. A tradition is making the same pie every Thanksgiving, not a bald eagle attempting murder," Zoey pointed out.

Hazel tossed her hair and opened the back door of the truck for the dogs. "I'm an author. You have to let me make up pretend patterns in real life."

Zoey opened her mouth to argue, but I had reached my limit.

"Just get in the damn truck," I muttered, yanking open the passenger door for her.

Zoey shot murder eye darts at me. "Don't expect a thank-you for being a shit waffle."

I blew out a breath between my teeth and started counting backward again. I was the nice guy, damn it. She just managed to drive me crazy every time we were in the same room. "Look. You scared the hell out of me. I thought you were hurt or worse." I reached out and tugged a twig out of her curls.

Zoey exhaled. "It's fine."

"But you should know better than to do something so stupid—"

Her eyebrows arched defiantly. "*Stupid*? Says the guy who fell off a roof the first time we met."

"It was a ranch house. And a bush broke my fall, not a half-ton pickup truck," I pointed out, feeling defensive. It wasn't stupidity that had knocked me off the roof. It was something a hell of a lot worse.

"Here's an idea, Gage. Let's play a game where you don't say a damn word while you drive us to the bookstore and I reward you by not hiding frozen shrimp under your floor mats for you to find later."

There wasn't a doubt in my mind that Zoey Moody, impulsive, fiery redhead, was willing to do exactly that.

"Just because you had one bad experience with a bald eagle—"

Zoey whipped around to glare at Hazel in the back seat. "*Two* bad experiences. You're forgetting the dead fish. And don't get me started on the breaking and entering raccoon or the free-range pig."

"I told you Rump Roast wasn't chasing you. He just wanted your Fish Hook leftovers," Hazel explained. "Besides, look at the progress you're making with all this exposure therapy. A few months ago, a snake to the head would have put you in a coma. Admit it. Story Lake has been good for you."

"Yay me," Zoey said dryly.

"Gage, do you know of any rentals in town? Zoey needs a place," Hazel said, changing the subject.

I opened my mouth.

Zoey held up a finger. "Uh-uh. One word and I buy an entire tray of shrimp."

My heart rate had finally returned to normal, but my brain was still turning over all the alternative grim outcomes. Every horrific what-if had me gripping the wheel tighter. Just beyond the justifiable anger at her being that irresponsible simmered a few shadowy what-ifs. What if I hadn't seen her? What if I hadn't stopped in time?

One thing was clear. Zoey and I had both gotten very lucky today, and only one of us cared.

The lake and town came into view, and I let the familiar sight of it calm me. It was postcard-perfect with tidy storefronts facing the sparkling water. We passed the new coffee shop and neighboring plant store that had taken up residence on Lake Drive. Rumor had it there was a cheese shop going in on the town square. More signs of Story Lake's growth. Growth that Bishop Brothers Construction was reaping the benefits of. The family business had gone from the brink of bankruptcy to a full schedule in less than a year. My law practice was benefitting from the boom too.

I pulled a U-turn on the street and eased into a parking space in front of Stories, a white clapboard corner shop with an eclectic window display of volumes old and new.

"Ride's over. Be more fucking careful," I said, feeling pretty confident I was safe from the threatened seafood.

Zoey rolled her eyes. "Jesus. Lighten up, Gage. Nobody died."

But on a different road, on a different day, someone had.

Hazel let out a strangled noise from the back seat between the dogs. A weighty silence fell over the cab. Even the dogs seemed to clue in to the discomfort.

Nana whimpered, and Zoey thumped her head against the back of her seat. "Shit. Haze, can you give us a minute?"

"Yep. Absolutely. I'll just take my dog and—oops. Make that both dogs since Nana is already on the sidewalk. I'll leave you to your…awkwardness," she said, sliding out of the back seat.

Zoey waited until Hazel had closed the door, then covered her face with her hands. "I'm so sorry. That was a really stupid thing to say. I'm having a bad day and wasn't filtering."

I shook my head. "It's fine. You scared the shit out of me,

and I took it out on you. That wasn't fair." *Even though she should be more fucking careful*, I added silently.

"Seriously though. I wasn't trying to throw Laura's accident in your face. Sometimes words just come out of my mouth, and it's like I have no control over them."

"I've noticed," I said dryly. "Maybe I'm slightly sorry for being an asshole, and I'm sorry Goose was being one too. Believe it or not, if he was sharing his lunch with you, it means he likes you."

"Great. I graduate from boys pulling my pigtails on the playground to a bully romance with a bald eagle. That sounds about right for how things have been going. Anyway, thanks for the quick reflexes and the ride." She reached for the door handle.

"I gotta collect my dog," I said, nodding toward the store.

We both got out of the truck and stood awkwardly on the sidewalk. There was something about Zoey Moody that bothered me. Several somethings. I'd made a study of it since the first second I met her. One thing was for sure, I had to keep my guard up around her.

I slid my hands into my pockets. "Sure you're okay?"

"I'm fine. My boobs feel like they went through a double mega mammogram, and my butt has felt better. But other than that, I seem to be intact."

"Why are you looking for an apartment?" I asked, changing the subject to a topic safer than Zoey's unmissable curves.

She sighed. "Long story involving me losing my apartment in New York. Which means I need to get my stuff out, which also means I'll need a place bigger than a hotel room to store it all. Plus, if I'm officially sticking around here indefinitely, I need to find a more cost-effective living situation."

She'd shuddered on the word *indefinitely*.

I grunted and tried not to notice the way the sun was hitting her hair, making the curls look like fire. I spent a lot of my time around Zoey trying not to notice things.

"There's worse things than staying here, you know." I gestured across the street to the gleaming waters of the lake.

"That's exactly the kind of thing someone who's never lived in New York would say. You sound like one of Hazel's heroes trying to entice a heroine to succumb to the charm of small-town life."

"Always figured I was hero material."

She theatrically mimed vomiting.

I gestured toward the bookstore door. "After you."

3

Sex drought

Zoey

"Bald eagle victims before gentlemen. I insist," Gage said, holding the door.

I rolled my eyes.

I'd suspected for some time that the man didn't like me. I usually had a sixth sense when it came to reading people. Gage Bishop was the nicest guy in the room…to everyone except me. It was like there was something about me he found inherently distasteful but he was too polite to actually say it. Which felt like a waste of time and energy to me. The guy was obviously still mad at me for my irresponsible, snake-induced fifty-yard dash into traffic and accidental insult to his family, yet here he was still being performatively polite.

It was annoying. Why couldn't people just be honest?

He was probably just as polite and gentlemanly in bed, I decided. *"Excuse me, ma'am. Do you mind if I insert my cock inside you repeatedly?"*

Hmm. Interesting. Imaginary Gage was surprisingly well equipped.

"What?" Gage asked.

I blinked myself back to reality to find him watching me closely, still holding the door.

"What what?" I asked, all feigned innocence and telltale hot cheeks.

Those bold Bishop eyes narrowed. "You look like you're up to something."

"You don't know me well enough to know when I'm up to something." I brushed past him into the store and took a deep breath.

Ahh, the smell of books. It was the smell of possibilities.

Thousands of books on shelves written by people who had done hard things, lived interesting lives, and managed to write entire novels about it. Bookstores always gave me hope that they held the answers I was looking for so I could finally get my life together.

"Outta the way." A prune-faced elderly white man with glasses so thick they looked like microscope lenses whizzed by me on a mobility scooter with airbrushed flames.

Ever the reluctant gentleman, Gage pulled me out of harm's way, putting my back in full contact with his front.

Damn. It was a very nice front. Hard, muscled, warm. And the flannel coat was giving just the right amount of romance-novel blue collar. My body foolishly delighted in the physical contact.

My sex drought was definitely getting out of control if just casually brushing against any male body could have me thinking about getting naked.

"You need a guardian angel," Gage complained, releasing me.

"That one was not my fault," I insisted.

"Watch where you're going, George, or they'll kick us out of here," warned the scooter man's compatriot, a tall, soft Black woman with springy silver curls. She was using her walker as a seat planted in front of a spinning rack of science fiction novels.

"Not my fault these aisles are tighter than a butthole in here," George the aggressive driver shouted back from the historical Western section.

I took a self-preserving step away from Gage. I needed to get away from the one-sided sexual tension before I did or said something I'd regret.

I glanced back at him and almost tripped over my own feet when I realized his gaze was locked on the general vicinity of my butt. Maybe he didn't hate *all* of me after all.

I cleared my throat smugly, and his eyes darted back up to mine.

"You...uh...have some dirt." He gestured at my rear end.

Damn it. Of course I did.

"Thanks," I muttered and ducked into the restroom.

When I came back out—dirt smears mostly replaced with water spots—Hazel and Chevy, the store owner, were already stacking paperback orders on her designated signing table. Both dogs were staring longingly at the jar of treats at the register that Gage had his hand in.

"Everybody sit," Gage said. The dogs plopped their butts on the floor in unison, tails wagging.

I pretended to be deeply invested in the back cover copy of a new celebrity biography so I could study him from behind the cover.

He was the clean-shaven, easygoing brother who was openly friendly with everyone who wasn't me. His hair, a warm brown, curled at the tips, giving him one of those permanently tousled look. He looked like the type of guy who would help an old lady load her groceries into her car. Could it be called boyish charm if it was coming out of the chiseled face of a man? I'd have to ask Hazel, the expert.

Not that it mattered, of course. The bottom line was Gage Bishop was so far from my type that I'd be more likely to date my own second cousin than him.

He crouched down, a treat in each hand, drawing my attention reluctantly to his muscular, denim-clad thighs. I sighed and gritted my teeth. Okay, the sex drought was officially a problem. *Lust 'em and leave 'em* was my motto. But this town was too small for that. Everyone would know about my tryst before I even unhooked my bra. And I absolutely would not lure Hazel's future brother-in-law—who didn't even like me—into a one-night stand.

Even though I totally could.

If I wanted to.

Which I absolutely didn't.

"You look like you want to eat him up."

Startled, I dropped the hardback on the table with a *thump*. The basket on the front of the woman's walker was full of novels.

"Who? Me? What? Him? No. Nope." I shook my head vehemently until I was dizzy.

She smirked. "Very convincing."

"He's so not my type."

She looked at me like I'd just offered to give her an unlicensed colonoscopy. "Who gives a shit? Life is short. Order dessert. Bang the hot guy."

"Thank you for the advice on my sex life, complete stranger."

"Opal," she said. "And you're wasting your time worrying about types and all that other garbage. You only get one life. Some of us might as well have some fun living it."

She clomped away with her walker, leaving me staring after her. People sure were nosy—and free with their advice—around here.

"Opal, when are you going to talk George here into taking my class?" Hazel called, pointing to the man on the scooter. Of course she knew both their names. She was an official Story Laker now, and knowing your neighbors was probably required by some obscure town ordinance.

Opal rolled her eyes. "Trust me, Hazel. You don't want this troublemaker in your class."

"I'll show up when I got nothing better to do, and I always got something better to do," George barked back as he executed a thirty-seven-point turn.

Hazel had recently started teaching a creative writing class at Story Lake Haven and seemed to be enjoying it. Author, town council member, now teacher. She'd come a long way from the unshowered introvert who refused to leave her apartment for weeks at a time.

I skirted a display of illustrated children's books and took a turn at the table laden with local history tomes mixed with glossy green plants.

"What's with the greenery, Chevy?" I asked.

The store owner looked up from the stack of Hazel's paperbacks he was organizing. He was a big guy in both height and width, dressed—as always—in baggy jeans, sneakers, and his musical artist T-shirt of the day. Today it was Miles Davis. Chevy had played college football for three seasons before an injury left him focusing on his dual library science and music history degrees.

"Trying out a cross-promotion with Leafy Greens. I traded them a stack of gardening books to display at their place," he said.

Inspiration struck, and I opened the note app on my phone. I scrolled through a few pages of previous brilliant ideas, shopping lists, and philosophical wonderings that I'd forgotten and was just getting ready to make note that I should drop off some of Hazel's books at the plant shop when I felt a presence looming over my shoulder.

"You know they let you make more than one note, don't you? You don't have to put them all in the same file," Gage pointed out.

I hugged my phone to my chest. "I have a system, Nosey McNoserton."

Okay. I didn't actually have a system. But I had the *intention* to create and utilize a system. That was basically the same thing.

"Doesn't look like a very efficient one."

"Don't you have several jobs to go do somewhere that aren't here?" I asked pointedly.

"You mean now that I'm not busy saving your life?"

"I'm putting shrimp on my grocery list," I warned.

"Do us all a favor and stay out of the road," he said. "See you around, Hazel."

"Thanks for the ride, Gage. Give Cam a kiss for me," Hazel called.

"Yeah, definitely not doing that. See you later, Chevy. C'mon, Nana. Let's go find your uncles before they do something stupid."

Nana made a pathetic-sounding grumble in her throat that had a fluffy black-and-white cat I hadn't noticed before vaulting onto the table next to me. I barely contained my squeak of surprise. What was it with this town and animals? In New York, I only had to worry about clouds of pigeons, the occasional dog walker with a dozen tiny Yorkies, and the rats on trash day. Story Lake was like wandering around a twenty-four-seven free-range petting zoo.

By the time Gage and his dog left the store—not that I was watching *or* admiring his dirt-free ass—I'd forgotten what I wanted to make note of. On an annoyed sigh, I plopped down on a spinning stool near the register while Hazel and Chevy worked their way through the signed orders.

"Hey, how are your preorders for the new release looking, Chev?" I asked.

"Looking good. Biggest preorder this store has seen. There's a sticky note on the register with the numbers as of this morning."

I leaned over the counter and plucked the sticky note off the monitor. "Hmm. Not bad. But I think we can get to *wow*."

Hazel snorted as she scrawled her name on the page.

"What's wow?" Chevy asked, opening the next book and sliding it in front of Hazel.

"I want bestsellers-list numbers. Numbers that have the rest of the publishing industry whispering uncomplimentary things about me behind my back because they wish they had Hazel as a client."

"You're officially ridiculous," Hazel said, reaching for the next book.

"Don't talk while you sign. You know you can't multitask like that," I warned.

George smacked his scooter into a shelf at the front of the

store, sending several books plummeting to the floor. "Clean up on aisle three," he barked, then wheezed out a cackle at his own joke.

Chevy gestured for me to take over flapping books for him while he went to right the damage.

"I'm just happy to be writing again. Can we not worry about the launch or the numbers?" Hazel asked, sliding a completed stack of signed paperbacks to the side.

"Lady buddy. Gal pal," I said, opening Hazel's next book to the signing page. "You stay focused on writing the best words ever, and I'll do the dirty work. That's the way this relationship works best. You keep your pretty little head in the creativity clouds and let me make deals with the devil to secure your success."

"Uh-huh. In this case, is Chevy the devil?" Hazel asked.

The man in question made finger horns atop his head.

The bell on the door jangled, sending Meetcute into a rabid fit of barking. He made a mad dash for the newcomer.

"Meetcute! Stay!" Hazel ordered. But the little dog was too excited to listen.

I dove for the end of the leash. We got tangled up around the legs of the stool and sent it crashing to the floor and into a display of used Sweet Valley High books.

Teenage mayor and cross-country star Darius Oglethorpe bounded inside. "Just the woman I was looking for," he said, sounding not surprised to find me on the floor.

"Me?" I asked, spitting out some of Meetcute's fur. The dog turned to lavish my face with exuberant, smelly dog kisses. "Ugh." I groaned.

Meetcute pressed his cold, wet nose into my neck and made a happy snuffling sound. I patted his back awkwardly.

"Sorry about my dog. He attacks with love. And at least he didn't pee in excitement this time," Hazel called cheerfully.

I held the twenty pounds of licky fur away from my chest and checked the front of my clothes to be sure. "Thank God." I put the dog down and shooed him back in the direction of his mother. "Shouldn't you be in school?" I asked Darius.

He held out a hand and hauled me to my feet. He was a tall, gangly teen with limbs like a colt that had earned him most of the school's cross-country records. He also happened to be a bit of a genius. "I have a free period. Principal Sprout lets me use it for mayoral business."

"What brings you to the bookstore, mayorally speaking?" I asked, brushing the dog hair off my tights. My outfit was not holding up well today.

He pushed his glasses up the bridge of his nose. "First of all, I heard about your run-in with Goose and wanted to apologize on behalf of the town. I hope you don't think that this unfortunate incident is indicative of all wildlife experiences in Story Lake."

"Damn that Garland and his gigantic mouth," I muttered. "I'm fine. It was horrifying and emotionally scarring, but I'm sure I'll recover." It was what I did. Bouncing back was an art, and I was the artist.

Darius beamed at me. "Wonderful. On behalf of the town, please accept this ten-dollar apology coupon good for a pontoon party boat lake cruise on the *Tiki Barge*."

"Didn't that pontoon boat sink last summer?" The neighboring town had managed to sabotage Story Lake's summer festival and sent a pontoon boat full of senior citizens to the lake bottom. Fortunately for all involved, the lake depth was only about four feet, and the passengers had enjoyed their refreshing swim back to shore.

"What a great memory you have. Yes, the party barge did receive a bit of water damage, but it should be afloat and good as new next month. June tops."

"I'll be sure to put it in my calendar," I said as I pocketed the coupon. My fingers came into contact with another piece of paper, and I pulled it out. It was my missing Christmas shopping list. Damn it! The Le Creuset casserole dish would have been perfect for Hazel instead of the intensely pine-scented bath set I settled for on Christmas Eve.

Darius clapped his hands. "Awesome. Now on to my next item of business. Hazel mentioned that among your literary agent duties, you've also dabbled on the promotion side of things as an unofficial publicist."

"She did, did she?"

"Don't pretend you don't know you're also my publicist," Hazel called from her table. "You organized that entire European book tour."

"The one where we both got the flu and a pickpocket stole my passport?" I reminded her.

She pointed her pen at me. "That's the one. You still managed to thrill six foreign publishers and get us home in one piece."

"I'd like to offer you a job," Darius announced.

I blinked. "Huh? Who? Me?"

He chuckled like I'd just told the punch line of a dad joke. "Yes, you."

I wondered if the stress of chasing valedictorian, leading the cross-country team, and running a town that had recently flirted with a sewer-related bankruptcy was getting to the kid. "Um, I'm flattered, but I already have a job. Literary agent to the diva back there singing to her dog."

Hazel was singing "Our Song" by Taylor Swift to an ecstatic Meetcute.

I was more of an "Anti-Hero" girl.

"Of course, of course," Darius said placatingly. "I meant a part-time gig for the town. I'd like to hire you to work a few hours a week as the town's publicist. We're coming into prime tourism season, and I want to show Dominion that we mean business."

Dominion was the neighboring town with a bustling year-round tourism business and year-round attitude problem. Their mayor had most recently tried to force Story Lake into giving up its town charter by turning one of our own town council members against us. Emilie Rump still lived in town and was bravely paying the price for her treason.

I patted him on the shoulder. "Are you too nice to say you want to kick Dominion's ass?"

He winced. "Yes. Please don't think less of me."

"Darius, my friend, you are talking to the queen of vengeance. I *live* for a good grudge."

"It's true," Hazel called out. "She *still* hates the girl in our fifth-grade class who reminded the teacher that he hadn't assigned any homework yet a minute before we were dismissed on a Friday."

"Fucking Gwendolyn Murphy," I hissed at the memory.

"Dominion tried to ruin our town. They tried to turn us into some loud, polluted spring break annex. I want them to pay. I want to hit them where it hurts. I want to make them rue the day they ever tried to mess with Story Lake!" Darius shook his fist at the ceiling.

"I like this side of you, boy genius. How exactly can I help?"

"The town needs someone who can work on convincing tourists that Story Lake is where they want to spend their summer vacation. We're already seeing a bump thanks to the retirement community opening and, of course, our famous resident romance novelist," he continued.

"That's me. He's talking about me," Hazel sang. Meetcute barked his agreement.

"But we need more. We need a concentrated effort to get people to come here and willingly spend their money, preferably all year round," Darius continued.

"I'll be back in New York by the fall." *Dear Lord, please*, I added in my head. "I might be willing to help you with the spring and summer tourist seasons. But you should know, I'm an agent, not an actual publicist."

"Don't listen to her, Darius," Hazel called from her table. "She's done my publicity for years. She's perfect for what you need."

I'd never been perfect for anything anyone ever needed.

"Excellent," Darius said. "There's a salary. A small one."

I crossed my arms. "Keep talking."

He glanced around the store and then handed over a folded gum wrapper as if it were his great-grandma's prized chili recipe.

The number was less than I'd made selling soft pretzels at the mall in college. But given my current situation, every cent counted.

"I know it's not much," he said quickly. "But it's all the budget could afford. Keep in mind, you'll be providing a much-needed service to the good people of Story Lake. *And* you get an unlimited supply of special town merch like *this*."

He produced a postcard from his backpack with a flourish.

It was an illustration of the town's welcome sign with a convertible smashed into it. A cartoon Goose was perched on top of the car with a fish in his beak. *Welcome to Story Lake.*

"You commemorated our arrival. That's hilariously sweet."

"The high school marketing and graphic design club takes their inspiration from real life. You and Hazel are the best things to happen to Story Lake since Dave Matthews's tour bus broke down here in 2013."

"What is it exactly that you want me to do?" I asked.

Darius pressed his palms together. "I want you to work with the council and local businesses to bring more people here. The more tourists we get, the more people fall in love with our beautiful town, the more folks move here and pay property taxes. We can upgrade the sewage treatment plant, build pickleball courts, and make our downtown and lakefront irresistible. And then we can rub our success in Dominion's face!"

I liked Story Lake. I mean, I didn't want to live here permanently, but it was cute and quirky. It reminded me of me. More importantly, I needed the money.

"Okay."

"Okay, like okay okay?" Darius asked.

I nodded. "Yeah. Let's do this. Do we shake on it or sign a contract?"

"We solemnly high-five," he said, holding up his hand.

"We what?"

He grinned. "I'm just kidding. I have a contract with me." He reached into his backpack again and pulled out a thin stack of papers.

"Better have a lawyer look at that," Hazel called.

"I'm sure Gage would be happy to answer any questions," Darius said, glancing at his smartwatch. "I have to get back for chemistry."

"I'll walk you out," I said, slipping my arm through his. "So, Darius. Is this like a biweekly-direct-deposit thing or a lump-sum-up-front?"

4

Meteor muffins
Gage

Story Lake Haven's entrance was a wide strip of fresh asphalt between two stacked stone pillars on the northern end of town. Phase one had begun on the rehab of the former hospital grounds and the small neighboring apartment complex that had once housed employees into a state-of-the-art assisted living facility and retirement community.

Bishop Brothers Construction was now spearheading phase two, the development of an independent living neighborhood on twenty acres of neglected farmland. All told, there would be fifty main-floor living cottages with attached garages, zero-entry front doors, and doorways wide enough to accommodate wheelchairs. The first dozen cottage occupants were slated to take possession in May.

I tossed a wave to the landscaping crew as they worked on the new flower beds along the drive and pulled up to the curb in front of a nearly finished bungalow with hunter-green siding. Pride pushed aside the lingering stress from the morning. We built this. Together. The latest generation of Bishops to leave our mark on Story Lake.

Cam's truck was in the driveway, and Levi's was parked across the street. Nana gave an excited shiver of anticipation. The dog loved jobsites. It was the perfect combination of people to pay attention to her and food carelessly left at golden retriever level.

We entered through the back slider, and I drew in a deep breath. Fresh paint, new carpet, and sawdust. It smelled like home, like family.

It sounded like it too.

"Fuck off. I don't know what you're talking about."

"You get fucking dumber since yesterday? How could you not remember? We spent hours on that thing."

My brothers' argument in the basement was loud enough to drown out the cabinet crew in the kitchen. After the appropriate number of greetings for Nana, we headed downstairs.

Cam and Levi hadn't accomplished a hell of a lot on the change order for a Lego storage room since I'd left earlier. They were both sitting on upside-down hardware store buckets, looking at their phones.

Cam looked up. "Gigi, you remember the pinball game Dad put in the barn when we were kids. Or are you an idiot like this one?" He pointed at Levi, who shook his head at me while yawning.

"Fun House?"

"I fucking told you," Cam said, springing to his feet to point victoriously at Levi.

Levi rolled his eyes. "I had him going. He was a minute away from driving over to Mom and Dad's to dig through the old photo albums. I was gonna nap in my truck."

"I knew you were fucking with me," Cam insisted.

"You look like shit, Livvy," I observed. He had dark circles under his eyes, and his hair was standing up in tufts.

He responded with a middle finger in my direction.

"What the hell's your problem? You out clubbing all night?" Cam asked.

I snorted. The day Levi voluntarily socialized was the day the devil took up snowboarding.

"I was writing," he said on another yawn.

"Great. Just what I need. Another part-time brother," Cam complained.

"Fuck you, Cammy. I don't wanna hear your shit when you didn't get a damn thing done since I left," I said, gesturing around the basement, which was exactly the same as when I'd left.

"Hey, asshole. We went across the street and swapped out the damaged tile in the laundry room," Levi explained, scrubbing a hand over his face. "Where's my sandwich?"

"Fuck your sandwich. Where's my spray foam?" Cam demanded.

"Here's your fucking spray foam and your goddamn sandwich." I whipped their respective bags at them.

Cam fished the can out of his bag. "What took you so long?"

"Where the hell's my mustard?" Levi asked, frowning down at his sandwich. Nana sidled closer to him, looking hopeful.

"Driving your bride and her irresponsible BFF around after an incident with Goose. And it's in the bag, dumbass."

Levi paused his condiment search. "Heh. You're fucked."

I picked up my tool belt. "Excuse me?"

He pointed the business end of his sandwich at Cam, and Nana leaned in, nose twitching. "That's how his whole deal started. Rescuing Hazel from Goose. You playing hero to Zoey? It's a sign."

Cam grinned, which I found disconcerting. I still wasn't used to my grumpy brother's newfound happiness. "I was fucking heroic," he announced.

I shook my head as I clipped on the belt. "Please. You can't rewrite history. You yelled at her and accused her of trying to kill a bald eagle. You should be kissing her feet every day for putting up with your crabby ass. And when the hell did you get so superstitious, Livvy?"

Levi shrugged broad shoulders and squirted a yellow river of mustard onto his sandwich. Nana let out a low grumble, and the drool started to flow. "Maybe it's the sleep deprivation. But it feels like a pattern," he said.

I did not like where this conversation was going. It was bad enough I had to keep reminding myself that I wasn't into Zoey. It would be a thousand times worse if my brothers caught on to the inconvenient, purely physical attraction.

"Let the record show that Goose is not a matchmaker. He's a bald eagle with asshole tendencies. He dropped a snake on Zoey. She ran out in the road and right into me," I explained.

That wiped the smile off Cam's face as he ruffled Nana's fur, distracting her from deli meat. "She okay?"

"She's fine." I would be too after a beer, a shower, and a good night's sleep so I could stop picturing her lying there motionless on the road.

"Then why do you look like someone pissed in your beer?" Cam asked.

"Maybe it's your imagination." I made a show of picking up a two-by-four and slinging it across the second pair of sawhorses.

"Liv?" Cam said, pointing at me.

"He's right," Levi said around a mouthful of turkey and cheese. "You look morose and shit."

"Maybe it's because I'm stuck working with my two idiot brothers on a nice spring day." Most days, at least one of us wanted to punch another one of us in the face. There was the occasion when we did throw a punch or two, but those were few and far between, usually settled with a cold beer, and involved a pact not to tell Mom.

"Bullshit," they said in unison.

I sighed. "Fine. I almost didn't see her in time. She got knocked down. I nearly had a fucking heart attack. Scared the shit out of me. There. Happy?"

The image of Zoey lying on the road, eyes closed, surfaced again, and my heart sped up.

"Why would that make us happy?" Levi asked, appalled.

Cam was already pulling his phone out of his pocket and dialing.

"Haze," he said into the phone. "Why didn't I get a call the second my brother tried to run down your best friend?"

"I didn't try to run anyone down," I said loud enough for Hazel and everyone upstairs to hear.

Cam held up his middle finger and stomped over to the far corner of the basement to continue his interrogation.

"That sucks," Levi said.

"She's fine," I insisted.

"Probably brought up some Laura-related shit," he guessed.

I shrugged. "Maybe." Our sister's life had changed when she and her husband had been out for an early morning run and a driver hadn't seen them. Laura was in a wheelchair now, and Miller... Miller was gone.

Were we all really one mistake away from ruining someone else's life?

It was a thought I didn't want to sit with. I was careful. I was responsible. I made plans, set goals, took action. I didn't make mistakes that carelessly destroyed families.

Levi nodded sagely, then took another bite of his sandwich.

"Good talk," I said.

He grunted.

Cam returned. "They're fine. So you gonna go into some 'reminded of Larry's accident downward spiral' shit? Because that would be stupid. And we're not equipped to deal with that, so we'd probably have to call in Mom, and she'd just kick your ass."

"He is," Levi said, ratting me out.

"I'm *fine*."

"Probably easier to believe him than to get Mom involved," Levi observed.

"Good point. Talk over. Problem solved." Cam glared at Levi. "Great. Now I want a damn sandwich."

Nana perked up and swiveled on her butt to eye her other uncle, who had said one of her favorite words.

I pointed to the third bag I'd deposited on the sawhorses. "There's two more in there. Plus chips."

"You're my favorite," Cam said, pouncing on the bag.

"Great. Now can we please accomplish something with this closet before I have to leave?"

"After sandwiches," Cam promised. "So back to the wedding. Picture this. Open bar with whiskey flights."

"You trying to get someone to puke on the bride?" Levi asked.

I checked my watch and swore as I hurried through the front door of the building. We'd finally gotten the Lego room framed out before being called down the street to mediate a dispute between the plumbers and electricians vying over schedules in another bungalow.

"You have fourteen minutes," my paralegal stated from the first-floor doorway.

Declan had fiery red hair and made adventurous fashion choices. I'd assumed that both factors would reflect a charismatic personality. However, after two months of working together, I had yet to see any evidence of a personality. At least the kid was efficient. Sometimes too efficient. I was glad business was picking up, because on days he caught up with his work, he listened to epic fantasy audiobooks and acted out the swordplay with a cardboard tube.

"I'll be on time," I assured him as I yanked my shirt over my head and charged for the door to the stairway with Nana galloping at my heels. The building I'd bought for my law office five years ago came with a small one-bedroom apartment on the second floor that I'd at one time intended to rent out, but instead it had defaulted to storage and shower facilities.

"You also have a report from the process server on your desk, and the mediator for client 1107 rescheduled tomorrow's meeting," he said, following me to the door.

"Client names, not numbers, Declan. And please get the tea started," I yelled back as I took the stairs two at a time.

"Shall I put out the cookies?" he called.

Mrs. Babcock had brought me muffins every visit, and while the woman was smart, stylish, and wealthy, she couldn't bake for shit. On the word *cookies,* Nana abandoned me and hurtled back downstairs to the office.

"No, she's bringing muffins again."

"I'll hide the trash can under the table by your chair," Declan promised.

I gave the door an unceremonious boot and was working on my pants when an unwelcome idea hit me. I paused, hand on my zipper, in the middle of the living room. It needed new carpet and a fresh coat of paint. And I'd have to get all the files out of the bedroom and living room. But overall, the place was in decent shape. I'd never done the landlord thing before, but for the right tenant... Except Zoey would be the absolute wrong tenant. It would be a huge mistake, a terrible idea.

"Thirteen minutes," Declan announced from downstairs.

"Fuck."

Eleven minutes later, I returned to the first floor, still tying my tie. "I know, I know. Two minutes," I said when Declan opened his mouth behind his desk.

I'd given my mom and Laura carte blanche on the interior design when I bought the building. Rather than dark and dignified like the standard law office, they'd gone with light and airy with light wood floors, white walls, and green accents. I'd managed to keep the plants they'd insisted on alive and even added a few pieces of farmland-themed art that they didn't hate. The overall effect was bright and calm. It suited me and my practice.

"Actually, it's one minute and forty-nine seconds," Declan said, gesturing to a digital timer, one of only two personal effects he'd brought with him. The other one was a plain white coffee mug.

"Appreciate the accuracy. Did you print out the copies?" Mrs. Babcock had changed her will three times in the last four months, and I couldn't wait to hear what the latest addendum was.

He nodded solemnly. "I arranged them in a fan next to the tea in the conference room."

From behind his desk, I heard the thump of Nana's tail. The guy might have been stoic as a statue, but he did let my dog sleep at his feet.

"Great. Thanks."

I was just poking my head into the conference room when the front door jingled open and Mrs. Babcock called out her customary, "Yoo-hoo."

She was a statuesque woman with dark, unlined skin that she credited to practicing what she preached in her successful dermatology practice, which she'd sold for a small fortune on her retirement. She favored colorful caftans and pricey-looking purses. Her single, straight granddaughter was tall as well but with a more bohemian vibe. Her long braids were secured in a high ponytail, and she wore an oversize floral cardigan on top of a pair of paint-splattered overalls. She was holding a cellophane tray of meteor-like muffins.

"You're early," Declan announced, looking mildly perturbed. My paralegal didn't handle it well when there were deviations from his carefully crafted schedule.

Nana trotted out from behind the desk and politely offered her paw to the visitors.

"There's my cutie patootie," Mrs. Babcock crooned, leaning down to ruffle Nana's fur. My dog dissolved in a puddle of ecstasy before wriggling over to the granddaughter.

"It's always good to see you, Mrs. Babcock. Declan has some tea in the conference room," I said. The tea helped the hockey pucks masquerading as muffins go down.

"Wonderful! Declan, you're a treasure. Now, Gage. This is my gorgeous granddaughter Gabby. Gabby, this is my handsome attorney Gage."

"Gram," Gabby said in exasperation.

"Pleasure to meet you," I said, offering my hand.

"I've heard a lot about you," Gabby said.

"I only told her what a perfect gentleman you are and what

a travesty it is that you're still single. Now, who's ready to talk about how much money I can leave to the most darling cat rescue I discovered?" Mrs. Babcock sang on her way into the conference room.

Gabby handed over the muffins. "The trick with these is to crumble them up on your plate so it *looks* like you ate more. And just so you know, I have a boyfriend. He's wonderful. I just haven't introduced her to him because of the whole overbearing and intimidating deal."

"Good for you and disappointing for me."

"Mmm. Gram always did have good taste," she teased. "Now let's go choke down some muffins and rescue some one-eyed cats."

Laura: Just got back from the gym. The rumor mill was working overtime today. According to the woman doing deadlifts next to me, Gage backed over a tourist from the city, but it's okay because it was a setup by Dominion to raise our crime statistics.
Hazel: Gage hit Zoey with his truck, but only after she ran into the road to escape an eagle and a snake. She's fine. No Dominion involvement, unless they've secretly been training our bald eagle.
Cam: Why were you at the gym?
Laura: To work out, dumbass.
Gage: Zoey's fault. My flawless driving record is still intact. Why were you at the gym without us, Larry? We work out together.
Laura: Codependent much?
Levi: According to the guy I just asked at the front desk, she's working with a trainer.
Laura: Does everyone in this town have a gigantic mouth?
Cam: What's a trainer know that we don't?

Hazel: A lot probably.
Gage: What are his credentials? Where did he get his degree?
Laura: This is why no one likes any of you.
Levi: My source says Wes started training with him a few weeks ago for basketball. Family discount?
Hazel: Is he attractive? Asking for research purposes.
Cam: I thought I was your research? 💪
Laura: I'm going to single-handedly raise Story Lake's crime stats by murdering most of you.

5

Sun's out, buns out

Zoey

I was late. Again. I'd gotten distracted putting the finishing touches on my presentation and worked straight through the alarm on my phone. And of course there was no parking left in the funeral home's lot. It was weird that Story Lake hosted town meetings in a building full of dead people, weirder still that no one else seemed to find it odd. But that was the vibe of this place: Weirdos welcome.

It had been a chaotic several days, and I felt like I was on a treadmill slipping closer and closer to flying off the back. In addition to prepping for Hazel's launch by shoving her story—romance novelist finds inspiration and her own happily ever after—down the throats of every journalist, podcaster, and influencer on my contacts list, I'd made a trip back to the city to start the monumental task of packing up my apartment.

I'd split one too many farewell bottles of wine with my cousin Inez and Mrs. Newville. In my drunken state, I'd impulsively purchased a box of Earl Wiggens's favorite cigars and had them overnighted to his house. Not only did sober me discover too late that they were obscenely expensive, I'd also forgotten to put my name on the card, thereby not receiving any credit for said obscenely expensive gift.

My financial and tactical regret was compounded by a nagging hangover, during which I'd turned in my rental car. I'd intended to get a modest, practical SUV. Instead, I'd fallen for a totally impractical ancient Mazda Miata convertible. The most recent owner had been a delivery driver, so its brakes squeaked and the interior smelled vaguely of cooked onions, but I'd just put the top down and let it air out while I sportily zipped around. Besides, I wouldn't be here by the time winter rolled around again, so there was no need to worry about the rear-wheel drive in Pennsylvania snow.

I still hadn't looked for an apartment yet in Story Lake. But that was next on my list...after tonight.

In between all my other duties, I'd spent a large and unplanned number of hours working on my first town council presentation as Story Lake's official publicist. Well, as "official" as I could be, seeing as I still hadn't reviewed or signed the contract. That was also on my list.

I entered the front doors of Pushing Up Daisies, out of breath. All three viewing rooms had been opened up to accommodate the crowd tonight. Since the Haven began welcoming residents, town meeting attendance had tripled. Apparently older folks liked alcohol and town debate.

Speaking of alcohol, I was too late to partake of tonight's fruit punch and vodka fundraiser for the girls' volleyball team. Alcohol sales stopped when the meeting started. So there went my chance at some liquid courage.

The local a cappella group, the Story Lake Warblers, was just finishing up their official "singing the meeting to order" when I spotted an empty chair in the middle of the room between Billie and Gage. I wasn't thrilled about the Gage part—his general disapproval of me wouldn't help my nerves—but Billie always packed snacks, so I figured it was worth the discomfort.

I apologized and excused my way down the row, climbing over legs and mobility implements to the chair.

"I hope this seat isn't taken, because I'd rather sit in someone's lap than crawl back out of here," I whispered, flopping down.

"All yours. Twizzlers?" Billie offered up her snack bag.

"Don't mind if I do. Hi," I said to Gage.

"Hey," he replied with little warmth. He looked irritatingly good as usual. His hair had a slight fresh-from-the-shower curl to it. Instead of his blue-collar-by-day look, he was wearing a zippered cardigan over a T-shirt, which I immediately decided to be turned off by.

Hazel gave me a finger wave from her spot on the dais at the front of the room between Cam and Kitty Suarez, the newest council member. Kitty had replaced Emilie Rump, the traitorous grump who had been removed for "treason against the town." Emilie was seated in the second row, tension visible in everything from her shoulders to her tight blond curls. I had to admire the woman's gumption for still showing up to town meetings when she knew she was unwelcome. It took ovaries of steel to bear the brunt of town-wide anger.

"I'm so happy to see so many smiling Story Lake faces," Mayor Darius announced from his end of the table. "We've got a lot of exciting things on the agenda tonight, so let's get started. First up, the status of the sewage treatment plant upgrade requirements."

It was a long-winded and technical explanation about the improvements that would take place over the next few years that had me tuning him out in the first two sentences. I ate my Twizzlers and hoped that my presentation would be more captivating. I wanted to make a good impression, show the town that I was the right person for the job. Even if it was a job I didn't actually want and had no intention of keeping, I still wanted to be good at it.

Gage leaned in, and my heart rate kicked up a notch in anticipation of an insult or barely detectable slight. I caught the clean whiff of soap. Just regular old off-the-shelf soap. What in the holy bananas was with the tickle of attraction in my belly? The man was in a *cardigan*, for Pete's sake. Cardigans weren't hot unless you were Pedro Pascal. I liked suits worn by unattainable men who were good in bed and bad everywhere else.

"Heard you're on the agenda tonight," he said, drawing my attention away from his confusingly sexy sweater.

I nodded. "First presentation as town publicist. Got any advice? Besides staying away from moving vehicles."

I scanned the crowd. It was a melting pot of ages, ethnicities, sexual orientations, and financial backgrounds. As far as I could tell, the only thing they all had in common was the fact that they were in this room listening to Darius talk about where poop goes.

"We're a fiercely loyal people," he said. "As long as you can convince everyone that this will benefit Story Lake, they'll get behind you."

"Good to know."

"By the way, weren't you supposed to stop by with a contract for me to look at?" he asked.

"How did you—"

He deigned to give me a smirk. "Small town, remember? Cam mentioned it last week. Then Hazel texted me to remind you if I saw you tonight. Oh, and Darius hired me to write the damn thing."

"Isn't that a little conflict of interest-y?"

"I give you my word I'm not trying to screw you."

"Right back at ya." The words left my mouth before my brain filter could catch them. "Uh. I mean, Twizzler?" I snagged another one from Billie's bag and offered it to him.

He looked at it like I'd just offered him a chalice of poison. "I'm good. Thanks."

Snack snob.

"So, uh, back to the contract. I didn't have time this week. Do you have any openings next week?" I asked.

"I can make room."

I pulled out my phone and opened my calendar app.

"Christ, woman. What the hell is that?" Gage demanded.

"It's my calendar."

"You have fifteen events every single day."

Every event also had at least two reminders or alarms attached to it, but he didn't need to know that.

"I don't want to forget anything. Stop judging me." I scrolled through my week. "I have time at four on Wednesday."

Gage consulted his own tidy, color-coded calendar. "That works." He looked like he was going to say something else, but a ripple of grumbles in the crowd had us both turning our attention back to the front of the room.

Emilie Rump was standing in front of the microphone set up for comments from the crowd. "I have a comment on town ordinance fifty-seven, subsection L."

The grumbling in the crowd grew louder.

To their credit, the council members refrained from eye rolling and began to page through their fat binders. Apparently organizing a town required at least a century's worth of paperwork.

"No need, folks. I've got it all up here," Darius said, tapping his temple. "Ordinance fifty-seven, subsection L, lays out appropriate means of fishing. Specifically that no one may catch a fish with their bare hands."

Cam kicked back in his chair next to Hazel and crossed his arms. The glare he delivered in Emilie's direction would have microwaved a lesser mortal.

"Oh, come on," someone called out behind us.

"Sit on your rump, Rump, and leave town business to people who actually care about Story Lake," someone else barked.

The audience started to boo.

"I have a right to comment about laws being broken," Emilie insisted. "I saw Willis Whimperschmidt pull a walleye out of the lake with his bare hands on Saturday at 9:17 a.m. I reported it to the chief of police, who said, and I quote, 'Why don't you mind your business before someone decides to feed you to the fish?'"

A ripple of laughter rolled through the crowd. Levi Bishop

was only a few months into his unwanted term as chief of police and had taken an unorthodox approach to wielding his authority.

Willis got to his feet in the fourth row. The man was always wearing some variation of flannel and overalls. "I hooked the damn fish, reeled the damn thing in, and my damn net had a damn hole in it, so I used my damn hands. Sue me," he snarled.

"I might be forced to if our law enforcement refuses to enforce the laws of our forefathers," Emilie said dramatically into the microphone. The woman clearly took the rules seriously.

"I don't care how many fathers you have. Quit wasting our time," someone yelled.

"Care to comment, Chief?" Darius asked.

All heads swiveled to the back of the room where Levi leaned against the wall. He was just as good-looking as his brothers, but where Gage was outgoing and charming—to people who weren't me—Levi was reserved. And where Cam was a straight up grouch, Levi was more broody.

He shrugged his massive shoulders. "It's a stupid law. I'm not enforcing it."

"Thank you for your comment, Emilie. I'll add ordinance fifty-seven, subsection L, to the list of ordinances to be repealed this year," Darius said.

"But it's the law *now*," she insisted. "Laws should be enforced."

A potato sailed through the air and hit Emilie in the shoulder. It exploded on contact and hit the floor with a dull thump. A low rumble of laughter spread through the crowd.

"I still don't get the whole potato thing," I whispered to Billie.

"Potatoing is an acceptable form of punishment reserved for citizens who have committed crimes against the town. Potatoes must be baked and no bigger than six inches long," she instructed as she reached into her tote and pulled out an actual baked potato. Billie winged it in Emilie's direction and hit her squarely on the left butt cheek. "See? It's a safe and entertaining way to show your displeasure. Also it's a great way to use up extra potatoes before they go bad."

On another wave of boos, the defeated, mashed Emilie

returned to her seat next to her husband, who looked as though he'd like to be removed from the situation via trapdoor.

"I almost kind of feel sorry for her," I said, cringing in secondhand embarrassment. "Maybe she just made a mistake?"

"You don't accidentally try to dismantle your own town just so you can rise to power," Gage said dryly.

But there was something about Emilie's "square peg in a round hole" situation that struck a chord with me. I'd heard she was the mediocre middle sister in an extraordinary sibling sandwich and could empathize. My older sister was the light of my parents' life. I was the punch line to the joke that started, "We should have stopped at one kid."

Laura, Gage's sister, raised her hand from the front row where she sat next to her parents. "I'd like to make a motion that only citizens who haven't committed treason against the town are allowed to speak at town meetings."

"Thank you for that motion, Laura," Darius said. "I'll add it to the list of motions for our town attorney to review."

Beside me, Gage heaved an irritated sigh as the crowd murmured their agreement.

"You're the town attorney, aren't you?" I asked him.

"Yep."

"You Bishops sure commit to the community involvement thing," I noted.

"This town has given us a lot. It's our turn to give back," he said, sounding defensive.

"Relax, Mr. Rogers. It was a positive observation, not a criticism."

Gage took a long breath, then blew it out, but he didn't answer. His two fingers tapped out a beat on his thigh, telling me I'd once again managed to irritate him just by breathing in his vicinity. I chalked it up as another win for me.

"Moving on," Darius continued from the front. "We have town publicist Zoey Moody making her first presentation. So put the potatoes down, folks."

"Good luck," Billie whispered as I crawled over her.

"Thanks. Excuse me. Sorry. Pardon me."

I made it to the aisle without breaking anyone's toes and only tripping twice. I straightened my blazer and made sure my skirt wasn't hiked up in the back.

"All set?" I whispered to funeral home director and audiovisual queen Lacresha on my way to the microphone. I'd emailed her my presentation before I left.

"Can't wait to see what speech goes with those slides," she said, giving me a toothy grin and a thumbs-up.

I'd basically been planning to read what was on the slides, which were pretty self-explanatory, so her comment made me nervous. But I turned to address the council anyway. "Uh, thank you, Mayor Oglethorpe. For those of you who don't know me—"

"We all know who you are, Zoey. Skip to the good stuff," the grizzled, tow-truck-driving Gator Johnson called from the second row. His elegant wife, Lang, elbowed him in the ribs and gave me an encouraging smile.

"Uh, right. Okay. So I'm here to discuss a town-wide education initiative—"

"I don't like education! School's for fools," bellowed a man on a mobility scooter and wearing a shirt that read *I farted*. Just my luck, it was Grumpy George from the bookstore.

"You might not hate this since it could make it easier for you to get to all those Western novels you like so much, George. So I suggest you temporarily zip it and save your comments for the end. Otherwise, I'll lose track every time you interrupt me and have to start over. We'll be here all night," I warned.

He harrumphed but shut his piehole.

I signaled Lacresha to cue up the presentation. "Now, as you can see here, Dominion attracts tourists who are mainly in their twenties and thirties. They're often unmarried recreational drinkers looking for action-packed adventures."

A general chuckle rose up, punctuated by a few wolf whistles. I turned around to face the screen and immediately joined Emilie's husband in wishing for a trapdoor. This wasn't my presentation. These were my beach vacation photos from three years ago. I'd grabbed the wrong drive, and now everyone in town was staring at me in a hot-pink bikini, holding a margarita the size of an aquarium.

"Oh my God," I squeaked.

"I stand corrected. Education ain't so bad," George shouted.

I frantically stabbed buttons on the remote, looking for a way to turn it off, but only succeeded in flipping through several more photos before a video of me showing off my sunburned butt cheeks in a thong appeared. The whistles got louder, and my face cheeks burned brighter than the ones on-screen.

"For the love of God, Lacresha, turn it off!" I yelped.

The screen went blank, and the crowd applauded. "Whatever it is you're selling, we're in," joked Quaid, our resident bodybuilder.

"For the record, that was not my presentation," I said into the microphone.

"Well, you've certainly got everyone's attention," Darius said, eyes still averted. "Please continue."

"Okay. All right. Let me just…organize my thoughts." I closed my eyes for a beat and tried to think my way through the embarrassment. At least no one had thrown a potato at me. Why was I here? What were the ideas I'd crammed into the slide deck? Education. Right. I could do this.

"You got this, Zoey," Billie called.

Scattered applause broke out, and I opened my eyes. "Look, the bottom line—ha—is Dominion sucks."

The applause was louder, more organized now, and people were nodding. My eyes locked on Gage, who gave me a grudging nod.

"They think just because they have the market on tourism cornered that they can push Story Lake around. But they can't. I've seen firsthand Story Lake pushing Dominion right back."

"Yeah, right off the dock," Laura crowed from the front row.

"Shit waffle!" someone shouted.

It was Hazel's turn to go bright red. She was the one who had shoved Dominion's mayor off the dock into the lake last summer and coined the term *shit waffle*. It had become Story Lake's unofficial town insult.

"Exactly. Well, I want to talk to you about pushing back harder. There are a lot of people out there who want a lake vacation without the poor-quality food, expensive drinks, and unfriendly atmosphere of Dominion. With a little education and some help here and there, you can find a way to welcome everyone that Dominion excludes. Families with young kids, people over the age of thirty-five, retirees, book clubs," I said, pointing at Hazel. She grinned. "My brilliant best friend who writes novels you all should be reading was on the right track with Summer Fest. Story Lake isn't some diesel-fueled, Jet Ski–propelled spring break rager. You're better than that, and it's time tourists took notice."

The applause gave me the confidence of a late-night talk show host with a captive audience.

"So let's talk about how you do that," I continued. "I'm proposing Story Lake schedules a series of educational…" I glanced at George, who looked like he was about to complain again. "Er, parties," I continued. "There will be food and drinks and official speakers who can help you implement town-wide initiatives like autism-friendly protocols, sign language lessons, accessibility plans to make your retail and restaurant spaces safer and more convenient for people with mobility issues. You've already done a lot of work to provide access. Now you just need to turn that access into welcome. Everyone who gets excluded in Dominion will be welcome here."

"Who's gonna do this educating?" someone asked.

"And how are we going to get people to show up?" another townsperson asked.

"I've got some ideas about both of those things. Starting with putting up billboards of my vacation photos. I'm absolutely just kidding."

"You were *awesome*," Billie said, hugging me around the neck as I returned to my seat. "Is this what you've been working on downstairs in the bar every night?"

"That and my alcohol tolerance," I joked. My heart was thumping like I'd just run a 5k uphill, and I had a waterfall of sweat sluicing down my back, but I'd done it. I'd recovered from catastrophe, winged my presentation, and gotten a unanimous yes from the council to proceed with my plans. As a bonus, hardly anyone had fallen asleep, I hadn't gotten pelted with cooked vegetables, and George had no complaints after I'd finished presenting. To be fair, he'd been one of the sleepers. But I still counted it as a win.

"By the way, your butt looked amazing in that video. I'm saying that as a friend, not just as a member of the LGBTQ community," Billie said, offering me an open bag of marshmallows.

"Thanks." I spared a glance in Gage's direction. "What did you think?"

"I think you didn't blow it," he said, keeping his gaze straight ahead. "You were smart and entertaining. You didn't just get the buy-in. You got everyone excited about it."

"I meant about my butt."

For a brief, shining second, he grinned, still not looking at me. "That was pretty impressive too, Disaster."

I'd had worse nicknames.

I was flirting. It was a bad idea for a variety of reasons, but I was riding high, and he'd grudgingly called me smart. Which meant I'd really earned it. It felt good. *I* felt good.

I was just about to jam a marshmallow into my mouth before I could say anything too risqué when I saw Laura leave her spot in the front row. Her face was ashen as she wheeled herself out of the room. Frank and Pep Bishop watched her go with twin looks of concern. "Is your sister okay?"

"Why?" Gage asked with a frown.

"She just left in a hurry. Your parents look worried."

He pulled his phone out of his pocket. The screen was already lit with some kind of alert that I couldn't quite read without climbing into his lap.

Gage lifted his gaze to me. His green eyes locked on my face, though I could tell his thoughts were already far away. "I gotta go." He rose and worked his way to the aisle. A moment later, his parents followed. Cam scowled from his seat on the dais and showed his phone to Hazel, who looked like she was going to be sick. I twisted in my seat and noticed Levi was gone from his spot at the back of the room.

No one else appeared to be paying attention to the fact that nearly every single Bishop had vacated the room. But I felt consumed with an inexplicable tension. Cam was getting antsier by the second, and Hazel was rubbing his leg under the table.

I suffered through another ten minutes of "town business" before Dr. Ace called to adjourn the meeting.

"Second," Cam said, springing to his feet. He gave Hazel a possessive squeeze, then bolted for the door just as the motion passed.

"What's going on?" I asked when I finally threaded my way through the crowd to Hazel.

She shook her head again and grabbed my arm. "Not here."

We ducked out into the lobby, and since half the town was exiting the building at the same time, Hazel pulled me through a door marked PRIVATE. It turned out to be a small staff kitchen with death-related magnets decorating the refrigerator.

She closed the door and leaned against it.

"What? Is one of the kids sick?" Laura had three teenagers who were the center of her world.

Hazel scraped her hands over her face. "No. They're fine. The driver who hit Laura and her husband, Miller, was finally charged."

6

A carpet tack in the ass
Gage

I took a swing, sending the head of the sledgehammer through stud and 1990s beige drywall with a satisfying crash. It wasn't entirely clear to me when I'd decided to fix up the upstairs apartment, but it probably had something to do with the primitive desire to demolish something I'd had since hearing the news earlier that week. I felt like I was suffocating in anger.

I was just teeing up again when Cam appeared in the bedroom doorway.

"What the hell? I thought this was just some cosmetic patchwork, and you're fucking rearranging walls?" he complained.

Levi poked his head into the room and grimaced. "Where's my dog niece?"

"With our human niece. I paid Isla twenty bucks to take her for the day so Nana doesn't chew any more sheets of drywall," I said, dropping the hammer on the plywood floor and picking up my thermos. "And for your information, I'm not rearranging walls. I took out the pantry to make a bigger bedroom closet. Got a problem with that?"

Cam snorted. "Yeah, I do. You said 'touch up.' You can't 'touch up' a gaping hole in the wall."

"First of all, stop using air quotes. It makes you look like an even bigger dumbass than usual. Second, we do this for a living. You think I can't reframe a closet in a day?"

"I think you look like you wanna take out a few more walls," Levi observed evenly.

"Well, fuck you too, Livvy."

He held up his hands in surrender. "Just sayin', man."

"What exactly are you just sayin'?" I demanded, taking an angry swig of cold water from my thermos. But nothing cooled the fire in my chest.

The driver who had killed my brother-in-law and destroyed my sister's life had been charged. But the middle-of-the-road charges were a goddamn slap in the face after everything my family had lost.

"If you're gonna be a temperamental dick, then I'm gonna reclaim my Saturday and go get my fiancée naked. *Again*," Cam announced smugly.

My brother was an asshole. A well-sated asshole who didn't seem to be angry enough, in my opinion. Was that what love and consistent sex did to a man?

I shrugged and tossed the thermos back in the corner. "Fine. You don't wanna lend a hand? I don't need you. I can have this place done by Wednesday by myself."

"What's the rush?" Levi asked, sliding down the wall to the floor and kicking his legs out like he had nothing better to do. Levi, like me, was single and therefore lacked any fiancée to get naked.

"That's when a prospective tenant is coming over. Hence turning it into less of a shithole. Got a problem with that?" If anyone should have a problem with it, it should be me. I shouldn't even be entertaining the idea of letting Zoey Moody move in. I wasn't myself around her. She knocked me off-kilter every damn time I saw her. I knew better than to get closer to her. Yet here I was, demoing a closet with her in mind.

"That's his second 'got a problem with that' since we got here," Levi observed.

Cam glared at me. "I'm starting to have a problem."

"What?" I demanded.

"Who's your prospective tenant? And it better not be who I think it is."

"I don't care who you think it is."

"I think it better fucking not be Zoey Moody," Cam said. "I forbid it."

"You *forbid* it? You forbid me to rent out the apartment in a building *I* own?" Suddenly the idea of renting to Zoey seemed more appealing.

"I forbid you from using an apartment to make a move on my wife's best friend," he said, giving me a shove. There was that anger I wanted to see.

I shoved him back. "I'm not making a move. I'm offering her a place to stay."

"Oh, so you're just 'offering' her a place to stay that 'just so happens' to be above your law office out of the 'kindness of your heart'?" he pointed out.

"Gigi's right. You look like a dumbass with all the air quotes," Levi cut in.

I ignored him. "First of all, it would be weird—not to mention illegal—if I broke into someone else's property and started expanding the closet. Second, I'm not offering her the place for free. There's this thing called 'rent' that tenants are required to pay."

Cam shook his head at Levi. "I'm not buying it."

"Why not?" Levi and I asked at the same time.

"You've been sitting on this apartment for what? Five years? And the second the hot girl with the curly hair and the big—"

"Hey!" I warned him.

"I'm practically married. I was going to say *eyes*. The second the girl with the big *eyes* says she needs a place to stay, you turn into Mr. Let Me Renovate You a Closet. Ergo, you're trying to get into her pants."

"No more air quotes and no more ergos. You sound like an idiot," Levi said.

"Er-fucking-go," Cam doubled down.

"Come on," I complained. "Zoey is practically family. This is what we do, you gigantic shit burger. Or did you forget how you moved in with Laura after the accident? It's what family does."

If silence could be loud, our eardrums would have burst. I'd gone and done it. I'd brought up the thing we were all trying to pretend hadn't happened.

"Exactly!" Cam exclaimed as if I'd made his ridiculous point for him. "She and Hazel are practically sisters, which makes her *my* sister-in-law, which makes her off-fucking-limits to you."

"I think the wedding planning has finally made him snap," I said to Levi.

"I'm gonna snap you if you try to mess around with that girl."

"Holy hell, Cammy. It's an apartment, not a box of condoms," I said in exasperation.

"I didn't think you liked her," Levi said.

"I *don't* like her. She's annoying, she's irresponsible, she's always late, she says everything she's thinking, she's terrified of animals, and she hates Story Lake. She's more likely to move to the Caribbean and open a nightclub than settle down and start a family. Also, what made you think I didn't like her?"

"You're kind of an asshole to her all the time," Levi said.

"I'm not an asshole."

"You're an asshole who put a lot of thought into that list to be able to fire it off like that," Cam pointed out smugly.

"You wanna settle down?" Levi asked. "As in marriage?"

It was my turn to shrug. "Well, yeah. Don't you?"

"Dunno. Hadn't really thought about it. I've been too busy being fucking *chief of police* and plotting my revenge against you assholes."

"Great. We're gonna have to listen to him whine about being chief *and* the Great Paintball Incident for the rest of our lives now," I complained.

"You two clowns would be lucky if a woman was ever desperate enough to shackle herself to your stupid faces for life. You mean to tell me you don't have any feelings whatsoever for Zoey?" Cam asked, returning to the original subject.

Did finding her distractingly attractive count as feelings? "Only negative ones," I insisted.

Levi frowned. "What's your problem with her? She's great, and you like everyone."

"I don't like either of you." I pointed at Levi. "Why aren't you jumping all over him, Cammy? Livvy clearly has feelings for Zoey."

"You're an idiot," Levi complained.

"Because Livvy didn't decide to renovate an entire apartment that will put Zoey in forced proximity with him," Cam announced.

"I'm not kidnapping her," I said defensively.

"Forced proximity is a trope," Levi explained. "It means the main characters are physically stuck with each other."

"We're not stuck with each other. Believe me, that's the last thing I want," I insisted.

"So you expect us to believe this is all out of the goodness of your heart?" Cam pressed.

"I'm a nice guy, fuckface."

"You fell off a roof the first time you saw her," Levi pointed out.

It was true. I'd just hoped that no one else had noticed that I'd taken one look at that beautiful face, all that wild hair, and that my punch-in-the-gut reaction had knocked me right off Erleen Dabner's roof. Further proof that Zoey was dangerous.

"Whose side are you on anyway?" I asked.

"Mine. I came to paint walls and drink beer, not talk about feelings," Levi said.

Cam was pacing in front of the pile of old carpet I'd ripped up yesterday. "No. Nope. He says he doesn't have feelings. But that's exactly what *I* said when I *did* have feelings. Because we Bishops suck at having fucking feelings." He pointed at me violently. "You're gonna get tangled up with her. Then you're gonna get crushed. And I'll be stuck listening to you whine about being crushed. *Or* you're going to be a dick to her, and I'll have to kick your ass because she's basically my sister. Which makes her *your* sister. Which makes you disgusting."

"You really need a lesson in biology."

"I really need a beer," Levi complained.

"I'm not having *my* wedding ruined by a groomsman and a bridesmaid who fucked around and found out," Cam insisted.

"If I *were* interested in Zoey—which I absolutely am not—why wouldn't it work out? You and Hazel did," I argued with flawless logic. I wanted a fight, and if I couldn't get a satisfying legal one over our family's enemy, I could score an intellectual victory over my brother.

"Me and Haze are different."

"How? It's the same exact situation. Beautiful burned-out woman from the big city lands in a small town and meets a charming blue-collar hero."

"You've been reading Hazel's books," Levi observed.

"Hell yeah I have. She's a good writer. Maybe you could learn a thing or two from her." That was the thing about Bishop fights. No one was safe from the front lines.

"I'm trying. I'm taking her writing class at the Haven," he said.

"Really?" I asked, temporarily distracted from my anger. "How's it going?"

"It's going great because my wife is a fucking genius. Now back it up. I can only deal with one brother at a time," Cam said. He pointed at me again. "Me and Hazel are completely different. Hazel came here looking for something, and she found it. 'It' being *me*. Zoey is here for moral support, and everyone knows she's counting down the seconds until she can move back to the city. Also, I'm fucking irresistible, and I wore Hazel down."

"I believe he's saying you're not irresistible, Gigi," Levi said.

"At my worst 'three days into the stomach bug with a high fever' moment, I'm *still* more irresistible than Cam is on his best day," I insisted.

"Hate to be the voice of reason, because I would love to see you two shove each other's heads through drywall, but you're basically pissed at something else and making up shit that's less shitty to fight about," Levi said.

"When did he become Mr. Know-It-All?" I asked, hooking a thumb at Levi.

"Yeah, Mr. I'm Better Than Everyone Else Because I'm a Tortured Writer Guy," Cam said, changing alliances.

"It's called 'character motivation,' and I learned it from your fiancée, who would have you sleeping on the couch with a raccoon in a hot second if she heard you making fun of writers, you shithead."

I wasn't sure who started the pushing match—I liked to think I was the bigger man and was goaded into it—but within seconds, all three of us were shoving each other into walls.

"This is so fucking stupid," Levi complained as he fought to secure his headlock around Cam's neck.

"Yeah, but it feels kinda good," I said, sweeping his legs out from under him and making them both land in the pile of ripped-up carpet. "Doesn't it?"

"Better than talking about shit," Cam agreed, kicking me in the thigh at the same time Levi got a lucky hold on my opposite ankle and dropped me to the floor.

"No one better tell Mom about this," Levi said as he shoved my face into the underside of the carpet.

Something sharp poked me in the ass. "Who just stabbed me in the ass? The rule has always been no weapons!"

"Uh, hello?"

Fearing for our lives, we all froze and looked toward the door. Thankfully, it wasn't Mom. It was my paralegal, Declan, dressed in a baby-food-green sweater-vest and white cargo pants, holding his coffee mug.

"Uh, hi, Declan," I rasped, fighting to sit up. I winced at the sharp stabbing pain. "We were just…"

"Fighting," Cam said, booting Levi in the ass.

"I came in to change out my mug. I heard a struggle so I investigated," Declan announced, eyeing us dispassionately.

"Yeah, if you could not mention this to anyone, especially our mother, that would be great," I said, elbowing Cam in the ribs.

"Okay. Bye." And with that, he was gone.

"Weird dude," Cam observed. "I like him."

"Me too," I agreed.

"You know, I was just thinking while I was pummeling both your asses," Levi said. "If Zoey doesn't move in here, she can just live with you and Hazel, Cammy. Wouldn't be so bad. You just couldn't have sex in the living room or the dining room or the kitchen anymore. And you'd have to wear pants outside the bedroom."

Cam processed in silence for about ten seconds. Then on a growl, he got to his feet. "Gimme that sledgehammer."

"Speaking of asses, I think I have a carpet tack in mine," I announced.

I blamed Zoey for it.

Cam's sex life effectively threatened and the rusty carpet tack removed from my ass, we worked in silence for an hour, communicating only in grunts and the occasional middle finger. There was something therapeutic about demolition and construction. Working with your hands to build something new, something better, was good for the head. And an acceptable way to blow off enough steam so you didn't implode. We all needed it.

"Anyone want another beer?" I asked. After the minor ass surgery, we'd managed to clear out the carpet and demo materials and frame out the new, bigger closets. I'd also scheduled a tetanus shot for the next day with Dr. Ace.

Both brothers grunted.

I popped the lid on the cooler and handed out icy lagers.

We took the beers into the living room where there were fewer carpet tacks to sit on and arranged ourselves against the walls.

"So this writing class. How's it going?" I asked Levi.

He hefted his shoulders and took a pull of his beer.

In general, we Bishops were tougher than a bad clam to get to open up. But Levi made me and Cam look like Chatty Cathys. He'd always been the strong, silent type, and after Miller's death, he'd only gotten stronger and more silent. Levi had served with Miller in the army, forging a brotherly bond that rivaled our own.

"Good," Levi said. "We've only had a few classes so far."

"Why are you taking a class with a bunch of senior citizens?" Cam asked.

"Classes are open to the public. There's other people from town taking it. Scooter's in it to help his songwriting for the Warblers," Levi said.

Cam grimaced, which brought joy to my heart. He'd been the target of some vindictive a cappella after breaking up with Hazel last summer.

"How's the writing going?" I asked Levi.

He tilted his head against the wall and closed his eyes. "Depends on the day. I thought the better I got at it, the easier it would be. But Hazel assures me that's bullshit."

Cam shook his head. "I don't know how either one of you fucking does it. Gimme a nail gun and a stack of drywall, and I'll make shit happen. But put me in front of a blank page and tell me to make something up that someone else is gonna want to read, and I'd rather nail-gun my head to a wall."

"I feel like I'm nail-gunning my head to the desk on a daily basis," Levi admitted.

"We're gonna have to break into his place and read what he's working on," I told Cam.

Cam smirked. "It's probably about a guy who murders his two brothers."

"Or a sister who murders her three brothers," I guessed.

They studiously avoided eye contact with me. I'd done it again and brought up the one topic on everyone's mind that none of us wanted to address.

I cleared my throat. "Has anyone talked to Laura since the meeting?"

We'd converged on her house, and she'd sent us all packing with the insistence that she was fine and didn't need our asses hovering over her.

Levi scratched the back of his head. "Nope," he said.

Cam busied himself picking at the label on his beer. "She hasn't responded to any of the hilarious memes I sent."

"The kids say she seems okay but she's been quiet," I said.

Levi raised his beer. "Using the niece and nephews to spy. Nice."

"What the hell are we supposed to say? Sorry the monster who killed your husband is looking at only three years in prison?" Cam said bitterly. "It's a fucking joke."

A joke that none of us found remotely funny. I prided myself on being the easygoing one, but I didn't know what to do with the rage that simmered under the surface besides tear down walls with sledgehammers. I believed in justice. I fought for it on a daily basis. But this didn't feel like justice. It felt like more trauma.

"What did Mom and Dad say when you talked to them?" Levi asked me.

I blew out a breath. "Not much. I explained vehicular homicide and the potential jail time. Three years is the minimum, but given how reluctant the DA was to file the charges in the first place, it's likely she wouldn't get more than that. Obviously it's not enough. But as Mom pointed out, nothing is going to bring Miller back or get Laura back on her feet. This is the new normal."

"The new normal sucks," Cam muttered.

"Nothing we say or do is gonna make this less fucked up," Levi pointed out.

We were saved from further discussion by the buzzer downstairs.

I got to my feet. "That's the new bathroom vanity."

"Let's get back to work so we can stop talking about shit," Cam said, polishing off his beer.

"I'll drink to that," Levi muttered as I hit the stairs.

I found two delivery people at the front door balancing a dolly with a box between them. "This here's one big-ass vanity. Where do you want her, Gage?" the suspender-wearing woman asked in her Georgia-tinged accent as she peered over the massive box.

"Second floor, Ida. Thanks. How'd you get stuck doing Saturday deliveries?" Ida and her husband owned the hardware store just outside town limits.

"Hubs is back in Atlanta helping our oldest put a deck on her place. My nephew here is earning a few bucks and a peach pie for helping out today." She clapped a hand on her helper's shoulder.

"More excited about the pie than the cash," the kid said with a quick grin. "Auntie Ida makes the best peach pie."

"I appreciate your priorities. Let's get this upstairs so you can get back to your pie."

It took the three of us and some creative maneuvering, but we made it to the second floor with the vanity and all body parts still intact.

"That's not a vanity. That's a continent," Levi observed when they left.

Cam glared at me.

"What?" I asked in exasperation.

"You know what," he muttered.

"Why don't you go ahead and spell it out for me?"

"The huge-ass vanity, the closet remodel. I'm back to thinking you're into Zoey."

"Christ. I am not into Zoey. Do I find her attractive? Of course I do. I'm a man with two eyes. Anyone would find her attractive. But I'm serious about getting serious. And Zoey is the opposite of serious. She's…" I searched for the words that would convince me to stop thinking about her. "A disaster."

"He could be lying to himself. But since I already pulled one carpet tack out of someone's ass today, I don't feel like fighting anymore," Levi said.

Cam crossed his arms. "What are you suggesting?"

"I'm suggesting that as long as Gigi stays away from Zoey, the conversation is over."

"And if I don't stay away from her?" It was in my blood to argue both sides.

"Cam and I get to kick your ass, and you have to tell Mom you were the one who paintballed the barn door," Levi said.

I snorted. "I'm not taking the blame for that."

In our teens, we'd gone through the usual teenage-boy-paintball phase. However, someone had unleashed a neon-green torrent on the freshly painted barn door. Neon green was Levi's color, so he'd been blamed and punished, though he never once wavered in his insistence of his innocence.

"I've taken the blame for almost two decades!" Levi barked.

"Well, you shouldn't have shot up the barn then," Cam said.

"I *didn't*!" It was nearly impossible to get a rise out of Levi, and given the fact that we'd already ended up in one wrestling match, I figured it was smarter to change the subject. None of us needed more carpet tacks in the ass.

"How's the wedding planning going, Cammy?" I asked.

Cam scoffed. "Get this. Hazel was thinking about satin for the bridesmaid dresses. *Satin*."

"I take it you don't like satin?" I guessed.

"They're gonna look like crumpled-up napkins by the end of the night in satin. And don't even get me started on stains. You ever been to a good party where you didn't end up wearing at least half a beer?"

"Satin sucks," Levi agreed, opening the bag of chips I'd squirreled away in the cooler's zipper pocket.

"You wanna keep bitching, or do you wanna finish the job?" I asked.

Cam smirked. "Keep bitching obviously."

"Obviously," Levi agreed.

We managed another hour and a half of productivity without throwing punches. Even I was pleased with the progress. The new vanity, with its excess of drawers and counter space, was in place. The old one had been hauled downstairs to the truck. The new sheets of drywall had been screwed into place in the kitchen and bedroom and were ready for the first coat of mud.

It was starting to look like an actual apartment.

We heard footsteps on the stairs followed by a cheery, "Knock knock!" Hazel stuck her head in the front door, eyes going straight to Cam.

"Hey, Trouble," he said, suddenly in a better mood than he'd been all afternoon.

"Hi," she said, crossing to him and laying a kiss on him that belonged on the pages of one of her novels.

Levi and I did the brotherly thing and pretended to dry heave until they broke apart.

"Oh my gosh, Gage! This place is looking great. Zoey's gonna love it," Hazel said, clasping her hands under her chin. She was wearing leggings, a ball cap, and a long sweater. Meetcute's leash was wrapped around her wrist.

"Hold on. You knew he was fixing this place up for Zoey?" Cam demanded.

Hazel slipped an arm through his. "Of course. He texted me. I thought it was a great idea."

Cam glared at me. "Seems like an awful lot of work for just a rental if you ask me," he said pointedly.

I ignored him as Levi and I both competed for the attention of our dog nephew.

"Who's a good dog?" I asked, ruffling Meetcute's fur.

"That's what you do for family," Hazel admonished my pain-in-the-ass brother over her shoulder as she headed in to take a look at the bedroom.

"Yeah, Cam. That's what you do for family." I flipped him the middle finger behind his fiancée's back.

"Oh, she'll love the closet," Hazel called.

"But will she love the idiot that made the closet?" Cam mused in a stage whisper.

I threw a clean paintbrush at him and mouthed, *Shut the fuck up.*

Make me, he mouthed back.

Levi sighed and squished Meetcute's face in his big hands. "Your uncles are morons."

Hazel reappeared. "So I have a confession."

We froze warily.

"What kind of confession?" Cam asked.

"I didn't stop by just to see the apartment. I came to guilt-trip you all into paying Laura a visit."

"She doesn't want to see anyone," Levi insisted.

"Are you saying that because you think she doesn't want to deal with the situation or because you don't want to deal with it?" Hazel asked.

"Both," the three of us said in unison.

"You're family. Family is there for each other, especially when it's awkward and painful."

"You don't know Laura like we do," Cam said. "She's mean when she doesn't want to be disturbed."

"She throws things," Levi added.

"So do the rest of you. Now get your asses in the car."

7

Definitely not my type
Zoey

I stabbed the doorbell a second time and added a brisk knock on the purple front door for good measure.

"For the love of God. Keep your pants on. I'm coming," an irritated voice called from inside.

Yeah, this was probably a mistake. But Laura was a friend. A new, usually grumpy friend. And I hadn't seen or heard from her since the news about the accident charges had broken at the town meeting. So here I was on a sunny Saturday afternoon after emerging from a tornado of work, forgoing laundry at Hazel's to stick my nose where it didn't belong.

"What?" Laura demanded, swinging open the front door. She was wearing workout clothes and a scowl. Her silver-blond hair was swept up in a hot-girl, gravity-defying pompadour. Loud rock poured forth from behind her.

"Hi. I have wine," I said, hefting the bottle.

Laura's eyes narrowed as she considered me. "Fine. But if you ask me anything stupid like how I'm doing, you leave and I keep the wine."

"Deal."

I followed her inside as she spun her wheelchair around and headed deeper into the house. The living space was cozy and lived-in. After a lifetime of living in Manhattan, spacious living rooms still left me gawking. There was a tangle of pillows and blankets on the couch and floor from what looked like a family movie night.

Laura's gigantic bear of a dog, Melvin, was snoring belly up and taking up a significant amount of couch.

There was a mountain of folded laundry sitting at the foot of the stairs just outside the door to Laura's first-floor bedroom, a recent Bishop Brothers renovation. The dining room showed the chaotic leftovers of family breakfast, and the kitchen beyond looked as if it had been abandoned mid-mess. The dishwasher was already running, but there was still a hefty mound of dirty dishes piled next to the sink.

Laura picked her phone off the kitchen counter, and the music cut off mid-howl.

"Where are the kids?" I asked, noting the peace and quiet.

"Isla is babysitting her uncle's dog while *studying* with a *friend*. She doesn't know that *I* know that's code for making out with a cute, dumb boy. My cute, dumb boys are both working the afternoon shift at Angelo's and trying to figure out how to sneak out to the underage bonfire tonight," Laura said, rummaging through a low cabinet and producing two wineglasses.

"Ahh, the teenage years."

"Were you a hellion? You look like hellion material," Laura observed, setting the glasses on the counter and pointing at the magnetic wine opener on the fridge.

"Still am," I said, making quick work of the cork and pouring two oversize portions of chardonnay.

Her lips quirked. "Me too."

I slid one of the glasses in front of her. "I'm shocked. Shocked, I say."

We each took a sip.

"Are you worried about them?"

She looked past me to the collage of family pictures on the wall in the dining room. "Every second of the day since before they were born."

"I can't imagine." I toyed with my necklace, comforting myself with the edges of the disco ball charm. There had been a time when I'd assumed I'd have a family like everyone else. But I wasn't everyone else. Every once in a while, I still got the twinge of regret. But all I had to do was remind myself how I was barely functioning as an adult on my own. It was for the best that I wasn't going to add "responsibility for tiny humans" to my plate.

"But it's nice seeing them be kids again. As long as I can stay a step ahead of them, of course," she added.

"They've been through a lot," I observed stupidly. Of course they'd been through a lot. That was like stepping outside naked in a mid-January blizzard and saying, "Golly, it's cold." I was toeing the line of asking the question she didn't want to answer. The stupid question with only equally stupid answers.

We carefully avoided eye contact and both lifted our glasses again.

A pivot was necessary. I rounded the island, turned on the hot water in the sink, and grabbed the bottle of dish soap. "If you had to do it all over again, would you do anything differently during your teenage hellion years?"

"You're doing my dishes?" Laura asked with suspicion.

"Yep," I said, shoving the first plate under the water.

"Okay. Fine. You can stay. Until you piss me off."

"I'm honored," I said dryly.

We drank and cleaned, chatting about nothing in particular. I steered clear of any topics related to the latest news on her accident while covertly studying her for any signs of downward spiraling. Miller's presence was everywhere from the photos of him on the wall to the military dog tags hanging from the light fixture above the kitchen sink.

"I'm fine, you know," she said abruptly as I tossed a wad of used paper towels into the garbage can she held for me. "You can report back to everyone else and save me the onslaught of unwelcome drop-ins since I called off work today."

Laura ran the family-owned general store on the town square and had only recently returned to work full-time. She and her parents had hired a few part-timers to fill in, freeing up the rest of the Bishops, who had been taking turns working shifts.

"You're entitled to a day off. Although it *is* kind of pathetic that you took a day off to clean your house."

She smirked. "It wasn't *all* disinfecting countertops and folding laundry. I had other things to do."

"Hmm, cryptic. But unless those things involved shoe shopping or a massage, I'm still judging you for doing it wrong."

She groaned. "Oh God. I haven't had a massage in nine thousand years. When all this is over, I'm booking a ninety-minute 'turn me to spaghetti' massage."

I was just debating whether I should ask her about "all this" when the back door burst open.

"Oh good. You haven't been kidnapped and/or entered the witness relocation program," Gage announced cheerfully from the mudroom as he led Hazel, Cam, and Levi inside.

His sudden appearance had my heart rate kicking up a notch.

Gage's gaze landed on me, and he raised a sexy eyebrow in question. I bobbled the plate I was drying and nearly dropped it.

God, since when did I find eyebrows sexy?

He was in what I liked to think of as his blue-collar clothes. Ancient jeans and a ripped-up flannel. It was a good look. Cam, Hazel, and a reluctant Levi each kicked off their shoes as they entered. Meetcute followed and began shoving his snoot in every discarded shoe.

Melvin, sensing the home invasion, appeared in the kitchen on a grumbly yawn.

Laura shot me a glare. I held up my hands. "I swear I had nothing to do with this."

"We missed you, Larry," Cam said, ruffling Laura's hair in that brotherly way designed specifically to incite annoyance.

"No, you didn't," she said, batting his hand away.

"It's almost like she's not happy to see us," Gage teased, still eyeing me.

"I don't need any of you idiot babysitters hovering over me, trying to hold my hand," Laura insisted.

I could understand her desire for privacy. Hell, I'd been known to hide in bathrooms just to get a breather during parties and work functions. However, I also would have given several nonessential internal organs to be part of a family that inserted themselves into my life just to show their support.

"Have you met any of us?" Levi asked his sister as he leaned on the counter and rummaged through the basket of snacks.

"We all wanted pizza and thought why not have pizza at your house?" Hazel explained brightly.

All three Bishop brothers pointed at Hazel behind her back, mouthing things like *her idea* and *don't blame me*.

The back door burst open again. "Someone say *pizza*?"

Laura's twin sons, Wesley and Harrison, entered the mudroom, looking hopeful and hungry in that bottomless-pit, teenage-boy way. They had identical mops of curly dark hair and were wearing matching polo shirts from the Italian restaurant where they both worked.

"Shoes!" Laura barked, pointing at the twins. "And you just came from Angelo's where you probably had pizza for lunch."

The boys sent their shoes flying and padded into the kitchen. "That was hours ago, Mom," Wes said, giving Laura a one-armed hug.

"Yeah, Mom," Harry added, hugging her from the other side and flashing impressive puppy dog eyes at Laura. "We're starving."

Not wanting to be left out, Melvin muscled his way into the family hug.

"Ugh. Fine," Laura said, feigning irritation. But I saw her give both boys a hard squeeze before releasing them.

"Hi, Zoey," Harry greeted me with a flirtatious smile.

"We would have been home sooner if we knew you were here," Wes said, pushing his brother out of the way.

"Stop flirting with Zoey," Cam said. "She's practically your aunt."

I grinned. "Hi, guys."

"So are Mom and Dad magically gonna pop out of a closet now?" Laura demanded.

"Nope," Cam said, swiping Levi's bag of chips. "They're on their way to pick up some llamas."

"Alpacas. A pair of them," Gage corrected, joining me at the sink and leaning against the counter.

"What the hell are they going to do with alpacas?" Laura wondered.

"What does anyone do with alpacas?" Levi pointed out, snatching the chips back from Cam.

The back door opened again, and Nana entered with her brand of chaotic enthusiasm, followed by sixteen-year-old Isla, who floated dreamily inside. Her usually glossy black hair looked like she'd just driven through a tornado in a convertible. She had a faraway expression on her pretty, freckled face.

Laura looked at me and rolled her eyes. I covered my laugh with a cough.

"How was *studying*?" Laura asked her daughter pointedly as Nana hurled herself at Gage.

"Great," Isla said as she all but melted against the island next to Levi, leaning down to stroke Melvin's thick fur.

Cam's eyes narrowed as he studied his niece. "What the hell were you studying? The airspeed velocity of unladen sparrows?"

Isla's hands flew to her hair, and her eyes went wide. "I–I was trying on hats. Lots of hats. I have to go upstairs to…do something…for school."

I bit my lip and refused to look at Laura as Isla dashed for the stairs.

"Take your laundry with you," Laura called after her.

"Hey, Mom. Harry and I were gonna hang out with Hung and Dae-Ho tonight if that's okay. Their parents are getting a big coffee bean order tonight at the coffee shop."

It wasn't a bad attempt. A distracted parent probably would

have made the leap and assumed the boys were going to help unload the coffee bean order. But Laura was not a distracted parent.

"How did I get so lucky to have two boys who are so thoughtful and willing to help others?" Laura mused sweetly.

Levi frowned at his nephews as he munched another chip. Wes became suddenly fascinated by the hole in his sock, and Harry looked like he was going to throw up.

"That's so generous of you to volunteer to help. Tell Mr. and Mrs. Jang that I'll be in tomorrow to try the coffee you helped unload," Laura said, twisting the motherly-guilt knife a little deeper.

The boys slunk out of the room with Melvin and Meetcute on their heels.

"Laundry," Laura yelled.

"You know your sons are going to that bonfire tonight," Levi said the second the boys were out of earshot.

"You know your niece was making out with a boy, right?" Laura shot back.

All three uncles looked pained.

"I liked it better when they were over five and under ten," Gage complained.

"Back when they thought we were cool," Cam said wistfully.

"Back when they knew we were smarter than them," Levi added, crumpling up his empty bag of chips. "I'm gonna be pissed if I have to arrest my nephews tonight."

"Imagine how you'll feel arresting your brother for threatening Isla's boyfriend with bodily harm," Cam noted.

"How about I call in the order?" Hazel announced, steering the conversation back to pizza.

"I'll pick it up," I offered.

"I'll go along," Gage volunteered.

"Uh, why?" I asked.

Was I imagining the warning look Cam shot him? No. I was definitely not.

"Just being helpful," he said, flashing Cam a shit-eating grin and rubbing his eye with his middle finger.

"How did we end up with all three dogs?" I complained as Melvin shoved his gigantic head between the front seats. Meetcute and Nana were jogging from window to window in the back seat, pressing their noses against the glass. Both tails wagged furiously in delight, and the entire truck cab smelled like hot doggy breath.

"You can't take just one for a ride," Gage explained as he pulled away from the curb. "That's cruel and unusual."

Nana stuck her snout around my headrest and gave my ear a slurp.

"Eww. Gross. Thank you for the wet willy, Nana."

"Where does the whole 'I'm terrified of animals' thing come from?" Gage asked.

"I'm not terrified. I'm…skeptical."

"And that feels like an important distinction to you?"

"Vital," I agreed.

He glanced at me pointedly, and I rolled my eyes.

"Fine. I was eight and I wanted a dog so badly. Someone to keep me company when I was at home. My parents gave me all the usual parental and Manhattan reasons why I couldn't have a dog. I was too irresponsible. The apartment was too small. Who was going to walk it in the middle of the night in the dead of winter, blah blah blah. But I was persistent."

"I'm shocked," he said.

"My mom realized I wasn't going to give up, so she took me to visit a friend of hers in Brooklyn. She told me they had a Pomeranian I could play with, and I was *so* excited. I used my allowance to buy a bag of fancy dog treats and everything. I was determined to make that dog my friend and prove to Mom I would be a good pet owner."

I glanced out the window as we passed the general store. Dusk was falling, and the town square was lit up with the cozy glow of streetlights and storefronts.

"Long story short, the Pomeranian was named Jaws, and he hated children, a fact my mother knew. He bit me twice. Once on the hand when I tried to give him a treat and then in the ankle when I ran away. I'll never forget my mom laughing at me as I ran past her, crying and bleeding with a damn six-pound monster locked onto my Achilles. 'See? This is why you can't have a dog,'" I mimicked.

Gage shot me an alarmed look minus his usual condescension. "Jesus, Zoey, that's not okay."

I shrugged. I could understand how the story sounded to someone who had grown up with Pep and Frank Bishop as parents. "She set me up to fail to prove a point. She won, but at least I inconvenienced her by requiring stitches."

Gage surprised the hell out of me by reaching under Melvin's torso and squeezing my hand.

"No offense, but your mom sounds like an asshole," he announced before quickly releasing my hand. But I still felt the current of his touch even after it was gone. Maybe I should talk him into bed after all.

"She kinda is. But you get used to it after thirty-some years. Subject change before it gets awkward. How are you? I mean with the whole 'charges filed, preliminary hearing' thing?" I asked.

"I'm fine," he said automatically as we passed Emilie Rump's house. It stood out from its neighbors thanks to all the brown lumps of mangled potatoes on her front porch and walkway. Story Lake sure knew how to hold a grudge. I appreciated that.

"Uh-huh. Sure."

"It is what it is," he said. "We'll all be better when justice is served."

His index and middle fingers silently drummed out a few beats on the steering wheel.

I could just imagine getting to a place where life was starting to feel normal-ish again, only to be reminded of wounds that had barely begun to heal. I wondered about the driver. Had she gone back to normal? Or had taking a life ruined her own?

My overinflated empathy wanted to point out that sometimes good people made mistakes. But Gage didn't seem like the type who was willing to accept imperfection.

"Thanks for checking in on my sister, by the way. She doesn't open the door to just anybody," Gage said.

"Then I'm flattered. She seems like she's doing okay."

"It can be hard to tell with Larry. She's tough on the outside, and she's real good at hiding what's going on inside."

His fingers were still performing those tiny, almost imperceptible taps.

"She's not the only one," I guessed. "What's up with Cam being mad about you volunteering to pick up dinner?"

Gage's fingers stopped, then started again. "My idiot brother thinks there's a danger of the two of us hooking up, imploding, and then ruining his wedding."

I choked out a laugh. "Excuse me? *We* as in *us*?"

Gage let out a reluctant chuckle. "I think the wedding planning has warped his brain."

"It's laughable," I insisted. "We couldn't be more wrong for each other. You're an uptight, calendar-worshipping nice guy."

"And you're messy, disorganized, impulsive, and late for everything."

I rolled my eyes. "Let's fight after we pick up the pizza."

"It's not a fight. It's a discussion," he said, as if that made even the slightest difference. "You have to admit we have nothing in common. You're about as far from my type as exists."

I scoffed in his general direction as we turned into Angelo's parking lot. "Back at you. If I wanted to be micromanaged, I'd go get a job with a time clock. And you look like the idea of spontaneous fun would make you constipated. Give me an exciting one-night stand with a finance guy just getting out of a messy relationship over 'what are we having for dinner' any day."

"Sounds stable and fulfilling," Gage observed dryly, pulling into a spot at the back of the lot.

"Please. I'm not about to be judged by someone who probably has a picket fence tattoo somewhere on his body. A temporary one."

"You don't take anything seriously, do you?" he asked, turning off the engine.

"Oh, come on. Lighten up, Judgy McJudgerson."

"I'm not judging you. I'm trying to understand your logic."

"Bullshit. You are absolutely judging me."

Melvin sneezed violently.

"See? Even the dogs agree with me."

"I'm just trying to wrap my head around you being Hazel's best friend and doing what you do for a living and not believing in some kind of happily ever after. Seems kinda hypocritical if you ask me."

"See? Judging," I said, poking his shoulder with my finger.

Gage thumped his head against the seat. "Does every conversation have to be a challenge with you?"

I threw my hands in the air. "*You're* the one making it challenging. I say I enjoy being single, and you accuse me of being a hypocrite. I mean, I thought you were a lawyer, not a judge."

He closed his eyes and drummed his fingers on his thighs. God, I enjoyed riling him up. He made it so easy.

"Fine," he said finally. "I apologize for making you feel judged."

I reached over and squeezed his face. "That wasn't so hard now, was it?"

"Every fucking conversation," he muttered.

I took pity on him. "Look, happily ever after isn't for everyone. You are someone who will celebrate your sixtieth wedding anniversary. I'm more of a 'happy for now' person. I don't want to be tied down and have to build my life around someone else's."

I gripped my necklace like a talisman. I'd tried it once and gotten burned badly enough to learn my lesson. There had been a time in my life when I'd wanted exactly what Gage did. But not everyone got to have it all. Some of us had to make do with what was left. But I was building a good life for myself, damn it, and I was having fun doing it. There was no need to mope about what I couldn't have.

"What do you want instead?"

Gage's tone took me by surprise. He sounded sincerely curious.

My eyebrows winged up. "Honestly?"

"No point in lying, seein' as how we're both vaguely disgusted by each other and not looking to impress," he teased.

"Excellent point, Attorney Man. Okay, here goes." I took a deep breath. "I want to be so good at what I do that no one can take it away or ignore it. I got fired before I moved here. I'm tired of people seeing me as just the mistakes I've made. Of telling me that I'm too much or not enough. I want to show them all they're wrong, that they underestimated me. I want them to realize they were the ones who made the mistake."

He nodded. "All right. How are you going to do that?"

"By launching Hazel's book into the stratosphere and taking out billboards within a five-block radius of their office that say WHO'S THE LOSER NOW?" I joked.

Gage shook his head, a soft almost smile playing on the corners of his mouth. "What do you want after you've accomplished that?"

I blinked visions of revenge-themed billboards out of my head. "Huh?"

"After you prove them all wrong? What's next?"

"I don't know specifics. I just know I want to have a damn good time doing whatever I want."

He opened his door, then paused to look at me. "You are definitely not my type, Zoey. But I hope you get what you want."

8

Broken, sparkly things
Gage

Angelo's was packed. It looked as though everyone in Story Lake had the same idea for dinner. Servers zoomed in and out of the kitchen, cooks yelled, and the phone rang incessantly. I put a hand on Zoey's back and guided her into the fray, trying not to analyze why the touch seemed so natural.

I guided us past the ancient, grumpy hostess Jessie, more of an institution of Story Lake than the restaurant itself. It was loud and crowded, and all the TVs were tuned to different stations. After so many years of the town looking like it was occupied by a skeleton crew, it was nice to be inconvenienced by a busy dinner rush.

I nodded, waved, and shook hands the whole way to the bar. Nearly every face in the place was familiar and shared a history of some sort with me. I loved that feeling, that deep, unshakable sense of belonging.

I snagged the last barstool against the wall for Zoey and positioned myself behind her. The tropical scent of her hair teased my nose, making me want to lean in even as I reminded myself of the safety of distance. I'd argued myself out of this infatuation so many times I'd memorized every single point. She was irresponsible, irrational, completely unserious...and so was this physical pull I felt toward her.

Part of me—a small, illogical part—wanted to explore it. To see what adventure it would lead me on. Thankfully, I was an adult with maturity and self-control. I didn't bend to spontaneous whims.

Dahlia, the bartender, looked up from the drafts she was pouring and gave a jerk of her chin toward the kitchen. *Five minutes,* she mouthed.

I leaned down. "Want a drink while we wait?" I asked Zoey over the music.

She cupped her ear. "What? It's so loud in here."

Reluctantly, I moved in closer. The smell of coconuts got stronger. "Drink?" I repeated.

"Sure. As long as you're confident the three ravenous wolves in the car won't eat your steering wheel."

"Beer okay?"

She nodded.

I flashed Dahlia two fingers, and she nodded.

Zoey swiveled on her stool to face me, bringing her knees in contact with the tops of my thighs. She seemed unfazed, but my body reacted like she'd set fire to my pants, and I took a self-preserving step back.

I was trying to look anywhere but her eyes, so my gaze fastened on the glittering globe she wore on a long chain. "What's on your necklace?" I asked.

She held it up for me to study. "It's a disco ball."

"Why am I not surprised?"

Her grin was wicked. "Because you think you know everything."

"I make educated guesses," I pointed out, taking the charm in my hand. "Why do you wear a disco ball around your neck?"

"Because I like broken, sparkly things."

"Broken?" I repeated, taking a closer look at the charm.

"All those broken pieces add up to something everyone loves."

I frowned as my thumb skimmed over the seams of the disco ball. It was a deeper answer than what I was expecting from Zoey "Fun Is My Middle Name" Moody.

"Now, I was honest with you. So you owe me," she said. Her eyes sparkled, and her curls took on the deep red of the neon sign on the wall behind us. She might not have been my type, but I sure as hell liked looking at her.

I dropped her necklace and tried not to watch it nestle back between her breasts. "I do?"

"You do," she said firmly. "Since we've established that we're not interested in each other for relationship purposes—"

"That is on the record," I said warily.

"—and since you don't look like the 'hot, sweaty, one-night stand' type, we officially don't need or expect anything from each other," she continued.

I let out a surprised laugh. "What was that about a one-night stand?"

Zoey looked me up and down, then smirked. "Please. You wouldn't survive it."

"I'm having trouble surviving this conversation," I shot back, doing everything in my power to force all the images that came to mind out of my head.

"I'm just saying we don't need or expect anything from each other. So that means we can just be brutally honest with each other. Right?"

The beers arrived in front of us, and I called out a thanks to Dahlia over the noise. I handed one to Zoey. "Fine. I think all your skirts are about four inches too short."

Zoey sputtered into her beer, and I grinned.

"First of all, if I'm not your type, why are you looking at my hemlines?" she demanded.

"Zoey, honey, you don't have to be a man's type to get his eyes on you. And I'm kidding about the skirts."

She poked me in the chest. "Now you definitely owe me."

I grinned. "All right. Fine. Tell me how to settle up."

"You lied when I asked if you were doing okay about the accident and the charges."

"Who says I was lying?" I asked casually.

"Come on, ol' buddy, ol' pal. Tell your platonic friend what's simmering beneath that good-natured surface," she prodded. The finger in my chest shifted to a warm palm on my arm. "Seriously, Gage. I'm not invested. I don't need you to have the reaction I want you to have. I just want to know how you're doing."

I studied my glass for a beat. Maybe she was right. Maybe getting it out would loosen the tightness in my chest.

"Disco."

I blinked. "What?"

"Disco," she repeated, holding up her necklace. "That's our official safe word. Only instead of incredibly dirty sex stuff that you definitely wouldn't survive, it's our 'tell the truth' word. If one of us says it, the other one has to tell the truth."

I blew out a breath and gritted my teeth against the new onslaught of fantasy images that played out in my brain. "That's ridiculous."

"Don't care. I like ridiculous. Stop stalling. It's either this or we sit here in silence, waiting for pizza."

"I like silence."

"That's Levi," she said.

"Fine. No. I'm not okay."

"I noticed," she said wryly. She looked up at me expectantly with those jade-green eyes.

"Miller is gone forever. My sister wakes up in bed alone and gets into a wheelchair every fucking morning. And somewhere out there is the woman who put her there. She got to go back to normal. She didn't lose anything. Her life didn't change. There were days since the accident that the *only* thing keeping me going was knowing that someday, that driver would lose their normal. That there'd be some kind of justice. But these charges are…"

The bitter taste of anger was rising to the surface again, and

I took a swallow of beer to force it back down. Zoey's thumb stroked the inside of my forearm. A small, gentle movement that centered my attention on her again.

"They aren't enough," I rasped. "How can three years of her life compare to taking Miller from us forever? I can't fucking stomach that. That's not justice. That's a fucking slap in the face. To Laura, to the kids, to Miller's parents."

"To you," Zoey added.

I nodded tightly.

She wet her lips, and my attention snagged on them. Full, rosy, glistening.

"Were you and Miller close?"

I shrugged. "Not at first. I was younger, the tagalong in school. But after I graduated from law school and came back, we were tight."

Tight wasn't the word for it. He'd been another brother to me. A voice of reason, a reminder to loosen up. Someone who always had my back. I missed him every fucking day.

"What do you think would feel like justice?" she asked.

I shook my head. "Honestly? I don't know if there's anything less than what she took from us that would do the trick. And I don't like the way that feels. I don't get angry. I don't walk around carrying grudges. But, Zo, this is eating me alive."

She let out a long exhale and then dipped her head to my chest and wrapped her arms around my waist. The contact, the comfort of it, shocked the hell out of me.

"That fucking sucks," she said into my shirt.

I dropped my chin to the top of her head and breathed in that tropical scent. It was like a vacation, a moment away from all the darkness. "Yeah. It does."

We were both silent for a beat in the middle of the bar's Saturday night chaos. I could feel the steady beat of her heart under my hand on her back, the warmth of her breath against my chest. She was small and warm and solid. Somehow, with my senses occupied by Zoey, my anger inched away from the edge.

"Good disco. That was just a platonic hug, by the way," she

said, pulling back and grinning impishly. "So don't get any ideas about trying to propose."

I snorted. "Please. Ten minutes alone with me and you're already thinking about trading in your convertible for a minivan," I teased.

"Nice try, pal. You're not wrong or bad for wanting justice," she said, going serious again.

"Yeah, well, I'm starting to realize that sometimes the law can't deliver true justice." I didn't know how to operate in a world like that.

"Hey, here's a thought. Have you tried numbing your pain with meaningless sex?" She fluttered her eyelashes at me.

Miracle of miracles, I found myself letting out a reluctant laugh. I ruffled her hair with affection.

She wrinkled her nose and tried to right the damage to her curls. "Can you imagine if we did hook up? It would obviously go horribly wrong."

"Horribly," I agreed.

"And then we'd have to spend every Thanksgiving and Christmas together because of Hazel and Cam," she said.

"I'd have to tell my future wife that I had a torrid affair that ended badly with the hot redhead at the table."

"She'd hate me."

"She'd have no choice," I agreed and picked up my beer. "I think Cam can unbunch his undies. We're obviously not going to get involved with each other. We have *disaster* written all over us."

"It's tattooed on our foreheads," Zoey said.

"Subject change," I said, using her segue. "Tell me about your work."

"What?" She cupped her hand to her ear again.

I inched closer. "Your job. What did you do today?" I asked.

She looked baffled. "Why?"

"I'm interested." Her baleful look made me smirk. "In what you do, not you."

Appeased, she pulled out her phone and opened that godawful calendar.

"Well, I had a heated emergency Zoom call with one of Hazel's foreign publishers over their failure to publish one of her backlist books in their language by the contract deadline. I took great pleasure in ruining their weekend by explaining that since they are in violation of the contract, we will be selling the rights to their direct competitor, who made a significantly higher offer. Then I answered a dozen editorial and marketing emails from Hazel's North American publisher, put some feelers out to two publicity firms because I am willing Hazel's launch to be so big she's going to need a publicist. I accepted a Finnish offer for the backlist and touched base with the audiobook production company. After that, I packed up twenty advance copies and dropped them off at the post office to be sent to some of my favorite influencers."

"Jesus, Zoey. It's Saturday."

"Yeah, well, I had to make up for all the time I lost packing and buying cars this week. Now, if I don't get laundry done in the next few days, I'm going to be breaking all the town nudity ordinances."

"We don't actually have any of those. One of Story Lake's founders was a nudist. You haven't been here for Pantless Day yet. It's in June."

"I can't tell if you're joking, and I kind of hope you're not."

"Aren't most literary agents off on Saturdays?" I asked, steering us back on topic.

"Only agents who have more than one client can usually afford to take a day or two off," she joked. "And I wasn't finished with my day. That was all before lunch. Which was late because I forgot that I'm human and I require fuel. So I microwaved SpaghettiOs, proceeded to spill them, cleaned up the mess, and *then* I had a harebrained idea that would promote Hazel *and* the town and accidentally did an hour of down-the-rabbit-hole brainstorming. Which completely exhausted me, so it was either crash for a nap, do laundry, or go visit your sister. And since lying down immediately after eating gives me acid reflux and I hate laundry, I decided to visit your sister."

I was impressed. "What's the harebrained idea?"

"It's nothing. It's barely a thought."

"Disco," I said pointedly.

She rolled her eyes as she polished off her beer. "Fine. I kind of thought it would be fun and beneficial if Story Lake hosted a Reader Weekend to celebrate Hazel's launch. Readers could book rooms in the lodge. Chevy could host a signing at the store, and then the rest of the businesses could offer book-themed sales or specials to entice readers to visit. You know, kind of a 'see the small town that inspired this small-town rom-com' deal. If it's done right, I could invite some influencers and raise both Hazel's *and* Story Lake's profiles."

"Zoey, that's—"

She winced, bracing herself. "Stupid? Terrible? Impossible?"

"Genius," I corrected.

"Shut up. We're honesty buddies, not actual friends. I don't need you to kiss my ass."

"I'm serious."

She perked up. "Really? I mean, her launch is only, like, six weeks away. It's short notice to pull together, but maybe it could be awesome, right?"

We were interrupted by Dahlia's appearance with our order. I traded food for credit card.

"I think you should go for it. It's an obvious win-win," I told Zoey.

She cocked her head. "Thanks, Gage. I need to flesh it out, do some preliminary planning and research before I mention it to anyone. But maybe it could be something."

The unexpected earnestness surprised me. It mattered to her, I realized. And I liked seeing that side of her. Thankfully, before I could do something stupid like tell her that, Dahlia returned with the receipt and a bag of dog biscuits.

"You better hit the road," she said. "Jessie just reported there's a golden retriever blowing the horn out in the parking lot."

"Damn it, Nana."

The biscuits lasted all of fifteen seconds, and the food barely survived the drive back to my sister's. Zoey had to hold it in her lap while I used my arm on the back of the front seat as a safety gate barricading the hungry dogs.

The lights were on in every window when we made it back, something that would have made my brother-in-law complain if he were still with us. Miller took his electric bill the way he'd taken all life's normal responsibilities: seriously. However he'd always managed to balance that with a sense of humor that had entertained us for most of our lives. He'd been my constant reminder to lighten up and have a little fun once the hard work was done.

The dogs piled out of the truck in a delirious surge of joy, and I took the pizza boxes from Zoey. The spring evening still carried with it a lingering winter chill.

"I'm glad we settled our overwhelming sexual tension," she joked as we trudged up the ramp to the back door.

"Me too."

"We'll always have disco. Now you can go back to barely tolerating me," she said, opening the door.

I didn't know what to say as all three fur demons streaked past us inside. I knew I wasn't as warm and friendly toward her as I was with other people. It was self-preservation, plain and simple. But it bothered me that she'd noticed.

"Food's here," she announced over the noise.

My nephews descended on us like twin locusts, relieving me of the food before I was fully across the threshold. Zoey slipped out of her shoes and, with an over-the-shoulder smile at me, joined the chaos in the kitchen.

I took my time slipping out of my shoes and hanging up my coat as laughter erupted around the kitchen island.

"Paper plates, you heathens," Laura yelled over the noise. "Zoey and I already did every dish in this house once today."

It was good to see that there was still life in this house. That we could still laugh together. Maybe we didn't have the highest emotional intelligence or the best communication skills, but I knew for certain that we always had each other's backs.

I dug out the spare change I always carried in my pocket and found a shiny dime. With a furtive glance in the direction of the kitchen, I bent and placed it against the baseboard under the hook for Laura's bag.

"Move your ass, Gigi, or there's gonna be nothing left but crumbs," my sister called from the kitchen.

I made a show of positioning my boots under the bench before straightening. Zoey's gaze locked with mine, an unasked question in those pretty green eyes.

I pretended not to notice as I entered the warmth and noise and light of the kitchen.

"Larry, back me up on this. You hate satin, right? It's unforgiving as fuck," Cam demanded, gesturing with his pizza. Hazel was grinning from her perch on his knee where she was eating a slice of her own.

"Hold up, Groomzilla. Before you poll everyone on their stances on bridesmaid dress material, Zoey needs to tell you all about her Reader Weekend idea," I announced.

"What Reader Weekend idea?" everyone demanded.

With her mouth full of pizza, Zoey shot me a convincing death glare. "Damn it, Gage."

"You didn't have me sign a nondisclosure agreement."

She wrinkled her nose at me. "You're such a pain in the ass."

And all was right in my world again.

9

Monogamous biceps
Zoey

"Haze? Hello?"

Story Lake Haven's Grandma Moses Community Room, which thanks to the informational card posted outside I learned was named for the successful and prolific American folk artist who hadn't picked up a paintbrush until her late seventies, appeared to be empty.

I checked my watch. Yep. I was five minutes late. So either Hazel had scared off all her creative writing students already, or I'd gotten the time wrong in my calendar.

"Damn it, me," I muttered. I was just about to dedicate the next ten minutes of my life to figuring out exactly how I'd screwed up when I heard a faint groan coming from inside.

I spotted a pair of feet poking out from behind the desk at the front of the room and headed in that direction. Hazel was lying on her back staring up at the ceiling. Her laptop was open to a blank page on the desk above her.

"Sooo, how's the writing going?" I joked.

"What if I forgot how to write a book? What if I used up all the magic in the last one?"

"Do you want Active Listener Zoey or Ass-kicker Agent Zoey?"

"Active Listener. I don't think I'm emotionally stable enough for one of your ass kickings."

"Okey dokey." I sprawled out on the floor next to her and admired the ceiling tiles. "What makes you feel like you forgot how to write a book and used up all the magic?"

Writing was hard, and authors were delicate people who often experienced episodes of paralyzing, whiny self-doubt. I'd learned it was important to acknowledge their feelings even when they were completely ridiculous.

"That last one came so easily. Like it flowed out of me almost like it was writing itself."

"Mm-hmm," I said, biting my tongue to prevent myself from reminding her of the dozen creative crises she was choosing not to recall.

"And *this* book. Ugh." She shoved her fingers under her glasses to rub her eyes. "I don't know the characters. I don't know what the hell their problems are, what's keeping them apart, what's going to blow them up, or how they're going to solve it all so they can find their way back to each other."

"Mm-hmm. All those do sound like important story elements. What do you have so far?" I asked.

"He's hot and she's quirky."

"I'd read that."

Hazel karate chopped me with a lazy backhand that missed my shoulder and hit my boob.

"Ow."

"Sorry. I was aiming for your face."

I rolled to my side. "Apology not accepted. What was different about this last book?"

She shrugged morosely as well as one could shrug while lying on an industrial tile floor. "I don't know. It was kind of the story of my life. But I can't just keep writing about me and Cam."

I drilled my index finger into her ribs and teased a weak laugh out of her. "You had real-life inspiration with the last book. Maybe that's your thing? Maybe you just need some new inspiration?"

Her head lolled in my direction, and she frowned. "That's not a terrible idea."

"Gee, thanks."

She sat up. "Maybe all I need is to find a new couple to follow around."

I rolled into a seated position. "I was thinking less stalking and more rewatching and rereading all your favorite rom-coms. Less effort, lower odds of being arrested."

"No, this is good." She gripped my arm. "Please tell me you're secretly lusting after someone."

Gage's face immediately popped into my head. Okay, fine. It was his face *and* his butt. Both had been making regular unscheduled appearances in my mind since Saturday night. "Nope. Sorry. My sex life here is as nonexistent as the narwhal."

"Narwhals are real."

"You're not serious. It's a freaking aquatic unicorn. That's not a real thing."

Hazel's laugh ended abruptly in a loud snort. "They're one thousand percent real. I'll show you on this thing called the internet after you admit there's someone around here who you've at least had naughty thoughts about."

I thought of Gage's quick grin. The weight and heat of his hand on my back when he steered me into Angelo's. "Well, I wouldn't say *lusting*."

Hazel jumped to her feet, a notebook magically appearing in one hand, a pen in the other.

"Where did those come from?" I demanded.

"Tell me *everything*."

"I was joking," I insisted, working my way back to my feet.

"No, you weren't."

Another problem with being friends with someone for so long. Lying wasn't really an option.

I blew out a sigh. "You're just going to get weird about it, and there's nothing to get weird about because nothing is going to happen. I literally just thought, *That dude is reasonably attractive*."

"Which dude? Where? What was it about him that made you fall instantly in love? And don't say his eyes or his cute butt. Give me some kind of interesting personality trait that I can exploit."

"You are literally the worst."

Hazel put her notebook and pen down and took me by the shoulders. "Zoey, my friend, my agent, my sister from another mister. We both know that when I get like this, I won't stop. I'm more tenacious than a house raccoon that's been locked out. I'll do *anything* to get back in. So you might as well tell me now, or I'll just have to break into your hotel room and get it out of you while you talk in your sleep."

"Fine. It's Gage."

Her hands flew to her face, and it took me a beat to realize the high-pitched squealing noise was coming from her.

"Stop squealing! I'm not interested in him. He's not interested in me. In fact, he's kind of been a jerk to me ever since that whole thing last summer when we got your book rights back from your stupid ex-husband, drank our faces off to celebrate, and then held hands on the way home."

I might have been intoxicated, but I'd been sure Gage was going to ask me out after that. Instead, he'd grown increasingly annoyed every time I entered a room.

"You did *what*? That was months ago, and you're just now telling me?" Hazel's voice was two octaves higher than usual.

I scoffed. "It was drunken hand-holding. I've gotten further with strangers on the subway during rush hour."

"But obviously something happened between now and then."

"We just had a…moment."

"How do you know he's not interested?" Hazel demanded.

"Because we already had the 'you're not my type' talk. We couldn't be more wrong for each other."

Hazel's brown eyes sparkled behind her glasses. "You beautiful, oblivious fool. Normal people don't have the 'you're not my type' conversation with people they're not interested in."

"Oh my God. What are you saying, crazy pants?"

"You've been here how long?"

"It feels like a lifetime," I complained.

She brushed away my dig at her adopted hometown. "When did you tell Darius he's not your type?"

"Darius is eighteen years old, you disgusting weirdo."

"How about Dr. Ace? Or Chevy? Or Cam?"

"They were all cc'd on the 'you're not my type' email I sent out the week we moved here," I quipped.

Hazel snatched up her notebook again. "This is good. I can work with this."

"No, no, no!" I took the notebook from her and tossed it over my shoulder. "There is no inspiration here, unless you find a sex drought inspiring."

"You don't have to take your sexual frustration out on a poor, innocent notebook."

"I'm not sexually frustrated. I don't want to date or bang Gage Bishop! Just because we have the tiniest unexplained attraction between us—"

Hazel bodychecked me out of the way and pounced on her notebook. "Tell me everything. Leave no detail undetailed."

"Thank God for editors. By the way, aren't you supposed to have a class right now? I thought I was late, but there's no one here. Did you scare off your students by trying to connect with them through a rap you wrote?"

"No rapping. I just told you class started earlier than it did so you'd be on time. Now back to Gage's overwhelming sex appeal. What is it in particular that you noticed first about him?"

"Please tell me you're not talking about my brother."

We whirled around to find Levi standing in the classroom doorway. He looked like he was considering throwing up.

"Now look what you did," I complained to Hazel.

"Hey, he's the Bishop least likely to repeat any of this. Levi, when did Zoey tell you you're not her type?" Hazel asked, evading my renewed attempts to grab her notebook by holding it over her head.

"Uh. She hasn't. Yet."

"And have you told her she's not your type yet?" Hazel asked triumphantly.

"Can I come back when things are less…weird?"

I covered my face with my hands and wished to be teleported anywhere but here. "I'm going to tell Cam you're the one who ran over his palm sander thing in the yard because you still can't park," I threatened Hazel.

"I already confessed, because that's what people who love each other do. They talk about things like palm sanders and sexual chemistry."

"I'm gonna go anywhere but here," Levi announced, but his exit was blocked by the rest of the students, who began to file noisily into the room. His broad shoulders slumped in defeat.

"This isn't over. You and I are going to have a long, detailed chat about you-know-who if you ever want to see another manuscript from me," Hazel said with a maniacal gleam in her brown eyes.

I waved to Scooter Vakapuna and Hana from the lodge as they took their seats. "Ugh. Fine. But you are sworn to the Sisterhood of the Noninterference rules. Okay?"

"Deal."

"Now why am I here?"

She beamed at me. "Oh right. The other thing. Okay. You know how grateful I am to you for moving here and holding my hand and being my biggest cheerleader, right?"

"This sounds rehearsed. Are you breaking up with me?"

"Stop being dramatic. I'm telling you I know you put all your eggs in the Hazel Hart basket. And while your loyalty and confidence mean everything to me, I know you can't survive on just one client," she said.

"I'm also Story Lake's publicist. So technically I have two clients."

Hazel crossed her arms. "Look. You gave up a lot for me. You lost your job because of me. You're living here because of me. You're the best friend and best agent a woman could have. I just want to show you how much I appreciate you."

"If you write me a pity best friend check right now, I'm going to be seriously pissed while I deposit it."

"I have a wedding and a honeymoon to plan. I'm not writing you a check."

"Fine. Help me move, and we'll call it even."

"I think I found a new client for you," she announced.

"Uh-huh. Does this mean you're not going to help me move?"

She rolled her eyes.

"Okay fine. A new client. Where did you find them? At ultimate bingo?"

"Here," she whispered gleefully.

"Like *here* here? In this class here?" I turned to eye up the prospects. In addition to Levi, Hana, and Scooter, the only other OG Story Laker was Kitty Suarez. The rest were retirement community residents with a combined age of probably close to five hundred.

"Please tell me it's not Menace on Wheels George," I whispered, recognizing the troublemaker from the bookstore and town meeting. Today he was wearing track pants, a sweatshirt that said *I Will Put You in a Trunk and Help People Look for You*, and—if my eyes were not deceiving me—a pair of $1,400 Dior sneakers.

"It's not. But I *am* going to make you guess."

"You know I hate guessing games."

"You're not going to get this wrong. Trust me."

I hated when people said that. As if only a true moron could miss the obvious and then I would proceed to do exactly that. Then everyone always had to pretend that "oh just kidding. It actually was kind of tricky," so I wouldn't feel like a big dumb idiot.

"Is it Levi?" I asked hopefully. I could definitely exploit his handsome face to sell a few books.

"He's only shown me a few chapters. He's good and getting better, but there's someone else I think you're going to want to talk to."

"Can't you just tell me?" I begged. My brain was already too tired to play games today.

"Are we starting class today, or are you gonna wait until one of us has an old age–related medical emergency?" a woman with an impressive gray bouffant demanded from a table against the windows.

"It's nice to see you again, Mildred," Hazel said, unruffled by the complaint.

"Who's your friend? She single?" asked a man in a large cowboy hat. He used the finger and thumb of his left hand to smooth down the hair of his fluffy white mustache. His right hand was a cool, robotic-looking prosthesis.

Hazel grinned wickedly at me. "She's definitely single, Terrance, and if you sit tight, I'm sure she'll tell you if you're her type."

"I hate you," I whispered.

"You could never," she shot back with a flutter of eyelashes.

I reluctantly tromped over to the empty seat next to Levi. It was closest to the door so at least I could fake an agent emergency and duck out if necessary.

"Hey, let's maybe never talk about what you overheard to anyone ever," I suggested to Levi.

"Never talking is my favorite," he said.

"I like that about you."

He grunted.

Hazel turned to the whiteboard at the front of the room. "Last time we met, we discussed world building…"

"All I'm saying is back in my day, we didn't go shouting it from the rooftops," George harrumphed from his scooter.

"Back in your day, you didn't have rooftops. Everyone still lived in caves," his friend Opal shot back.

The rest of the class snickered appreciatively.

"Thank you for those...interesting thoughts on...whatever that was, George," Hazel said from the front of the room. "Your characters are the foundation of the story, but the world is the foundation for everything that happens to your characters. I love the samples you chose to share from other authors. Especially you, Mildred, for picking a scene from one of my books. You're definitely my favorite. But now it's time to be the writer. For the next ten minutes, I want each of you to write a short scene, paragraph, or even just a sentence that shows, not tells, what kind of a setting your characters are in and what it means to them."

While everyone settled in to tackle their assignment, I scanned the room.

It was an eclectic group of students. So far, I wasn't having any luck identifying the potential client Hazel had teased me with. Half of them seemed to be taking the class seriously, and the other half were treating it like the last class before lunch.

Handsome, hard-to-read Levi sat quietly, his fingers moving methodically on the keys of his laptop. Town councilwoman and renowned hat knitter Kitty Suarez was filling a spiral-bound notebook with words and doodles. The guy with the cowboy hat was frowning at the ceiling, fingers perched on the tiny Bluetooth keyboard for his tablet. George was flipping through a magazine. The white-haired woman next to him was asleep. At least I hoped she was sleeping.

Movement in the courtyard caught my eye, and I felt a knee-jerk zing of excitement that I immediately tried to extinguish.

Gage was outside with a helper, and they were muscling some large timber beams into the open space. The midafternoon sun was apparently warm enough for short sleeves, which meant biceps. Nice ones. That was what had caught my attention. That was what had caused the spark. It wasn't excitement, I decided. It was a generalized appreciation for the fine male form. Yeah. That was it.

Crisis averted, I dragged my eyeballs away from the manly, muscly scene through the window and tried to read Levi's screen.

In true author fashion, the man shifted his body and screen to block my view.

Against my will, my gaze returned to Gage, who was shouldering another beam into place. A small crowd of female residents had already gathered outside to watch. I couldn't blame them. The view was...pleasant.

Something flicked me in the ear, and I snapped back to reality to find Hazel behind me. She tossed a folded piece of paper on the desk in front of me. "Two more minutes, everyone."

I unfolded the paper and rolled my eyes.

You liiiiike him! Don't be such a... I peered closer at the rudimentary sketch and squinted.

What the hell is this? I mouthed, pointing at the drawing.

Hazel stopped behind Levi, tucked her hands into her armpits, and waved her elbows like chicken wings.

I pretended to dig something out of my eye with my middle finger as she moved on. I wasn't actually into Gage. Was I? No. Of course not. It was just a good ol' forbidden fruit situation. The second he'd said I wasn't his type, my lady parts decided his man parts were worth a closer look.

This was just a boring, grown-up version of that time my parents had insisted that the nineteen-year-old dog walker by day, bass player by night from the eighth floor was a bad idea. Trip had only gotten hotter in my eyes after I was forbidden from seeing him.

This explained it all.

Two minutes of definitely not peering out the window later, Hazel clapped her hands from the front of the room. "Okay. Time's up. Who wants to go first?"

Three hands shot up. Every class had their teacher's pets, I supposed.

We sat through Terrance the cowboy's paragraph describing his sock drawer in vivid if not riveting detail. Hana was next with a descriptive scene set in a restaurant kitchen during the dinner rush. Mildred followed, painting a wordy picture of the Wisconsin gas station where she met her second husband.

"Every time I smell the salty, hot scent of rotisserie hot dogs, I think of my Norman," she concluded with a bow.

My stomach growled on the words *hot dogs*, and I realized it had been a long time since breakfast.

"That's wonderful, Mildred," Hazel exclaimed. "I think you took everyone there in their minds. Levi, how about you?"

The man looked as if he wished the ceiling would collapse on top of him so he'd have an excuse to disappear.

"Come on, Chief. Don't be scared. We'll only be judging every word," Opal teased, smugly placing her hands behind her head and leaning back in her seat.

On a sigh that bordered on a growl, Levi began reading, keeping his head down, eyes on the screen. "The fallen leaves created a carpet of reds and golds. A bed for the body lying twisted and broken atop it."

"Now we're talkin'," George said, slapping the table.

"Zip your lips, George," Hazel ordered.

"How many people had walked the tree-lined trail, eager enough to get to the overlook that they missed this final resting place? How many families had soldiered on, sandwiches in backpacks, binoculars around necks, excited for their next great adventure, while behind a mossy boulder not ten feet away, a killer finished his job?"

I pursed my lips. Not bad for a newbie. I shot Hazel a questioning eyebrow wiggle, which she returned with a smug smile that told me nothing.

Levi shut his laptop screen and crossed his arms over his broad chest.

Why wasn't I into him? He was big and broody and clearly not looking for a relationship. Yet here I was, thinking about Gage's stupid monogamous biceps. There was something wrong with me.

"Really great work, Levi. You gave us a sense of time and place while showing the reader how close danger lurked to the innocent. How about you, Opal?"

Across the room from me, Opal in her black stretchy pants

and gray tunic sweater blew out an aggravated sigh. But instead of arguing, she licked her finger and paged back in her yellow legal pad.

"The mud smelled like death, sucking at her knees, holding her frozen to the spot. Blood dripped from the gaping wound on her shoulder and pattered like frozen rain on the fallen leaves. The sulfuric fog slithered its way through the forest, advancing on her like the fingers of a silent silver wraith. Beneath her boots, the ground trembled, a warning of the evil that was to come. Her hand flexed around the hilt of the sword, so much heavier and less useful than the wand she was used to wielding. But they'd taken it from her as they'd taken everything else.

"The scream of the beast was inhuman. A fiery bellow that promised pain, so much pain. But she didn't care. Not with *him* sitting on the deadly throne, watching her every breath from the cathedral of trees. She was going to die here in this field at the mercy of a monster, and *he* would be witness to it all. Her mortal enemy. Her untenable ally. The man responsible for stealing her magic and sealing her execution. She would spend the last seconds of her life with his icy gray eyes on her, and he would spend the rest of his never forgetting her. She could accept that. A smile tugged at the corners of her mouth as the *whoosh* of wings and the burn of fire cut through the fog."

Opal flipped her notebook back to the first page and leaned back in her seat. "That's all I've got."

The room was post-record-scratch silent.

My mouth was hanging open like I was trying to consume an entire foot-long sub in one bite. Hazel was wearing her best "I told you so" face.

"Daaaamn," George said, finally breaking the silence.

"Pipe down, you old bag of farts," Opal said.

"Is there more?" I asked hopefully. "Like who is she? Who is he? Did he betray her?"

"Are there dragons? Dragons are so hot right now," Kitty said.

"What happens next?" bellowed Mildred.

Opal harrumphed. "It's a writing exercise. You people need to get out more."

I was pretty sure I was going to vibrate out of my body by the time Hazel dismissed the class.

Levi closed the lid of his laptop with a snap and disappeared out the door before anyone else had moved a muscle. I got up, keeping my eye on Opal, thinking I should corner her here in the room before she escaped and I lost her in a sea of retirees.

"Hey there, pretty lady. You remind me of my granddaughter. Hang on. That came out creepy. Dang it! I'm new at this whole 'meeting new people thing,'" Terrance said. "Anyway, I'm Terrance, and I just moved here, and you really do look like my granddaughter but she's too busy to visit me. Crap. Now I just sound pathetic."

"Terrance, I'm Zoey. I'd love to help you work on your small talk, but I have to go tackle someone right now. We'll chat later," I promised.

"It's a date," he said enthusiastically as I fought to untangle my purse strap from the chair.

By the time I liberated it, Opal was already in the hallway. I all but vaulted over George and his scooter, but my quarry had a head start on me. The woman was faster than I thought she'd be with a walker. It didn't help that I got stuck behind two white-haired ladies with those four-footed suction cup canes in the hallway.

By the time I got around them, Opal was heading outside into the courtyard.

"Opal! Wait," I called after her.

She paused and glanced back.

I dodged an adorable elderly couple holding hands and caught up with her. "Have you ever been published before?" I asked, sucking in a breath.

She looked me over from head to toe. "You need to sit down or something?"

"No. I'm fine. I just haven't done cardio since 2010. Have you ever been published?"

"Is *published* slang for some kind of drug you wanna sell me? 'Cause I'm not buying."

"No, ma'am. What you wrote in class was good. Really good. Opal, you can write."

She snorted. "I know. I can also fry an egg, but you don't see me applying for jobs in the cafeteria."

"So what you shared back there, was that part of a larger work? Do you by chance have a finished manuscript lying around?" I asked hopefully.

"Who's asking?"

"Sorry. I'm Zoey Moody. I'm a literary agent. Hazel's agent. And I think you're really good."

"Listen, I gotta get to happy hour before George sucks down all the good whiskey."

"Wait! Let me give you my card. We can talk when you have more time. Or I can come to happy hour with you. I love whiskey." I shoved an arm into my purse, praying I actually had a few of my old cards left in the bottom. I'd meant to make new ones, but it had slipped my mind.

"I don't need a card or some pretend publishing deal. I'm perfectly fine just the way I am. Now get out of my way, or I'll stomp on you with this damn walker."

I stepped aside and watched her go.

"How did it go?"

I jumped out of my skin and spun around to find Hazel lurking nearby. "Great. She threatened to stomp on me with her mobility aid."

Hazel cracked open a Wild Cherry Pepsi and slurped heartily. "Yeah, she's a tough cookie. Now tell me all about you and that fine specimen of manhood not having sex," she insisted, pointing in the direction of sweaty, handy Gage. He raised a hand to us. We both returned it.

"Fine. I'll give you every detail *if* you do my laundry for me. I haven't had a clean pair of underwear in a week."

"Deal. Since when did you start wearing underwear?"

10

So many nipples
Gage

"You keep looking at the clock," Declan announced.

My paralegal had appeared, silent and catlike, in my doorway and was sipping his coffee out of his plain white mug. Nana poked her head around his legs with a large stuffed hammer in her mouth.

I dropped my pen on the documents I'd been scanning. "My next appointment is late." I'd expected nothing less of Zoey. What I *hadn't* expected was the sense of anticipation I'd had all afternoon leading up to the appointment that she'd probably forgotten.

"Six minutes. Should I reschedule Ms. Moody?"

"Using clients names. Impressive, Declan."

"I still think the numbers are more efficient," he complained.

"It's not always about efficiency."

He didn't look like he believed me.

The door jingled open, and suddenly there she was. Zoey entered like a tornado, windswept and energized, in designer jeans, a silky sheer blouse, and a velvet blazer.

"Sorry, sorry, sorry! I'm late. I'm awful."

"Six minutes," Declan admonished.

"It's fine," I insisted, rising from my chair and meeting her in the reception area.

"Would you believe I thought I was actually going to be early for once?" she asked, using the crook of her elbow to shove her sunglasses up on top of her head. "So I thought I'd stop and get us all coffees, but then there was a line. A *line*! In Story Lake. Can you believe it? Then I realized I didn't have my keys, so I had to retrace my steps, and long story short, throwing your keys in the tip jar just confuses everyone."

"Hi," I said and took the tray of drinks from her.

Her shoulders dropped as the frenetic energy left her. "Hi. I'm sorry for being late. I hope a black coffee and an Earl Grey with almond milk will make up for it. I asked Jennifer Jang what your usuals were."

"Apologies aren't necessary, and the drinks are appreciated," I said as Nana pranced up to Zoey, bonking her in the knees with the stuffed hammer.

"Hello. Yes, I'm sorry. I should have greeted you first, Nana," Zoey said, leaning down to give my dog a cautious pat. "Ah, to have the confidence of a golden retriever believing that everyone is delighted to meet me."

Nana appreciated the effort enough to throw herself on her back to give Zoey belly access.

"Yeah, I don't know what to do with that part of your anatomy," she said.

I took my coffee and handed Declan the tray and his drink. "She likes belly rubs," I said, demonstrating.

Zoey tentatively mimicked me and patted Nana. "Oh God. Why does she have so many nipples?"

"Why don't we get started?" I suggested. I thought about holding out my hand and helping her up but decided the less physical contact, the better.

We rose together, not touching, but our gazes locked.

"Why are you staring like that?" Declan asked, peering at us from an uncomfortable proximity. Not one to be left out, Nana wedged herself between us, tail wagging, hammer squeaking. "Does she have something in her teeth?"

"I'm not staring," I said defensively.

"Do I have something in my teeth?" she asked, rubbing a finger along her gumline.

"You're fine."

"Would you like me to bring my floss to your office?" Declan offered solicitously.

"Thanks, Declan. No need for floss. Shall we?" I gestured toward my office, making sure to give her a wide berth.

"Are you sure I don't have something in my teeth?" Zoey asked hastily when we settled in across the desk from each other. "Because once, I gave an entire presentation to the marketing and sales departments, and I had multiple chia seeds stuck between all my visible teeth the entire time and no one told me."

"There is nothing in your teeth. Now, I didn't see any red flags in the contract, but that's because as the town solicitor, I wrote it." If I kept the conversation professional, I wouldn't think about her comments about a one-night stand like I had every day since the weekend.

"How conflict-of-interest-y," she teased.

"Since you're a nonpaying client and I'm doing this out of the kindness of my heart, I figured you wouldn't mind. What questions do you have?"

"What's that trophy for?" she asked, pointing at one of the bookcase shelves.

"High school baseball state champs. Senior year. Back to the contract—"

"You've got a real time capsule vibe going on in here," she observed. She got up and prowled the room with her coffee.

It was true. In addition to the requisite degrees, law books, and inoffensive office art, I'd included several pieces of personal memorabilia. Family photos, framed newspaper clippings, and mementos occupied shelves and wall space. "I like keeping what's important to me close."

"Is that why you chose to stick around and play the hometown hero?" she asked, picking up the shadow box with a nail from the first job I'd ever worked with my brothers.

"When I said *questions*, I meant questions about your contract."

"You got to ask me about my job. It's my turn."

"Then yes. It was never the plan to move away. I'd always intended to stay in Story Lake."

"Was construction by morning, small-town law by afternoon always part of that plan?" she asked.

"I thought I'd be a full-time attorney. But despite the fact that they're absolute raving assholes some days, I love working with my brothers. It's the best of both worlds."

"What kind of legal conundrums are you solving here in Story Lake?"

I leaned back in my chair and studied her as she examined a family photo from Laura's wedding.

"Mostly family law. Estates, divorces, custody agreements. There's the occasional court case to keep me sharp, and then there's the town solicitor responsibilities, which amount mostly to contracts and bylaws."

She meandered back to the desk and sat. "So what did you do today?"

"I played project foreman over at the Haven's bungalows and inspected three kitchens. Then I met the electrician at a fourth cottage to figure out why the hell the bathroom vanity lights flicker every time the bedroom ceiling fan turns on. I swung by the general store, added some shelves in the stockroom for Laura, then got conned into helping my dad fix a section of fence on the farm that the cows ran through last week. Nana rolled in some otherworldly combination of farm animal shit, so I had to hose her and then myself off. After that, I grabbed a sandwich and shower at home, met a client over in Dominion, fired off three piracy notices for a local romance novelist who shall remain nameless, and gave your contract another once-over. Now I'm making small talk with a woman whose calendar said she only had a thirty-minute window for me today, and I need to get through the contract so I can show her something."

"Wow. First of all, my five o'clock was rescheduled…after I realized I put it into the calendar wrong. Second, my brain has already jumped to six different ideas for what you could possibly want to show me, and three of them are incredibly dirty."

She was flirting with me, and the smart, logical move would be to put a stop to it. "You'll just have to be patient and find out."

Christ. So much for smart.

"Ugh. Patience." She said it like it was a four-letter word.

"Back to your contract," I said, gesturing at the papers spread out in front of me. "I assume you have concerns over the length."

She rested her elbow on my desk, chin in one palm. "I'm *very* concerned over length. Just how long are we talking?"

"Twelve."

Zoey blinked and dropped her hand. "*Twelve*? What are you? Part stallion?"

Great. Now I was being inappropriate. I needed to get things back on a professional keel.

"Months," I said quickly. "The contract is for twelve months."

She slumped in her chair, looking amused. "You got me. And I'll be honest. I didn't read the contract. It's six pages of legalese. I used to depend on a very expensive, very patient attorney that I can no longer afford. I barely stayed focused long enough to print it out."

She looked embarrassed, like she was expecting me to chastise her.

"Zoey, no one but lawyers like to read contracts. That's why you're here. I'll go point by point and put it all into English."

"English like I'm seven years old?"

"Yes."

Relief danced across her gorgeous face. "Thank you."

We ran through the particulars of the agreement without hitting any serious snags or devolving into flirtation again.

"So I'll get more specific with the wording of the deliverables, and you'll let me know what you want on the length of term," I summarized.

She chewed on her lower lip. "The idea of committing to a whole year here gives me hives."

"I had a feeling," I said dryly. "Think about it for a day, and get back to me. Darius is going to be flexible, especially since he's already in an ecstatic lather over your Reader Weekend idea."

She grinned. "Fine. Now can you show me your trouser snake or your collection of Swedish royalty–themed commemorative plates?"

"That's what you narrowed it down to?"

"Hazel isn't the only one with an active imagination," she pointed out.

"Come on," I said, exasperated.

Zoey waved goodbye to Declan, who was using a metal square to align manila folders to perfect right angles on his desk. Nana was belly up in a sunbeam, snoring with the hammer still in her mouth.

I held the door for Zoey and gestured toward the stairs. "We're going up."

"I'd like to amend my list to now include eight baby bunnies you rescued on the side of the road or your collection of Eagle Scout badges."

"You're ridiculous," I said, giving her a nudge toward the first step.

She started up the stairs. "A wall of every compliment you've ever been paid written on sticky notes?"

"No."

"Oooh! I know," she said, spinning around on the step above me. "It's a slide deck of selfies with every old lady you've ever helped cross the street!"

"Definitely not. Go." Without thinking, I put my hands on her hips and nudged her forward. The feel of her curves under my palms short-circuited my brain for a beat. What the hell was I doing? In this moment, she was a client. An unofficial, unpaying client, but there were rules.

She started climbing again, and I dropped my hands. "How about a scrapbook of all the times you've been pulled over by the cops just so they could tell you what a good driver you are?" she pressed.

"You say you're not into commitment, but look at you commit to this bit," I said as we reached the second floor.

"I'm a woman of depths," she said sunnily. "And you seem to be holding up just fine."

I led the way to the door and pulled out the keys. "Hurling insults is my family's love language. I'm used to it."

"I like your family. They don't suck."

"That's a false assumption. They absolutely suck. They just suck in charming, entertaining ways, not emotionally scarring ones."

She cocked her head and studied me. "Do you know how lucky you are?"

"I do. I don't know if you know this, but my brothers and I are all adopted. Our parents died when we were young."

Zoey nodded. "Hazel told me. Not that she goes around blabbing your entire family history or anything. It's just we talk a lot about stuff."

"It's fine. Everyone talks here. We were split up in foster care. I landed here with Frank and Pep Bishop. When they found out I had two older brothers, they moved heaven and earth to reunite us. Now here we all are. I don't remember much about our birth parents, but I do know how lucky I am to be a Bishop." I unlocked the door and waved a hand for her to enter.

She stepped inside cautiously. "It's an empty room. I gotta say, I'm disappointed."

"Yes, but it could be *your* empty room in your empty apartment if you stop annoying the landlord."

Interest sparked in those green eyes. Her eyebrows arched in surprise. "Ohhh. I'm done being disappointed."

"Now don't you feel like a brat?" I asked smugly.

"Gage, this is twice the size of my apartment in Manhattan."

I liked the way my name sounded on her lips, and admitting

that made me want to punch myself in the face. She wasn't the right one. I shouldn't be having any of these feelings. Why the hell couldn't I remember that? "A dollar stretches a little further out here," I said.

"What's this room?" she asked, stepping through the cased opening off the living room into the area just off the galley kitchen.

"It's what we non–New Yorkers call a dining room."

She tapped a finger to her chin. "Hmm. A room just for eating? What will I do on my couch?"

"How do you feel about oversize bathroom vanities?" I asked.

"I feel like you should keep talking, handsome potential landlord."

"Flirting will not get you a discount on the rent, as it's already been confirmed that we're not interested in each other."

"You know who is interested in us?" Zoey said as she made a beeline for the bathroom door. "Hazel. Oh my God. It's huge!" she announced gleefully. She looked back at me, grinning.

"What did I say about flirting?" I said, leaning against the doorframe. "Why is Hazel interested in us? Did Cam get to her too?"

Zoey hopped up on the corner of the vanity, feet swinging. "Get this. She thinks she needs some new real-life inspiration for the book she's writing, and she's trying to concoct a romance between the two of us."

"Where did she get that idea?"

"From me telling her I wasn't interested in you."

"You were talking about me? That doesn't sound disinterested to me."

She rolled her eyes. "There's that Bishop ego. I knew it couldn't be *that* far under the surface. Anyway, I just wanted to give you a heads-up. If you see a brunette romance novelist lurking behind your trash cans, trying to force romance, that's why. As her agent, I'd appreciate it if you humor her so she can start hitting those word count goals."

"How much humor do you suggest?"

"Keep your pants on, Tiger. *I* might be willing to one-night-stand it with you, but then you'd be hypnotized by my body and start following me around town, begging for another night."

"Someone woke up cocky today," I observed.

She looked around the renovated bathroom and sniffed. "Why does everything smell new? Fresh paint, new carpet." She hopped down from the counter and whipped back the shower curtain on the tub. "Aha! New tile."

"Because it is new."

"Gage."

"Zoey."

"Did you redo this apartment for me?"

I thought about lying. Then I thought about how Santa Claus got all the credit for the best gifts. "I did. It was vacant, and I was using it for storage," I admitted.

She looked around the tiny room again. "This is the nicest thing anyone has ever done for me. Literally ever. And you don't even like me."

"It's not that I don't like you," I said in exasperation. "I just don't enjoy spending time with you."

"You're an ass," she said with a laugh. Then she was rising on her tiptoes and placing a smacking kiss on my cheek. "Now, pardon me while I ruthlessly judge your closet space."

She skirted around me and left the room, leaving behind the scent of coconut and a scorching sensation where her lips had touched my skin.

Fuck. This was not good. I was playing with fire, and I never played with fire.

"Oh my God, I could fit almost all of my wardrobe in here," she squealed from the bedroom.

I glanced in the vanity mirror and rearranged my face so it looked less dumbfounded. "Get it together, Bishop," I told my reflection before tracking her down.

"I'll need some shelves in here and a three-month lease,

because we both know there's no way I'll still be here in a year," Zoey called from the closet.

"Nine months," I countered.

She pirouetted to the closet doorway. "This is eight times the size of my closet in the city."

"I told you Story Lake isn't all that bad."

"It's definitely growing on me...like a fungal infection," she admitted.

She was joking, but Story Lake had a way of sinking its hooks into a person.

"There's a partial lake view through the dining room windows, and there's a back staircase off the kitchen that goes directly to your parking space," I explained. "Maybe if you're not too much of a pain in the ass, your landlord will help you carry groceries."

"Six months," she decided. "You can make my contract with the town the same length."

"Deal," I said and held out my hand.

We shook on it, and I ignored the sparks I felt against my palm. I wasn't going to just put off my future for a little fun in the present. I could absolutely handle close proximity. I was a fucking adult with admirable self-control. Attraction and lust were obstacles for teenagers, not grown men well into their thirties.

She let go of my hand and ran a victory lap through the entire apartment before throwing herself at me and wrapping me in a one-sided, violent hug. "Thank you thank you thank you, Gage!"

She released me and danced off to inspect the kitchen.

"What the fuck have I done," I whispered to myself.

Exactly how was I supposed to line up the next Mrs. Bishop when I had a redheaded apocalypse living upstairs?

I'd just have to keep my distance. Which shouldn't be hard. She was busy. I was busy. Two busy people didn't have a ton of free time to bump into each other all over town.

She skidded to a halt in front of me. "You know what's funny? If we *were* into each other, this would have been downright romantic. That lease puts me right on top of you. Hazel would eat this up with a spoon."

11

Vodka splatter
Zoey

I checked my teeth for lipstick in the glass of the hotel's revolving door as it shut out the sounds of Manhattan's Friday night traffic on the street behind me. I'd had a long day of throwing shit into boxes for the big depressing move tomorrow and wanted nothing more than to curl up in my bed for one last night. But I wasn't about to miss this.

The Italics was an annual publishing industry gala that benefitted New York literacy programs. It was attended by publishers, agents, and authors who either hadn't yet figured out how to say no or required an evening of ego stroking. Each year, the Italics Icon award was presented to an "industry titan."

The award had historically gone to wealthy old white guys who spent more time on their sailboats in the Hamptons than at the helms of their companies. The wealthy, old, yacht-owning CEO from Hazel's former publisher had won the last three years in a row. He'd also once famously hurled the glass Icon award at an intern who had mixed up his lunch order with a vegan director's in publicity. Thankfully, he'd missed the intern and instead shattered the door to his office.

But the face of publishing was changing. This year, the recipient was the president of Hazel's new publisher. Navya was a sharply intelligent first-generation American whose five-year-old company was disruptive enough to give the big guys a run for their money.

I couldn't pass up the opportunity to stop by, drink a few glasses of overpriced champagne, and rub my former coworkers' faces in their loss. I would only stay long enough to congratulate Navya and touch base with a few contacts before heading home at a reasonable hour since the movers were coming at the butt crack of dawn.

I took the elevator to the third floor and admired my outfit in the mirrored doors. I'd skipped the New York standard black and went with an eye-catching scarlet Tracy Reese dress. The suede stilettos I'd paired with the dress had seemed like a good investment when I'd purchased them on a full-time salary. Given my current financial predicament, they only taunted me.

Packing had led to a rather painful inventory of my life and assets. I was sitting on a gold mine in used luxury-brand wardrobe items. Unfortunately, I was fairly sure my new landlord wouldn't accept payment in shoes and dresses.

The elevator doors slid open, and I followed the sounds of corporate networking into the ballroom. It looked like every other generic industry event. White linens, fancy canapés, two cash bars swathed in purple table skirts to match the ostentatious lighting. I nodded at a few acquaintances and headed for the nearest bar.

"Champagne please," I said when the bartender slid a cocktail napkin in front of me.

"That'll be twenty-two dollars," she said.

"Seriously? Are the grapes made out of diamonds?"

She flashed me an apologetic smile. "Bottom shelf markup. I can offer you a truly terrible fourteen-dollar tequila that will peel the paint off a wall."

"I'll stick with the 'highway robbery' champagne," I decided and dug out my credit card.

"Well, look what the cat dragged in," a familiar voice crooned behind me.

"Valentino!" I leaned in for a cheek kiss. "Why do you always put me to shame?"

My longtime friend did a runway-worthy spin so I could properly admire his cropped ivory trousers and fitted jacket. His purple suede loafers were bedazzled with chunky crystals.

"You like? I was going for a Cinderella–Prince Charming mash-up."

"Nailed it."

He handed me my champagne and tucked an arm through mine. "Let's take a lap while you tell me everything. I'm hearing buzz that your Hazel is about to drop an absolute gold mine."

"I started that buzz, but it's still true. It's her best book yet, and I'm not just saying that because she's my best friend and only client, and my entire life is riding on it."

I could be honest with Valentino. We went way back. We had started out as editorial assistants together in our early twenties. He was now the head of a successful sci-fi imprint for one of the Big Five publishing houses. And I was…barely keeping my head above water.

"Chin up, my little salmon croquette. We all have to trudge through the dark night of the soul once or twice. It makes the victory so much sweeter. What is this I hear about you living in some tiny village in New Jersey?"

We meandered past the canapé table. "Pennsylvania, and it's temporary."

"I never pictured you as a small-town gal."

"Believe me, it's been an adjustment. There's a free-range pig that just wanders around. A bald eagle that throws snakes. And the entire town turns out to watch people play bingo. But there's a gorgeous lake, and the population has an unusually high percentage of good-looking men."

"I'm coming to visit. The dating pool here has dried up, and I'm subsisting on repeats."

I laughed. "I think you might actually enjoy yourself."

"I enjoy myself everywhere…except the dentist and the waxer. Hmm, maybe I could buy one of those sporty vests outdoorsy people seem to like? Now please tell me you haven't heard the latest about Jim so I can be the one to fill you in."

I dragged us to a stop near the empty stage. Jim was not only my former horrible coworker at the literary agency Beau Monde, he was also Hazel's ex-husband, who had swindled away the rights to the first three books of her Spring Gate series in their divorce settlement. Thanks to me, Cam, Gage, and Hazel's mother's legal team, she had finally won back the rights.

"Is he going to jail? Did he contract some kind of incurable foot fungus?"

"He dropped his newest client after her debut fizzled."

"That's not surprising or salacious," I pointed out.

"Dear me. Did I forget to mention that he'd been sleeping with her since he signed her to what looks to be a rather predatory contract? She's a twenty-three-year-old grad student who had the brains to report him to the powers that be. They're keeping it hush-hush for now, but I don't think it's going to go well for him."

"In my heart of hearts, I want to be a better person. I don't want to be the kind of person who revels in schadenfreude, but sometimes karma is *so* satisfying," I said.

"Some people deserve our joy at their misery. It's a law of nature," he said, holding his glass of overpriced alcohol aloft.

I clinked my glass to his. "I've missed you, Valentino."

"Try not to be gone so long that I forget how much I like you. Now, if you'll excuse me, I see a baby author who needs rescuing from having his soul crushed by Earl Wiggens."

"Wiggens is here?" I asked, craning my neck.

"They tempted him out of his cave with the promise of red meat and a bogus lifetime achievement award."

"I'd love to steal him away from BM." I always took great joy in shortening the agency name, Beau Monde, to the abbreviation for bowel movement.

Valentino reacted as if I'd slapped Dolly Parton. "Why on earth would you ever want to do that? The man's an amoeba."

"An amoeba who makes Beau Monde a shitload of money."

"You know I adore you, my little cheese Danish, but that man is a bag of shit disguised as a human. He farts in elevators. He asks pregnant women why they're out in public. He still smokes in restaurants."

"And BM depends on his farty, chauvinistic royalties."

Valentino shook his head. "Darling, I'm afraid this sounds more self-destructive than vengeful."

I snorted. "I can handle him, and maybe I can even break him of a few of his caveman ways. Go, save your protégé."

He parted the crowd with the confidence of a celebrity, and I trailed along in his wake to do some Wiggens reconnaissance. I took up a position at a nearby cocktail table and surreptitiously studied my quarry.

He was short and doughy in the middle. His tinted glasses hid his eyes so one could never be sure where they lingered. Though as he was on wife number five, an athletic, twenty-nine-year-old swimsuit model, I could guess what was usually in his line of vision. He was in the middle of telling off a young man who was clutching a copy of Earl's latest release and looking positively stricken.

"Bottom line, sport, I ain't signing that book to your mother or anyone else. Real men don't ask other men for autographs," he barked.

"Mr. Wiggens, how *interesting* to see you again. If you don't mind, I'm going to steal Raphael away and introduce him to some actual humans."

Wiggens gave Valentino a curmudgeonly once-over. "What are you supposed to be?"

Ugh. The man was reptilian with a king-size ego. I envisioned myself hitting him in the face with a catering tray. So satisfying. God, maybe my plan really was garbage. Did I really want to have to deal with a guy like that on a regular basis, or was this just another impulsive idea I'd gotten attached to?

Valentino threw his head back and laughed. "Ah, such a *vintage* sense of humor. I'm so happy to see you haven't started listening to the surgeon general. Enjoy that incredibly smelly and off-putting cigar."

"Well, if it isn't Zoey 'I Dropped the Ball' Moody."

My eyes narrowed to slits as I turned to greet another someone who deserved a catering tray to the face.

"How's fired life?" Jim Whitehead, the ex-coworker and ex-husband, sneered at me in Hugo Boss. He was a medium-height, medium-build nothingburger of a man with the ego of a nepo baby reality TV star. Next to him, I recognized Colin, fellow agent at BM and Wiggens's current representation. I had no beef with Colin other than he had the poor taste of being friends with Jim.

"How's 'getting punched in the face' life?" I asked Jim, referring to our last meeting when Cam had decked him in a conference room.

"I'm surprised to see you here," he said, ignoring my insult.

I nonchalantly polished off my overpriced champagne and set the glass down. "Oh really? And why is that?"

"Well, for one, I'd be too embarrassed to show my face after being let go like that. I heard a rumor you're making the move to that hovel of a town permanent," Jim said smugly.

Publishing in New York shared a striking number of similarities to the gossip tree in Story Lake. "I've heard a few interesting rumors myself recently. How's that new author you screwed and screwed over?" I asked.

He scowled at me and opened his mouth to deliver what was sure to be a smug insult, but Colin interrupted. "I hear you've been reaching out to my client."

So Wiggens *had* received at least some of my communications. And he'd thought enough of them to tell his agent. Good. I pasted on a professional smile. "My noncompete is over. If you're doing your job well, I'm sure you have nothing to be concerned about."

Jim snorted into what I could only assume was a fifty-dollar glass of mediocre scotch. "Like anyone with half a brain would choose you over Beau Monde."

"Your ex-wife did," I said pointedly.

"Hazel was let go the same way you were. We don't waste our time on subpar hacks. It's a shame really. If she had just taken my advice, she could have been a respectable author."

I was looking for a conveniently placed catering tray when we were interrupted by yet another new arrival.

"There you are, Zoey," Navya, the woman of the hour, said as she extended her hands to me. We'd met a few times before, but I was struck as always by her elegance. She was gorgeous and glittering in a black cocktail dress. Her dark hair was threaded with silver and swept back in a sophisticated twist. She had the posture of a ballerina and the quiet confidence of a queen.

Every time I was in the room with her, I found myself standing taller.

I took her offered hands. "Navya, congratulations. It's so nice to see this award go to someone who truly deserves it."

Colin cleared his throat. Jim didn't bother hiding his sneer.

"You know Hazel's ex-husband, don't you? The one who tried to take her books in the divorce?" I said, introducing her to Jim.

I knew from the surprised wing of Navya's eyebrows and the deadly glare Jim sent my way that I'd gone just a smidge too far. *Damn it.* It was one thing to spar in private, but to air dirty personal laundry publicly was an amateur move. Why couldn't I keep my inside thoughts to myself?

"I'm surprised you took a chance on the 'dream team,' Navya," Jim said, snidely hooking his thumb in my direction. "It's only a matter of time before Hazel breaks down again or Zoey here drops the ball and ruins a launch. If you're ever interested in publishing a few legitimate authors with professionals backing them, I'm more than happy to take you to lunch."

My blood was boiling, and my mouth was open, which I knew from experience was not a good combination.

Fortunately, Navya responded first. "What an interesting pitch," she said archly.

Unfortunately for us all, my mouth was still open, and it intended to do its job. "Yes, Jim. So interesting that you've changed your tune. What did you call Navya's publishing house at their first launch party? Oh, right! A tabloid of trash that wouldn't last a calendar year."

Colin looked as if the olive from his martini had gone down the wrong pipe.

"Such imagination. I can assure you, Navya, I would never disparage you or your company like that," Jim said, lying through his weaselly teeth.

I snorted.

He turned on me. "Even if Hazel's next foray into maudlin bodice rippers is a commercial success—which it won't be—eventually she's going to realize what everyone already knows. You are a talentless child with the attention span of a flea, and she could get much further with a real professional behind her. Not someone just playing dress-up."

I didn't think. There was no premeditation when I snagged the vodka and soda out of the hands of the woman walking past and tossed it in Jim's face. Instant satisfaction. However, I hadn't accounted for the splatter, which not only soaked me but also Navya's gorgeous dress.

A gasp went up from the nearby bystanders.

"Women. They're so damn emotional," Wiggens complained, blowing a nauseating smoke cloud toward the ceiling.

"Oh, shut the hell up, you ancient primate," I said to him.

Fuck, fuck, fuck.

I backed away from the horrified faces and bumped into a cocktail table behind me, knocking over a few more drinks. Whispering apologies, I made a hasty exit.

"Stupid," I murmured to my reflection in the gilt-framed restroom mirror.

Shame was a ball of fire in my stomach.

Why couldn't I have just kept my mouth shut? Why couldn't I settle for just *imagining* I was throwing a cocktail in Jim's smug face? Once again, my impulses had led me astray. He'd known exactly what buttons to push to activate my deepest, darkest fears. And I'd reacted like a child mid–temper tantrum.

Only this time, I'd done it in front of the one person who'd believed in Hazel enough to give her a shot to prove herself… and a roomful of people who had already written us both off.

"I'm such an idiot," I whispered morosely as I dabbed at the vodka-scented wet spots on the bodice of my dress. I was going to grovel to Navya, and I would have to apologize to Jim *and* make it seem like I meant it. And I wasn't that good an actress. No, thanks to my impulsiveness, the entire publishing industry knew that I was an unstable mess.

"Are you all right?"

I spun around, horrified to see Navya in the doorway.

"I am so sorry. Unbelievably sorry. I ruined your beautiful dress on your big night. You must think I'm horrible," I babbled. Why couldn't I just be like everyone else? Why couldn't I just think mean thoughts instead of acting on them?

I handed her a huge wad of paper towels, a pathetic apology gift.

She accepted them and put them down on the counter. "Zoey, as satisfying as it was to see vodka and soda dripping from that idiot's nose, you can't let people like that get to you. Especially not in a professional setting."

I winced. "I know. I know. I just…couldn't help myself. Please. Whatever you do, don't let this affect Hazel. She's amazing. She wrote an amazing book, and she deserves all the good that's coming her way."

Navya chuckled. "I'm in this business for two reasons. Because I love books and I love making money. Hazel wrote a brilliant story that's going to connect with readers around the world and make us a lot of money. And you, my dear, were smart enough, brave enough, and passionate enough to be her champion when no one else was. I believe in you just as much as I believe in her."

To my ultimate embarrassment, my eyes filled with hot tears. "Really?" I whispered.

"Really. There are enough toadstools like Jim Whitehead gatekeeping wonderful books from the world. You have a drive and a loyalty that reminds me of me when I was your age. But you have got to learn to take that pause between stimulus and response. It does you no favors to let imbeciles like that know they've gotten under your skin. It's much more satisfying to make them think they mean nothing to you at all."

I closed my eyes. "I know you're right. He's going to tell everyone how 'unstable' and 'emotional' I am. I basically just handed him the perfect weapon to use against me."

"Learn from your mistakes. Find a way to control your impulses. If you can channel that passion in less self-defeating ways, you'll be unstoppable."

I wanted to believe her. I wanted to believe that it was possible to finally uncover an untapped well of self-control. But I was starting to worry that my parents were right. That I was a lost cause.

"Now I suggest you get back to what's most important. Getting Hazel ready for the launch that will change both your lives."

I nodded. "Thank you. And again, I'm so sorry, Navya."

"Don't apologize. And don't slink out of here with your tail between your legs. I expect to see you in the audience, head held high."

"I can do that." At least I'd give it my best shot.

12

Step away from the lady's underwear

Zoey

Whoever had scheduled the movers for 8 a.m. was a masochist. And whoever dictated that we had to be on the road no later than 9:30 was a monster. A horrible, cruel, masochistic monster. Oh right. It was me.

I was the hungover monster hurtling toward Pennsylvania with the top down and a hoodie laced around my face so tight I could barely see because the Miata's roof latch was broken. Between no working roof and the incessant rattle in the door panel that was worse at highway speeds, I was starting to think I'd made a mistake in my choice of vehicle.

On the last pee break, I'd pulled out a trick from Hazel's old bike messenger days and wrapped my hands in plastic bags to keep them warm since all my gloves were packed in a box somewhere.

I had seven pairs. Which was far too many pairs of gloves. I had far too many of everything. Which had led me to my new plan. Earl Wiggens was out. That farty old dinosaur was one interview away from getting canceled anyway. So I, Zoey Moody, longtime fashionista, was going to liquidate my wardrobe to save my bottom line. Much as it pained me, if I was going to survive financially, I was going to have to say goodbye to some of my less practical pieces.

I gagged.

My new plan made me a little bit nauseous. But a little poverty was still better than dealing with the Wiggenses of the world on a daily basis.

A gust of April wind rocked my tiny car and ruffled my plastic bag mittens. I was probably leaving a comical trail of pretty bras and toiletries across rural Pennsylvania as they blew out of the boxes that I'd run out of tape for. Hopefully the moving truck behind me was slightly more secure.

This was such a me situation it was almost laughable. I stuffed an ice-cold McMuffin into my mouth. I got a little bit of plastic bag with it but managed to spit out most of it. I didn't know if half-frozen grease was as effective in curing a hangover as hot, fresh grease was, but I was desperate.

Once again, I'd failed to stick to the plan. I'd followed Navya's advice and stayed through her acceptance speech, during which she—thankfully—did not mention her vodka shower. I'd certainly had more than my fair share of eyes on me but found my spirits buoyed by a small but mighty phalanx of publishing industry insiders who all agreed that Jim was a tool who deserved a schnoz full of alcohol.

I drank too much, cheered too loudly, and then organized an impromptu after-party before crawling home at 2 a.m.

Home. I winced as another strong spring gust rocked the Miata.

I no longer had a home. For the first time in my entire life, I didn't have a Manhattan address. And after last night, I was scared down to the tips of my fuzzy socks that this was the beginning of the end. Jim's words had been echoing in my head since last night, and I couldn't shake them.

Would Hazel be better off without me? Would a better, more "professional" agent be able to take her places I couldn't? I hated that the worm might have a point.

I was wallowing so deep in what-ifs that I missed the exit to Story Lake and had to double back. "Get yourself together for *once*, Zoey," I muttered to myself. The van had been paying attention and made the exit, so now I was going to have to come up with an excuse or confess that I was too hungover and wallowing in self-pity to follow the GPS's directions.

Finally, the town limits came into view. I slowed to a crawl when I passed the welcome sign. Last summer, Hazel and I had made a spectacular entrance to Story Lake by plowing into the sign thanks to our first run-in with Goose. As if triggered by the memory, a shadow fell over me in the open car.

I shook my plastic-bagged fist at the eagle as he arched lazily overhead. "Don't even *think* about it, Goose!"

The feathery jerk turned around and made another pass directly over my head. At least he didn't have any fish or snakes in his talons this time. I still had concerns about the capabilities of his back end. Eagle shit was probably toxic or something. To be on the safe side, I accelerated out from under the bird and headed into town.

I found the moving van parked in front of my new temporary lodgings with the lift gate folded down and the door rolled up.

I took a fortifying swig of sports drink and a deep breath. It was going to be a long-ass day made all the worse by the inconvenient hangover. Maybe I could just assemble the bed and go to sleep for the next fourteen hours? I'd unpack next week. Or next month.

"You ready for this?" the driver asked with a thick Queens accent.

"No. But I have no choice."

I got out of the car and brushed McMuffin chunks off the front of my sweatshirt.

"Surprise!" shouted someone with no empathy for the hungover.

It took me almost a full ten dizzying seconds to realize it was Hazel, accompanied by all the Bishop brothers. They were hanging out of the apartment windows on the second floor.

My apartment windows. Between them, Hazel had unfurled a WELCOME HOME banner.

"The hell happened to you?" Cam demanded. "You look like shit."

Gage smirked, then slapped his brother in the back of the head as I hastily untied my hood and shoved it down. I could *feel* my hair defying gravity as it took on a life of its own.

"Leave her alone, Mr. Sensitivity," Gage said.

"What are you guys doing here?" I rasped, trying to prevent my own voice from snapping my head off my neck.

"We're helping you move in," Hazel yelled back sunnily.

"And apparently fixing whatever's wrong with your car roof," Gage added.

"On it," Levi volunteered and disappeared from the window.

"Get on up here. There's food and coffee," Gage said.

I was so grateful and relieved and hungover I almost started crying on the spot.

"That your boyfriend?" asked the impressively biceped female mover.

"That's my landlord."

"Damn, girl. Nice work. My landlord looks like Bigfoot."

"Need a hand?" Gage asked, poking his head into the bedroom.

My surprise moving crew was hard at work putting things to rights in the living room and kitchen while the movers unloaded the rest of my belongings. Nana was overseeing the chaos by completing a lap of the apartment every two minutes. Gage had offered to leave the dog in his office downstairs. It was nice that he'd offer, but I was too hungover to be afraid of the golden retriever today.

While Nana was hairy and slobbery, she was also soft and pretty and had this way of making me feel like she was really happy to see me. Plus, there was absolutely nothing going on inside her noggin, so I didn't need to feel threatened by her.

I was trying valiantly in my hungover state to hook the bed

rail into the headboard but had only succeeded in smacking the freshly painted drywall…twice.

"I could use, like, six of them," I said, collapsing in a sweaty, headachy mess on the carpet to stare at the ceiling. It was a nice room with a quiet blue on the walls and fresh white trim. The two windows faced north and overlooked town.

"Found these in the Kitchen and Maybe Some Bathroom Stuff box," he said, holding up a baggie of bolts labeled *Bed Hardware*. "Thought you might need them."

"Ugh. Thank God. I was starting to think I left them somewhere on the highway."

Gage nudged me aside and competently slid all the tabs into all the slots, then got to work on the mattress supports. "You're lookin' a little under the weather," he observed.

"I'm hungover as hell is what I am. Apparently every time I start a new chapter in this town, I have to do it with a hangover."

"One last hurrah in the city?"

"More like one last catastrophic mistake. I threw a drink in Hazel's ex's face in front of the entire New York publishing industry last night."

"He's lucky you didn't throw a punch. His nose probably still isn't healed from Cam."

"I think I did more damage to myself than him. He got under my skin like he always does, and I failed to control myself like I always do."

Gage gave one of those smirky smiles as he tightened one of the bolts with a wrench that I assumed he'd brought with him.

I watched him move on to the next bolt. "It must be nice to be handy and have tools and know how to fix things," I observed.

"I like to be prepared," he said, stepping out of the bed slats. "Feel up to moving the mattress with me?"

It was my turn to smirk. "If any other guy said that to me…"

"Yeah, yeah. Come on," he said, pulling me to my feet. "If you help me with the mattress, I'll close the door and tell everyone you're unpacking 'lady things' so you can grab a quick catnap."

"Deal," I said.

I helped him muscle the mattress into place and immediately face-planted on top of it.

"Do you think I'm bad for Hazel?" I asked, lifting my head only long enough to ask the question.

The mattress dipped, and then I was unceremoniously rolled onto my back. Gage sprawled out next to me, and we lay there staring up at the ceiling.

"Now what idiocy would have you asking that?"

"Jim the shit waffle said Hazel would be a lot further in her career if she didn't have me holding her back. And I kind of can't stop thinking about it."

"Zoey, honey, you can't listen to people like that."

"That's why I'm asking you. Am I bad for Hazel? Disco," I added hastily.

He rolled on to his side and propped his head on his hand. His bicep bulged in a pleasant, manly way. "If you want the disco, I'll give you the disco."

I closed my eyes and braced myself. "Okay. I'm ready for the disco."

When he didn't say anything, I opened one eye and found him grinning at me. "You're adorable."

I wrinkled my nose even though my stomach swooped like it was on a roller coaster. "I'm well aware of my adorableness. What I don't know is if I'm dragging my best friend down to my level instead of helping her live her dreams. Also, you have a nice smile."

"I'm well aware of my nice smile. And Hazel is lucky to have you. No one is going to care more about helping her succeed than you. I've seen you hold her hand. I've seen you kick her ass. I've seen you cheer louder than anyone every time she gets a win. That guy is an idiot. He was her husband, and he treated her like a commodity. You'd do anything for her, and I can't think of a better quality to have in an agent. Any imaginary deficiency you're worried about, you more than make up for with loyalty and love and hard fucking work. Now quit wasting time worrying about the opinion of an asshole who wears driving moccasins."

I let out a laugh and immediately regretted it when my head started thumping again. "Ow. Thank you for the disco and the ass kicking."

Gage reached over and ruffled my disastrous hair. "Hang here. I'll try to find your ibuprofen."

"Thank you," I called after him. I'd barely shut my eyes when the mattress dipped again. It was Hazel, gleefully clutching two bed pillows to her chest.

"I saw you two *in bed* together," she whisper-screamed.

"Jesus, Haze," I said, snatching one of the pillows and pulling it over my head. "He put my bed together and moved my mattress. We were taking a break."

"A *horizontal* break. With sexy smiles and lingering looks. It looked like you were talking about something serious."

"We were discussing driving moccasins."

"Hmm. I think I'll have you discussing something more meaningful and character arc-y. Like maybe he was heroically calming your fears about starting this new chapter in life."

"I don't know why I put up with you," I groaned into the pillow.

"Ooh! What if you had a muscle cramp and he offered to rub it for you? Is the thigh too sexy for this early in the story?"

"Hazel!" I groaned in exasperation.

She grinned and threw her pillow over my stomach before curling up with me. "I know it's selfish, but I'm so glad you're here and that you're staying."

"Temporarily," I said, twirling her ponytail.

"I'll take it. I feel like this place might be a little bit magic, and now it's your turn."

"Oh my God. I'm *not* going to fall in love with Gage and find some storybook-worthy HEA here."

Suddenly, a red-blond furry face appeared in my line of vision as Nana joined us on the bed. Deciding she was an integral part of girl time, she curled up next to my head and rested her face in my hair.

"It doesn't have to be Gage, but it would be so convenient for me," she insisted. "And his dog obviously loves you."

I reached up blindly to pat Nana. "Nana also loves lampposts. Don't take her opinion too seriously. Haze?"

"Yeah?"

"Do you think you might be better off without me? I mean like if we were still friends but you had an agent with more… experience?"

Hazel sat up and looked horrified. "Where in the hell did you ever get a stupid-ass idea like that?"

"From a stupid ass."

"We're in this together. And yes, we have both made mistakes. If you're looking for a very recent example, let's examine me letting a *stupid ass* destroy my mojo for two entire years until there was barely a career left to salvage while you stood by my side and moved away from everything you love to help me through it. Don't let one word that comes out of my ex-husband's mouth land anywhere near you."

"Ugh. Who told you about Jim?" I asked. Nana shifted and covered my face with her chin, giving me dog-face beard.

"Valentino. And Jamila. And Sara. I wish I could have seen him snorting vodka out of his nose for the rest of the night. You're a good friend, Zoey. And that makes you an even better agent."

I turned my head as much as the weight of dog face allowed. "I didn't move away from everything I love."

Hazel raised an eyebrow above the rim of her glasses. "Oh?"

I pointed at her.

She pointed at herself, eyes going misty. "Me?"

"Yeah, and I'm hungover as hell, so I'd appreciate it if you could keep it together so we don't have to have a whole moment. I'm so dehydrated I might die if I formed any tears."

"Fine. I've got this." She sniffled dramatically and waved her hands in front of her face.

"You know that works better when you're not wearing glasses."

"I love you too, Zo."

We were recovering from our nonmoment when Gage returned with a bottle of ibuprofen and a glass of water. "Found it in a bag of extension cords and phone chargers."

Hazel poked me. "I told you to let me help you pack."

"You have a book to write. That's more important."

"Well, I *am* feeling inspired," she said pointedly, looking back and forth between us. Nana's tail thumped on the mattress.

Cam poked his head in the doorway. "Got a medium-size problem downstairs," he reported.

"Oh God! It's not any of the boxes labeled *shoes*, is it?" I demanded. By my rough, hungover calculations, I had a few thousand dollars in fabulous footwear that I could sell.

"You need to see it for yourself."

I downed the water and ibuprofen on my way out the front door and into the sunshine.

It was not the box of shoes. It was much, much worse.

Levi was standing on the sidewalk, arms crossed over his chest, attention on my car. The movers were lined up at the back of the moving truck, each armed with a cell phone, recording.

"What's going on?" I asked.

Levi looked my way. "The good news is I fixed your roof latch temporarily. You'll need to take it into a garage for a permanent fix."

"Thanks, Levi. I owe you. What's the bad news?"

Cam pointed to my car. "He didn't close the roof after he fixed it, so that's your problem."

"Seriously? Damn it, Goose!" I shrieked.

The eagle was perched on the last box in my passenger seat. The cardboard flaps were open, and the bird had a hot-pink bra with tiny crystals in his beak. It was one of my nicest bras. My favorite bra.

Gage and Cam arrived at my side. Cam laughed while Gage did his best to hide his amusement.

I groaned. "That's a three-hundred-dollar bra that he's slobbering eagle germs on!" I'd been planning to sell that bra, but who was going to buy it if it had eagle beak marks?

I made a move toward the macabre scene, but Gage stepped in. He took me by the shoulders and marched me backward.

"With your luck with animals, I'd prefer if you didn't engage the bald eagle."

"But that asshole's going to eat my bra!" I waved my hands at the bird over Gage's shoulder. "Drop the bra and fly away, or I will make sure every tourist in this town is issued an umbrella upon entering town limits, and you'll never get to shit on anyone again, Goose!"

The gigantic bird looked at me as if contemplating my threat.

Cam and Levi dissolved into manly snorts of hysteria.

"Not helping, guys," Gage complained before turning his attention back to me. "Don't move."

"What are you gonna do? Wrestle the bird for the bra?" Cam asked.

Gage responded with a brisk middle finger in his brother's direction before marching off to his truck parked at the curb.

He opened the door, dug around for something, and then returned to the scene of the crime in progress.

"Happy move-in day—uh, what's happening?"

Pep and Frank Bishop joined me on the sidewalk. Frank was holding a festive gift bag, and Pep was carrying two bottles of wine with curled ribbon around the necks.

"Goose has a crush on Zoey," Levi reported.

"Am I the only one still working?" Hazel hollered out of the second-floor window.

"We're watching Goose steal Zoey's underwear," Cam yelled back.

"Well, that's new," Frank said, handing me the gift bag and joining his sons in their armchair eagle quarterbacking.

Gage shook the small bag in his hand. "Come on, you feathery pain in the ass. You'd rather have a snack than some expensive underwear."

A muffled bark came from behind us, and I spotted Nana with her nose and tongue plastered against the glass front door, triggered into delirium by the word *snack*.

Goose seemed interested in Gage's offer. He shifted his weight from foot to foot and eyed the bag of God knows what eagles considered treats.

Gage opened the pouch, and Goose hopped onto the passenger door.

"Drop the bra, and you can have this," Gage instructed, holding up the treat.

"What is that?" I asked.

"Organic dried beef dog treats. Turns out they're not just good for stray dogs. They're Goose's favorite. Although we do have to watch his sodium," Pep explained. "If you're having this much trouble with him, you might want to start carrying them."

"Won't that just encourage him to continue being an asshole?"

"Look at it like redirecting a toddler," she suggested.

We collectively held our breath as Goose spread his wings. On a disgruntled squawk, he opened his mouth and dropped the bra. I breathed a sigh of relief when it draped neatly over the Miata's door.

"Good pain in the ass. Nice pain in the ass," Gage said. He tossed the treat in the air, and Goose caught it neatly in his terrifying beak.

The eagle snarfed it down the way I attacked a midnight microwave burrito: with aggressive enthusiasm.

"Now how about we step away from the lady's underwear," Gage suggested, shaking the bag again.

The eagle took a tentative step toward the back of the car.

"Thank you thank you thank you," I said, sidling closer to the bra.

Goose whipped his head in my direction and pinned me with a creepy bird eye. I squeaked and froze on the sidewalk. We stared each other down for several beats, and I swear to God, the demon fowl *winked* at me.

"You listen here, bird. I am exhausted and hungover. I can't be held responsible for my actions. So don't. You. Dare," I hissed.

But oh, how he dared.

With a graceful dip of his head, Goose snatched up the bra in his beak, unfurled his wings, and took off.

I covered my face in my hands and groaned. "I'm being bullied by a bald eagle. I need more ibuprofen."

"Bird's definitely got a crush," Cam said, shielding his eyes from the sun to watch Goose soar away with a week's worth of gas, grocery, and wine money in his stupid beak.

An SUV pulled to a stop in the street. Hana and Billie from the lodge stuck their heads out of their respective windows.

"We were just coming to drop off a housewarming present. What's Goose have?" Hana asked, shading her eyes against the sun.

"A three-hundred-dollar D-cup," I said morosely.

Pep patted me on the shoulder. "Look at it this way. Goose now has the most blinged-out eagle's nest in history."

"Sorry, Zo. Guess he wanted the bra more than he wanted the food," Gage said.

"We've all been there," Cam said sagely.

I took a step backward and nearly went ass over feet over Emilie Rump's free-range pig, Rump Roast. He spit out an apple at my feet and oinked happily.

"This is not an auspicious beginning," I muttered.

The pig grunted in agreement.

"Sometimes the best new chapters start in disaster, kiddo. You'll see," Pep said with confidence. She scratched the pig on the head and then tucked the bottles of wine into the open box on my passenger seat. "Let's get this inside before Goose decides to come back for the matching underwear."

13

Don't say sperm
Gage

Neighborly: "Town eagle loots new resident's belongings. Will authorities respond to the crime? Read the whole story!"—Garland Russell

---

Three hours after Goose departed with his new treasure, our small army had nearly every box of Zoey's unpacked. A miracle in itself given that the nightmarish labeling system had included boxes labeled *Rando Junk I Might Need Someday* and *Makeup, Socks, and Mail to Open*.

The apartment had gone from blank walls and bare floors to a home…a home for someone with chaotic taste. Zoey favored color, lots of it, from the green velvet couch to the distressed turquoise chest she used as a coffee table. Her art was splashy and vibrant, as was her excessive collection of throw pillows. And everything had a story. The two purple swivel chairs on the long wall of the living room had been a graduation gift from her favorite great-aunt. She'd paired them with the raw-edged console table that Hana and Billie had delivered earlier. Apparently it had been in Zoey's room at the lodge until an unfortunate run-in with a can of SpaghettiOs had left a blotchy orange stain on the top.

There was no unifying theme, no cohesive plan that I could identify in the tie-dyed plaster human skull and the string of disco ball lights she'd hung on the wall. But somehow it all said "Zoey Moody."

My parents had gifted Zoey a practical selection of picture hangers and had therefore been tasked with putting up Zoey's framed photos and artwork, including the Do Epic Shit print now hanging proudly on the bathroom wall above the toilet. Cam and Hazel had curtained off the dining room and were doing God knows what inside. Zoey, my dog, and my mother were sprawled on the couch, taking a break to watch me and Levi hang the TV on the living room wall.

And I was still thinking about that damn bra.

I was a responsible, reliable adult with two successful businesses. Yet here I was, trapped in some ridiculous mind loop, wondering what Zoey had on underneath her sweatshirt right now. Did it have sequins? What color was it? The more time I spent with her, the more time I spent thinking about her. It was definitely a fucking problem.

"Are you even trying to hold up your end?" Levi demanded.

"Sorry," I said, adjusting my grip on the TV.

"This place turned out great, Gage," Mom said, helping herself to one of the housewarming brownies town council member Erleen Dabner had dropped off along with a dream catcher and a large hunk of rose quartz.

"Thanks, Mom," I said as we slid the TV onto the wall bracket. "I'm the favorite," I whispered to Levi.

"We helped," he announced.

"Yeah, Mom," Cam called from the dining room. "Be impressed with us."

"They've always been competitive," my mother explained to Zoey.

"First I'm seeing it," Zoey deadpanned, pulling her hood back up and resting her head on the back of the couch.

My mother grinned. "You're so sweet to lie to my face."

The sound of heavy furniture scooting across the dining room floor had me wincing. "You better not be scratching that floor," I warned.

"Mind your business," Cam grunted from behind the curtain.

I pointed at Zoey. "Whatever they do, it's coming out of your security deposit."

"Calm down, By the Book. You've been a landlord for five whole minutes," she said.

"Good banter," Hazel called from the dining room.

"Thank you," Zoey said. "And thank you to everyone else for helping today. I'd have been living out of boxes for the next six months if it weren't for you."

"That's what we Bishops do. Usually without any ulterior motives. However, if you're not too under the weather, Frank and I have something we'd like to discuss with you. Professionally," my mother said to Zoey.

Levi and I stopped browsing the brownie tray and eyed our parents with suspicion. We usually knew everything Mom and Dad were up to at almost all times.

Zoey held up a hand. "Full disclosure. I'm not under the weather, I'm hungover. And I'll understand if you don't want to discuss anything professional with me until I stop looking like a goblin."

"Kiddo, we raised four kids. Everybody deals with unplanned midlife hangovers," Mom said, patting Zoey's sweatpants-clad knee. "Frank, stop hammering before the poor girl's head falls off."

Dad stowed the hammer he'd borrowed back in my tool tote. "Sorry, Zoey. Don't hold it against us when we present our project."

Zoey stroked her chin theatrically. "The Hangover Goblin is intrigued. What project is that?"

"Yeah, what project?" Levi and I repeated.

Cam poked his head out of the dining room curtain a beat late. "Yeah, what project?"

"Too late. You ruined it," I told him.

He shot me a middle finger.

"Come on out for a brownie and beer break, and we'll tell you," Mom said.

Cam and Hazel ducked out from behind the makeshift curtain. "Beer? Beer? Beer?" he asked, pointing at each of us in turn.

Everyone except Zoey said yes. "I'll take a ginger ale if you can find one."

Once everyone was settled in the living room with their beers and brownies, Mom and Dad shared an excited look. "Well, we didn't want to say anything until there was actual news to share. But since we just won our first small grant, we're taking Hazel's idea for a petting zoo a step further and turning the farm into an animal sanctuary."

"Congratulations! That's so exciting! And what a great setting for a romance novel," Hazel mused.

"You're gonna need a bigger barn," Cam said.

"And a hell of a lot more feed," Levi added.

"Where are you with the paperwork? The nonprofit application process isn't easy to navigate," I pointed out.

"Ignore your buzzkill sons, and let's focus on the me-related fun stuff," Zoey suggested.

"We're not buzzkills. We're the voices of reason," I insisted.

"Why don't you reason that brownie into your mouth and let your adult parents discuss their plans for the property they own?" she said.

"We're thinking we could do farm tours, let visitors come and help feed the animals. Host birthday parties and goat yoga. Cow cuddle therapy," Mom announced.

"You want people to cuddle Fart Blaster 2000?" Levi asked incredulously. Fart Blaster was one of my parents' Holsteins, named by my niece and nephews.

"Does this mean we have to start telling people you rescue livestock instead of hoarding it?" Cam joked.

"Yes," Mom and Dad said, shooting him twin parental warning glares.

Mom turned to Zoey. "Since you're doing the town's publicity, we're coming to you to help us get started. We're going to need a website, email, a way to collect donations online."

"Then there's the biggie," Dad said, plopping down in one of Zoey's swivel chairs. "How do we get visitors to show up, enjoy themselves, and make big fat donations? The more donations we bring in, the more animals we can help."

"We realize that animals aren't exactly your thing," Mom said apologetically to Zoey, who was reluctantly cradling Nana's head and upper body in her lap. "But we could really use your help."

I didn't like where this was going. The woman was already going to be living above my office. The last thing I needed was her running around on my parents' farm, which was adjacent to my own home. I should be putting distance between us, not getting closer.

"Think of it as immersion therapy," Hazel suggested, squeezing onto the couch between Nana's ass end and my mother.

"Stop trying to immerse me in animals," Zoey shot back.

Nana's tail thumped happily against Hazel.

"I'm just saying you've got a dog in your lap."

Zoey chose to ignore Hazel's observation. "As long as I'm not personally required to participate in cow cuddling, I'm happy to work with you," she told my parents.

"Cow cuddling is optional," Dad promised.

"Then I'm in. We'll need bios on each animal. And not just their sad, heartstring-tugging rescue stories. Include funny things about their personalities. Make people feel good about those big fat donations. Think less emotionally scarring than those dog rescue commercials and more overly honest personal ads."

Mom grinned slowly. "Oh, I like that."

Dad slapped his knee. "Sounds perfect. One question. How do we get started?"

"We'll work together on the logistics," Zoey promised them.

"Your first step should be making an appointment with your smartest son so he can help you with the filings," I said sternly.

"Why would they make an appointment with me?" Cam quipped.

"You wouldn't be the smartest son if Livvy and I were both in comas," I quipped.

Levi grunted his approval of my brotherly burn and held up a fist. I bumped it.

"Gage wants to wife someone up," Cam announced.

I groaned. "Shut the fuck up, Cammy."

"That's nice." To her credit, Mom was unfazed. She was too used to us to take the bait.

Zoey was openly smirking at me.

"I'm so glad I opened up to you idiots. I have no regrets at all," I said, heavy on the sarcasm.

"Got any candidates lined up?" Dad asked with a straight face.

"Not yet," I said evenly.

"How do you feel about arranged marriages? Livvy and I could find a bride for you," Cam offered.

I scoffed. "I wouldn't trust either of you to pick out an avocado."

Hazel pointed at me. "Hey! Offended."

"What I meant to say is that Cam got lucky when the perfect woman appeared in front of him. Some of us can't just wait around for a car to crash into a sign in front of us."

"So what are your qualifications for the ideal candidate?" Zoey asked, joining in.

"I motion to change the subject to literally anything else."

"Motion denied," Hazel said. "We should definitely discuss what you're looking for in a life partner. Spare no detail."

"Where did you get that notebook?" Zoey asked her.

"Don't worry about it," Hazel insisted, briskly clicking her pen open. "Let's start with personality traits. How important is a sense of humor to you?"

"Mom? Help?" I prompted.

She held up her hands. "Sorry, sweetie. We all just want to see you happy. You might as well give them something, or they'll hound you to death."

"Fine. In no particular order, I'm looking for someone who's organized, thoughtful, smart, financially independent, and responsible."

Zoey, Levi, and Cam all feigned snoring fits. Zoey pretended to wake suddenly. "Sorry, your future wife just bored us to sleep."

My mom snickered in appreciation.

"I'm not loving this collaboration," I told them. "And what exactly is wrong with my list?"

Levi grimaced. "You just described yourself, dumbass."

"What's so wrong with that?" I wondered.

"Son, if you don't know, I'm not sure how to explain it to you," Dad said.

"Oh, this is so good," Hazel said, making notes on the page. "It's like he doesn't know how love works."

"I know how love works," I argued.

Cam snorted. "That's what everyone says before they've been in it."

"I love you assholes," I pointed out.

"Yeah, but you didn't pick us out. You got stuck with us," Levi reminded me.

"Look, I appreciate the unsolicited opinions, but allow me to point out that there's only one happily married couple in this room, so the rest of you can keep your opinions to yourselves."

"Haze and me are happily engaged," Cam insisted.

"Cam's right," Hazel said, pointing her pen in his direction.

"Please," I scoffed. "He's one dumbass mistake away from making you come to your senses and locking him out with the raccoon."

"Gage is also right," Hazel mused.

"So how are you planning to meet the lucky young lady?" Mom asked.

"Maybe he hired a matchmaker," Cam guessed.

"Ohmygod, did you? I've never had a hero do that before. What if he falls for the matchmaker?" Hazel pushed her glasses up her nose and started scribbling again.

"As delighted as I am to be your entertainment, can we get back to these boxes so we can let Zoey enjoy her new place?" I didn't care to have this conversation period, let alone in front of the woman I'd been fantasizing about.

"Oh, I'm enjoying my new place already," she said with a sly grin.

"I'm raising your rent. Hey, who wants to see my carpet tack wound?" I offered to the group.

"Have you tried speed dating?" Mom asked, batting her lashes innocently.

"I expected more from you, Mother."

"I don't know why you would," she teased.

"Dating apps!" Hazel announced, pointing her pen at me.

"Yes, I'm on a couple of dating apps. Now can we please—"

"Sounds like a good way to get murdered by a stranger," Levi said, finally sounding interested.

"Which ones?" Zoey asked, pulling her phone out. "Dating apps, not murders by strangers."

"I plead the Fifth."

As the youngest, I was usually quicker on my feet. I could see a sneak attack coming from a mile away. But I blamed Zoey for distracting me. Cam and Levi's attack caught me by surprise. I put up a good fight, but they managed to wrestle me to the floor in less than a minute.

"Get off me!" I complained as Cam held my arms behind my back and Levi rummaged through my pockets.

"Got it," Levi said, triumphantly holding up my phone. He keyed in my passcode—our family was definitely too close—and tossed the phone to Zoey, who caught it midair.

"Mom!" I yelled.

"Boys, get off your brother," she said mildly.

"We're just having fun," Cam said, happily shoving my face into the rug.

"I hope they don't do this at the wedding," Hazel observed.

"Can't promise anything," Levi said.

Dad stepped in and grabbed Cam's ear.

"Ow! Mom!"

"Hmm, well, he's on Everafter, and his profile pic is not shirtless. So that's something," Zoey reported.

My brothers abandoned me to lean over the back of the couch.

Zoey looked up at me while I climbed to my feet. "You have a dozen unopened DMs," she said.

"I've been a little busy fixing up *your* apartment," I pointed out.

"And I so appreciate that. Now it says here your interests include cooking and spending quality time with your family. I think we could jazz this up a little bit so you sound less…"

"Less what?" I challenged.

"Boring as fuck," Cam interjected.

"He said it, not me," Zoey said.

"You should listen to her. Zoey is an app expert," Hazel said.

"Let's open his messages and pick his new bride," Cam said.

I stomped over, snatched my phone out of Zoey's hands, and shoved Cam in the forehead. Levi reached out quick as a snake and locked his hand around my arm.

"Boys!" Mom yelled. "No fighting with three innocent women in the middle."

Nana barked.

"Sorry. Four innocent women," Mom said.

"Hey, maybe it's time for Zoey's present before someone loses an eye," Hazel suggested brightly.

"Did someone say *present*?" Zoey said, shoving back her hood.

"Cam and I wanted to do something special for you," Hazel explained, extricating Zoey out from under my dog.

"I wanted to get you four puppies," Cam cut in wickedly.

Hazel jogged back to the curtain hanging over the dining room doorway. "Thankfully, I'm a much more thoughtful gift giver. So ta-da!" She Vanna White–ed her arms toward the curtain, but nothing happened.

"What's happening?" Zoey asked.

"The curtain, Cam. Pull the curtain," Hazel said out of the side of her mouth.

"Oh, right." Cam unceremoniously yanked down the duct-taped curtain.

"Ta-da!" Hazel said again.

"Oh my God," Zoey breathed. "I have an *office*?"

"You have an office!" Hazel squealed.

I joined Cam in the doorway while the two best friends started hugging and jumping and squealing.

They'd positioned a desk and chair in the middle of a colorful pink and orange rug. A matching canvas with wild swipes of color was centered between the two windows on the wall behind the desk. A long, skinny console table in matching wood was pushed up against the front wall. It was topped with a series of wire bins and cups of colorful writing implements.

Nana strolled inside and immediately threw herself down to wriggle all over the fluffy rug.

"Now you have room for your printer *and* you can still keep all your piles but they'll *look* organized," Hazel explained. "Oh! And here's a filing cabinet. I prelabeled as many folders as I could think of so you don't have to. And there's office supplies in there, including your favorite highlighters." She pointed to a tall, skinny cabinet shoehorned into the corner.

"Did you go notebook shopping for me?" Zoey asked, opening the cabinet door.

"Mostly for me, but I got you a few too," she said.

"Frank, we need to redo our office," Mom noted, admiring the setup.

"Great. Thanks a lot, Campbell," Dad complained.

Zoey turned to Hazel. "I love it. So much. I can't believe you did this for me."

"It's gonna be a big year," Cam predicted, shoving his hand in his pockets. "Figured you needed a place to ringlead."

Zoey surprised him with a hug. Then she released him to grab Hazel. "Thank you. Thank you both of you. I'll make sure this year is the most kick-ass year of your lives."

Nana nosed her way in.

"And thank you, pretty girl," Zoey said, cupping the dog's face between her hands and pressing a kiss to her furry forehead. Nana's tail wagged violently.

"Hey, I helped too," I pointed out. "Those walls didn't paint themselves."

"How could I forget Nana's dad?" Zoey said, turning her attention to me. She cupped my face and delivered a noisy, close-mouthed kiss to my lips.

There was nothing sexual about the kiss, but my body didn't seem to register that fact. I felt like my lips were on fire.

"That better have been platonic," Cam said.

Hazel clapped her hands. "Ooh! What if it *was* platonic, but with the most innocent of physical contact, the hero suddenly realizes he wants more? And with the heroine living upstairs, there's obvious forced proximity. Imagine the landlord-tenant situations that would ratchet up the sexual tension."

Fuck. My. Life.

"Here we go again," Zoey said.

"You don't mind if I borrow one of your notebooks, do you?" Hazel asked, already reaching for one.

"What did you do with the one you had five seconds ago?"

"It's full."

"Whatever. If it turns into another book, I don't care if you write on my walls."

"*My* walls," I pointed out.

Zoey took a seat in the chair behind the desk and spun it around while Nana barked wildly. "My associate Nana and I have called you all here today to tell you—" She stopped the spin abruptly and put her head on the desk. "Hang on. Hangover goblin vertigo. I might barf."

"You need some electrolytes and some good old-fashioned grease," Mom suggested.

The conversation was interrupted by an automated voice.

"Your siblings are assholes. Your siblings are assholes," the voice announced flatly.

"What the hell is that?" I demanded as Levi patted his pockets.

"It's the ringtone for my fucking chief of police phone," Levi said, producing a phone from his back pocket. He answered the call. "Yeah? Uh-huh. Did you try explaining to them that the streets are for motor vehicles? Fine. I'll be there in five." He disconnected the call and heaved a sigh. "Apparently a mobility scooter company decided it was a great idea to host a demonstration at the Haven's happy hour. Now we've got a dozen intoxicated retirees cruising through town on stolen demo scooters."

"Classic Story Lake," Zoey said.

"They give you a cop car yet?" Cam asked with a shit-eating grin.

"No. Just a magnetic emergency roof light."

"Maybe you can roll down your window and make siren noises so they know you mean business," I suggested innocently.

"I hate you both. I'd punch you in the face, but I have to go do a job I never signed up for. Why?" Levi pointed at me and Cam.

"Because your siblings are assholes," we announced proudly.

"Have fun restoring law and order," Zoey called after him as he left with both middle fingers extended in our direction.

"We love you," Mom said.

"Don't get hit by a scooter," Dad suggested as the door slammed behind him.

"That should do it," I said as I sank the last screw into the wall through the bracket. Everyone else had left to nurse sore moving muscles. Or in Levi's case, to handle the eight pounds of paperwork from the Great Scooter Incident.

"I always thought hardware like that was just extra pieces. You know, like with a Lego set," Zoey said from the bed.

"Wall anchors aren't extra pieces. They prevent horrible furniture-related accidents." I gave the bookcase a demonstrative shake.

"Believe it or not," Zoey said from her belly-down position next to Nana, who was once again asleep, "I've yet to have a horrible furniture-related accident." She had her chin in her hands and had provided an attentive audience while I'd assembled her new bookcase out of the kindness of my heart, *not* out of the desire to spend more time with her.

"And now you definitely won't. That's what friends are for."

"Friends." She pursed her lips. Her color had come back after a dinner of delivery chicken fingers and boxed macaroni and cheese. "I haven't had a guy friend since junior high."

"I prefer the term *man friend*. Aren't you friends with any of your exes?"

Zoey let out a surprised laugh. "If you knew some of my exes, you'd know why that's a completely ridiculous question."

I joined her on the bed like I didn't have a choice. My body wanted to keep her close while alarm bells rang in my head. I stacked my hands under my head, careful to keep my snoring dog between us. "Give me some examples."

"Okay. Well, there was Keith, the deadbeat guitarist in an eighties cover band. He had more hair than I did, and even though he was playing weddings and bar mitzvahs, he thought he was entitled to groupies. Then there was Darren, the investment adviser. We met when he was flirting with someone else at the bar. When she went to the bathroom, I told him his pickup lines were weak. Turns out not only did he have a short attention span, he was engaged…to be married and also in insider trading."

"If you know these guys are so horrible, why do you go out with them?"

"Don't know. Just broken, I guess," she said airily.

"Disco."

She rolled her eyes. "Fine. Uh, I guess maybe because they can't surprise me. I know exactly what to expect, and I'm not inconvenienced by their departure."

"Zoey, you're a smart girl. I refuse to believe your entire dating history looks like that."

She sighed. "There was a guy once, Sam. Very handsome, very responsible." She narrowed her eyes at me. "Come to think of it, you remind me a little of him. Always doing the right thing. Anyway, it was serious…for me at least. But it was college, and you can only get so serious in college. I thought I was in love. He wanted more of what I couldn't give him and less of…well, me. He broke up with me, and I was just crushed enough that I realized I never wanted to be in that position again. At least not until I knew how to stand on my own two feet."

"It sounds like there are significantly more details to that story," I noted.

"Yeah, well, let's not taint my new start with an old sob story. How goes the wife hunt?" she asked, changing the subject.

"I've been too busy making sure my new tenant doesn't get crushed by her bookcase to do much hunting."

"Better get on that. Those sperm aren't getting any younger," she teased.

I sprang off the bed like the mattress was made of bees. *Sperm* wasn't exactly a sexy word, but hearing it come out of Zoey's mouth while we were lying on a bed together was too close to the line. I was playing with fucking fire here.

"I'd better get going. I have…things to do."

"Things like cooking and spending quality time with family?" she quipped.

Things like putting some much needed distance between Zoey Moody and my sperm.

14

Sexy swamp beast
Zoey

"Come on. You know you want to," Wes prompted.

"You'll like it. I promise," Harry assured me with a wink.

I groaned. "This is the weirdest peer pressure I've ever experienced."

"Just hold out your hand," Isla advised.

"How did my life come to this?" I wailed as I held out a palm full of dried pellets to a farm beast that was big enough not to notice when it trampled me. I was really going to miss that hand when it was bitten off.

Fart Blaster 2000, the ridiculously named Holstein, lumbered her black-and-white body toward me. I automatically took two steps back, which only made the cow pick up speed.

"She won't hurt you," Wes promised, trying to hide his amusement.

"Unless she accidentally steps on you. She weighs a shit ton," Harry warned as the advancing cow boxed me in against the pasture fence.

I squeezed my eyes shut, preparing to face the end of my life.

I'd always known my demise would involve livestock. "I changed my mind! I don't wanna be the town publicist!"

That was what had gotten me into this mess. Frank and Pep had insisted on giving me a tour of their property since I was going to help them launch their nonprofit farm sanctuary. It was a Sunday, and Laura's kids had volunteered to conduct the tour, which was definitely going to end in my tragic death.

But the anticipated squishing never came. Only a soggy, velvety brush against my palm. I opened one eye to find the cow neatly snacking on the pellets in my hand.

"Aww! Fart Blaster 2000 knows you're nervous, and she's being gentle," Isla observed.

"Until the cow food is gone and then it eats my entire arm," I said, bracing for the attack.

"Gramps calls her a therapy cow because she can tell if you're sad or scared or if you want to play," Harry explained. "When I failed my driver's test, she almost crushed me when we were sitting in the field."

"Not a great time to share that story, bro," Wes pointed out.

The food was now gone, and Fart Blaster was staring at me with bland brown eyes. "Moo?"

"Ah! Tell Hazel I want to be cremated!" I screeched as I covered my head with my arms.

Once again, the murder by farm animal I'd expected didn't happen.

Isla giggled. "She just wants you to pet her."

"Like a dog?" I asked.

"Yeah. Just think of her as a bigger Melvin," Harry suggested.

"I'm not petting this thing's belly," I said, eyeing the udder with terror. I did *not* want to find out how many nipples a cow had.

On cue, Melvin and Bentley, Frank and Pep's beagle, jogged up proudly, each carrying a stick that should have belonged to the other. Harry wrestled the tiny twig from Melvin's massive mouth while Wes took Bentley's leafy tree limb. The boys hurled both deeper into the pasture, and the dogs took off after them, barking joyfully.

I gave Fart Blaster's nose a tentative stroke. Hmm. Who knew cows were kind of soft and fuzzy? It was…not terrible. The cow sighed and leaned into my hand.

"Look! You're making friends," Isla said.

"Do you wanna meet the new alpacas?" Wes offered.

"Watch out. They spit a lot," Harry warned.

"I'll pass on the alpacas. So what are you guys all doing on the farm on a sunny spring Sunday?" I asked, continuing to stroke the giant cow.

When I was a teenager, I spent my Sundays in coffee shops, crushing on baristas, or at friends' apartments, crushing on their older brothers. But even I had to admit Story Lake's farm life had a certain aesthetic appeal. April sunshine bathed the rolling green pastures in warmth. The trees were showing off fresh, new leaves. And the sky was the kind of blue I never got to see back home. Spring had a whole different vibe here compared to Manhattan, where the season was traditionally marked solely by the return of the sundress and pollen on parked cars.

"Family workday," Harry said, hoisting himself up to sit on the top rail of the fence.

"We take one Sunday a month to come and help out around the farm. The uncles take another one. Mom and Dad always said they wanted us to understand the value of hard work, but we figured they were into the idea for the free babysitting. Gramps and Gram were cool with it because it's free child labor," Wes explained, giving the cow's haunches a pat.

"What do you all get out of it?" Fart Blaster shifted her weight and leaned against me as I scratched around her ears.

"Lunch," they said together.

"And it's nice to help out and be all outdoorsy and stuff," Isla added. "Plus, driving the tractor was pretty fun."

"She's really good at it too," Harry said. "She's the only one of us Gramps will let back it into the barn."

His pride in his sister's abilities struck a funny chord in my chest. I couldn't remember the last nice thing my own sister ever said about me. Hell, I couldn't remember the last time we'd even texted.

"You can drive a tractor, and you don't even have a driver's license yet? Maybe Cam should have hired you to teach Hazel to drive," I joked.

Isla grinned. "He tried. He couldn't afford my rates."

"So what do you guys think of the whole farm rescue idea?" The cow angled away from me to munch on the grass at my feet while I stroked her back. Her tail twitched and flipped in what I hoped was happiness.

"I think it's awesome. Gram and I always wanted horses, and now we'll be able to rescue some," Wes said, greeting the dogs as they raced back, this time sharing one regular-size stick.

"It's good for Gramps too," Harry said. "After he had his stroke, the day-to-day of running a farm got to be too much. So they leased some of the fields to another farmer and focused on the animals. I know he misses the work. With a rescue, they can take on volunteers to help with a lot of the physical stuff."

"*If* Gramps learns to delegate," Wes pointed out.

"We Bishop men are stubborn as hell," Harry said proudly.

An earsplitting bray interrupted our conversation.

"Jesus! What the hell is that?" I asked, bewildered.

"That's Pepe," Isla said. "Come on! You have to meet him. He's so cute I can't stand it."

"Who or what is Pepe?" I asked, following the teenagers and dogs out of one pasture and into the next.

Harry cupped his hands to his mouth and yelled. "Come on, Pepe!"

There was another horrible screeching cry, and a short gray blob galloped into view.

"That's Pepe. He's a mini donkey," Wes said.

"Hazel named him Pepe after some movie called *Romancing the Stone*. Something about 'my little mule'?" Isla offered.

I gasped. "You've never seen *Romancing the Stone*? You poor, deprived child."

Pepe looked as if he had a regular-size donkey head attached to a barrel body and stumpy, matchstick legs. And his teeth. Dear Lord, his teeth. The yellowed buckteeth looked like they could gnaw through a human leg in under four seconds flat.

The dogs greeted the donkey with enthusiasm.

"Usually donkeys aren't safe to have around dogs because they're bred to protect other livestock from predators like foxes and coyotes. So they have a tendency to kick and stomp anything that size," Harry lectured.

"Jesus," I said, stepping nervously toward Bentley. Melvin was the size of a compact car and could probably hold his own, but the beagle was definitely stomp-size.

"It's okay. They're friends," Isla promised. "Pepe was raised on a farm that bred German shepherds. He grew up with litters of puppies and thinks he's a dog. He gets along better with them than he does our full-size donkey, Diva."

Pepe trotted up to us with another horrific donkey greeting.

"I can't believe that noise comes from nature," I said.

"You can hear him all the way over at Uncle Gage's," Wes said, giving the donkey a friendly slap on the back. A cloud of dust wafted up into the spring air.

Pepe accepted the kids' greetings and then pranced up to me expectantly. His weirdly cute donkey ears only came up to my chest. He looked perky and enthusiastic about life and bore an uncanny resemblance to the donkey in *Shrek*.

"Hi. Ooooph!" I lost my breath in a rush when the donkey headbutted me in the chest. "Um, ow!"

Harry grimaced. "Sorry. That's just how he says hi."

Pepe looked at me expectantly.

"What does he want?"

"Your undying love and affection," Isla said.

As if to prove her point, Pepe nudged me in the hip with his nose. I was glad I'd dressed in my least expensive jeans and a sweatshirt that I'd spilled an entire glass of red wine on. "Okay, more pets. Got it," I said, reaching out to tentatively stroke his wiry hair. "Gross. Did you take a dirt bath or something?"

"He likes to roll around in the dirt. It's hilarious when

you see his spindly little legs flailing around in the air," Isla explained.

I wiped my hand on the butt of my jeans.

The roar of a small engine caught our attention. Wes pointed out a dirt cloud cresting the hill to the farmhouse, and one of those weird little utility vehicles the size of a small car came into view. There was a man behind the wheel and a golden retriever in the passenger seat.

"Looks like Uncle Gage is coming to say hi," Harry said.

As if annoyed at having to share the attention, Pepe's lips parted over his obscene teeth, and he grabbed my sleeve with a sharp tug.

"Excuse me, sir. That's my shirt," I complained. I reached out and ruffled the bristly black hair between his ears, and the donkey released my sleeve.

Gage pulled alongside the gate and got out of the vehicle. He looked annoyingly good as usual, this time in worn jeans, a T-shirt that hugged all the best chest places, and a backward ball cap. I didn't want to say *yummy*, but I definitely thought it.

"Hi, Uncle Gage," Harry called, dropping to his knees to wrestle with Nana, who was, as always, delighted to see literally everyone.

"Gramps said he needs your help stripping the stalls in the barn. Gram sent me to take over the tour."

Pepe shoved his head between my arm and my body so I had it draped around his neck. "I think I've seen enough," I said wryly.

"We didn't take her to the pond yet," Wes said.

"We'll head there now. Hop in," Gage told me.

At least in a vehicle, I'd have fewer opportunities to be mauled by a farm animal.

"Thanks for the tour. Bye, Pepe."

The donkey followed me forlornly to the gate.

"Maybe I'll see you at Angelo's sometime?" Harry asked hopefully.

"She's too old for you and out of your league," Gage scolded.

Harry grinned. "I like to aim high."

Gage shook his head and adjusted his ball cap. "Get in before he starts trying out his pickup lines."

I congratulated myself on managing to open and relatch the gate without completely embarrassing myself and climbed in next to Gage. Nana had graciously moved to the back seat of the vehicle.

"You really don't have to do this," I said. "I think you've had enough Zoey time this weekend, and I have more than enough information to work up a plan for your parents."

"If I take you back to the house now, you'll be forced into mucking stalls, and you don't look like the type that would enjoy shoveling shit."

"To the pond," I announced grandly.

"I thought you might say that," he said.

He waited until I'd buckled up before shifting into drive and pointing us into the sun. I appreciated the warmth on my face and relaxed against the seat as the fields rolled out on both sides of the trail. It was not my usual way to spend a Sunday, but I had to admit, it didn't entirely suck.

"I've been thinking about something you said," Gage said, breaking the silence as we crested a hill.

"I say a lot of things. You're going to have to narrow it down for me."

"You said I don't like you."

Nana shoved her head between us and rested it on my shoulder with a happy sigh. "Uh, yeah. I do recall something like that." I wondered if a regular laundry cycle would take care of cow snot, donkey dust, and dog slobber or if there was some industrial farm wash cycle I should be aware of.

"I don't not like you," he said.

"Good to know. Hey, do you use some special laundry detergent that gets animal out of your clothes?"

"I'm serious."

"So am I."

"Regular detergent is fine."

"Great," I said, giving scratches to Nana's neck.

"I just wanted to set the record straight. I don't want you to think that I don't like you."

I peered over the dog's face. "But you are less friendly to me than you are to literally the entire world."

His fingers tapped out a soundless rhythm on the wheel, and I turned so he wouldn't see my grin. Gage was uncomfortable, and I was enjoying it.

"It kind of hurts my feelings," I said, putting a quaver into my voice.

"Shit, Zo. I'm sorry. I just… You're just…"

"I'm kidding. Relax. You don't have to like me. I mean, could you have been nicer at times? Sure. But you *did* just give me an apartment and help me move. And sometimes when you're not being a jerk, you're flirting with me. I'm perfectly content with our relationship."

"I feel like I owe you an explanation." He steered us off the main trail onto a smaller, bumpier one.

"If this explanation involves telling me all my flaws that you don't like, I would prefer to skip the whole 'Mr. Darcy' thing."

He veered off the track and into the field. Ahead of us, I spotted a small body of water next to a picturesque copse of trees.

"When you first moved here, I found you…unsettlingly attractive," he continued.

I turned to look at him. "I see. Did I get less attractive since I got here?"

"No."

"And what do you mean *unsettlingly*? You sure know how to take a compliment and turn it into an insult."

"I took one look at you and fell off a damn roof. You have—*had* that effect on me. And since you don't fit the plan, I thought it was safer to keep my distance. I didn't realize I was coming off like I didn't like you. You're likable. Extremely likable."

"I think we're moving back in the direction of compliment territory."

He stopped the utility vehicle next to the pond and shut off the engine. Nana jumped out and began peeing on a variety of flora. "Look, you already know I'm looking for something permanent," Gage said.

"And you already know *permanent* gives me hives," I supplied.

"What I was going to say is you're one hell of a distraction."

I fluffed my hair theatrically. "Thank you for noticing. Also, why the hell would you rent me an apartment if you're trying to avoid me and my irresistible feminine wiles? I mean, talk about rookie mistake."

"I knew you were going to be a pain in the ass about this," he complained.

"You'd better be talking to Nana," I warned. The dog in question was nosing around the waterline.

"Oh, I'm talking to you, Disaster."

"I think about you naked too, Gage," I admitted spitefully.

He closed his eyes. "Christ."

"Yeah, try not to think about *that* next time you hear me showering above your head," I joked. "Now what's the significance of this quaint little swamp?" I waved my hand in the direction of the pond.

"Mom wants to rescue some ducks and put them here. We'll put up a picnic pavilion over th—Nana, no!"

Nana had apparently tired of looking at the water, because she took a running leap and gracelessly belly flopped into the shallows.

"Son of a bitch. You literally had a bath yesterday," Gage complained, climbing out from behind the wheel.

The dog showed no remorse as she happily paddled into deeper water. To his credit, Gage didn't slow down. Nope, he just took off his hat and shirt, threw them over his head, and plowed right on into the water.

"What are you doing?" I demanded on a laugh.

"She'll never get out unless I drag her out. It's a little game she likes to play called being fucking terrible," Gage called as he slogged after the golden retriever, who appeared to be living her best life.

"Are there snakes in there?"

"How the hell should I know?"

"It looks like snake water."

I got out of the UTV and cautiously approached, phone in video mode.

"Are you seriously videoing me right now?" Gage demanded grumpily.

"Think of it as content for the sanctuary," I said chipperly. "Your parents might go viral with their first post."

"My life was a hell of a lot easier before you two redheads showed up."

Before he could say anything else uncomplimentary, Gage stumbled and, with a "fuck this" expression on his face, went under. Nana immediately changed direction and swam back to investigate. Her human father surfaced sputtering but managed to hook his fingers in her collar.

"I don't think you should be drinking that water," I called.

"Yeah? Well, I don't think I should have to drag a dog out of every body of water after spending five hundred bucks on obedience classes." He looked down at the delightedly drenched dog. "Your recall still sucks."

Nana didn't look offended.

Swearing under his breath, Gage trudged back to shore with the dog in tow.

I met him at the edge of the muddy lip around the pond and held out his T-shirt to him. He snatched it out of my hands and tossed it over his rippling, muscular shoulder. Wet, shirtless Gage Bishop made quite the picture.

"Don't even think about laughing or I'll pick you up and toss you in," he warned.

"I wouldn't dream of it," I said, pocketing my phone and holding up my hands in surrender.

"Damn it, Nana," Gage grumbled as the dog dug her heels in and pulled backward. "You're not winning this one."

But fate was not on Gage's side. Because Nana managed to slide backward out of her collar. However, instead of diving back into the water, she hurled herself into the dank, smelly mud on the bank. She rolled over and over again until all traces of her reddish fur were gone, replaced by a soggy mud monster with a grin.

"Oh. My. God," I said.

"'Bout done?" Gage asked the dog, his hands on his hips as if waiting out a toddler's temper tantrum.

Nana sat and gave a cheery bark. What I could only assume was her tail swept muddy ripples back and forth behind her.

"You might wanna take several steps back," Gage warned.

"Me or her?" I asked.

Nana answered for him by shaking her body vigorously, sending mud splatters raining out in an impressive blast radius that included me.

"Gross!" I groaned as the cold, wet mud hit me in the head, face, and chest.

Thwap. Thwap. Thwap.

Gage was standing with his back to me, hands still on his hips, head hung low.

"Are you—" I spit out a fleck of mud. "Are you okay?" I asked.

"Honestly, Zoey? I'm just trying not to hate my life right now."

He turned slowly, and I clamped a hand to my mouth. The man was covered in soupy brown mud. *Covered*. Nana looked extraordinarily pleased with herself and trotted in my direction.

The laugh burst out of me despite my best efforts. "You can't blame me for this. I didn't make your dog go skinny-dipping in a mud bath."

"No. But if I hadn't been enlisted to take you on this tour, I doubt I'd be covered from head to toe in slime."

"Yeah, I think that points the blame at your mother for making you do it. Also, I'm sorry. I'm really trying to take you seriously, but all I can see are the whites of your eyes and your teeth, and I want to start calling you Sexy Swamp Beast."

He yanked his T-shirt off his shoulder, found a clean, dry corner, and swiped at his face, which I found hilarious.

"You think you look much better? You look like Jackson Pollock decided to paint with only browns."

"It's not that b—" I was cut off by fifty-five pounds of muddy golden retriever launching itself at me.

Under normal circumstances, I probably would have kept my footing. I'd taken my first self-defense class in junior high, so I knew how to brace for an attack. But the ground beneath my sneakers was marshy and slick. I felt myself tipping backward in slow motion as I lost the battle with gravity.

I landed flat on my back in a body-size puddle. "Please, *please* tell me this is a mud puddle and not a river of cow pee," I whispered.

Nana pounced, landing her dirty paws squarely on my chest, knocking the wind out of me.

The dog disappeared from my chest, and Gage's smirk appeared above me. "You were saying?"

I sputtered out a breath. "Ouch. Are you sure you sent her to obedience school and not deviance school?"

"I'll demand a refund."

I took his offered hand and let him haul me back to my feet. I had two perfectly placed paw prints that looked like pasties. The rest of my front was a mud-splattered work of art. My back from hair to heels felt significantly…squishier. "I don't know what to do in this situation. I've never been this dirty before," I confessed.

"I find that hard to believe," Gage said, making a lightning-quick grab for Nana and reattaching her collar.

"You are *not* flirting with me right now. Not when I look like something you'd grow mushrooms in."

"Come on. Let's go get cleaned up," Gage said.

15

You sure you're not the one?

Zoey

I was still trying to figure out how I was going to get all the mud out of my hair when Gage brought us to a stop alongside a two-story red board and batten barn with windows. There was another smaller building with garage doors next to it.

"Uh. Where are we?" I asked, frowning in confusion.

"My house."

Nana hopped out of the back of the vehicle and trotted up to the tiny side porch, where she sat next to the door, tail still wagging.

"You live in a *barn*? I know we're not keeping a list of all the reasons we're pathologically incompatible, but if we were, this would go at the top."

"It's a converted barn," he said dryly.

We climbed out and approached the structure, squishing and sloshing as we went. "How many animals live with you?"

"Just the swamp monster on the porch." He gestured for me to go up the two steps ahead of him.

"I can't go in there like this." I gestured helplessly at myself. "I wouldn't go inside an actual barn like this."

"Relax. You don't grow up on a farm without learning how to contain the mess." He nudged me up onto the porch and opened the door. Nana bolted inside, and I followed her.

"Is this your *laundry room*?" I demanded, spying the washer and dryer across from the door. The back wall was made up of natural wood cabinets and a strange-looking sink under a huge window with a striking view of the backyard. There was a long, skinny island in the middle of the room.

"It's more of a mudroom–laundry room."

Nana gave another happy shake, sending an arc of muddy water everywhere.

"Literally," I said under my breath.

Gage pulled a towel out from a cabinet and handed it to me. "Leave your clothes here. You can wrap up in this and go shower. Bedroom's through there," he said, pointing at the doorway with the doggy gate across it.

"Uhhhhh." I looked at the towel like I'd never seen one before.

"Don't tell me you're going shy on me," he teased.

"Pfft. Me? Shy?"

"I can just hose you off outside if you're more comfortable," he offered with a wicked grin.

"Shower's good," I said, grabbing the towel from him. "So I guess I'll just strip then?"

He smirked and pointed to the door behind me. "You can change in the bathroom."

"You're such a jerk," I said, opening the door to find a small utilitarian powder room.

"That's payback for laughing at me while I almost drowned," he called as he turned on the sink.

I slammed the door on the annoying man and his dastardly dog.

When I came back out wrapped in the towel, Gage had lifted Nana into the weird sink and was spraying her down with the faucet.

"Oh! It's a dog shower," I observed.

He glanced over his shoulder at me and gave me a slow once-over. "Comes in annoyingly handy."

Nana was sitting pretty in the hammered copper sink, tail thumping as Gage carefully washed the mud from her fur.

"You aren't really mad at her, are you? She was just having fun."

Gage pressed Nana's soppy wet jowls together. "It would be nice if she'd have a little less fun so my days wouldn't be consumed with cleaning up after her. But it's hard to be mad at this stupid face."

Nana licked his face in response, then made a horking sound like she didn't like the flavor of mud she'd pelted him with.

"I'll just leave you to wash your swamp monster while I go snoop through all your possessions and find your shower," I said, leaving my wet clothes on the tile.

"Don't let the pigs out of the living room," he called as I slung a leg over the doggy gate.

"The *what*?"

His gaze flicked to me again, and he grinned. "I'm joking, Zoey."

"I didn't know you could do that," I quipped.

I tiptoed over the blond hardwood, trying not to rain mud everywhere. The mudroom opened into a handsome kitchen with dark green cabinets. There was another island with a stack of neatly printed recipes next to a pile of dry ingredients.

Ugh. Of *course* Gage Bishop was a meal prepper.

The kitchen flowed into a dining room at the front of the house, which in turn opened into a spacious living room anchored by a stacked stone fireplace on the back wall. Thick wood beams ran the length of the high ceiling. Stairs with a rustic wrought iron railing led up to the second floor, and at their foot was an open door.

A large sectional faced a billboard of a television. The walls were a warm honey color. Everything was tidy. Too tidy. It looked like a model home. He needed some colorful throw pillows, a basket of blankets, some books and photos and art. Maybe a showstopper chandelier in addition to the functional yet boring can lights recessed into the ceiling.

"Aha. The bedroom."

I double-checked my feet for mud splatters before stepping onto the creamy, plush carpet. All matching furniture, I noted, from the four-poster bed to the nightstands and the dresser. I would have gone with heavy velvet curtains in a jewel tone over the off-white shades he'd picked. And added a bench at the foot of the bed and a lounge chair in the corner. But not everyone could have my good taste.

I stepped into the bathroom and nearly swooned when I realized the floor was heated. There were two full-size vanities with large mirrors, a freestanding tub big enough for an orgy, a linen closet, and a room that looked like it was supposed to be a walk-in closet but was mostly unfinished drywall and a sad single closet rod. Best of all, there was a tiled shower with body jets. It was big enough for eighteen muddy Nanas.

"Oh, thank you thank you thank you," I said, turning the water on and cranking up the temperature.

I ditched the towel and dove under the spray. It took me three rounds of shampoo and half the contents of Gage's body wash bottle before the water finally ran clear.

When I got out of the shower and wrapped myself in a fresh towel, I found a neatly folded stack of clothing sitting just outside the doorway. The T-shirt was crisp and white and about four sizes too big. But it was better than putting my muddy farm clothes back on. The waistband of the sweatpants came up to my boobs, and the whole outfit smelled like manly dryer sheets.

I padded out of the bedroom and followed the sound of Gage's voice.

"You really need to put more effort into behaving," he was saying sternly.

I turned the corner of the dining room and spotted him at the kitchen counter, beer in hand, deep in conversation with a now clean Nana, who was too busy snarfing up dog food to pay attention to him. He'd showered too and was wearing a Philadelphia Eagles T-shirt and delicious gray sweatpants.

"Hey," I said, suddenly feeling self-conscious with my wet curls, makeup-free face, and bralessness. It would be less weird if this were a postsex kitchen meetup, but this "physically platonic with a side of active attraction" situation was awkward.

"Hey," he said, green eyes flicking over me in his clothes. "Your clothes are in the washer."

"Thanks," I said, trying not to admire the impressive outline of sweatpants dick. Nana finished her meal and trotted up to me like she hadn't seen me in months. I leaned down and ruffled her still damp fur. She burped enthusiastically. "And thanks for lending me some wardrobe."

"No problem. Wine?" Gage offered. He held up a bottle. "Figured you deserve a drink after your unscheduled mud bath."

"God, yes please."

His phone vibrated on the counter as he poured a glass. He rolled his eyes. "Mom is concerned that I abducted you."

"Oh God. If I show up at their house freshly showered and wearing *your* clothes, it's going to look like we just had sex. And in this town, the rumors will be everywhere by dinnertime."

"Or," he said, handing me the glass, "it's going to look like my dog is a lovable asshole that ruined your clothes. You forget, we live on a farm. My parents are used to us coming home covered in mud or worse."

I took a fortifying gulp of wine. "First of all, I forbid you from telling me what the 'or worse' entails. Also, I don't want them to think that we were fooling around while I'm supposed to be here helping them. It looks like I wasn't taking them seriously."

Gage leaned against the counter, putting his back to the window above the sink. "Mom and Dad won't think we were doing anything other than touring the farm. Cam, on the other hand…" He let the sentence trail off.

I groaned. "Oh God. Hazel is going to have a field day with this. Great for Agent Zoey. But for Personal Life Zoey, it's gonna be a whole pain in the ass."

"Boo-hoo, baby. So someone thinks you're hooking up with the hot attorney. *I'm* the one who's supposed to be finding 'the one' here. How am I going to do that if the entire town thinks I'm fooling around with Little Miss Disco Sparkle?"

My smile was smug over the rim of my wineglass. "I can't believe you just referred to yourself as 'the hot attorney.' I'm so embarrassed for you."

"Remind me, why did I let you in my house?" he asked in exasperation.

"Between this and the whole 'you giving me an apartment thing,' I'm starting to think you're in love with me."

"I didn't give you an apartment. I rented you an apartment," he argued.

"And you're clearly in love with me. Now let's figure out how to get me back to my car without raising any suspicion before you propose marriage."

"Let's go over it one more time," Gage said.

We were hunkered over his hand-drawn diagram at the kitchen island, a bowl of salsa and a bag of whole grain tortilla chips in front of us.

I stuffed a salsa-laden chip into my face. "Okay. You're going to drive me in your truck back to your parents' house and park here to block the view of my car." I parked a chip on the diagram. "Hey, why do you have so many dimes?" I asked, noting a small bowl of them on the kitchen counter.

"Stop getting distracted. People have change. Now, back to the plan. If anyone happens to be lurking outside, Nana and I will distract them while you sneak into your car." He bit a chip in half and put it on the diagram next to his chip truck. "You'll wait until everyone is out of the front yard before you leave."

"And you'll tell your parents that the tour went well, I have lots of ideas, and I'll get back to them with an official plan in a few days. Meanwhile, no one will have the opportunity to think that we were doing anything that would end up in one of Hazel's books," I summarized.

Gage held up his beer. "I'll drink to that."

"There's just one problem."

"What's that?"

"My car keys are in my purse...in your parents' kitchen."

"Shit."

"Okay. What if we bribe your niece to sneak my purse out to us?"

He shook his head. "That opens us up to future blackmail. Believe me. It wouldn't be the first time."

"That Isla is one smart cookie," I said.

"Here's another option. We wait until your clothes are dry."

I winced. "That's an...embarrassingly obvious solution."

"It is," he agreed.

"Then why did you let me craft an entire unnecessary, over-the-top plan?" I demanded.

"I kinda just wanted to see what went on in that brain of yours." He looked at his watch. "We have about an hour. What do you want to do until your clothes are dry?"

I could think of a few things that didn't involve clothes but *did* require sweatpants dick. That would be a fun way to end my sex drought but probably not the smartest move. Probably definitely. "You can give me the grand tour and tell me if you were literally raised in a barn," I suggested.

"Fine. But first give me your wine."

"I'm not done," I complained as I handed the glass over.

"I know. But I saw the destruction your SpaghettiOs wrought on that table from the lodge. I'm taking no chances." He opened the cabinet above the coffee maker and poured the contents of my glass into a tumbler. He secured the lid and handed it back. "Let's go."

I followed him out of the kitchen. "You're adorably anal."

Gage gave an entertaining and educational tour, and I made note to mention that fact to Pep and Frank, who could inconvenience him in the future by insisting he give the tours.

The upstairs had another three bedrooms, two full bathrooms, and a cozy study he used as a home office. Downstairs, he showed me the small den I'd missed during my muddy wandering. The doors at the back of the living room on the first floor opened onto a sizable deck with a grill and an accessibility ramp. The front door led to a covered porch.

"Our grandfather built the original structure when my dad was five years old," Gage said, crooking his finger at me. I approached, and he pointed down at our feet. There on the edge was a childlike *Frank* etched into the concrete.

"Much as I want to make fun of you for living in a barn, it's pretty cool that you wanted to preserve this part of your family history."

"Preserve it and build on it," Gage said, pointing to the extension of the porch where in the front corner I spotted *Cam. Levi. Laura. Gage.*

I didn't know if it was the wine or the mud bath trauma, but something had my nose and eyes tickling. Sometimes the yearning for what could never be still snuck up on me.

"You're very lucky," I said, forcing a note of brightness into my tone.

"I know. What's your family like? You don't talk about them much."

I toyed with the disco ball charm on my necklace. "We're just not as close as you Bishops. You have something special here."

"That's why I want to share it with someone," he said, his voice husky.

I looked up from the names immortalized in concrete and found he'd stepped closer. For a second, I irrationally considered closing the distance and snuggling into his chest. Which was totally stupid. I didn't snuggle. I didn't require emotional support from hot attorneys who adopted dogs and loved their families.

His eyes were fixed on me, that deep forest green holding me immobile as he took another half step forward into my space.

His jaw clenched once, and I watched him swallow. We were standing too close for it to be innocent, and I fantasized about what would happen if those last few inches disappeared.

"Zo," he said on a gravelly rasp.

"Yeah?" I squeaked. I cleared my throat. "I mean, yeah?" I said in a lower octave.

"You sure you're not the one?" he asked.

"P-pretty sure. Almost positive." I couldn't be who he needed or give him what he wanted. And in the moment, part of me almost hated myself for it.

His lips looked like they'd be really good at kissing. Like *really* good. His fingers trailed little licks of fire down both sides of my waist. I was wondering if I should be shocked or thrilled that he made the first move when I realized my hands were fisted in his shirt.

I cleared my throat. "I bet my clothes are dry," I announced at an unnecessary volume.

Gage's jaw clenched once more before he removed his hands from my hips and took a step back.

He looked down at his watch. "Looks like it."

"We should probably—".

"Avoid each other at all costs?" he filled in.

"I was going to say *go* but also definitely that thing that you said."

"How hard could it be?" he muttered.

Me: Hey. It's been a while. Let me know if you have time for a sister video chat.
Carla Moody: Pretty busy for the next few weeks. If you need something it's probably faster to tell me over text.

16

They're breasts, not rabid wolverines

Gage

It was a hell of a lot harder to avoid the woman living over my office than I thought it would be.

Every time I drove by, my gaze was pulled to the second floor, where colorful curtains fluttered during the day and string lights glowed at night. When I was in my office, I was being brutally and unfairly reminded of her existence with every creak and footstep from above.

Then there was the endless stream of people knocking on her door. I had no idea who half of them were or what they were doing. Their visits rarely lasted long, and according to my building security cameras, most of them arrived empty-handed and left carrying something. I didn't want to get involved, but as her landlord, I felt it was within my rights to discuss safety measures with her. Which I would do as soon as I'd avoided her long enough that I wasn't worried I'd feel compelled to kiss her.

First kisses were calculated, choreographed. They were delivered at the right time to maximize the romance of the moment. They were memorable, meaningful. Yet I'd stood on my own front porch and nearly kissed the hell out of Zoey just because she'd locked eyes with me.

I was a man with self-control, damn it. It should be easy to *not* kiss someone. There were plenty of women I currently wasn't kissing. Zoey Moody shouldn't be an exception.

I jogged into the vestibule outside my office and paused long enough to brush the sawdust off my jeans. I was in desperate need of a shower before my meeting in an hour, but first I wanted to review the LLC agreement Declan had drafted before my afternoon appointment. Work with my brothers had run over the time I'd allotted, and I was running behind. I'd have to make it up by either skipping lunch or eating it in the shower, I decided.

I stomped my boots one last time and pushed open the door to my office. Declan was at his computer, staring off into space and typing at an alarming rate. A pair of sparkly stilettos caught the sun from their perch on the corner of his desk.

"What are those?" I asked, accepting the messages he handed over, still typing one-handed.

"Shoes."

"I can see that. What are they doing there?"

"Zoey asked me to keep them here until the person she sold them to comes to pay for them."

I pinched the bridge of my nose. The irritation that had been building all day spiked to the surface. "The office is not a thrift shop."

"She brought me tea," Declan said, a hint of defensiveness in his usual monotone.

"We are a law office, not an indoor yard sale," I insisted. A telltale *thud* sounded from the second floor. "And if she's here, then she should be responsible for getting *herself* murdered by selling shit to strangers on the internet. Not my employee."

"Would you like me to relay the message in a formal letter?" Declan offered as I stomped into my office.

"Yeah. Sure," I said.

"You have a meeting in fifty-eight minutes," Declan called after me.

I closed the door at a reasonable volume, mostly to prove to myself that, despite the fact that I was annoyed, I was still in control of my impulses.

I had just settled behind my desk and opened the folder when I heard another thump followed by a muffled screech. Visions of Zoey leaving her window open and Goose flying in to take a look around assailed me. Was an indoor bald eagle attack unlikely? Yes. But anything was possible where Zoey was concerned.

"Shit." I threw my pen down and exited my office.

"Fifty-seven minutes," Declan reported as I snagged the shoes off his desk.

"Thank you, Declan," I said dryly. "I'll be back in time."

I stormed up the stairs to the second floor and had just raised my fist to pound on Zoey's door when I heard a loud moan coming from inside. She was either hurt or having sex. And I didn't want to walk in on one of those situations.

I paused and listened. "I'm going to die like this," I heard her say before there was another thump.

I rapped my knuckles on the door. "Zoey? You okay?"

There was a pause and then a morose, "No."

"Do you need help?"

There was another long pause. "Yes. Please."

There was a note of hysteria in her voice that had my adrenaline pumping. "What's wrong? Open the door."

"You're about to see something you're not ready for," she warned.

If she let a bald eagle into her apartment, I was going to be fucking pissed.

"I think I can handle it," I assured her.

Her laugh was humorless. "We'll see."

"Let me in, Zoey."

"Ugh. Fine. It's unlocked."

I pushed open the door. "We need to have a conversation about locking—"

The rest of the sentence, along with my breath, abandoned me. The blood flow to my brain made an abrupt U-turn and headed straight to my cock.

Zoey stood in the middle of the living room with her arms suspended over her head. Her curls were exploding out of a high ponytail. Her cheeks were flushed. Something that looked suspiciously like a sports bra was rolled up and banded tightly above her breasts. Her *bare* breasts.

"Fuck," I breathed.

"My sentiments exactly. A little help here? I feel like I'm being strangled by an anaconda, and I'm not proud to admit it, but I'm really starting to panic."

Pep and Frank Bishop had raised good men if not full-time gentlemen, but the pivot to avert my gaze and close the door was at least three seconds slower than it should have been.

"What do you need?" I asked the door as visions of her perfect breasts seared themselves into my brain permanently.

"I need you to make me a sandwich. *What the hell do you think I need?* Get me out of this thing before I die!" she screeched.

"Calm the hell down."

"Are you saying that to me or the door? They're breasts, Gage. Not rabid wolverines."

"Yeah, Zoey. The evidence strongly suggests they're breasts," I said, still facing the door, willing my instantaneous hard-on to also calm the hell down.

"Oh my God. Please stop pretending to be a gentleman and get me out of this thing! I'm suffocating!"

I sucked in a shallow breath and turned to face her.

Yep. She was still topless, and I was never going to recover.

She was built like a goddess. Her full, teardrop-shaped breasts were on display like some art exhibit by a master. My cock was harder than the marble a sculptor would have chosen to immortalize her in.

"Help," she said in a whimper as her arms dangled above her head. "I'm too sweaty. I can't get it off."

I took matters into my own hands and turned her around so I wasn't facing the most perfect set of tits I'd ever seen in my life.

"Where's the clasp?" I said gruffly as I felt along the band over her shoulder blades. It had been rolled over on itself half a dozen times.

"There isn't one. It's one of those pull-on things, which I will *never* wear again. It wasn't very supportive anyway. Too much jiggling."

"Stop. Talking," I begged through gritted teeth.

"Start *working*."

I pressed my thumbs against her back and tried to slide them under the twisted band, but it was too tight.

"Hold still," I ordered.

I slid my hands around to her sides and tried to get under the band at her armpits.

She let out a panicked giggle and jumped. Her legging-clad ass came into direct contact with my throbbing dick, and we both froze.

"Uh, I'm ticklish," she whispered.

"Yeah. Got that," I said as my vision started to go dark. One wiggle, one too-deep breath, and I was going to humiliate myself by coming in my jeans.

"If I weren't panicking about being strangled by my sports bra, I'd be flattered," she said finally. "It feels pretty impressive."

"Zoey, I need you to stop talking about your tits and my cock now."

"Sorry. Shutting up now," she promised.

I tried again to get my fingertips under the band, but it wasn't working. The twisted material was too tight. "Listen, I kinda have to get…in there. Do you want me to call—"

"Oh my God, Gage. You've touched tits before, haven't you? I don't care if you have to motorboat me. Just get me out of this thing!" Her voice pitched into hysteria territory.

"Can you please stop saying things like *motorboat* and *tits*? I'm trying to be a gentleman here, but you're not making it fucking easy."

On a frustrated groan, Zoey spun around to face me. She grabbed my hands and slapped them on her breasts. "There. Welcome to second base. Can we focus now?"

I stood there, rooted to the spot, cupping her full breasts. Her skin was slick with sweat, and her nipples pebbled against my palms.

My hands squeezed reflexively, and I would have apologized, but I wasn't even remotely sorry. Zoey's breath was coming in pants, making her breasts rise. My breath was nonexistent, something I didn't realize until I started to see black dots.

I dipped my forehead to hers. "You're killing me, Disaster."

"Yeah? Well, it's about to be a double homicide, seeing as how this bra is murdering me," she hissed shakily.

"Fuck," I muttered. It took every brain cell I could muster to concentrate, but by sliding my hands up and over the breasts I would spend the rest of my life fantasizing about, I managed to get my thumbs under the band above her sternum. I gave it a tug, then a harder one.

"Ow," she whimpered.

"Sorry," I said, ceasing my ministrations.

"Okay. What if I, like, bounce?" she offered.

"*Bounce?*" Was this some kind of cosmic joke? Was I being punished for some past indiscretion? I couldn't think of a worse idea.

Apparently Zoey thought I didn't understand what the word meant, because she demonstrated by bouncing up and down, making her tits jiggle.

Some kind of uncontrollable biological impulse in me clamped my hands down on her breasts. My mouth watered. My cock flexed behind my zipper, demanding to be set free. She was trying to kill me. That was the only possible explanation that made any sense to my blood-starved brain. "No bouncing," I rasped.

"Great. So I'm just going to die like this?" She waved her arms helplessly overhead.

There were worse ways to go, but I didn't feel like she was open to that kind of philosophy in the moment.

"Scissors."

"What?" she asked.

"Scissors. I'll cut you out."

"Yes! You're a genius! I have some…somewhere. Let me think. Gah, I can't think. My oxygen is being cut off."

"Focus, Zoey. Think about the scissors." Sweat broke out on my brow.

"Shit. They're in a box. Probably with my missing box cutter. I've been punching boxes open. Do you have any downstairs?" Her breath was coming faster and faster. "Gage?"

Those emerald eyes locked on my face with fear and need.

"Fuck it," I muttered. I gripped the fabric just under her neck with both hands and yanked.

The bra ripped in two, and we sprang apart.

"Oh, thank God!" Zoey bent over, hands on her knees, and sucked in an unhindered breath.

I dropped like a stone onto her couch and covered my face with my hands. My hands that now smelled like her. I bit my tongue until I tasted blood so I wouldn't be tempted to reach for my cock.

"So what did you want?" she asked.

"What?" I dropped my hands to see her standing straight, hands on hips, still not wearing a fucking shirt, her breasts heaving hypnotically. There was only one thing I wanted right now, and that was to pull her into my lap and make her ride me while I sucked those perfect pink nipples until we both came.

"You knocked on my door. I assume you wanted something besides this delightfully humiliating field trip to second base."

It felt like a lifetime ago since a much younger, more innocent me had climbed those stairs. I scrubbed my hands over my face. "I don't fucking know. Something about shoes. I was going to yell at you."

"You were going to yell at me about shoes? Oh, do you mean the ones I left with Declan?"

"Yeah. My office is not a place you sell things in."

"A store?"

"Yes. That. And my employee is not somebody who sells shit. Now for the love of God, will you please cover up so I can work on getting some blood back to my head?"

Zoey pulled a purple crochet throw off the chair and wrapped it around her like a cloak. "I knew my boobs were good, but I didn't know they were *this* good. It's like discovering a superpower in middle age."

"You're doing this just to torture me, aren't you?" I demanded.

She rolled her eyes. "Yes, Gage. The entire world revolves around you. Everything I do is to get you to notice me."

"This whole getting-stuck-in-a-bra thing can't be a thing that happens in real life," I insisted.

"Next time you and your brothers are drinking, I want you to play 'take off the sweaty sports bra' and see what happens," she said, flopping down next to me.

"Too close," I growled.

"Sorry." She didn't sound the least bit apologetic as she scooted farther away from me. "Thank you for saving my life. And I'm sorry for asking Declan to babysit my shoes. I was on a Zoom call with Hazel's publisher's marketing department that was supposed to go longer than it did, and I didn't want to miss the shoe guy. It's a birthday present for his wife."

"Why are you selling your wardrobe?"

"So my evil new landlord won't kick me out when I can't make rent."

"Zoey," I said.

"What?" she said defiantly.

"If money's tight, I can give you a break—"

"Absolutely not. I'm not taking a charity discount. I'm fine. I just have to be a little frugal until Hazel's next advance installment kicks in. I'm not frivolous with money, by the way.

I had savings. It's just been a long time since I've had a regular paycheck."

"How much do you have to sell?"

She shrugged. "I'm starting with the 'cute but really uncomfortable' things. So far, it's going well, and you won't have any money-related reasons to evict me."

"If you need—"

She cut me off again. "I don't need anything from you."

I looked pointedly at her shredded bra on the floor.

"Besides undergarment removal," she corrected.

I looked at my watch and grimaced. "Fine. Then can I ask a favor from you?"

"Sure."

"Can I use your shower?"

"Of course," she said, picking up a discarded tank top from the floor and pulling it over her head. But not before giving me another look at her spectacular tits. "You earned it."

"Thanks," I rasped. I stood abruptly and made my way into the bathroom, kicking the door shut behind me. "Fuck. Fuck. Fuck," I muttered to myself as I wrestled my belt open. I shoved my jeans down my thighs, and my cock sprang free, leaking precome like it was a fucking fountain.

I stripped like it was an Olympic sport and I was going for gold, then turned on the spray. It was ice cold when I stepped under it a second later. I braced one hand on the tile and fisted my cock with the other. I gave a testing stroke and bit back a groan. This was *not* okay. I shouldn't be doing this. Jacking off in Zoey's shower, thinking about how warm and full her tits had been in my hands while she was just on the other side of the wall.

I was pathetic. I was undisciplined. I was disrespectful.

I was…going to come.

My release had my balls tightening. Electricity charged up my shaft. The pleasure I needed was one violent stroke away.

There was a knock at the door. "Hey, Gage? Do you want a shower beer?" Zoey asked, her voice husky.

"Fuck." I came on a low, barely muffled growl.

I left the bathroom with damp hair and a slightly more controlled libido. I wanted to feel guilty, but I was having trouble seeing past the absolute biological necessity of what I'd done. I wouldn't have been able to walk downstairs, let alone perform any lawyer duties had I not taken care of the problem.

Zoey met me in the living room and wordlessly handed me a beer.

I took it and drank half of it down.

She rolled back on her heels. "Sooooo," she said awkwardly.

"Yeah." Her destroyed sports bra was still lying in a clump on the floor.

"Maybe we shouldn't tell anyone about this…situation. They might read something into it if they found out I encouraged you to fondle my breasts."

I choked on the sip I'd been about to swallow. "Damn it, Zoey."

She grinned up at me. "I'm just messing with you. Thank you for saving my life."

"You're welcome."

"And feeling me up. It's been a while since the girls have gotten any action."

"Zoey," I barked.

"You make it too easy, Gage. Most guys would be high-fiving their friends by now. But you…" She trailed her fingers down my chest. "You're a good guy."

She said it like it was an insult. And I'd had enough of feeling completely out of control. I captured her hand with my own and had her pinned against the wall in a split second. She looked up at me with delight.

"Sweetheart, just because I'm the good guy when my clothes are on doesn't mean I go to bed that way."

"If you want sex, say the word," she said. "I'm willing to risk your heartbreak to find out how good you are in bed."

I let my hand coast over her ribs until it fit under one full breast. "I want more than sex. A lot more."

She looked smug and relaxed, but her heart hammered against my palm, and her nipples formed perky points against the snug fabric of her shirt.

"That's a shame," she said finally.

With effort, I drew my hand back from her. "You are a goddamn disaster."

Apparently there was one woman in the world who could turn me on to the point of desperation. And she wasn't the one I was going to marry.

17

Routine butthole maintenance
Zoey

"So there goes Cam, out the front door in his underwear, chasing a raccoon. Felicity next door almost threw up from laughing so hard. Thankfully she managed to get a picture of him for Neighborly before she dry heaved in her azaleas," Hazel said, turning her screen so I could see it. "It might have been the best morning of my life."

I shook my head while admiring her fiancé's near nakedness. The Bishop men were certainly well-built.

We were at a table in the window of Perked Up with a mountain of baked goods between us. The coffee shop's owners, the Jangs, had gone with a puzzle cat theme. Not puzzles of cats but puzzles *and* cats.

The puzzles were donated, and the cats were rescues up for adoption. I was sure that on paper, the combination of the two would have been appealing to some, but the reality was more chaos than cute. I'd managed to click two pieces of the Eiffel Tower into place before a leggy gray kitten had hopped up on the table and rolled over on his back, blocking out the entire night sky. It had eventually left, but now a hefty calico named Brenda—who didn't take no for an answer—was snoring in my lap.

"Your life is a romance novel. Everything is inspiration," I said, eyeing my empty mug. I'd already pounded a double espresso and was wishing for a second. I hadn't slept well last night. Probably because I'd stayed up too late trying to formulate a schedule of events for Reader Weekend, which was proving to be tricky since I couldn't seem to interest any businesses in discussing how they could participate. Or maybe it was the constant fantasies of Gage's capable hands on my boobs. The sports bra incident had definitely messed with my resolve to avoid the man at all costs.

I decided to go for sugar instead of more caffeine and snatched an apple fritter out from under Hazel's hand.

"Speaking of inspiration," she said pointedly.

I shoved a hefty portion of fritter into my face. "Wha?"

"How are things with Gage? I heard that your farm tour ran a little long while you two were alone."

"We weren't alone. We were chaperoned by Nana, who needs to go to doggy obedience boot camp. Ow! Stop stabbing me," I said to the cat in my lap.

Hazel slumped in her chair. "Come on, Zoey. Give me *something*."

"You know what I miss? The days when you'd make things up and put them in books."

"Yeah, but it's so much easier when I can just steal from real life."

"Ugh. Fine. But only to keep you from accosting poor innocent townsfolk and trying to matchmake them."

Hazel clapped. "Yay. Okay, spill it. Pep said you had crazy hair when you came back from your 'tour.' Was it from hot tub sex?"

"Gage doesn't have a hot tub," I said dryly.

"Uh-huh. That's fine. Fictional Gage does. So where exactly did the sex having take place?"

A long, lean black-and-white cat jumped up on our table,

swatted two puzzle pieces onto the floor, and then sat down on the windowsill to perform some routine butthole maintenance.

"There was no sex having. He showed me the pond, and his problem-child golden retriever went for a swim. He had to wade in after her and drag her back out. It was kind of funny. At least until Nana decided to add mud wrestling to the itinerary. She got us both. Gage looked like he'd been birthed by swamp people."

"Please tell me you have pictures."

"I have better than that," I said, proudly producing the video that I'd watched a few dozen times since the weekend.

Hazel's snort drew the eyes of nearby patrons. "Yeah, that's definitely going in a book," she announced. "So what happened after the mud wrestling?"

"Gage took me back to his place, we showered *separately*, and then I went home." Brenda clawed me in the legs as if she knew I was withholding information.

"What did his soap smell like? Did you find anything kinky in his nightstand? What's his closet space situation?"

"His soap smelled like whatever manly soap smells like. Maybe like wood chips and chainsaws? I didn't go through his nightstand. And his closet situation is pathetic. He's got a whole room off the bathroom with one measly clothing rod. No drawers, no hooks, no velvet jewelry trays, no full-length mirror. Just a sad, droopy rod of T-shirts and button-downs."

"Uh-huh." She made several notes. "And why does that annoy you?"

"I'm not annoyed," I argued.

Hazel lifted an eyebrow.

Brenda reached out to swat the windowsill cat's tail, which apparently was not enough for it to stop lavishing its butthole with attention.

I sighed. "I really don't like that we know each other so well."

"Yeah you do," she insisted cheerfully. "Back to you being annoyed. Is it because he lives in a converted barn? It's not like he shares a bathroom with actual farm animals."

"No. The house was kind of…nice," I admitted.

"Then what? Did he use too much legal jargon? Sometimes he does that to piss off his brothers."

"It's not that. I'm just…confused."

"How did the hot guy with a barn house confuse you?" Hazel asked.

I threw my hands up in frustration, and my lap cat started purring. "I don't know. I have all these conflicting feelings. I'm attracted to him even though I know without a shred of doubt that he's a terrible fit for me. And while *I'm* perfectly willing to have some nice, healthy sex, *he's* shopping for Ms. Right. And he knows I don't do relationships, but we had this intense eye-contact-y moment, and he asked me if I was sure I wasn't 'the one,' and obviously I'm *not* the one because he wears cardigans but somehow makes it hot, and I know the right thing to do is avoid him, which I was trying to do, but then I got stuck in a sports bra, and he saved me and touched my boobs. And now I can't stop thinking about him."

Hazel was staring at me open-mouthed, pen hovering over the notebook.

The cat on the windowsill looked up at me with what I considered to be an unfairly judgmental expression for something that had just spent five minutes licking its own butt. While still maintaining eye contact, it slapped a paw over a corner puzzle piece and dragged it off the table.

"No wonder you're freaked out," Hazel said finally.

"I'm not freaked out. Men don't freak me out. I must have just inhaled some toxic mud from the pond or something."

"Clearly that's the only explanation. So did you jump up and wrap your legs around his waist, or did you pull his hair to get him down to kissing level?"

"Neither. I shouted something about laundry and ruined the moment."

"Okay, the old Zoey would have scaled Gage like an aggressive mountain goat. What's going on with you?"

"You can't seriously think it's a good idea for me to have a fling with your soon-to-be brother-in-law," I pointed out.

"Why not? You're both adults. Hot, sexy, consenting adults."

"Trust me. He's way more adult than me. He's ready to wife someone up and start making babies in a minivan."

She reached out and gave my hand a squeeze. "Is that why you don't want to get involved?" All teasing was gone. Her voice was gentle now.

I shook my head. "I came to peace with it a long time ago. I'm fine with it. I promise."

"I just don't think you should expect all relationships to end the way you and Sam did."

"I don't," I insisted without knowing if it was true. Sam had loved me the way I'd always needed someone to…right up until he found out just how lacking I was.

"Good, because that was college. No one is a fully realized adult in college. Besides, families happen in a lot of different ways," Hazel said.

I held up a hand. "I'm going to stop you right there. You've met my family, Haze. Why would I ever want to give it a try?"

"You would make different choices than your parents," she insisted.

I wasn't so sure those different choices would be any better. "I lose my grocery list between home and the store. How would I even begin to keep another human alive? Sometimes nature is all like 'There can be only one' for legitimate reasons," I joked.

"I know you're deflecting with humor," she began.

"And I know you mean well, but the point is Gage and I are very different people who want very different things. I also can't give him what he wants, so I need you to put this muffin in your face before you bring me down."

"Fine. But only because I want to, not because you managed to distract me. Let's go back to Gage and your boobs."

Relieved, I acquiesced. "I'd been walking around town trying to talk to businesses about participating in Reader Weekend and got all sweaty. When I got back to my apartment, I couldn't get out of my sports bra."

"Ugh! I hate when that happens. The panic sets in, and you feel like you're suffocating."

"Exactly! Anyway, he knocked on my door to yell at me about shoes, and instead I yelled at him and made him feel me up."

Hazel's pretty brown eyes fluttered behind her glasses in some inspiration-induced fugue state. "Walk me through the choreography."

"No."

"It's for the book, Zoey. Also my own personal entertainment."

"Ugh. Fine."

I made a move to stand up, but Jennifer Jang appeared at the table and plopped down a table tent in front of me. It said, *If a cat sits on you, you are legally obligated to stay put for at least ten minutes.* "Sorry, Zoey. House rules," she said.

Like me, Jennifer and her family were new in town. An avid reader and fan of Hazel, she'd talked her husband into a weekend getaway to Story Lake last summer. Apparently quirky was their vibe, because they packed up their house and their boys and moved here to open a much-needed café. I liked to say—loudly to journalists—that Hazel Hart inspired real-life happily ever afters every day.

"But she was just going to demonstrate how she was trapped in a sports bra and made Ga—ouch!" she said when I kicked her under the table. "A completely random guy you don't know grab her boobs," Hazel corrected.

"I hate the sweaty sports bra trap, and I love a good second base scene," Jennifer said. "I'll help."

"Yay!" Hazel clapped her hands and stood up.

"This is ridiculous," I said, gesturing to encompass the cat, the sign, and the two women eagerly awaiting my instructions.

"You've got at least five minutes left on the cat clock. You might as well give us all the dirty details," Hazel insisted.

"Did you have your back to him or were you facing him?" Jennifer asked.

I reluctantly obliged and directed them through the scene, making sure to replace Gage's name with Adonis to protect the innocent.

"There. Happy now?" I demanded when it was over. The rest of the café patrons broke into spontaneous applause, startling Brenda, who finally vacated my lap. Jennifer took a bow while Hazel fired finger guns at everyone.

"Stop that," I hissed at her as she took her seat.

"Sorry. You know I get awkward when I get excited. So when are you not going to have sex with this Adonis again?" she asked.

"Don't you have enough inspiration yet?"

"This will give me a few chapters. But I'm thinking about you and real life right now. It's not like you to be so angsty over a guy."

"I just don't get it. He's so earnest and respectful. Ugh. I mean, shouldn't I be more into Levi? He at least looks like he's emotionally unavailable. Do you think I should get my brain scanned? Like what if this is the first sign of a significant personality change?"

She snort laughed and pushed her glasses up her nose.

"I'm serious, Haze. I'm not into nice guys."

"Zo, Gage isn't the nice guy. He's the *good* guy. There's a big sexy difference."

"Oh, what do you know anyway? You're so full of orgasms and wedding plans you think everyone needs to be in love," I complained.

Hazel picked up her pen and drummed it on the table. "I say this with love. Don't you think it's time you outgrew the whole 'my parents got divorced; therefore I believe all relationships are doomed' thing?"

"I say *this* with love. Stop trying to character-arc me. I have a right to my feelings, and I don't need to change. I'm perfectly happy where I am."

"But are you though?"

I glared at her.

She held up her hands in surrender. "All I'm saying is maybe you should think about whether you really don't want a relationship or you just think you can't have one."

"I will do no such thinking," I said and began stuffing the remaining baked goods into my bag. "Now, if you'll excuse me, I'm going to go hunt down Opal and ply her with sugar until she agrees to let me represent her."

"Have fun. I'll just go pump Gage for his side of the story."

I ceased my baked-good packing. "Don't. You. Dare."

"How else am I going to get the hero's voice right?" she asked innocently.

"If you go harassing him about our almost moment, he'll know that I told you, which means he'll know I'm still thinking about it."

"Oh no. How terrible," Hazel deadpanned.

"Do *not* go near Gage," I warned her. "Or I'll tell your publisher you changed your mind and you want to go on a twenty-city tour for your launch."

Hazel grinned. "You're a monster and I love you."

"Love you too, shit waffle."

"You're so stupid, Zoey. When are you going to grow up and be responsible?" I said under my breath as I rummaged through my bag for the phone I knew was in there somewhere. Because if it wasn't, I was going to have to go back to the café and ask if I'd left it there…like my car keys. It served me right for carrying such a big purse, I thought as I headed through the automatic back doors of the Haven's main building.

I had cat hair on my pants and an unwrapped brownie crumbling in my purse, and I couldn't remember if I'd locked my car, which didn't really matter since the roof clip had broken again.

"Whose voice is that?" a gruff voice asked.

"What?" I glanced up from my fruitless search.

The question had come from Opal. "'You're so stupid, Zoey. When are you going to grow up?'" she quoted back.

"Well, it came out of my mouth, so I'm gonna say it's mine. Aha!" I triumphantly pulled out my phone from under a now-squashed muffin.

Opal glared at me for a long beat, then rolled her eyes. "Come with me."

"I was actually just coming to see you," I explained as she shoved a shopping bag into my arms.

"My lucky day," she grumbled as she set off down the path that connected the Haven's main building with the apartments. The wildflower garden was starting to bloom, and every bench was occupied by residents soaking up the warmth of the spring sun.

I jogged ahead and hit the open button for the Keiko Fukuda apartment building's glass front doors. "If you give me five minutes, you might actually mean that. I wanted to talk to you about letting me represent you…as an agent."

Opal said nothing as she trundled past me with her walker.

I assumed she wanted me to follow her since I was carrying her groceries, so I followed her inside to the bank of elevators. The doors opened, and Opal stepped in. "Let's go before my ice cream melts, Curly," she said.

We headed up to the third floor, and Opal hung a right. The doors were all seasonally decorated with green leafy wreaths, sprigs of fake spring flowers, and cheerfully worded welcome mats. Opal stopped at the end of the hall in front of the only unaccessorized door.

"Are you allergic to festive decor?" I asked her as she let us into her apartment.

"What the hell's there to be festive about? It's spring. Big whoop-de-do. Time marches on until you die. Then it keeps marching on without you."

"I see you're one of those optimists who annoy everyone with your zest for life," I observed.

"Bite me."

This was going well.

Opal's apartment was small but cozy. Well, it would have

been cozy if the curtains hadn't been shut tight against the spring sunshine. There was a TV against the wall on a console table, with drawers and a single recliner facing it. A dining table was buried under stacks of books that didn't fit on the overflowing shelves that took up the space on both sides of the windows. Sci-fi, romance, thrillers, and nonfiction all warred for space.

"Wow. So you're definitely a reader. No wonder you're so good at writing."

"Stop kissing my ass," Opal said, leaving her walker by the door and limping over to the table.

"Are you supposed to do that?" I asked.

She grabbed the cane that was hooked over the back of one of the chairs. "You a narc?"

"I'm just trying to make conversation with a grumpy brick wall."

"I had a hip replacement. The know-it-alls in rehab pretend like I need to be on the walker for another few weeks."

"Yes, Opal. I'm sure the mean medical professionals are just making up the rules as they go for their own entertainment without any scientific basis."

"I'm wounded by your sarcasm. Do you have a hard time following conversations in noisy places?"

"Huh?"

"Do you have a hard time—"

"Sorry. I didn't realize we were starting in the middle of a conversation. Uh, yeah. I guess. I actually stopped going to my favorite wine bar in the city because it had concrete floors and brick walls, and the noise just echoed off everything."

"Do you have a hard time following verbal directions?"

"What?"

"Do you sometimes ask, 'What?' even though you heard the question, but it feels like it takes your brain a few extra seconds to process what you heard?"

"How did you…?" I trailed off.

"How many times do you have to rewash the laundry you forgot was in your washer?"

"I don't know what's happening here. Are you some kind of crabby psychic?"

Ignoring me, she turned her attention to her wall o' books. "If I said I wanted to teach you to play a card game right now or that I needed you to assemble my new coffee table, would you immediately start looking for excuses to leave?"

"Obviously. Why? Are you trying to get rid of me?"

"Do you interrupt others mid-conversation?"

"No." Relief coursed through me that the all-knowing lady didn't quite know everything.

"Or did you *used to* interrupt others but got corrected as a kid so now you spend all your effort in every conversation trying not to interrupt while still holding on to the point you wanted to share until you realize you're not even hearing what's being said?"

Damn it.

"At home, do you have to leave important documents or items sitting out so you don't forget they exist?"

"Lots of people have an 'important' pile," I said defensively.

"Do you feel ashamed all the time? Like you're a bad person and you're terrified one day everyone is going to find out?"

Baffled, I slowly sank down onto the recliner.

"Do you drink alcohol not because you crave it but because it makes your brain quiet?"

"Who are you, and why do you know stuff?"

Opal plucked a book off the shelf, then moved to the table. "Do people close to you call you impulsive? Did you have a temper that got you into trouble when you were younger? Do you catch your belt loops on drawer pulls? Do you have a voice in your head constantly criticizing you? Do you feel like an underachiever compared to everyone else in your life?"

I held up my hands. "Are you some kind of fortune teller?"

She picked up a second book and limped across the room to me. She dropped both titles in my lap. "ADHD."

"Wait. What?"

She poked the top book with the tip of her cane. "ADHD.

Attention deficit hyperactivity disorder. My guess is you have it. A raging case of it. Those will help."

I glanced down at the books in my lap. "Sorry, isn't that, like, an 'elementary school boy' thing?"

"Are you an elementary school boy?"

"Not to my knowledge." Though I did have the sense of humor of one.

"Then no, it's not."

"What makes you think I have…that? Is your weird hobby diagnosing strangers with conditions?"

Opal pointed at a frame on the wall. "Sorry, kid. Real doctor. Psychologist specializing in neurotypical diagnoses for forty years."

"Okay, but like, no offense, were you any *good* at your job? Because your people skills are kinda iffy."

She gestured to an entire shelf of awards and certificates. "I wasn't good. I was the best. Now I'm old and retired, so I don't have to let the patient find their own answers. So I'm telling you. You got ADHD. Now go do something about it."

"I came here to talk to you about writing. I don't know what to do with this." My brain was swirling like bathtub water down a drain.

"Read the books. Take one of the eight million online assessments. I bet you a hundred bucks that your score is off the charts. And given that I've worked with a few hundred ADHD patients, I wouldn't bet against me if I were you."

I closed my eyes for a second and opened them again. "Are you saying there might be a reason why I am the way I am? Like I'm not actually stupid and irresponsible?"

The note of hope in my voice sounded pathetic to my own ears.

Opal took pity on me and pulled up one of her dining chairs. "Look, girls and women are usually diagnosed late because their symptoms look different. Which usually means you grow up with exasperated parents and teachers who think you're just not applying yourself. It creates this whole pain-in-the-ass shame spiral. Blah blah blah. Bottom line: It's treatable. Read the books."

"So there's actually something I can do about this…mess that is me?"

"Yep. Lucky you, having one of the most treatable chronic conditions in the world."

I scoffed. "Lucky me."

"Read the books. Go talk to someone who isn't me, because I'm retired and I don't want to do the work with anyone. I've done the work. I'm over the work. Okay?"

"Okaaay."

"Good. Now, back to me." She heaved herself out of the chair.

I looked up from the books. "Back to you what?"

"I didn't drag you here out of the kindness of my heart, you know. I'm not some weird do-gooder diagnosing strangers and giving them hope for the future. I'm old. But maybe I'm not ready to be completely invisible." She crossed to the console under the TV and used the hook of her cane to pull open the bottom drawer.

I craned my neck to see what was inside, crossing my fingers it wasn't a scrapbook collection. "Oh my God. Are those…" I jumped out of the recliner and dropped to my knees on the floor.

"I spent forty years trying to fix people in real life. Sometimes it was easier to make them up and then fix them on the page."

"You have a literal drawer full of manuscripts. May I?" I asked, spirit fingers at the ready.

"I'm already regretting this."

I was too busy gathering fat manuscripts in my arms. Some of them were yellowed with age on the old printer paper with the perforated borders.

"How many?" I asked.

"Six. Well, five and a half. It's whaddaya call it when you smash epic fantasy together with romance?"

"Romantasy," I whispered reverently. I was already skimming page one. "Opal, I could kiss you right now."

"Yeah, yeah. I'm a fucking catch. Let's keep this professional," she said, flopping back down in a chair.

I looked up. "What made you change your mind?"

She blew out a breath. "I've been successful at a lot of things in life. Maybe I don't want to fail this close to the end."

"Jesus, you're not dying, are you?" Fulfilling the dreams of a dying woman was a lot of pressure.

"We're all dying."

"Then maybe you should enjoy living while you're doing it. You're what? Seventy?"

"Seventy-three."

"Seventy-three is the new fifty-three. Stop acting like you're on death's welcome mat."

"When I want your opinion, I'll give it to you," Opal said.

"Look, I know I'm the last person to give advice about failure, but—wait, that's not true. I know failure better than anyone. And this isn't failure. This is perseverance, and if they're a quarter as good as what you read in class, you're not going to fail."

She harrumphed. "It's just a hobby."

"Opal, no one writes five and a half entire novels as just a hobby. You're an author."

"No. I'm a retired old lady who just wants to be left alone," she said with a derisive sniff.

"If that were true, you wouldn't have opened the drawer for me," I pointed out. "Now, how long does it take you to write one of these babies? When do you think you'll finish the one you're working on?"

"How in the hell should I know?"

"Well, you wrote five of 'em, so ballpark it for me."

She stared down at her feet. "I don't know, okay? I was writing for pure entertainment purposes, but I've been having an inspiration problem."

"Pfft. That's my specialty. How long have you been blocked?"

"Four years."

"Okaaay," I drawled. "Can I take these and read them?"

"Fine. But do me a favor and use some young-person technology to scan them and back them up in a cloud somewhere. The first couple are only in hard copy."

Shit. Could I be trusted with that? "I'll guard them with my life," I promised. "Are we done with your thing?"

"Why?"

"Because I have some more questions about my thing."

"Never should have opened my damn mouth," she muttered.

"It's just I've been so bad at so many things over the years. If I get this stuff figured out, will I get better?"

"How the hell should I know?"

"Well, you're the professional, Opal. And I was today years old when I learned—rudely, by the way—that adult women can be diagnosed with an attention disorder."

"Some people get better at some things. And some things you shouldn't waste your time on bettering."

"I don't know what that means."

"Stop wasting your time berating yourself for not doing things you can't do. You know how many things I can't do? Do you see me having a self-worth crisis because I can't change the oil in my car or make a damn pie crust from scratch? No. Because I'm fucking great at a bunch of other things, and that's where I'm going to spend my time and energy."

"Okay. Then be great at writing books I can sell."

"You're like a terrier with a Snausage."

"Thank you for noticing. But also, aren't we supposed to work on our weak points?" I pressed.

Opal threw up her hands. "What the hell for? Why spend time and energy bringing yourself up to mediocre when you could spend that same time and energy getting exponentially better at what you're already good at? What's going to get you better results?"

"I know I shouldn't be saying this after you so innocently agreed to let me hold on to your manuscripts, but I'm a failure at adulting."

"Who gives a shit? Nobody is good at everything. What are you good at?"

I blinked. "I don't know."

She threw a scratchy throw pillow at me. It bounced off my face. "Yes, you do."

"Ow! Okay, I'm good with people. I–I'm good at predicting what's going to happen. Uh. Um, I'm good at focusing on things…but only if they're interesting. I'm good at coming up with ideas. Oh, and I'm good at looking good, which is probably not a skill to be bragging about, but you're stressing me out, and I'm basically just babbling at this point."

"So do what you're good at, and give the crap you're not good at to someone else."

"I don't know what you think a literary agent gets paid but—"

"Outsource it, or make it interesting."

"I bet you were terrifying as a therapist."

That got half a smile out of her. "Are we gonna seal this deal with a drink or what?"

"It's eleven thirty in the morning," I said.

"What's your point?"

18

A brick to the face
Gage

"Sometimes I think it might be easier to just stay."

My client leaned back in her chair at the conference table, arms crossed, shoulders slumped. I could see the girl I'd known in high school in the woman before me. Audrey still had the nose ring she'd gotten on her sixteenth birthday and still dressed like an edgy musician, in cargo pants and graphic T-shirts. But now, instead of a daring pixie cut, she wore her dark hair in long twists pulled back from her face. She'd added more tattoos to both forearms. She toyed with the wedding band on her left hand.

It was strange to be sitting across from someone I'd known since I was five years old and be in completely different places. While I was just now ready to find a wife, Audrey was looking to end her marriage.

She'd met Gerald, a scrawny white guy who bartended on the weekends, while he was pursuing a business degree. The young couple had gotten pregnant just after graduation. After a difficult pregnancy and labor, Audrey had left her fledgling career in microbiology behind to focus on being a full-time mom. They'd had another kid a few years later, and while Audrey eventually balanced parenting with part-time work at a lab two towns over, Gerald had grown into a waste of space who drank like his liver didn't matter.

The more he drank, the shorter his fuse and the worse his decisions got.

The final straw had been the DUI he'd gotten two months ago with their sons in the car. When Audrey had confronted him at the hospital, he'd punched a hole in the wall and been escorted out by security.

I closed the file on the divorce papers I'd drafted and interlaced my fingers. "Audrey."

She closed her eyes. "I know what you're going to say."

"What am I going to say?"

"The same thing my therapist says. That the sucky same feels comfortable because it's familiar. That making a change feels scary because I'm entering the unknown. That just because something is familiar doesn't mean it's actually good for me or the boys. That it's going to be hard in the short term but better for everyone in the long term."

"Your therapist and I sound pretty smart."

She gave me a half-hearted eye roll and pulled her hair over her shoulder to run her hand down it. "I know all this. But I also know what a shit show the divorce is going to be. He's going to fight me on visitation even though he doesn't spend time with them now. He's not going to pay a dime in child support because he hasn't had a job in over a year. And I'm the *only* reason he hasn't ended up in the hospital for binge drinking. If I'm not there to stop him, he's just going to get worse."

"Then you should totally stay. Since you're responsible for a grown man's decisions and health. It's bound to get better, right? If you just find the right way to enable him, he'll finally see the light and get better because you want him to. Besides, we all know that marriage is about giving up your own goals and dreams to take responsibility for your spouse's behavior and choices."

"I see you've gotten even more annoyingly good at arguing since high school," she observed dryly.

"You try growing up with Cam, Levi, and Laura."

"If I had, they never would have let me marry Gerald in the first place."

"They definitely would have kidnapped you from your rehearsal dinner and locked you in a basement until you came to your senses. But you're rescuing yourself now. You know he's not going to get better. You know the damage that living under the same roof with him is doing to your boys. You know that you've been supporting your family single-handedly for the last year, so you know you can make this work as a single mom. You know that Gerald has to decide to get better on his own. You know that this is the right thing for all of you."

"I keep telling myself that. But it's still scary."

"The good shit is always scary," I said, nudging the plate of cookies closer to her.

The whimper from under the table had Audrey laughing and stroking a hand over Nana's hopeful head. Her tail thumped expectantly on the floor.

"'The good shit is always scary,'" Audrey repeated to herself. "Can you turn that into a motivational poster? I'll hang it up when Gerald moves out."

"Consider it a divorce present from me…and Nana," I added when my dog whimpered pathetically. "Now how about you walk me through your plan of how you're going to tell Gerald about the divorce?"

I spent another half an hour with Audrey, going over the plan she and her therapist had come up with to break the news to Gerald and the boys and how she was going to get her ex to leave the family home with the least amount of fuss. She promised he'd never been violent with her or their kids, but women were at the highest risk of violence when they left a relationship.

"Talk to Levi," I suggested. "He's a friend and law enforcement. He'll be able to help if Gerald refuses to leave. And if he pulls anything like he did in the hospital, we'll get that restraining order."

"He's the father of my kids. I really don't want it to come to that," she whispered.

"Do you feel safe around him, Audrey?" I asked.

She shook herself and sat up straighter. "Of course."

"If that changes, I want to know."

"Thanks," she said, gathering her things. "For everything, Gage."

"Figured I owed you for beating you out for class president sophomore year," I teased.

"By five whole votes, and I beat you the next year," she reminded me.

"A win's a win."

When Audrey left, once again resolute that she was making the right decision for herself and her family, I gave Nana a treat—fine, two treats—and gave myself a five-minute break. I had a lot left on my plate for the day before I could officially call it the weekend. There was the back-ordered bathroom hardware I told Cam I'd follow up on since he'd previously pissed off the retailer. And then I had to finalize the adoption paperwork for the Clarks and make sure I reviewed my notes for a mediation scheduled for first thing Monday morning.

It wasn't all work on my to-do list though. I had my first official dating app date the next day with a woman who, on paper, seemed like solid life partner potential.

I closed my eyes and tried to bring her profile picture to the front of my mind. But instead, a curly red-haired calamity surfaced. I'd gone back to doing my best to avoid Zoey since this week's sports bra incident. And while I hadn't talked to her, I'd done a hell of a lot of thinking about her. In the mornings while I was swinging a hammer. In the afternoons while I navigated family law. And at night when I had nothing else to distract me.

It was becoming a problem. I hoped to hell this date tomorrow would have the power to wipe my tenant from my mind.

But I wasn't delusional enough to believe it would. Zoey Moody was as forgettable as a brick to the face.

Nana let out a happy *woo-woo*, and I removed my hands from my eyes to watch her jog into the waiting room.

My sister, followed closely by a woman holding a pouting toddler, wheeled inside and fixed me with one of those looks that I didn't understand but knew wasn't good. Declan knew it too, and I watched him slowly slump down behind his desk until he was no longer visible.

I got up and met her in the doorway. "What's wrong?"

"Can we talk?" Laura said.

The woman with her looked familiar in an unsettling way, but I couldn't quite place her. She had long brown hair pulled back in a limp ponytail and was wearing yoga pants and an oversize sweatshirt. She was getting paler by the second. "Laura, I don't think this is a good idea," she said. The toddler on her hip started fussing, and Nana whined in sympathy.

"You just have to trust me," Laura told her. "He'll help."

"It's not fair to ask." The little girl squirmed in her mom's arms, rapidly entering full-on meltdown mode. "Shh, it's okay, sweetie. We can go play in a minute," the woman promised.

Nana whimpered pathetically at being deprived of sticking her wet nose in the child's face.

"I'm sorry. She missed her nap today. We shouldn't have come. I didn't know Laura was planning this," the woman said. The words, tinged with panic, were directed at me, but she wouldn't look anywhere but my feet.

"It's fine. Declan has some coloring books and cookies," I said pointedly in the direction of my paralegal's desk.

"Thank you, but I think we should go."

"Val, we're doing this," Laura said in her "I'm the boss" tone that my brothers and I were oh so familiar with.

The recognition was a lightning strike to my brain. Val. As in Valerie Hillport. ICU nurse and supporter of her local high school's music boosters. Wife to Brian. Mother to two young girls.

Driver of the sedan that had hit Laura and killed Miller.

I'd never seen her in person, just photos on social media from the hours of digging I'd done after the accident. But now she was standing in my office next to my sister.

I couldn't breathe. Couldn't think. There was a dull roar in my ears drowning out the conversation happening around me as Declan reappeared with coloring supplies and cookies and reluctantly tried to tempt the little girl out of her mother's arms.

Laura took a deep breath. "Gage, this is—"

"I know who she is. What I don't know is why she's in my office with *you*." My tone was ice cold, but inside I was volcanic.

Valerie winced and looked like she was about to bolt for the door. But I didn't care. She could run all the way home to her husband, because *her* life hadn't been destroyed by her carelessness. Only my sister's.

"I'm so sorry. I didn't know we were coming here until we pulled in. I would never ask for your help," Valerie said to me.

She was thinner than in the pictures I'd seen before. No, *thinner* wasn't the right word. Gaunt. Older too than the twenty-six she should be now. Either the profile pictures I'd seen were years old or she'd aged drastically. *Good.* I hoped it was the guilt eating her alive.

"Then we're on the same page, because I would never offer it," I said coldly.

"Gage," Laura snapped. "Stop being a dick."

"Dick!" the little girl said before happily sharing her sugar cookie with Nana.

"No, it's fine. I absolutely deserve it," Valerie said, looking nervously toward the door.

"You don't," Laura insisted before turning back to me. "I want you to defend Valerie against her charges."

My laugh was humorless. "You've got to be kidding me."

A child's peal of laughter rang out, startling in its discord with what was happening in this room.

"Give us a minute, Valerie," Laura said, giving the woman's hand a squeeze before pushing past me into the conference room. Laura waited for me to close the door before turning to face me, breathing fire. "I brought her here to you because I *trusted* that *you*, out of everyone in the family, would do the right thing."

"What's the right thing here, Laur? That woman ruined your fucking life, and you want me to do what? Make sure she doesn't pay the consequences? What the hell is wrong with you? She killed Miller." I pointed at the framed photo of Miller in his army dress blues on the bookcase.

"Do you honestly think I don't know that, you jackass? Do you think there's a second of any day that goes by that I don't miss him?"

"Then why? What the fuck is this?"

My sister took an exaggerated inhale that I knew was her attempt to rein in her temper. It never worked. "We talked. It started a few months after the accident. She reached out. At first I didn't really want to hear anything she had to say. But she didn't give me any excuses. Just apologies. She was fucking devastated, Gage."

"Good. Welcome to the fucking club."

"She'd just gotten off a twelve-hour night shift as an ICU nurse. Her baby—that baby," she said, pointing through the glass to the little girl in the waiting room, "had kept her husband up all night because she was teething."

"I don't want to hear any of this." I didn't want to humanize the woman who'd taken everything from my sister. She was a criminal, a monster, deserving of punishment.

"Well, tough shit, because I had to live through it, so the least you can fucking do is listen."

I held up my hands in an angry, wordless surrender.

"She packed the baby and their toddler in the car to take them out to pick up breakfast so her husband could get some sleep. The sun was rising. The baby was crying at the top of her lungs. Valerie was trying to keep it together."

I didn't want to see the picture she was painting, because I knew how it ended.

"The toddler threw her pacifier at Valerie and started

screaming. Val took her eyes off the road for *one second* to reach for the pacifier, and that was it."

I pressed the heels of my hands into my eyes.

It. The end of a life. The end of normal. The beginning of an emptiness that could never be filled.

"She put you in a wheelchair, Laur. She killed Miller," I said quietly. The strongest, bravest, funniest man I knew.

"It was a goddamn horrible accident. And she's the only other person in this world who knows exactly how horrific all those minutes were before the first responders showed up."

I opened my mouth to argue, but she cut me off.

"No. Gage. She held my hand in that ditch while I screamed for Miller. While her babies cried in the car." A single angry tear carved its way down her cheek.

"I thought you didn't remember." My throat felt like I'd swallowed a pack of razor blades.

"It was easier for me if none of you knew. I remember enough."

"Christ, Laur."

"I know that we all lost something on the side of the road that day. Part of her died there too, and I will *not* let another family lose *another* parent over this. She's paid every second of every day since then. She had to leave her job because of panic attacks. Her husband is divorcing her. She's lost enough. It was one second, one tiny mistake, Gage. So if you want to do the right thing, if you want an action item on your to-do list that will actually make my life better, you'll do this for me."

"Laura, she doesn't even want me to take her case," I said wearily. I felt like the world was a carousel spinning out of control. I felt like instead of continuing on the straight line I'd planned, I'd just run face-first into a brick wall.

"Because she thinks she deserves to lose more."

"Yeah? Well, so do I."

"I need you to get the fuck over that, Gage, and do your goddamn job. For me."

"You're asking a hell of a lot," I said.

She reached over and gripped my wrist. "I know I am. Just like I know you're going to do it, so you might as well skip over this moral outrage part."

"She deserves to be punished," I insisted. It had been the only thing to keep me going in the early days. A law had been broken, a crime committed. Justice would be served.

"What about me?" Laura demanded, pointing at herself. "I was the one who suggested we run on the road because there were puddles on the shoulder. Miller was running on the line behind me because *I* didn't want to get my new sneakers muddy. Do you know how that memory ate me alive for months after the accident? I didn't even need the miles that day. I could have gone the next morning. I had more time then, and Miller wanted to sleep in. But *I* wanted to get the training session checked off the list. *That's* why Miller's dead."

"That's bullshit. He died because that woman carelessly got behind the wheel with a bunch of distractions in the back seat."

"I need you to do this for me, Gigi. You can't bring Miller back, but you can sure as hell make sure that little girl doesn't lose her mother."

"Sometimes you're the fucking worst, and I hate that I can't tell you that often enough anymore because of all the shit that's happened."

Her smile was quick, sharp. "I can still kick your ass any day, little brother."

"Fuck you."

"No, fuck you."

"I can't say yes. Yet," I added when her eyes narrowed. "Let me talk to her, and then let me think about it."

"Fine. But you have to be polite, and you only have until Monday to decide. She needs to enter a plea at the preliminary hearing."

Fuck. This was a big decision, and I never made those on the fly. I'd always weighed my options, talked through all the possible outcomes. I looked at Miller's picture again. He'd been the voice of wisdom, a sympathetic ear, and a shoulder to lean on.

I'd never get to go to him for advice again. Because of the woman in my waiting room.

"I love you, Gigi," Laura said quietly.

"You've got a funny way of showing it," I complained.

"I know that I'm asking a lot of you, but I'm only doing it because I know you can handle it. Also, I'm going to need your help when I start inviting Valerie and the kids to family dinners, because you know Cam is going to lose his shit."

I swiped a hand over my face. "Fuck me."

"I'm going to send her in and rescue Declan from Tilly the Terror. Don't be a dick," Laura warned. She pointed two fingers at her eyes and then at me before wheeling back into the waiting room.

"Fuck," I muttered, staring blankly into my empty coffee mug, wishing it was full of bourbon.

The tentative knock on the doorframe drew my attention. Valerie stood at the threshold, looking like she was about to be sick.

I stood and gestured for her to take a seat. "Sit." There was a bite to my tone that I couldn't quite control.

She closed the door and took a chair that gave her a direct line of sight into the waiting room, where my sister was allowing the sticky-fingered Tilly to feed her crumbled pieces of cookie.

"You don't have to do this. You shouldn't do this," she said in a rush. "I already told Laura that I'm going to plead guilty. I had no idea she was bringing me here to you."

I got a bottle of water out of the mini fridge and put it on the table in front of her before taking the seat across from her.

I was an adult, a goddamn professional. I could sit through this horrific five-minute interview and send her on her way. I was going to say no. I already knew that. Laura couldn't fault me for it forever, and the rest of the family would have my back. This woman had taken too much from us.

"Why don't you start at the beginning? Tell me about that day," I said.

She fiddled with the bottle. "I had a plan. After my shift, I was going to make breakfast, start the laundry, sleep until three, and then make cupcakes with the girls for my husband's birthday the next day. We had a meeting at the bank before my next shift to talk about a loan so we could buy a house since we were outgrowing our rental."

She paused and opened her water to take a drink.

"But when I got home, it was chaos. My husband was just coming off the flu and was exhausted because Tilly had kept him up all night. The dishwasher had stopped mid-cycle. Molly, my oldest daughter, was begging me to play dollies with her. I told her I would after breakfast. I had a list of things that needed to be accomplished before fun."

Valerie stopped and pressed her fingers to her mouth, eyes glassy with tears that I didn't have empathy for.

"I would give anything now if I'd made the choice to sit on the floor and play dollies with my daughter for ten minutes. *Anything.* If I'd been a better mom, more focused on the present moment than some stupid list of responsibilities, Miller would still be here."

The sound of my brother-in-law's name from the mouth of the woman who'd cost him his life was almost too much for me to take. He'd been closer in age to Cam and Levi, so they had more history, but we'd had our own bond. I was the one he'd asked to take care of his family while he was deployed. I'd promised him I'd make sure they had everything they needed.

"What happened next?" I asked evenly.

She swallowed hard. "I loaded the girls up in the car, told my husband to go back to sleep. I was going to stop by the grocery store and then pick up breakfast and get the girls out of his hair. An hour, I thought, was all it would cost me. But it cost so much more."

"So you're in the car with your daughters," I prompted without emotion. But my heart was hammering behind my ribs, knowing I was about to hear the person responsible for my brother-in-law's death describe exactly how she'd ended his life.

She nodded and took another drink. "The sun was up but low in the sky. You know how it flashes through the trees like a strobe? I forgot my sunglasses. I had the radio on and was singing to the girls. Tilly was crying, because at that point in her life,

Tilly was always crying. Molly was fine for the first few minutes, but she started to have big feelings about being in her car seat. She took out her pacifier and threw it. My husband always said she had an arm on her. It landed in the front seat, and she started crying. I was exhausted. It had been a tough shift, a tough night. And I was about to break down in tears with my daughters. I needed the peace. So I reached for the pacifier."

She looked up at me for the first time, square in the eye.

"It wasn't my daughter's fault. It was mine. I should have stayed home and played dollies. I should have remembered my sunglasses. I should have been able to withstand ten minutes of my own children crying. But I didn't do any of those things, and your family paid the ultimate price for it."

She slumped back in her chair, fingers toying with the bottle cap.

"I didn't see them," she whispered. "But I will never forget the sound, the feel, the knowledge of what I'd just done. How everything that I'd thought was so important one minute earlier was now meaningless."

She was crying now, silent tears slipping down her cheeks. She didn't even bother to wipe them away, like she'd resigned herself to their presence long ago.

"I'm so very sorry." Her words were barely audible.

I cleared my throat to dislodge the emotions that had taken roost. "Look, Valerie. Despite whatever my sister told you, I can't give you an answer today. I need to think about this. All of it."

"I understand, and I'm fully expecting you to say no. Just the fact that you're willing to think about it is more than I deserve. I know you probably don't want to hear anything from me, and I certainly can't blame you for that. But Laura loves you. And she's proud of you. She's told me a lot about your whole family and how you've all been there for her through this." Another tear escaped, but again she didn't brush it away. "It's something special when you have a family that's so supportive like that," she said.

"You should go now," I said, abruptly getting up from the table.

19

A big ol' but
Gage

"As you can see from my test results, I still have a significant number of viable eggs, and if you flip to page four, you'll find a summary of my general health as well as an overall score for my fertility. The number isn't from a medical source, but I was able to create a scoring range based on a number of data points," she explained, clicking a pen and hovering it over a blank notebook page. "Now, have you had a recent sperm count?"

Jill, my date, looked at me expectantly with intense brown eyes.

"Uh…" I wasn't often at a loss, but thanks to recent circumstances, my ability to roll with the unexpected had been compromised. I should have canceled. I should have stayed home, plotting out the best way to tell my sister I wouldn't defend the woman who had killed a man who was like a brother to me. I should have been drinking copious amounts of bourbon, not feigning interest on a first date.

"A sperm count?" I repeated.

It was a rainy Saturday afternoon. We were thirty minutes from Story Lake in a noisy farm-to-table bistro with—inexplicably—live accordion music. I was trying hard to concentrate on the woman across from me, but it was taking a Herculean effort, and I didn't have the energy for Herculean.

On paper, Jill had seemed like an ideal candidate. Potential marriage material. Her texts were intelligent and witty, her spelling impeccable.

Jill was in her late thirties. She worked in insurance, had a master's degree in actuarial science, and felt it was important that children grew up in homes with pets. When we were scheduling our date, she told me she was slotting me in between a scheduled oil change and her monthly video chat with her grandparents in Utah. Responsible and respectful of family, both key criteria for me in a partner. However, either my criteria didn't result in chemistry, or I was too distracted to put forth a decent effort.

She nodded briskly. "Your profile said you were ready to start a family, so I assume you've done the appropriate testing. What's your blood type?"

We were five minutes into our first date and hadn't even gotten our drinks yet. Yet my mind had wandered to my sister, Valerie, and Zoey a half dozen times already, and Jill wanted my sperm count and blood type.

I forced myself to do a mental inventory. Jill was a tall, attractive woman who looked as if she had her life together. More pluses in my column. She carried a briefcase instead of a purse, which on a Saturday meant either she valued functionality over fashion or she was a workaholic.

Her shoulder-length hair was swept back in a low, nononsense ponytail. From my limited knowledge of cosmetics, she was wearing minimal makeup, or what my niece would call "nomakeup makeup." She was dressed in business casual slacks and a thin sweater. I hadn't noticed them when I'd shaken her hand, but Jill had assured me her hips were "ideal for childbearing."

"A positive," I said, relieved to have at least one answer to her questions.

"Do you have a specific religious faith that you feel strongly about raising your children in?" she asked, continuing down her actual checklist.

"Is there a Church of No Assholes?" I joked.

Jill put her pen down and interlaced her fingers on top of her leather-bound portfolio. "Gage, it's important that I'm clear with you from the beginning. While I usually appreciate a sense of humor, especially on a date, I'm thirty-eight. I have an incredibly rewarding job. I exercise four times a week. I'm closing on a four-bedroom house in a great school district in two weeks. I have a group of interesting, supportive friends. My parents are still married and in great health. I have a 401(k), a robust portfolio, and a vacation property in Asheville, North Carolina."

"That's, uh, wow."

"I know what I want, and I explore all the possibilities in getting what I want. Right now, I want a family. So while I'm going on dates with men who say they're ready for commitment, I've also submitted paperwork to begin my journey as a foster parent and am exploring other options, including but not limited to IVF."

I nodded, still not having anything worthwhile to contribute to this conversation.

She opened her arms. "This is me. I don't enjoy coming on so strong, but I'm excited about this next step in my life. The timing is right, and I've found it's best to weed out the inappropriate candidates as quickly as possible."

"I understand and appreciate your candor," I assured her.

She picked up her pen again. "Great. Think of this as a preliminary interview. What I need to know from you is are you actually interested in starting a family, and if so, in your limited experience with me, do you think we would make successful co-parents?"

Our drinks arrived, a club soda with lime for Jill and a draft beer for me. I grabbed mine like a lifeline. My mouth was dry, and I was starting to sweat. I took a fortifying swallow, then returned the glass to the table.

"Jill, while I appreciate your efficiency, I'm not quite there yet. I'd need a few more dates. Then I'd want to introduce you to my family before I could answer that with any sense of accuracy."

She made a notation. "Mm-hmm. And is your immediate family important to you?"

I thought of Laura's demand. Of Valerie's tearstained face.

"Unfortunately, it's the most important thing to me."

She flashed an approving smile as she took notes. "That's lovely. I'm glad we have that in common. How's next Thursday?"

I blinked. "For what?"

"To introduce me to your family."

"Jill, you've been honest with me. I think I owe you the same."

"Of course. You have the floor." She looked at me expectantly as she sipped her club soda.

"If we had met a few weeks ago, this would be an entirely different conversation. I appreciate a woman with a plan. I admire someone who has built a life as successful as yours. You're exactly the kind of person I was looking for to explore the next step."

"I'm an actuary, so I'm great at predicting patterns. You're about to say a big ol' *but*."

"Unfortunately, I am. I'm in the midst of some family turmoil that has not only divided my attention, it's left me with some questions that I can't seem to find the right answers to."

"This turmoil doesn't involve you already having a wife and children out there somewhere, does it?" Jill asked.

"No. Definitely not."

She scratched through a line on her legal pad.

"I guess what I'm trying to say is I'm having second thoughts about…" What? My plan? My goals? My *life*? "Where I've focused my attention."

It was true. For the past twenty-four hours, my brain had continued turning over Valerie's words. *"Everything that I'd thought was so important one minute earlier was now meaningless."* She and my sister had both expressed twin regrets of prioritizing the wrong thing that day. As someone who had lived my entire life dedicated to the next goal, it had gotten in my head.

"Hmm," Jill said.

"I'm a lawyer, and something happened to my sister that was terrible, and then she asked me to do something I really don't want to do. It's not illegal or anything. I'm not *that* kind of lawyer. But my brother's getting married, and the happier I see him get, the more I want that. I want to share my life with someone. Someone who makes sense and fits the bill. But there's this woman who lives upstairs, and she's all wrong for me. And I can't stop thinking about her, and I'm starting to worry that it means something."

Great. Not only was I word-vomiting all over an innocent bystander, my brain's other obsession had entered the chat. I was going to go down in Jill's history as the worst date ever. She closed her portfolio again and gave me a perfunctory smile.

I winced. "I'm sorry. I'm making a mess of this. I'm usually more coherent, less rambly. What I really want to say is you're great. I'm a mess. I can't in good conscience pursue co-parenting with you right now."

"Say no more," she said, sliding the portfolio and pen into her briefcase. "I appreciate you saving me the time. You would not believe how many guys on the apps pretend they're open to a committed relationship and then on the first date offer to 'put a baby' in me."

"I apologize for my gender. Some of us are still Neanderthals."

The server returned and asked if we were ready to order.

I pointed to the menu. "I at least owe you lunch."

Jill checked her watch. "Actually, I'd prefer to leave since it's not going anywhere. I have another interviewee with some earlier availability, so I'll just text him."

"Ah. Yes. Well, good luck. I hope he's the one."

"Thanks. I hope so too," she said, crossing her fingers. "That would put me a full month ahead of my timeline."

"Jill, you seem like a focused, motivated person."

"I am."

"Do you ever feel like sticking to the plan makes you miss out on some of the fun of life?"

She stood and shouldered the strap of her briefcase. "I've found that my FONA is stronger than my FOMO."

"FONA? I don't think I'm familiar."

"Fear of not accomplishing. The people who are wasting their time having fun might look like they're enjoying themselves, but happiness can't buy a financially secure retirement."

I rose from the table with her. "This has been enlightening, Jill. Good luck on your journey."

"I like to think of it more as an action plan. But thank you for the sentiment. Good luck with your...trauma."

I watched her leave and sat back down with the menu.

"Bad first date?" the server guessed.

"For her. Can I get the salmon?"

I was halfway through my meal when my phone vibrated on the tabletop.

Laura: Here's Valerie's number again since you still haven't called her.
Laura: In case that last text was too subtle. CALL HER!

I dropped my fork, appetite officially lost. I needed to just tell my sister I wasn't doing it, that it was insanity she'd even asked me. A new text rolled onto the screen.

Laura: Stop trying to come up with ways to tell me you aren't doing it and just do it.

Swearing under my breath, I picked up the phone and called her.

"Stop harassing me," I said when she answered.

"The preliminary hearing is Monday," Laura said, crunching on something in my ear.

"Are you eating chips?"

"You know I snack when I'm stressed, and you're stressing me out."

"Me? How the hell do you think I feel?"

Laura sighed. "Gigi, I get that I've had more time to work through all this, and I get that it's unfair of me to dump you in the middle of it. But I need you. You've asked me a thousand times since the accident what I need. I need this."

Fuck. The problem with coming from a close-knit family was that every member knew exactly what buttons to push to make you do things you didn't want to do.

"Miller was the most forgiving person on the planet. He's not sitting around in the afterlife plotting vengeance. He would want you to do this."

"Low blow, Larry."

"Yeah, well, that should tell you how much I want this. It may not feel like it at the moment to you, but this is the right thing to do."

"I'm swamped with work," I said, trying a different tack.

"Too busy to keep a mom out of prison? Too busy to keep a family together? Too busy to make sure one mistake doesn't ruin a woman's life? Wow, man. Your priorities really have changed."

"You're the worst sister in the history of sisters."

"What's that? I can't hear your insults over the noise of my wheelchair."

"That's not the thing to guilt me with right now," I warned her.

"Sorry. Force of habit."

She didn't sound sorry at all.

"You always said you'd do anything for family. Please do this for me, Gage."

It was still raining, and I still wasn't sure what I was going to do when I knocked on the door of Unit B, the middle brown brick town house. The exteriors were dated but tidy, and there were kids' toys in each postage stamp–size front yard.

I heard footsteps approaching, a pause, and then the slide of a dead bolt. Valerie opened the door and looked at me nervously. "My kids are home," she said, shooting a glance over her shoulder.

I didn't know if she was more concerned about her daughters hearing the details of what she'd done or the possibility that I'd behave the way I had in my office.

"We can talk out here if you feel more comfortable," I offered.

"I just caught the little one with craft scissors, running for the bathroom, so I'd feel better if I could keep my eye on them." She opened the door wider. "Come in."

She led the way into a cramped living room where a large couch and a mound of toys vied for floor space. Her daughters, curly-haired carbon copies of their mother, were engaged in some sort of block building battle. There was more throwing than building happening.

"Can I get you something to drink? I have water, juice boxes, and milk," she said, gesturing toward the small kitchen that opened into the living room via a pass-through.

"I'm fine."

"We can talk in there. You can sit and I can make sure they're not cutting each other's bangs again," Valerie said loudly.

"Sorry, Mommy," the oldest girl said, looking not the least bit apologetic.

"Yeah, sowwy, Momma," parroted the youngest. "I have snack?"

"In a few minutes. I'm going to talk to Mr. Gage in the kitchen," Valerie promised. "Come on in."

The kitchen was even smaller than it had looked from the living room. The green linoleum had to be original. The cabinets were builder grade, and the countertops were an ancient yellowed Formica, but the surfaces were clean, and the white refrigerator door was plastered with photos and drawings. There were no photos of Valerie and her husband.

She poured a glass of water out of the tap and set it in front of me, then winced. "I'm sorry. You said you didn't want anything. I'm nervous. We probably should have done this over email."

"Done what?" I pointed to the chair opposite me at the tiny round table.

"You telling me what you're about to tell me," she said, sinking into the seat.

Twin peals of girlie giggles erupted from the living room.

Valerie closed her eyes. "I love that sound so much. I don't know what I'll do when I can't hear it anymore."

"Is your husband here?"

She shook her head. "No. He's at home. His home. Our former home. We split up last year. We share custody of the girls."

I'd forgotten that. Or had I brought it up to wound her?

"I didn't realize you'd gotten divorced," I said and hoped it wasn't a lie.

"We're not officially divorced. Separated. Things were... tough after the accident. I was in a dark place, and I had to leave my job at the hospital. I kept freezing when I saw blood. I couldn't sleep. Couldn't function. Eventually my husb—the girls' father asked for a divorce."

She said this to the top of the table, where she was tracing an old stain with her finger.

"I'm sorry to hear that." It was a reflexive platitude, and I could tell that it hadn't carried any genuine emotion with it when she flinched.

"Nothing for you to be sorry about. I'm working at an assisted living facility now. It's not what I was doing before, and the pay is, well, kind of terrible. But we share fifty-fifty custody."

I didn't know why she was telling me all this. I didn't want to know about her personal life. It was easier to think of her as some distant, faceless criminal than an actual person. Which, most likely, had been Laura's point all along.

I took a breath and reached into my briefcase, producing a legal pad. "It's easier to discuss your case in person, Valerie."

She blinked. Once. Twice. "I'm sorry. I think I misheard you."

I cleared my throat. "Regardless of my personal feelings, my sister asked me to do this. And I would do anything for her. Anything."

She nodded meekly. "I understand."

"And that anything currently involves representing you."

She swallowed hard. "I–I don't have much money for a retainer, but I can get a loan. My parents—"

I shook my head. "This is a personal favor for my sister. Which means I won't be charging you. But I will be holding this over her head for the next decade or so."

"Th-thank you," Valerie squeaked, pressing the white knuckles of her hand to her mouth.

"Look, Valerie. It's important to me that you know that while the personal aspects of your case aren't going to be easy for me, I am legally bound to provide you with the best defense possible."

Tears slid down her face, but instead of yesterday's despair, I saw something else in her brown eyes. Hope. "I can't believe you're willing to do this. I don't deserve your help."

"Let's let the court decide the deserving part."

Valerie's oldest skipped into the kitchen with a front-toothless smile and her hands behind her back, her little sister on her heels. "Mr. Gage, I made you a present!" Molly announced, whipping out a crayon drawing of God knows what and presenting it to me.

"Wow, Molly, this is really…something. Did you draw this just now?"

"Yep. I'm a good drawer," she said with the confidence of a well-loved kid.

"It's amazing. Thank you. What's this part over here?" I asked, pointing to a pink scribble.

"That's a dragon spider. See all its legs? Then those are the wings, and this is the fire," she explained.

"Momma sad?" Tilly asked, laying a sticky hand on Valerie's arm.

"No, baby. Momma's happy," Valerie promised.

"Good. Snack now?" Tilly asked.

Valerie managed a laugh. "All right. Snacks for everyone."

"Mr. Gage too?" Molly clarified.

"Mr. Gage too."

20

I can't believe I thought you'd be polite in bed

Zoey

I was mentally and physically exhausted when I stepped into Rusty's Fish Hook. It was a busy Saturday night. Spring meant the deck was open again, and tonight it was packed with people clustered around the patio heaters and the outdoor bar.

I didn't feel like socializing, but I also didn't feel like being alone, so I veered off to the indoor bar. It was quieter, and there were several barstools open. On the very last one, I spied my morose-looking landlord in a stupidly sexy cardigan, staring into his glass of liquor like it might hold the answers to the universe.

All plans of drinking alone abandoned, I headed in Gage's direction. "This seat taken?" I asked, gesturing at the empty stool next to him.

He looked up at me, and the sadness in his eyes almost took me out at the knees.

"What's wrong?" I demanded, slinging my giant bag onto the bar and sliding onto the stool.

He took a closer look at me. "Why do you look like you haven't slept in days?"

"Because I was up most of last night pursuing twin unrelated rabbit holes, and I think I may have broken my brain. What's wrong with you?"

"Hey, Zoey. What'll it be?" Rusty of Rusty's Fish Hook himself was manning the bar tonight.

"Can I have a really big white wine? Like a wine and a half?"

"I'll serve it in a margarita glass," he said.

"I love you, Rusty," I called after him.

"Care to expound?" Gage asked.

"About my deep and abiding love for Rusty?"

"About your rabbit holes."

"You first," I said, tapping a finger on his booze. "What's this? Scotch?"

"Bourbon."

"You're usually a beer man," I pointed out.

"Yeah, well, tonight I'm a bourbon man."

I fished my necklace out of my cleavage and flashed the charm at him. "Disco."

He picked up his glass. "Zoey, honey, I'm sure you've got better things to do on a Saturday night than listen to your landlord bitch about things."

"Not to ruin your image of me but not really. It's either this or *NCIS* reruns. I have a weird crush on Jethro Gibbs."

The corner of his mouth hitched up.

I nudged him with my elbow. "Come on, ol' buddy, ol' pal. Tell the girl you freed from a sports bra all about it."

"Fine. But I go, you go."

I opened my mouth to argue, but he silenced me with a sexy pointed look. "Ugh. Fine. Now disco me, baby."

"Well, up until yesterday, my biggest problem was an inconvenient attraction to my tenant upstairs."

"This is way better than Jethro Gibbs reruns," I decided.

Rusty returned with a margarita glass filled to the brim with wine.

"You're my favorite person in the world right now," I told him.

He threw me a salute before disappearing down the bar.

I scooted the glass closer and leaned over to take a noisy slurp. "Ahh! Refreshing. Now back to the problem that eclipsed all your fantasies about my boobs."

Gage managed a reluctant chuckle. "My sister emotionally blackmailed me into doing something I don't want to do."

"How bad is the something? Is it 'go dress shopping in the city' bad or 'give a kidney to an undeserving asshole' bad?"

"She wants me to represent the driver who hit her and Miller."

I choked on my wine.

Gage patted me on the back until I stopped coughing into a bar napkin. With tears burning my eyes and a throat on fire, I turned to him. "Why would she ask you to do that?" I rasped.

"Apparently they bonded over the…trauma. Laura is convinced it was just a mistake. But she doesn't get that it doesn't fucking matter if it was accidental or intentional. The result is my sister is in a wheelchair and Miller is dead," he said flatly.

His pain was so palpable I laid my hand on his arm. "I'm so sorry, Gage. What are you going to do? Wait, why am I even asking that? I know what you're going to do."

"You do?" He eyed me over the rim of his glass.

"I'm willing to bet twenty bucks that you already said yes."

"How did you know? Laura doesn't even know yet."

I gave his arm a squeeze. "Because there's nothing you wouldn't do for family, no matter what it costs you."

Gage's eyes narrowed. "You pay a lot of attention to the landlord you're not interested in."

"I'm not *not* interested. I'm just *only* interested in dirty, sweaty sex," I said, batting my lashes at him as I leaned in for another mouthful of wine.

"Why is it you're the only person in the world who could make me smile right now?" he asked.

"I like to think it's the breasts."

It was Gage's turn to cough into his drink. Somehow he managed to make it look sexier than I had. "You're one of a kind, Zoey Moody."

"That's what they tell me. What else is on your handsome brain?"

"What makes you think there's something else?"

"You already made the decision to represent the driver, which means you're already working out a strategy for the case. There's something else that has you drowning that handsome face in bourbon."

He sipped his drink and stared straight ahead for a beat. "You ever run across a message enough times you start to wonder if you're supposed to listen?"

I scoffed. "Uh, yeah. Why do you think I don't do relationships? You can only have so many people in your life tell you that you're too much or too hard to love before you have to start taking it seriously."

He put his drink down and leveled me with a look. "Who told you you're too hard to love?"

I laughed. "Well, my parents for starters. When your own parents find it too difficult to love you, you know you're the problem."

It was strange to think that now there was a reason, a label for what had been wrong all these years. Not that it changed anything.

"The more I hear about your parents, the less I like them," he said.

"They're really not that bad. They did the best they could. It's just their best wasn't very good." I helped myself to more wine. "You know, I used to be like everyone else. I wanted to have someone look past all my flaws to the special, unseen beauty that everyone else missed. I wanted to have that person who made me think anything was possible. Who could prop me up when I got shaky, who would even out my deficiencies, maybe even find them charming. But not everyone gets to have that. Some of us are just a little too messy for normal."

"You're really hard on yourself. You ever consider knocking it the hell off?"

I shook my head. "You grew up with two sets of parents

who loved you. They probably thought you were a special gift from the universe. I was nothing but a burden to mine. They *still* complain to me about how much I cried when I was a baby. Like I was trying to ruin their lives when I was a newborn. I was an unplanned 'surprise' that derailed all their perfect plans with my perfect sister. They couldn't go to Europe for the summer because I failed math and needed to go to summer school. I got suspended for a week in high school for punching a boy who put his hand up Hazel's skirt. I failed a college course because I forgot to drop it. Zoey Moody: ruining lives since birth."

He turned on his stool to face me. "You didn't deserve to feel like a burden."

I shrugged. "Eh, well, it evened out. I was pretty hard on them during my teenage years."

"A parent's job is to support their kid, not keep a profit and loss statement."

"That is such a you thing to say."

"I'm just glad you didn't ask for my sperm count."

"Uh, has someone else asked you for your sperm count today?"

"I had a first date," he announced. "First and last."

"No spark?"

He shook his head. "I feel like I went on a date with myself." He filled me in on his brief yet spectacular failure of a date. "Between Jill, Valerie, and Laura, I feel like the universe is beating me over the head with a brick."

"About what?" I asked, resting my chin on my hand.

"I'm very goal-oriented."

"Nooo. You don't say."

"Don't disparage me while we're discoing."

"You're right. I'm sorry. I'll hold my insults until the end."

His brow furrowed. "I'm starting to think that maybe there's a problem with my priorities."

"In what way?"

"Everything I do is to get me a step closer to the next goal. I prioritize success over everything. But what if I'm missing out on what's really important? Valerie said if she'd just taken ten minutes to play with her girls, she wouldn't have been on the road. Laura wouldn't have been there at all if she'd slept in like Miller wanted, but she wanted to squeeze in an extra training run. I would have made the same decision. Accomplish, check off, move on."

"I can see how that would get in your head."

He looked at me with suspicion. "Isn't this where you tell me how superior your choices are?"

"*Mine*?" I barked out a laugh. "Gage, I'm a certifiable dumpster fire."

"I prefer human disaster."

"I'm serious. Yesterday, this thing happened, and then today, some more things happened, and it's like now I'm so hopeful but sad and pissed off and also scared."

"That's a lot of feelings about this mysterious thing that happened. Are you going to explain?"

"I…I don't know how to talk about it intelligently yet."

"I'm looking for a conversation, not a dissertation, Zo. And don't even try to think about getting out of it, because I just laid my soul bare for you. So you're legally obligated to share now."

"Pretty sure that's not how the law works."

"I'm the lawyer here. You're just going to have to trust me."

"I got weird news. And I don't know what to do about it, and it's kind of messing with my head," I admitted.

He sat, waiting and watching.

When I didn't continue, he reached out, and for a split second, I thought he was going to gather me in his arms and kiss the bejeezus out of me. Instead, he tapped the disco ball charm on my necklace.

I took a breath and let the words escape like a deflating balloon. "Fine. Yesterday, I went to harass Opal about the whole book-writing thing, and instead she basically just yelled at me and told me I'm neurodivergent. Which shouldn't have been news to me. She was kind of mean about it, because she's a retired psychotherapist, and I guess there's no politeness requirement when you're retired. But also it gave me like... I don't know. A sense of hope. Because if there's a reason why I've had such a hard time being normal, maybe I can actually do something about it and fix some of the bigger problems. And from last night's rabbit hole and today's emergency session with a non-Opal therapist, it's kind of sounding like this might be the reason for just about every single thing I've struggled with. But also, I've failed so many times before, I don't want to get my hopes up."

I picked up my cauldron of wine and forced myself to take a sip so I would shut the hell up.

"ADHD?" Gage guessed.

I nearly fell off my stool. "How did you know?"

"Harry was diagnosed in junior high. The whole family took a crash course in it so we could help with his accommodations."

"Side note: I love your family. Main note: I didn't even know adults could have it. I thought it was just something that little boys who couldn't sit still were diagnosed with."

Gage patted my hand. "Sorry, sweetheart. That's not how executive dysfunction works."

"That's what Opal's psychiatrist friend—who was much kinder than Opal—said today." I patted my bag. "I've got a reading list, my psychotropic report card, and a new prescription in here. And I'm scared shitless."

"Scared about what?" he asked. When I didn't answer immediately, Gage turned me to face him, tucking my knees between his legs and resting his hands on my thighs.

I liked the contact *a lot*.

"What if the therapy, the resources, the meds don't work? What if it all just stays bad? What if I'm just...broken?" I asked.

"Only one way to find out. Do the work."

I rolled my eyes. "Ugh. I know, but aren't I allowed a few hours of existential panic?"

Gage looked at his watch. "I'll give you until eight a.m. tomorrow."

I gave him a wobbly smile, then looked away. "What if I'm not actually stupid or lazy?"

His hands squeezed my legs. "You were never either of those things. Talk to Harry. He's kind of an expert."

I bit my lip. "Maybe I will." Or maybe I would just wake up tomorrow and nothing would change, and I'd stay the mess I'd always been.

"Look, Zoey. This is a lot for anyone to take in. Anybody in your shoes would feel like their head was spinning. And I'm sure this is in your extensive reading materials, but one of the things I remember Harry dealing with is this god-awful shame spiral. He'd see his friends pick things up in school and move on while he was getting further and further behind. He could have easily been labeled a problem kid, which would have stuck with him for a long time had it not been for my sister and her husband being so proactive. You didn't have that. You didn't have an early diagnosis, which means you've got a few more decades of shit to unravel. But you're gonna be okay. Better than okay."

A shame spiral. The words resonated with something deep inside me. "Thanks, Gage. I should probably go."

"You barely touched your vat of wine," he pointed out.

I looked down at the glass and found yet another small relief. I didn't actually want the alcohol. I wanted the quiet it brought my brain. "I think I'm good." I made a move to push my barstool back and escape, but Gage's warm, callused hands tightened on my legs, holding me in place.

"Don't go."

"I should…"

"Look, Zoey. I don't know what it is about you, but I feel better when you're around. I watch the door for you. I sit next to you every chance I get."

Every cell in my body was vibrating with something. But I couldn't tell if it was excitement or fear. "What are you saying, Gage?"

"Nothing that changes anything. We don't fit. We don't make sense. We want different things. But maybe we want the same thing tonight."

I wet my lips. "What do you want tonight?"

"I want to forget. Just for the night. I want to get out of my head and feel good for a few hours. No plans, no expectations."

"I wouldn't mind forgetting for a little while," I admitted. Then I looked at his drink. "Exactly how much have you had to drink? Because as tempting as it is, I'm not the kind of girl to take advantage of Bad Decision Drunk Gage."

He held up his glass. "I've had exactly half a glass of bourbon."

I was going to regret this. I'd never been more sure of anything in my life. But damn did I want this. "Good enough for me. Fun fact. Did you know impulsivity is a hallmark of ADHD?"

"Did you eat tonight?" he asked.

"That's a weird foreplay question."

"I have wine and frozen pizza at my place."

"You also have farm animals."

"They're outside, and Nana is having a sleepover at my parents'."

"This is a mistake. We both know it," I said, trying to convince myself. But I wanted to be close to someone. Him. I wanted to feel Gage's hands on me. I wanted to put my head on his shoulder. I wanted him to make me feel good, just for a little while.

"Big time," he agreed. He released my legs and pulled away.

I wanted to reach for him, but he was standing up and pulling out his wallet.

He threw a few bills down on the bar. "You coming?"

I looked up to find him watching me. "You're sure?"

"Yes. You, Zoey Moody. Will you come home with me and let me touch you until we both forget everything else?"

I lost the power of speech. My breakup with words was immediate. My jaw was somewhere between my waist and my knees. I managed a floppy-necked nod and slid off the stool.

Gage's hand settled on my lower back as he guided me out of the bar.

I didn't even miss the thump of music outside because my heart was doing an impressive drum riff in my chest.

"Are you sure you—"

My last-ditch attempt to be a decent, selfless, not-dying-of-horniness human who wasn't taking advantage of Gage's state of mind was unceremoniously cut off when he tugged me off the sidewalk around the side of the building. He positioned me against the wall and moved in close.

Every neglected erogenous zone on my body screamed with giddy delight.

He took possession of my body with a casual confidence, one hand on my hip, the other threading through my hair at the nape of my neck.

I tipped my head back to look up at him.

"I'm sure. But I'm more concerned with you right now. Are *you* sure?"

I nodded a little too wildly, nearly hitting him in the chin with my forehead. "Yes," I whispered. "Totally sure. I just wasn't expecting…this."

"How about we ease into it? See how that goes?" Gage offered.

At least that was what I thought he said. It was hard to tell over the thrum of blood in my ears. I nodded again, more carefully this time. "Sounds cool."

Sounds *cool*? What was I? A 1990s teenage extra on *My So-Called Life*?

A smile played on his lips. Lips that were dangerously close to my face. "I was watching the door for you tonight," he said.

My knees buckled. I panicked and fisted both hands in his sweater. "Oh hell." I couldn't afford to lose any more sexy points. I had just decided to take the offensive and kiss the hell out of him to hopefully make him forget how incredibly uncool I was when he moved first.

Gage Bishop didn't kiss like a gentleman.

He didn't use his tongue like a nice guy.

And there was nothing respectful about the way his hands roamed my body.

Thoughts pinballed around in my brain, getting lost in raw

physical sensations. He was hot and hard against me, pinning me against cool brick. His mouth tamed mine with an aggressive kiss that had me reconsidering whether I required oxygen to survive.

His belt buckle and another piece of impressive hardware were pressed against my stomach. I poured myself into the kiss, savoring the flavors and scents of him. A whimper worked its way up my throat, and Gage swallowed it with a growl. His hand flexed over my breast, setting off flares of desire in my downtown.

"Christ," he muttered against my mouth, and then he was picking me up and wrapping my legs around his waist.

His worthy-of-a-romance-novel hard-on speared between my legs.

"I can't believe I thought you'd be polite in bed," I whispered when his teeth streaked down the sensitive skin of my neck.

"You know what they say about making assumptions," he said before nipping at the exposed curve of my breast.

"Something about asses. Speaking of, I'd really like to see yours."

He pulled back slightly and ran his thumb over my swollen lower lip. "Still sure?"

"You don't have to be so cocky about it."

"Let's get out of here. I'm driving," Gage said.

"I can't believe you're making me ride in the back seat," I complained five minutes later.

His gaze met mine in the rearview mirror. "Baby, it's for your own safety. I'm not confident I could operate heavy machinery with you sitting next to me looking like you want my mouth on you again."

I pouted. "I want a hell of a lot more than just your mouth."

"Which you can explain in explicit detail as soon as we make it home safely."

If it had been anyone else but Gage, I would have taken my

underwear off and thrown it into the front seat. But it was Gage, and he was responsible. I wanted to respect that. Also I wasn't wearing underwear.

"You're thinking," he accused. "Second thoughts?"

"I was thinking about the fact that I'm not wearing underwear."

Gage punched the gas hard enough to make me laugh as I was thrown back against the seat.

21

Holy fucking penis
Gage

We made it to my house in record time. I left my SUV in the driveway, not willing to waste the time it would take to park in the garage. Zoey seemed to share my sentiments as she was already opening her door before I came to a complete stop.

"Hazel is going to laugh her ass off when I tell her you made me ride in the back seat. Oh! Speaking of Hazel, is Cam going to kick your ass for this? Because Hazel won't be able to keep her mouth shut," Zoey announced breathlessly as I grabbed her hand and towed her up onto the porch toward the mudroom door.

"How about we not talk about my brother when I'm five seconds away from taking your clothes off?" I suggested, ushering her inside.

"Right. Of course. Focusing on the impending nudity," she said.

She made it two whole steps before spinning around and launching herself at me. I caught her mid-leap and had my mouth on hers before I'd even managed to kick the door shut.

I dropped her on the mudroom counter, muffling her yelp with my mouth. She tasted like fucking dessert. And I was a starving man.

"Are you definitely sure about this?" I demanded as I helped her wrestle free of her shirt. God, only Zoey Moody would be wearing a hot-pink push-up bra fit for a burlesque show under a fucking sweatshirt. My mouth watered as I unhooked it.

"Tell me you're not one of those 'I need your verbal consent at every progression' guys, or if you are, lie to me because I want it fast and dirty, not gentle and boring," she complained, shrugging out of the bra with a sense of urgency I appreciated.

I sank my teeth into her shoulder.

"Ah! Okay. Biting. That's cool and fun and unexpected. Yes, I am giving you verbal consent to give me one hell of an orgasm. Now hurry the hell up!"

"Only one?" I repeated, brushing my mouth over the curve of one perfect breast.

"I really hope for my vagina's sake that you're not just a big talker," she said breathlessly as she clawed at my chest through my shirt.

Her breasts were full and warm in my palms, and I wished I'd thought to snap on the light when we'd walked in. "This isn't going to end well," I predicted between hungry kisses.

"Yeah, but think of how much fun we'll have in the middle."

If this was what I'd been missing out on by sticking to the plan, always pursuing the goal, I was changing my middle name to Fun.

"I don't know what it is about you, Zoey, but you sure take up a hell of a lot of real estate in my brain," I confessed as I started to work her leggings down her thighs.

"Why didn't I wear sexier-to-remove pants?" she grumbled, flinging her sneakers in different directions. One landed with a clang against Nana's food bowl.

"I don't know if I could survive sexier pants," I said, finally wrestling one foot free.

She was naked in the dim light except for her leggings,

which now dangled from one ankle, and her disco ball necklace. I knew I wasn't going to make it all the way to the bedroom without at least a taste. I slid my hands under her perky ass and pulled her to the edge of the counter. Zoey hissed out a breath, delight flashing in her eyes.

"Laundry room oral, Bishop? I'm impressed."

"Hold your applause until the end," I advised before lowering myself between her spread thighs and finally, finally stroking the tip of my tongue through her slit.

"Oh fuck," we both groaned in unison.

Her taste was a goddamn aphrodisiac. It took my cock from hard to granite as I sampled her again and again. Zoey's fingers found my hair, sank, and gripped.

I was mindless with the need to touch and taste every inch of her body. Everything else disappeared, leaving behind nothing but the desire to fuck.

"Hey. How funny is it that I keep getting naked in your mudroom?" she asked breathlessly.

"Hilarious," I murmured against her clit as I sank two fingers into her wet heat.

The strangled sound she made was more cry than laugh. I wanted to hear it again and again, I decided as I pumped my fingers in and out of her quaking pussy.

"Okay, you're much better at this than I thought you would be."

"Do you always talk this much when someone goes down on you?"

"I don't know. Can't remember. Maybe you should go down on me five or six times. For science."

I decided to shut her up the old-fashioned way and lavished her clit with my tongue in rhythmic circles.

Her slick walls quivered around my fingers as I pumped them into her, and her hands tightened their grip on my hair. I could feel her orgasm start to build, her whole body shaking with the need to come.

"Gage!"

Her shout echoed in my ears as I felt her muscles contract with a powerful climax. I didn't just feel her release, I *tasted* it. My cock reacted as if it was inside her, precome welling up and out. I had never wanted anything in life as much as I wanted to be inside Zoey Moody when she came. It took every ounce of my self-control not to bury myself in her right then and there.

"Okay. That was"—Zoey panted—"nice."

"Nice?" I nipped at her inner thigh, then soothed the spot with my tongue.

She rose onto her elbows. "Sorry. Brain. Fried. Stupendous. Tectonic plate-shifting. Five stars."

"I suppose that's better."

She sat all the way up and sucked in a breath. "I'd like to pretend I'm not a greedy person, but since this is going nowhere and I don't have to worry about making a good first sexual impression, I'm just gonna be honest."

"By all means."

She grabbed my face in one hand and squeezed. "I want another one of those. And I want it with your cock inside me."

Fuck yes.

"I think we can come to an agreement," I managed out loud.

She reached for my zipper, and just the graze of her knuckles across my erection was enough to almost kill me.

"Bedroom," I announced, plucking her off the counter and wrapping her legs around my waist.

"Why are you not naked?" she murmured against my mouth.

"I got distracted by your nakedness."

"Well, catch up," she demanded.

"In the bedroom," I promised.

"God, you're hot," she said between kisses as her fingers grasped the lapels of my sweater.

"I was just thinking the same thing."

"Narcissist."

I pinched her ass. "About you, Disaster. You're fucking beautiful."

"I rescind my narcissist comment. Your bedroom's so far away. Why don't we test out the resilience of your dining room table?" Her mouth skimmed over my jaw to my neck, and the hot little flicks of her tongue were driving me to the brink of sanity.

"I don't want to break my table fucking you."

She grinned at me, and I felt everything go lighter and brighter.

"Practical and confident," she observed.

"It's not so much confidence as I've planned out every single possible scenario with you, and the best ones require a mattress."

"You've been busy since I made you touch my boobs."

It had started way before then, but I didn't feel like I was bound to our disco ball agreement in the moment. I booted the bedroom door open and crossed to the bed, dumping us both onto it. She giggled as I ripped off my sweater and T-shirt.

The laugh turned to a moan when I ranged myself over her body and ran my hands over her. Her reddish-blond curls were spread out like a fiery halo. Her lips were swollen, cheeks flushed. She was the picture of carnal sin.

"Two quick things," she said, pressing a hand to my chest.

"I'm all ears." And throbbing need.

"I have a birth control implant, and…shit. I forget the second one. You're very distracting when you're shirtless."

"Said the woman with the most perfect breasts I've ever seen."

"I'm really enjoying making this huge mistake with you," she whispered.

"Me too."

"Awesome. Now let's lose the fucking pants," she said, again reaching for my zipper.

"No offense, but I've seen you try to remove a sports bra. Let me handle the zipper."

"Fair enough." She wriggled up against the pillows and stacked her hands under her head like a goddess of temptation. Creamy skin scattered with freckles, hypnotizing curves, and eyes that glittered with emerald fire. She was utter perfection. "You may now entertain me...with your penis. And no, I'm not embarrassed that I said that, because none of this is real."

"I'll be secondhand embarrassed for you," I joked.

She hit me in the face with a pillow, startling a pained chuckle out of me. I had never in my life been on the receiving end of a pillow fight during sex before. This was yet another first when it came to Zoey. "Are we fighting or fucking?" I demanded.

She clapped her hands imperiously. "Pants! Now!"

I obliged, losing my shoes, jeans, and underwear. I knelt naked on the end of the bed and held my arms open, cock bobbing. "Well?"

"Holy fucking penis," she whispered. "You're...wow. Just wow." Her gaze seemed to be glued to my cock, and it liked the attention, flexing greedily toward her.

She reached for it, but I was faster. I'd wanted this—*her*—for so long I wasn't taking any chances. I captured her wrists and shackled them over her head, covering her body with mine.

The groan that clawed its way from my throat was inhuman as my skin skimmed over hers.

"Chest hair, abs, thighs, and the hard-on of the Greek god of debauchery. You, Gage Bishop, are an excellent surprise," she said, arching under me.

I'd gone as long as I could without using my mouth on her. With teeth and tongue, I worked my way down her neck, across one clavicle, to her breast. When my mouth closed over the already straining peak, Zoey bowed off the bed, levering her hips into me on a gasp.

I teased her nipple with a few strokes of my tongue before giving in to both our desires and suckling hard. It was an instantaneous chemical reaction. Her nipple pebbled against my tongue as I sucked harder, deeper. Her whimpers were music to my ears.

I'd had dreams, nightmares, fantasies about doing exactly this. But the reality was better than anything I'd ever imagined. Beneath me, Zoey opened her thighs, and I wasted no time settling between them. The wet heat of her sweet cunt seared my stomach. On a groan, I pumped my hips reflexively, thrusting my swollen cock into the mattress.

"Oh God, Gage!"

Her breathless cry made my head spin. I shifted my attention to her other breast, and we both bucked, desperately searching for the friction.

I released her nipple with a pop.

"You're going to be the death of me," she predicted on a moan. "Death by orgasm. I'll be a case study. Science will study me."

"Sweetheart, I'm just getting started," I warned.

"I'm going to hold you to that," she said before she wrapped a leg around me and rolled. It was more of an uncontrolled flail, and I heard something crash to the floor. I let her control the motion and found myself flat on my back with her straddling me. She looked better than every carnal fantasy I'd ever had in my entire life. "It's my turn to play."

"I have no issue with that," I assured her.

I might have been fine with it, but I sure as hell wasn't ready for it. She slid down my body, her breasts burning a path down my chest, across my abs, to my thighs.

"Go slow," I hissed.

But Zoey played by her own rules. That smart mouth curved just before whispering, "No." Then it closed over the crown of my cock, and I lost my grip on reality. She teased me, tortured me with flicks of her tongue around the head and down the shaft, one hand cupping my balls, the other gripping the base of my erection.

With a wicked gleam in those green eyes, she took me to the back of her throat. There was nothing slow about the slick glide of her mouth. "Jesus fuck!" I hissed, hands fisting in the comforter. I was fairly certain these were the last few moments of my life, and I had no regrets.

She slanted over me again and again, adding long, hard strokes with her hand. My balls were churning with the need to release my seed. There was no way I could hang on any longer.

Playtime was over. I jackknifed up and grabbed her under the arms.

She let out a little whine, which stopped the second I pinned her to the mattress. Blindly, I reached out and yanked the drawer out of my nightstand. It crashed to the floor but thankfully not before I got my hand on the box of condoms. "I'll fix that later," I said as I shredded the box with one hand.

Where the fuck was my finesse? I was ham-handing a box of condoms like a bear with a picnic basket. One look at Zoey sprawled naked beneath me and I knew I was more beast than man.

She snatched the roll of condoms from me, ripping the first one open and throwing the rest across the bed like Mardi Gras beads.

"I can't take any more foreplay or I'll die," she announced.

"I'm good with that. Jesus, woman!" I barked as she grabbed my erection.

"I knew you were nicely endowed thanks to the whole sports bra debacle, but I didn't know just *how* nicely endowed," she said conversationally as she rolled the condom down my length. "I mean, I was expecting a pleasant penis surprise and ended up with a cliché 'you might be too big to fit in here' situation. But I'm game if you are."

"You're fucking adorable," I breathed as I hiked her hips up and lined myself up at her entrance. "And you're sexy as hell."

I notched the crown of my cock in place, and she greedily accepted the first inch. Her head fell back against the pillow. "Wait wait wait. Are you sure?"

I dropped my forehead to hers. "*You're* asking *me* if I'm sure?"

"You're the one with the whole wife and kids fantasy. What if we do this and you get hypnotized by my sexy as hell vagina and decide to throw away all your dreams?"

"Do you honestly think no matter what happens that I'm *not* going to be thinking about what we've already done for the next decade or two? Is a few more inches gonna make a difference?"

She wriggled against me. "I sure fucking hope it does."

"You know what I mean. Whether we have sex or not, every time I see you from now on, I'm going to be thinking about how you tasted on my tongue when you came."

"Okay. Fine. I can live with destroying all your future dreams. Just fuck me already," she said and dug her heels into my ass.

Without preamble, I thrust home into her tight, wet heat.

"Ohmygod. Huge mistake. Huge awesome mistake," she said, writhing beneath me.

My jaw was clenched tight as I pulled out every trick in my playbook not to come right then and there. "Need you to relax." I gritted out the words. Sweat dotted my forehead from the effort not to pull out and slam myself back into her body's slick grasp.

"Relax?" she repeated, her voice a full octave higher.

"You don't have all of me yet."

"That's not something that a man says during real-life sex. That's romance-novel sex."

"Yeah, well, get used to it. Literally, Zoey. Get used to my dick so I can give you the rest of it."

She spasmed around me. "This dirty-talking side of you is unexpected and very appreciated."

"Fuck it," I growled, pulling almost all the way out.

"Hey! No one likes a quitter—"

Her teasing insult cut off when I drove back into her and held there until her body accepted all of me.

"Gah!" she groaned. "Oh, that's good. Really good."

It wasn't good. It was fucking heaven. It was everything.

Her nails raked my shoulders, hips grinding against me, and I began to piston into her. My consciousness slipped away, all logical thoughts tumbling out of my head, leaving me with nothing but sensation and need. I was meant to do this. I was meant to bring her pleasure. I was meant to take my own from what she offered.

We set a frantic pace, my wild drives moving us across the mattress. Zoey threw her arm out, and I vaguely registered a distant thump, but nothing was as urgent as the need to make her come again. To feel her sweet cunt tighten around my cock. To empty myself into her.

My cock throbbed, balls tightened to the point of pain. Every breath was agony as I chased the pleasure we both needed.

"Gage!" she cried.

"Zoey." Her name was an oath, a prayer, a threat.

And then she was closing around me, going impossibly tighter, her body tensing under mine.

"Zoey," I bellowed as the first wave of her orgasm crashed over her, dragging me under with it. The scorching-hot jet of my release felt like fire as it erupted from me. Volcanic. Violent. Her climax fed mine, making me mindless in the face of pleasure. I used the tremors of her body to ride out the rest of my release before collapsing, spent, hollow, and sated on top of her.

Fuck. I knew it was going to be like this. From the first second I saw her, I knew I'd never experienced anything like Zoey Moody.

A few minutes, possibly an hour of euphoria later, a rhythmic clapping brought me back into my body.

"Are you slow clapping me right now?" I murmured against her neck.

"I'm slow clapping *us*. That was a spectacular performance on both our parts," she said.

I was still on top of her, and my brain was working enough for me to have concerns about suffocating her. But if I rolled off her, I had a feeling she'd make a break for it. She had *runner* written all over her, and I didn't want her to leave. Regretfully, I managed to roll to my side. I was pleasantly surprised when she didn't immediately launch herself off the mattress, which by my calculations was at a forty-five-degree angle to the headboard.

"Water," Zoey announced decisively. Her hair was a wild mess of curls cascading over my pillow, my shoulder. I wanted it to stay there. I wanted *her* to stay.

I tore my gaze away from her hair. "What?" I was having trouble focusing on anything other than what had just happened between us. I didn't know how to play it cool, how to pretend it hadn't altered my entire being.

"Water," she said, sitting up. "And snacks."

"You're staying?"

"See? That's the kind of question that can get you in trouble with your future wifey. But I'm just here for the dick and the snacks."

"And the destruction," I noted.

My discarded clothing littered the floor. On one side of the crooked mattress, the nightstand had exploded, its drawer and contents strewn across the carpet. On the other, a lamp had crashed to the floor and lost its shade. There was only one pillow left on the bed.

I took a medium amount of joy in pulling it out from under Zoey's head to stuff under mine. "Since I'm not trying to marry you, you can get your own snacks."

She grinned at me, a full-on delighted smile. "Now you're getting the hang of it."

22

Needy anaconda of lust

Zoey

I was warm. Cozy. Wrung out. Limp as a noodle. But like a happy, sated noodle.

Awareness was coming back to me slowly. Crisp, clean sheets. Soft pillows. God, my bed was amazing. Why did I ever leave it?

I buried my nose deeper in the warm, smooth pillow under my face. Except it didn't feel like a pillow. It was harder, almost hot.

I cracked one eye open and barely managed to clamp my hand over my mouth to muffle the screech. I wasn't draped over a pillow. I was sprawled over a naked Gage Bishop. Delicious, orgasmic memories of last night flooded me. The sex had been nothing short of phenomenal. So obviously there was a problem. A gigantic one.

I'd fallen asleep. And not even in my own mattress zone. No, no, no. My stupid naked self was wrapped around Gage like some kind of needy anaconda of lust. I didn't stay. I didn't cuddle. I enjoyed myself and then I went home to my toothbrush, my bed, my ten-step skin-care routine.

But nooo. One unhinged night of multiple orgasms and

I was just breaking the rules willy-nilly. Which told me how messed up I was, because I'd never once in my entire life used the word *willy-nilly*. I blamed Gage and his magic willy-nilly.

Eyes glued to Gage's stupidly handsome sleeping face, I tried to ease out from under his arm.

A one-time, no-strings-attached fling did *not* involve spending the night snuggling. I didn't know what weird monogamous spell the man had cast, but he wasn't going to trap me here until he got tired of me. No matter how good in bed he was.

Holding my breath, I managed to roll to my opposite side and then carefully inch down the bed. I kept right on sliding until my butt hit the floor at the foot of the bed. Gage grumbled something in his sleep, and I stayed hidden under the comforter for several beats to make sure he wasn't awake. I popped my head up over the mattress like a prairie dog to take in the situation.

Gage's blissful expression had turned to a pinched frown at my absence. It would have been adorable if I had any interest in the man besides what his penis could deliver. But I was Zoey Moody. Wild child, party girl, fun haver. I was not Mrs. Bishop material. If last night had made one thing clear, it was that this man presented a clear and pleasant danger to my priorities.

Mr. Here Have Four Orgasms on Me mumbled something and rolled to his side where I'd been. Biting my lip, I grabbed my pillow and carefully smushed it against him. Pillow Decoy would buy me enough time to sneak out of the house…and… shit. My car wasn't here. It was back at the Fish Hook.

Damn it. I was going to have to call Hazel from the driveway. I'd never hear the end of it, but it was better than Gage waking up and us having some kind of awkward morning-after conversation.

Ugh. It was too early, and my brain was too fuzzy for a crisis. I was going to stick with my instinct and leave. Besides, since I was already awake for the day, I could spend the rest of the morning being productive and listing the next round of wardrobe items for sale online.

I army crawled around on the floor, picking up items of

clothing. I found my bra and leggings that I'd salvaged from the mudroom the night before during my snack run, but my sweatshirt was still missing in action. I snuck to the dresser and found another tin full of dimes on top.

This guy was really into his change.

I silently opened a drawer at random and snatched Gage's Ultimate Bingo Champion hoodie. It smelled like manly heaven. Since I was already going through the man's drawers and I'd never claimed to be a good person, I quietly pawed through the next drawer until I found the shirt he'd lent me after my mud bath. It was soft and didn't have an itchy tag, and frankly I deserved a souvenir or two after my services last night.

I belly crawled into the bathroom and quietly shut the door behind me before getting to my feet. Early morning light filtered through the blinds in here. My reflection caught my eye, and I clapped a hand to my hair, which had exploded in all directions. I was sure I had a hair tie somewhere around here, but I didn't have time for a treasure hunt. Not when I had to get out of here.

My skills shone during sex. It was once we got out of bed that men had historically realized I was a lot of work. I'd been through enough heartbreak to know the key was to leave them orgasmically dazzled and wanting more.

Just thinking about being forced to participate in the awkward "so do you want some breakfast?" conversation with Gage made me want to hyperventilate.

We'd shared one wild night together, and that was enough. I'd scratched my itch. Taken the edge off. Unveiled the man parts behind the cardigan. And it had been great.

But all great things came to an end. Usually a messy, ugly one, and I wasn't sticking around for that. Besides, there was a teeny, tiny part of me that was "what's that noise coming from the scary basement" terrified that all it would take was one sleepy-eyed smile from the man and I'd fall face-first back into bed with him.

God, I couldn't believe I'd been so suckered in by the whole nice guy facade. Gage Bishop might present as a "good guy with a heart of gold," but the man fucked like a villain.

My lady parts gave the genitalia equivalent of a standing ovation and spontaneously clenched at the memory.

I needed to preserve my sanity, get a little physical distance, and spend the rest of the day replaying last night's highlight reel from the safety of my own place.

Plan set, I yanked on my leggings, slid into the oversize shirt and hoodie, and tiptoed back into the bedroom. I gave my personal orgasm donor one last admiring look before slipping out the door. I didn't dare draw a breath until I made it into the kitchen. I paused long enough to steal a bottle of water from his fridge before tracking down my shoes and purse in the laundry room.

I winced when I dug out my phone and found it down to 5 percent battery life. Why didn't I carry a battery backup or a charging cord with me like an actual adult? Oh right. That was probably ADHD. Huh.

Hopefully 5 percent was enough for a call to Hazel, because I sure as hell wasn't hiking over farmland to ask Gage's parents for a ride.

I let myself out the mudroom door onto the side porch and was just stuffing my feet into my shoes on the top step when I was startled into a near cardiac arrest by an earsplitting bray.

"Hee-haaaaaaw!"

The unexpected noise destroyed my tenuous relationship with gravity, and I tumbled down the three steps to the asphalt.

A fuzzy leg and weird-looking hoof entered my line of sight at about the same time as my brain became aware of an intense shock of pain in my right wrist. A donkey nose prodded me in the shoulder. "Hee-haw?"

"Damn it, Pepe!" I groaned at the miniature donkey while cradling my aching wrist to my chest.

Suddenly, donkey legs weren't the only limbs in my vision. Fluffy reddish-blond ones appeared, and a split second later, my face was being lavished with dog kisses.

"Nana! Stop—" My protestations sputtered to a halt when the dog aggressively French-kissed me.

"Oh my."

The exclamation didn't come from me, the donkey, or the dog. Nope. It came from the mother of the man I'd spent most of the night boinking.

Pep Bishop peered down at me, the morning sunrise exploding behind her head. "What do we have here?"

"I was just…" Pain and embarrassment were scrambling my brain like eggs. "Not sneaking out of your son's house after having sex?"

"Christ. What the hell, Zoey? Are you hurt?"

"Oh no." I groaned and closed my eyes, trying to block out the image of Gage, dressed only in bright red boxer briefs, vaulting off the porch and landing next to me…and his mother.

"Can you move?" he asked, gently gripping my shoulders.

The donkey seemed to be concerned about that too and used his nose to prod me in the chest. Nana joined him and sniffed me frantically.

"I think she hurt her wrist," Pep said, wrestling the donkey and dog back a few steps. "I was just dropping off Nana. Pepe got loose and followed us. He startled your…uh…guest."

"Your mom knows we had sex," I announced. "And my wrist feels like it's on fire. That damn donkey scared the hell out of me when I was sneaking out."

I was in a torrential amount of pain—which I understand is not an actual measurement, but I was feeling dramatic—but not enough to miss the slight hitch to Gage's mouth.

"You wanna talk about why you were sneaking out?" he asked.

"Geez, Gage! Not in front of your *m-o-m*," I hissed as he helped me into a sitting position.

"Sweetie, I can spell. Did you also hit your head?" Pep interjected.

"I don't think so. But I need you to know it was just sex. I promise I'm not angling to become your next daughter-in-law."

"Okay, dear," Pep said, patting me on my good arm. "Gage, why don't you go get some pants on so you can drive your sex partner over to Dr. Ace for an X-ray?"

"I don't need an X-ray. I'm sure it's just…temporarily stunned." I tried to hold up my wrist to demonstrate its functionality and only succeeded in yelping as pain rocketed up my arm.

"You're going to see Ace," Gage insisted. He picked me up and gingerly set me down on the bottom step. He then proceeded to kneel in front of me and tie the shoelaces I'd been in too much of a hurry to bother with during my ill-fated escape. "Don't move," he ordered before jogging up the steps behind me and into the house.

Pepe clip-clopped closer and nudged me again with his big nose.

"I think he likes you," Gage's mom said as she once again shooed the damn donkey away.

I shook my head. "It's not like that. We were both just in a weird place last night and thought that getting naked would be fun."

"I was talking about the donkey," she said.

"Oh. Right. Quick question. Can someone die from embarrassment?"

"Answering as a mother of three boys who decided to host a fart contest into the unattended microphone onstage before their sister's elementary school choral concert? Unfortunately no."

"Good to know. Ow." I drew in a sharp breath between my teeth as a fresh wave of pain radiated up my arm.

Pepe let out an eardrum-rattling bray and tip-tapped in place on the asphalt.

"He's worried about you," Pep observed. "Donkey again. But also probably my son."

"I didn't mean to spend the night. I woke up and then did the least responsible thing possible as usual. I panicked."

"Gage consistently puts the rest of us to shame by always doing the most responsible thing. It's kind of nice to see he had a brush with fun for once," Pep said.

The door opened behind me and a fully dressed Gage, looking annoyed enough to commit murder, clomped down the porch steps. He grimly shouldered my purse and held a hand out to me.

I thought about not taking it. Look what had happened when I allowed him to put his hands—and mouth and penis—all over me. Then I thought about what a big baby I was being. So we'd had sex. Awesome, amazing, mind-blowing, body-exhausting sex. So what if I fell asleep and drooled all over his muscly chest? It didn't mean anything. I could touch the man's hand, for Pete's sake, and not sign up for a devastating breakup. Right?

"Do you want me to carry you to the car?" he asked when I didn't move.

I took his hand and pointedly ignored the electrical current that went straight to my nipples while he pulled me to my feet.

"I'll just go give Nana her breakfast and then take my wayward donkey home," Pep said. "Let me know what Dr. Ace says, Zoey."

I nodded.

"Thanks, Mom," Gage said. "Here, put your arm through this." He'd fashioned a necktie into a sling and used it to cradle my wrist to my chest.

We didn't speak a word on the drive into town, except for Gage's terse phone call to wake up the still sleeping doctor. The morning sun was low in the sky, warring with the clouds for supremacy. At least it was early enough I didn't have to worry about the entire town witnessing my walk of shame into the clinic with my grumpy one-night stand.

The clinic was in a small, tidy building on Lake Drive, painfully close to the apartment I'd been attempting to escape to. Gage pulled to a stop at the curb.

"Isn't there a parking lot in the back?" I asked, surveying the street for people with big mouths and a penchant for gossip.

Gage turned in his seat to look at me. "Zoey, you're starting to make me think you regret last night."

"I definitely do not regret the sex part," I insisted.

"Then what the hell's with the failed Houdini act?"

"There isn't supposed to be this much conversation after a one-night stand."

"Maybe you've been having one-night stands with assholes," he pointed out.

I was saved from answering by a pajama-bottomed Dr. Ace unlocking the front door and waving to us.

"You don't have to come in," I said hastily as Gage opened his door.

"Stop being a baby," he said as he got out.

Literally adding insult to injury, I got the seat belt tangled in my makeshift sling and needed Gage's help extricating myself. On a long-suffering sigh, he put me on my feet on the sidewalk, and I scurried like a rat on trash night toward the building.

"I'm so sorry for bothering you, Dr. Ace. It's probably nothing," I insisted. The good doctor was wearing checkered pajama pants, a Howard sweatshirt, and suede house slippers.

"She fell down a short flight of stairs and landed on asphalt. I think she might have a sprain or a break," Gage explained.

"It's nothing," I insisted again, then did absolutely nothing to help my cause by screeching when Dr. Ace's cool fingers prodded my wrist.

"Hmm. It certainly sounds like something," he said. "Come on back, and we'll have a look-see."

"I can't believe I broke my wrist," I muttered when we left the clinic.

"I can't believe you broke your wrist trying to sneak out after having sex with me." Gage said this cheerfully around the lollipop he'd pilfered from Dr. Ace's front desk.

I hissed out a breath through my teeth. "When you say it like that, it sounds pathetic."

"That's what I was going for," he said, slinging his arm around my shoulder. "If that brace doesn't fit, my parents have an inventory of them at home. Between me and my siblings, we managed to break or sprain at least one of every body part growing up."

"Every body part? Really? How about your penis?"

He sighed. "No, Zoey, I never sprained my penis."

"Sorry. I'm trying not to spiral into feeling sorry for myself. What am I going to do? I need my hand for stuff." I waved the bulky brace in his face.

"Get in the bush."

"Excuse me?" I was sure I heard him wrong.

But Gage was pushing me behind the large shrub outside Dr. Ace's front door.

"What are you—"

But he was looking past me. "Mornin', Ms. Patsy."

I peered through the foliage to spy a lady in a matching sweat suit with her white hair piled on top of her head in an impressive beehive style. She tilted her huge wraparound sunglasses down her nose and scanned Gage.

"You're out and about early today," she noted, squinting at him.

"You know what they say about early birds and worms, Ms. Patsy. You heading to the workout at the lake?" he asked.

She held up her hot-pink wrist weights. "You know it!"

I shook my head in the shrubbery. Of course the man knew what random townsfolk did with their Sunday mornings.

"Well, you have fun doing whatever it is *you're* doing," Ms. Patsy said pointedly.

"Will do. You have yourself a good day," Gage said, sending her off with a wave.

I waited until Ms. Patsy disappeared. "Can I come out of the bush now?"

Gage helped me out of the greenery. "Sorry. She's just got the biggest mouth in the tri-county area. Thankfully, she's also got the worst vision. If she'd seen you, the rumors about us would already be flying."

"You *pushed me* in a *bush*."

"To save *your* reputation."

I scoffed as I brushed leaves and twigs off me. "Mine or yours?"

He opened the truck door for me with a charming grin. "Does it really matter?"

I sighed as I climbed onto the seat. "Not really."

Gage slid in behind the wheel. "I'm hungry. Let's go get some breakfast."

"I don't know what kind of one-night stands you're used to, but you don't typically go out to breakfast together the next morning," I pointed out.

"I'm willing to bet most one-night stands don't involve chauffeuring your partner to the doctor. But since you're my first, you can explain the rules to me over breakfast."

Great. I'd taken the one-night-stand virginity of the man. He was definitely going to be a problem.

"I don't want breakfast," I said, pouting. I wanted to go home, crawl into bed, and list all the ways I'd screwed up last night…and this morning.

"Tough shit, sweetheart. Because I'm behind the wheel, and I could use about a gallon of coffee and a platter of bacon."

"I guess bacon doesn't sound awful," I admitted.

"We'll talk over bacon," he said cheerfully.

"We don't have anything to talk about," I said defensively.

Instead of answering me, he cranked up the radio to a peppy country song and steered us out of town.

I was full-blown starving twenty minutes later when he pulled into the parking lot of what looked like a 1950s diner on the side of the highway.

Gage was already out of the truck when I started digging through my purse with my good hand, looking for a hair tie and my lip gloss. I flipped the sun visor down and took a peek in the mirror.

I winced. Yep. I looked exactly like I'd spent the whole night having wild sex only to wake up, fall down, and fracture a goddamn bone. My curls were a snarled mess. Last night's eye makeup was smudged around my lash line. And if I wasn't mistaken, that was a hickey where my neck met my shoulder.

I was classy AF.

My door opened.

"I'm almost done," I said, hastily smearing lip gloss over my mouth.

"Take your time. I'm only wasting away here since you made me burn all my calories last night."

"I can't go in there with sex hair," I said, pointing to my unruly crown.

Wordlessly, he handed me a Bishop Brothers Construction hat.

I wanted to be annoyed at his ability to predict and meet my needs. But it had sure worked out in my favor last night. I jammed it down on my head, wishing I had more time to compose myself.

"You need another minute, or are you good to go?" he asked, reading my mind.

"How did you—what makes you think I need more time?"

"That thing we talked about last night. You know, before we got naked and started trading orgasms?"

"Oh, *that* thing." Forgetting I'd been diagnosed with ADHD was probably a hallmark for ADHD.

"Bingo," he said, tugging the bill of my cap. "People with ADHD can struggle with transitions like getting out of the car."

"I knew that," I lied.

"Come on. I'm starving." He took my good hand, and I followed him into the diner like a hungry little puppy.

To the credit of the hot guy who'd spent hours making me scream his name, Gage waited until our food arrived before ambushing me with "the talk."

"You tried to run out on me this morning," he said conversationally as I shoved the first flaky bite of waffle into my mouth.

"Mmmph."

"Did I do something that made you feel like you needed to escape like a recently freed hostage?"

"Of course not," I said, grimacing at the thought. "You were a perfect gentleman even when you weren't."

He cut a neat and tidy bite of his vegetable-stuffed omelet. "Good. Now that that's settled, what the fuck, Zoey? You'd rather throw yourself down a flight of stairs than sleep with me?"

"I didn't do it on purpose."

"You broke a bone trying to get away from me."

"Now you're just being dramatic," I complained, dumping a pint of syrup over my remaining waffles.

"Disco," he said.

"Oh, come on."

"Either you admit it, or I'll tell you what I think happened," he warned.

"This should be good. Be my guest." I snagged a strip of crispy bacon and prepared to tell him what a big dumb idiot he was.

"I think you woke up feeling vulnerable, and that scared you. So the first thing that popped into your mind was escape."

The bacon stuck in my throat, so I washed it down with what I hoped looked like a nonchalant hit of coffee.

"Tell me I'm wrong," he said.

"You're wrong," I squeaked unconvincingly.

He took a smug bite of his stupid wheat toast.

I rolled my eyes. "Ugh. Fine. I don't spend the night. Ever. It's too…"

"Intimate?" he guessed.

"I was going to say *inconvenient*, but whatever."

"You've never spent the night with a man?"

"Not since my college boyfriend, who ripped my still-beating heart out of my chest and stomped on it. He was the first and last."

"Zoey, I'm not out to hurt you. I had a great time last night. I understand that you're not looking for anything serious. And I'm up for you using me for sex again if and when you decide you can handle it."

"First of all, I can *handle* using you for sex," I insisted.

"Yeah, because that was so obvious this morning when you were writhing around in pain on my driveway."

"It was the damn donkey's fault!"

He gave me one of his charming, amused half smiles that made me want to punch him in the face.

I glued my eyes to my plate and tried to figure out how to carve my waffle stack into bite-size pieces with only one hand. "So you didn't hate having casual sex?"

Gage took my plate and utensils from me. "No, Zoey. I didn't hate having casual sex with you. As evidenced by the fact that I wasn't the one who woke up hysterical," he pointed out as he cut my breakfast into bite-size pieces for me.

"I woke up disoriented. I'm allowed to indulge in a moment of panic."

He slid the plate back to me. "If I were less of a gentleman and someone who was more concerned with being right than being kind, I'd point out that it sounds like you were catching feelings and you panicked."

I threw a packet of Splenda at him with my good hand. "You wish. I am the queen of casual sex. I'm allergic to feelings," I announced haughtily.

"Well, speaking as one of your loyal subjects, thank you for introducing me to the joys of casual sex. It was exactly what I needed last night. You were exactly what I needed."

I pointed my fork at him. "That doesn't sound very casual."

"This is the lightest I've felt in a while. And I wouldn't mind feeling it a little longer. If you're up for it."

"Are you suggesting a 'landlord-tenant with benefits' arrangement?" I teased.

"The lawyer in me doesn't like the sound of that. I'm suggesting we continue to provide stress relief for each other with no additional strings or expectations."

I did my best to chew while telegraphing my suspicion with my face. "How do I know you didn't fall in love with me somewhere around orgasm number three and are now plotting to keep me all to yourself?"

"Guess you'll just have to trust me."

"Seriously, Gage," I said, pointing my fork at him. "This whole new 'I just wanna have fun' leaf you've turned over isn't sustainable. Not for someone who organizes his socks by color and pattern."

He was going to get hurt. Dabbling in this kind of casual fun never went well for serious people.

"When were you in my sock drawer?"

"Don't worry about it."

"Look, I'm not saying Fun Me is here to stay. But it's what I need right now. I'm not gonna push you into something you can't handle. So think about it and let me know."

I took another bite of waffle and wondered if somehow sex had resulted in a *Freaky Friday* situation where I was now the responsible one and Gage was the impulsive troublemaker.

Hazel: Will you come over early before my virtual interview to tell me my top half looks nice?
Me: Of course. Let's make a breakfast out of it because I have some...news.
Hazel: What kind of news? Tell me now!
Me: It's more in-person news. There are visual aids.

23

The Fighting Vampires
Zoey

I stared at the prescription bottle on my nightstand with one bleary eye as my alarm chirped cheerfully from across the room. Opal's first manuscript was next to me in bed.

Monday. The beginning of the week. A new start. Despite my stupid broken wrist and an entire night of naughty dreams about a certain attorney-slash-contractor who shall remain nameless, I was going to have a productive day adulting.

I sat up, wincing when I put too much weight on my bad wrist.

"Here goes nothing," I announced to the empty room. I popped open the bottle and washed a pill down with a swig of water. I thought about lying back down and grabbing another thirty minutes of sleep, but it was my new start, damn it.

I got out of bed and turned off my alarm while wondering what a productive person would do to start their day. Probably a workout. But then I would need a shower, and it was hair wash day, which meant there went half my morning.

The curse of curly hair. It was cute as hell, but the maintenance was next-level. I should have gotten up earlier if I was going to turn over a new leaf *and* have clean hair.

"Great. A new start and I'm already behind," I muttered, shuffling naked over to my dresser.

An hour later, I had showered and was applying my makeup while my curl activator worked on my hair. I'd also only thought of Gage six or seven times so far.

I ran through the events in my calendar while I finished off a second coat of mascara, no easy feat using my nondominant, nonbroken hand. I was sitting in on Hazel's big interview with an online magazine later this morning. Then I had a call with an acquisitions editor about Opal. Then there was a meeting with some of Story Lake's talented young minds to see if they were opposed to a little child labor. Oh! I could take my laundry to Hazel's this morning, start it before the interview, and finish it this evening, possibly getting dinner out of the deal. I had to remember to bring the packages I'd picked up from Hazel's post office box along. I'd left them on the side table in my office next to the insurance card for my car—

I slapped my good hand to my forehead. "What's happening to me? Why am I remembering stuff?" I asked my reflection. I blinked in recognition. "Holy shit. Is it working?"

I burst into Hazel's house lugging a laundry basket and a whole lot of feelings. The foyer was a homey spot with a table that held a vase of flowers from the front yard and the framed newspaper clipping about the Bishop brothers that had brought Hazel to Story Lake. The napkin she and Cam had signed their no-strings sex contract on was in a frame on her office wall.

Meetcute rocketed down the hall toward me, his human mom on his heels.

"You're early! And…you're crying." Hazel's smile immediately shifted to concern.

"Is this how it feels to be a normal person?" I demanded.

She took the laundry basket from me. "I don't know if I'm the person to answer that. What's 'this' and what's 'normal'?"

"I'm on drugs, and I think they made me normal," I wailed.

"I'm gonna need more context. Do you want some oatmeal?"

I nodded and sniffled pathetically. "Chocolate chip?"

"Of course. Come on, my little curly-haired weirdo. Did you shower? Your hair smells good. What the hell happened to your arm?"

I held up my brace so she could examine it. "Opal diagnosed me with a brain thing. I had sex with Gage. Then I broke my wrist because of a donkey. And now I'm normal."

"I talked to you Saturday morning. When did all this happen?"

"I lived a lifetime this weekend."

"So mimosas then?" Hazel suggested as she led the way to the kitchen.

"I'm not sure where to start," she admitted ten minutes later when I'd finished verbally vomiting about my weekend. Hazel's kitchen was a nice place to have a crisis with its stylish navy-blue cabinets and acres of counter space. We were sitting at the table in the breakfast nook with spring sunshine slanting aggressively through the windows. "I mean, obviously I wanna start with you and Gage having sex. But I think that's the romance novelist in me. So let's start with how did you do your mascara with a broken wrist?"

"I held the wand still and blinked fast."

Hazel nodded her approval. "That's smart. How do you feel?"

"Sore. Happy. Hopeful. Confused. Sad. Sexually sated."

"One of my many stepsiblings had ADHD. It makes a lot of sense," she said, hooking her feet on the rungs of her chair.

"It does. And I think the reason I'm sad is that things could have been so much better for so much longer if I'd just known."

"That's awful, Zoey. I'm so sorry," Hazel said.

I scraped the last bite of oatmeal out of my bowl awkwardly with my left hand. Hazel polished off her mimosa. I'd decided to stick with just the oatmeal since I was barely hours into my new start. Also, I didn't want to challenge that big, yellow alcohol warning on the prescription bottle on day one.

"Speaking of Gage," she continued, cupping her face in her hands and batting her eyelashes at me.

"We weren't," I pointed out.

"But we are now," she said cheerfully.

"Unfortunately, we need to table this part of the discussion until later, because you have an interview," I said, holding up my phone to show her the time.

"Crap! But I didn't even get to interrogate you about the sexy times yet! How was it? Where did it happen? How many orgasms were had? What kind of endearing sexual maneuvers that readers would enjoy did he employ?"

"It was a one-time thing, and I promise I'll catch you up later. But first you have to go tell the readership of Thrive all about your amazing guaranteed-to-be-a-bestseller," I said, pulling her out of her chair.

"But I don't wanna talk to real people. I wanna hang out with the fictional ones in my head."

"Tough shit." I guided her into her office, a sunny room on the side of the house dominated by gorgeous bookcases. Sprawled across her desk was DeWalt, her tubby orange beefcake of a cat. I ruffled his ears and earned a disdainful *meh* from him. "No meowing on camera, buddy," I warned, then turned to the dog. "And you, Meetcute. If you even *think* about barking at a squirrel outside, you'll be living in Bertha's raccoon house."

"Well, that was just delightful," the editor announced cheerfully an hour later, after Hazel had finished dazzling her with the story of her real-life happily ever after. "Thank your agent for the advance copy, because I loved it, and so has everyone else who got their hands on it."

I jumped out of my off-camera seat and danced a boogie in front of Hazel's desk.

"Thank you so much, Shiloh," Hazel said, ignoring my celebratory shenanigans. "I feel like I put pieces of my heart and soul into the story."

"The women's entertainment division has been talking about organizing a trip for ages, and your book was the inspiration for actually making it happen. We've decided to come to Story Lake!"

Hazel kept her excitement professional, and Meetcute eyed me with suspicion while I performed a vulgarly comedic series of hip thrusts.

"That's amazing. I'll cook dinner for everyone," Hazel announced.

I stopped thrusting and started making a slashing motion over my throat. Hazel was great at a lot of things. Brilliant even. Cooking wasn't even close to one of them.

"A little curly-haired bird told me that you're hosting a local reader event for your launch," Shiloh continued. "We were wondering if you'd mind if we attended."

My thumbs-ups were so aggressive, the shock of pain that shot up my arm convinced me I might have broken another bone. I doubled over, hugging my wounded wrist to my chest and mouthing several colorful vocabulary words while Hazel beamed at her camera. "I think that would be perfect timing," she said.

"Great! I'll be in touch with Zoey, and we can coordinate," Shiloh said. "We're all looking forward to it. Not gonna lie, the idea that you escaped to this quirky little haven and your HEA is giving us single ladies hope."

"That's exactly what Story Lake gave me. Hope," Hazel said, ending on the perfect sound bite.

The second Hazel disconnected the call, she jumped out of her seat. Meetcute yipped and danced at her feet. DeWalt gave one of those weird cat scream yawns and readjusted his considerable bulk to take advantage of a sunbeam.

"Thrive, the wildly popular online magazine, is coming to *your reader event*!" I shouted.

"Give me all the sexy details about Gage!" Hazel demanded.

"Oh my God, you're tenacious."

"I'm stuck on chapter ten. There's only so much not-sex my characters can have before I get bored."

"Ugh. Fine. But I'm not giving you all the details, because that's weird. And also you're responsible for how much face breaking Cam performs on Gage if you tell him anything."

"I'll cross that bridge when I come to it," she said with confidence.

———

Me: Good luck today.
Gage: Thanks. Are you just using a preliminary hearing as an excuse to text me and tell me how you'd like to get me naked again?
Me: You wish. I've already forgotten what your penis looks like.
Gage: Are you asking for a dick pic?
Me: I wasn't. But I guess if you really want to send me one, I'd have to give it at least a cursory glance.
Gage: How's the wrist?
Me: Still attached. And I haven't broken any new bones yet today.
Gage: Success.

———

Story Lake High was a dated brick building that looked like the quintessential nineties-movie high school with a flagpole out front and a sign proclaiming it was the proud home of the Fighting Vampires.

"Interesting choice for a mascot," I noted.

I checked in at the front office and tried to keep the traumatic memories of my own teenage experiences at bay as I made my way through the halls. Back then, I'd been a flat-chested, brace-faced teen who hadn't owned a hair dryer with a diffuser. Now I'd finally blossomed into a busty, straight-toothed, almost respectable literary agent with good hair and—as of this weekend—an impressive sex life.

Not that I was thinking about Gage again or wondering what he'd been like in high school. Nope, definitely not. But if I *were* thinking about him, I'd be willing to guess he'd been Mr. Popularity.

It was just after 2 p.m., and I was running a few minutes late. Not due to any of my usual reasons but because I'd swung by the lodge to discuss Reader Weekend plans with Billie and Hana and had gotten caught up in the contagious excitement. Things were slowly starting to take shape. A vague, blobby, mutated shape. I just needed to find a way to get the buy-in of more town businesses.

If Hazel and I could make this launch a success with our own limited resources, maybe victory would taste even sweeter?

I found room 210 at the end of a mural that looked suspiciously like the battle scene from the final *Twilight* movie and poked my head in the open doorway. It was kitted out like a computer lab that had a fling with an art studio. There were a dozen students lounging in chairs, arguing about what appeared to be a logo for a cat litter brand.

Darius spotted me and hopped to his feet. "Guys! Our *client* is here. Zoey, this is Story Lake's Graphic Design and Marketing Club. Everyone, this is our town publicist, Zoey Moody," he said, making the introductions.

"Bro," a guy in a beanie said from his almost reclined position by the windows. I assumed it was meant as a greeting.

"'Sup?" I returned.

"Hi, Zoey." Laura's daughter, Isla, waved from behind a jumbo-sized computer monitor. She was painfully pretty, and judging from the boys in the seats surrounding her, I wasn't the only one who noticed.

"Can I get you something to drink, Ms. Moody? Coffee? Water?" offered a curly-haired boy with a spindly teenage mustache.

"Call me Zoey please. And a water would be great."

He blew out a sigh of relief. "Thank God, because I got busted sneaking into the faculty lounge for coffee last week, and they said one more infraction and I was looking at in-school suspension."

"Why don't we head over to the conference table?" Darius suggested, pointing toward a corner of the room that did not actually have a table.

The sound of screeching table and chair legs filled the room as the students pushed their furniture into the shape of a long, skinny conference table.

"Have a seat." Darius proudly gestured to the head of the table, which was currently occupied by an Avril Lavigne 2.0 type.

"Move, Kylie," Isla hissed.

Kylie rolled her smoky-lined eyes and, cracking her gum in what I could only assume was derision, vacated the chair.

"Here, Ms. Moody. I got this out of the water fountain that the wrestling team doesn't put their mouths over."

"Uh, thanks?" I said, taking my seat and my unmouthed water.

"Before we get into your project's specific needs, we put together a little presentation to show off our talents and some of our previous work," Darius said, gesturing toward the pull-down screen at the front of the room. "Bodie?"

The kid in the beanie dramatically stabbed a key on his laptop, and the presentation started.

"While we haven't executed many professional projects yet," Isla began, "you can see we have diverse experience in signage. These are the signs we designed for Mr. Rose's retirement last year."

"He was kind of an ass as a teacher so we didn't try very hard," Kylie said, tugging on her nose ring.

"Yeah, don't judge us on those designs. We were, like, purposely phoning it in. The dude didn't give A's because 'A's are perfect and no one is perfect,'" Bodie said with a snort.

"I hate that," I said, thinking of all Hazel's four-star reviews that should have been fives.

Isla pointed at the screen. "By contrast, here's the signage for Janitorial Appreciation Week."

"We love our janitorial staff," Darius cut in.

"I can tell by the balloon arch," I said.

The presentation lasted a solid twenty minutes, and at some point, the focused energy I'd enjoyed for most of the day left my body like it had been exorcised.

The urge to yawn was as overwhelming as a smothering lethargy stole over me. I was used to the midafternoon crash that plagued office workers like me with crappy eating habits and little to no physical activity, but this was like being exposed to a carbon monoxide leak.

"So what do you think?" Water Boy asked hopefully.

Crap. They were all looking at me expectantly.

"I think you've shown a wide range of talent and execution," I said.

"That's what we were going for," Darius said with enthusiasm. "Now what can we do for you?"

I fought off the exhaustion. "We're going to talk about how you all feel about books and farm animals and creating some promo material, but first I gotta ask: What's with the vampires?"

In unison, the students dramatically swept invisible capes over the lower halves of their faces and hissed.

"I'm suddenly feeling unsafe," I said.

"Sorry. The Fighting Vampires are our mascot," Darius explained.

"Go, Vampires!" Bodie barked.

"The *Twilight* series was big here way back in the mid-2000s," Isla said. "Stephenie Meyer's second cousin went to school here. The school took a vote."

"Of course they did," I said.

Story Lake loved to vote on things. Like high school mascots…or plow truck names. Which was why residents waved to Plowy McFuckYou when it went by in the snow.

"We used to be the Story Lake Stinkweeds, named for the invasive lake weed that was a problem back in the 1970s," Darius explained.

"The Fighting Vampires is definitely better," I decided.

24

Everyone is pissed off
Gage

The county courthouse occupied a corner on Main Street in downtown Dominion. Outside, it was an impressive classic revival brick building topped with a louvered belfry and clock tower. Visitors passed a large metal sculpture of the scales of justice to get to the front doors. Inside, however, it was a run-down warren of offices with cigarette smoke–stained ceilings, peeling floor tiles, and creaky furniture that had been around longer than I'd been alive.

It was a prime example of what was wrong with our neighboring nemesis. Dominion was flashy on the outside and falling apart on the inside.

Declan's face was, as always, impassive, but he kept rolling onto the balls of his feet as we waited next to the elevator outside the courtroom.

"Nervous?" I asked him.

"This is my first time in court. Do they disinfect all surfaces every night?" he asked, squeezing himself up against the wall as two deputies half dragged, half carried a man in cuffs past us. The guy looked green around the gills.

"Do *not* puke again until we get outside," the female deputy instructed him sternly.

"I'm never drinking Fireball again," he responded, dry heaving as they disappeared around the corner.

"Court's an adventure," I told Declan, who was now facing the wall and had a hand clamped over his mouth.

Great. This was like discovering your surgical intern had fainting spells.

The elevator doors opened, and a nervous-looking Valerie exited with two people.

"You're not going to vomit, are you?" Declan asked her. "I'm a sympathetic vomiter."

"I'm going to try not to. These are my parents," she said, introducing the older couple behind her.

Her father, a burly, bearded man who looked as if he was being strangled by his necktie or some kind of emotion, gave me a tight nod.

"Thank you so much for taking Valerie's case. You have no idea what it means to our family," her mother said, laying a hand on my jacket sleeve. She was small and matronly with big red glasses and a no-nonsense chin-length haircut. Both of them were eyeing me warily.

They looked like any other parents, any other grandparents. And right now, they were depending on me, the man who'd tried to make sure their daughter served jail time. I couldn't blame them for being worried.

I had conflicting feelings about the case. But I'd leave all that at the courtroom door. The only thing I had to do right now was be the lawyer I'd be for any other client. There was a structure, a process to it, and that was what I would rely on to balance my personal crisis and my professional responsibilities. Or die trying.

"I'm going to do my best for your daughter," I assured them.

"Declan, why don't you show Valerie's parents where they can sit in the courtroom?"

"I'll choose a spot away from the vomit," he announced before leading them away.

"Vomit?" the mother asked nervously.

"How are you doing?" I asked Valerie as she held the strap of her purse in a stranglehold.

"Fine. Totally fine." She was nodding like a bobblehead on a dirt road. "I'm lying. I don't think I can do this, Gage. I think I just need to plead guilty."

"Okay, come over here." I led her over to a pea-soup-green vinyl upholstered bench along the wall and sat with her. "Look. This is just a formality. You're not going to enter a plea. You're not going to be found guilty or marched out in handcuffs in front of your parents. The prosecutor is just going to present their evidence to support the case. I'll cross-examine if I think we can push an advantage, but we aren't here to try your case. It's going to move forward. The judge will find that the district attorney's office has a strong enough case to proceed, and then we'll get on the docket for a trial. That's it. That's all that's going to happen in there."

"But the evidence," she whispered.

"What about it?"

"I–I know this is selfish, but I don't know if I can live through it again. The pictures, witnesses telling the world what I already know. That I killed someone. That someone's husband, someone's father, didn't go home ever again because of me."

She looked so young, so lost. If she'd been anyone else, I'd say the right words to make her feel strong enough to walk in there. But a small ugly part of me wanted to know that she suffered. And that filled me with shame.

Fuck.

"Valerie, look at me."

She turned watery eyes my way.

"Your feelings of guilt don't matter. My feelings of…whatever don't matter. It sounds harsh, but it's the truth. The only thing that matters today is that this is what Laura wants. You and I are doing what she wants, and we're going to do it to the best of our abilities because she asked us to. So you are going to go in there, and you are going to survive. And I'm going to go in there and provide the best damn defense possible."

Valerie closed her eyes and drew in a shaky breath. "For Laura."

"For Laura," I repeated.

"Let's get this shitty party started."

We both looked up to find Laura wheeling off the elevator toward us.

"What the hell are you doing here?" I demanded.

"Laura." Valerie looked aghast.

"Showing my support, dummies," my sister announced. "I can't believe you guys thought I'd sit this one out."

"This isn't a good idea," I insisted.

"He's right," Valerie agreed.

Laura held up a hand. "Really? You think the victim showing up in support of the defendant in open court is a bad look for your case? Are you going to be Valerie's lawyer or my overprotective stupid brother?"

"Both. Minus the *stupid* part."

"Laura, they're going to go over every detail of the accident report. You shouldn't have to sit through that," Valerie said, her voice a full octave higher. Her knuckles were white on the purse strap.

This wasn't just fear of losing face, I realized. This was fear of losing Laura. Of all the things they'd both lost that day, they'd found each other. And a good lawyer would use that. I just hoped to God I could be that lawyer.

My sister reached out and gave her hand a squeeze. "We're in this together. I'm going in that courtroom with or without your permission, so suck it up and deal with it. Both of you."

"Laura?"

Another familiar voice, the concern and confusion in it, had my gut turning to ice.

Fucking fuck.

Laura and I shared a deer-in-headlights stare for a moment, but she recovered faster. "Fuck. I forgot how it feels to be in trouble with them. I've had a free pass for a while," she said out of the corner of her mouth. "Mom? Dad? What are you guys doing—"

"Gage?" Dad said my name like he couldn't believe what he was seeing.

I jumped to my feet as guilt drilled a hole in the pit of my stomach.

"What's going on?" Mom looked back and forth between me, Laura, and Valerie. "Is this—"

"Valerie," Laura said, her voice too bright, too forced.

Valerie looked like she was trying her hardest to be absorbed into the bench. I couldn't blame her. I'd give just about anything for a hedge to disappear into. Apparently the humbling fear of disappointing your parents could haunt adults well into their thirties.

"You didn't tell them?" I said to Laura without moving my lips.

"I was going to wait until after today," she murmured back.

"Since I can hear everything you think you're whispering, I think you'd better catch us up," Mom said coolly.

"Okay, but you're forbidden from freaking out. This is what I want," Laura preempted.

I knew it wasn't particularly brave of me, but I was relieved as hell that she was taking the lead on this one.

"Explain," Dad demanded.

"What the hell, Bishop?" I turned and found the district attorney steaming toward me like she was a bull and I was waving a red flag.

Weighing my options, I felt like the angry prosecutor was a safer bet than my pissed-off parents. "I'm gonna go talk to opposing counsel way over there. Nobody commit any crimes," I told my family. "Valerie, I'll be back to walk you in."

"Don't think this is getting you out of a serious conversation," Mom called after me.

I was absolutely going to run out of the courtroom and hide from my mother for the foreseeable future.

"Is that your mother?" Tarini was the county's youngest district attorney. I'd known her since law school where she'd repeatedly kicked my ass in con law. She wore her long black hair in a sleek ponytail, her sleeve tattoos were hidden under a tailored suit jacket in a classy navy, but the ink on her fingers was still visible. Tough but cool as hell was how nearly everyone described her.

"Yeah and she's pretty pissed right now, so let's go over here," I said, guiding her around the corner.

"What the fuck?" she said, crossing her arms once I could no longer feel my parents' disapproving gazes.

"I know what you're going to say," I started.

"Then let me say it. *You* pushed for these charges. *You* practically built my argument *for* me."

"I know."

"And now *you're* representing her? I repeat. What the fuck, Bishop?"

"Laura asked me to."

"If Laura asked you to hurl yourself off the top of the water tower into a pool of Jell-O, would you?"

"Probably. Look, Tarini, you don't know what she went through."

"Yes, I do. Thanks to your landslide of emails and phone calls. To your constant pressure on the investigating team. I think I have a damn good idea of what Laura went through because you *told* me."

"Okay fine. But here's the situation. Laura forgave Valerie. And she asked me to represent her. This is the *only* thing she's asked of me since it happened."

"Well, you should have said no, you colossal jackass. How the hell are you going to defend a woman you spent nearly two years trying to get my office to charge? I could have you removed from the case. I *should* have you removed from the case."

"I'll give my client the best possible defense, just like she was any other client."

"But she's *not* any other client, Gage. You know it and I

know it. In a perfect world, you could compartmentalize, and it wouldn't hinder your performance. But this is not a perfect world, and I will be on the other side, waiting to take advantage of every mistake you make, intentional or otherwise. She's the one who's going to pay for it. So if you aren't going to be able to give her the defense she deserves, you need to voluntarily terminate yourself right now."

"You're not scaring me off this case. I'm going to do my job to the best of my abilities. Laura forgave her, and that means something to me. It should with you too. Another family shouldn't have to lose another parent."

Tarini bent at the waist and sucked in an irate breath. When she straightened, I opened my mouth, but she pointed a bloodred fingernail in my face. "Is that not *exactly* what I said to you when you showed up in my office last year, demanding to know when charges would be filed?"

"It sounds vaguely familiar. Your rage is valid and terrifying. But people change…sometimes. And here we are."

"Yeah, here we are. Me wanting to slap you so hard your children are born with backward heads. But no, I can't do that, because I'm a responsible adult not ruled by my emotions. So now I'm going to be spending my time and energy prosecuting a woman who made a fucking mistake. And you're going to be right next to me, defending the woman you said didn't deserve to be off living her life after she destroyed your family's. Way to go, Bishop. You just fucked up both our lives. You are officially uninvited from PowerPoint Night."

"Come on, Tarini. You're just saying that because I won last year with my 'How Are Pandas Still Alive' slide deck."

She shook her head, clearly not in any mood for jokes. "I'm saying that because I haven't been this pissed off in months, and I just had a guy projectile vomit Fireball on my entire prosecution."

I flashed her my most charming grin. "You know, if you just dropped the charges, we could go back to being friends."

She gave me a long, steely stare that would have made my

mother proud. "You're an idiot," she announced before storming off in the direction of the courtroom.

"Well, that went well," I muttered, swiping a hand through my hair. I decided it was an act of self-preservation rather than cowardice to take out my phone and text Zoey instead of facing down my parents.

> **Me:** About to go into the courtroom and Laura showed up. Followed by my parents.
> **Zoey:** Did your parents know you were representing Valerie?
> **Me:** They did not. I might be grounded. Or shunned.
> **Zoey:** As soon as I get out of this meeting with the Story Lake VAMPIRES—seriously, make it make sense—Marketing Club, I'll find a way to redirect all blame to your sister.
> **Me:** I knew I liked more about you than just your hot body.
> **Zoey:** My hot body and my deviousness.
> **Me:** It's a winning combination.
> **Zoey:** Speaking of winning, stop hiding from your parents and go do some lawyering stuff.
> **Me:** Dinner tonight?
> **Zoey:** Either you're trying to get back in my pants or you're hiding from your parents.
> **Me:** Does it matter?
> **Zoey:** Not as long as you feed me.

Despite the absolute shit show of the last five minutes, I found myself smiling as I made sure my phone was on silent before stowing it in my pocket. That was the magic of Zoey Moody. The woman could take the worst moment of the day and turn it into something enjoyable.

Spirits lifted, I turned the corner and found Valerie leaning against the wall outside the courtroom looking pale and hollow-eyed.

She nodded toward the doors. "Your parents and Laura are inside."

"Was there any shouting or bloodshed?" I asked.

"Not so far, but I hope I can develop a mom face half as terrifying as your mother's," she quipped. Her smile faltered. "Not that I'll need it for a while if I lose."

"We," I corrected. "And we're not going to lose. We're going to fight."

"We don't have to. *You* don't have to."

"I committed. I told Laura I would do this, and I will. But you should know you have other options. If you have any concerns about me not giving this case my all, you can and should ask for new representation."

She shook her head, still staring ahead at the doors. "I committed too. This is what Laura wants."

"Okay. So when we go in there, it's not like TV. We don't have the courtroom to ourselves. There will be other defendants, plaintiffs, lawyers, and families inside. It can be a little unnerving, but you don't have to speak. You just have to sit there and get through it."

She swallowed hard. "I realize it's unfair of me to ask you to listen to my string of panicked thoughts, but in my head, what's on the other side of that door is what could keep me from my kids for the next three years…or longer. I could also lose a new, very dear friend in there. And I know it's absolutely shitty of me to be worried about that when you've all permanently lost someone and I was the one to take him away."

Her voice cracked, and she covered her mouth with a hand.

"Valerie, I'm not trying you today. The court is not trying you today. And if you and Laura got through this once together, you both can survive it again in there. So let's focus on that. Surviving this step so we can take the next one. Together."

She nodded. "Okay."

I ushered her to the door. "Whatever you do, don't throw up in there."

"I didn't know that was an option," she said slowly.

"It's not a good one," I advised.

We entered the courtroom and were about to take a seat in the back when the bailiff called our case. I steered Valerie to the front of the room. We passed Valerie's parents and then my parents with Laura on the aisle in the front row. My sister flashed us a thumbs-up as we crossed the railing to the defense table.

The Honorable Judge Ray was looking formidable as always at the front of the courtroom in her robes, her graying hair styled in thick twists down her back. She was peering at a fat stack of paperwork through a pair of bright blue reading glasses. I'd come up before her several times before. Tough but fair. Intimidating but with a few soft spots. She was a stickler for courtroom procedure, and I liked that about her.

Tarini swept in and took up her position behind the table opposite us, shooting me a withering look.

Valerie sucked in a breath.

"Don't worry. That's for me," I assured her.

"I can't believe I'm here. I used to be a regular person." Valerie said it so softly I wasn't sure if she meant for me to hear her.

"Keep it together," I said.

"State versus Hillport. Mr. Bishop, are you ready to proceed?"

I sure as hell hoped I was. Valerie was trembling beside me like she was sitting on her own personal earthquake. I was just about to offer her a glass of water when my sister snaked her hand over the railing and gripped Valerie's. I clocked the expressions on the faces of the judge, the DA, even my parents as each one glanced down at the joined hands. And for the first time since I'd walked in here, I breathed a little easier.

Cam: I need a raccoon removal volunteer.
Levi: Not it.
Cam: Literally all you need to do is hold the bag.

Levi: Is it a tooth-proof, rabies-proof bag? No? Still no.
Cam: Fuck you. I'm doing all the work with the fucking tennis racket, asshole!
Levi: I'm busy reluctantly chief of policing thanks to you. Enjoy your karma, dick.
Cam: Gage?
Cam: Dad?
Cam: Larry?
Cam: Mom?
Cam: Where the fuck is everyone?
Levi: No one likes you.
Cam: I just tried calling Mom and she didn't answer.
Levi: Mom always answers. What did you do to piss her off?
Cam: I didn't paintball her freshly painted barn door if that's what you're asking. Gigi isn't answering either.
Levi: Fuck off. Dad and Larry didn't answer either.
Laura: Stop fucking calling everyone, fuckfaces. We're busy.
Cam: Busy together?
Levi: Without us?
Mom: Your sister will explain how this is all her fault later. Now leave us alone before we all end up in contempt of court.

25

Corners

Zoey

I opened my door to find Gage standing there, a to-go bag in hand and a manly, shell-shocked expression on his handsome face. Nana was with him, wriggling in delight.

"That bad?" I asked, stepping back and letting him in. Nana crashed into my legs in some sort of brainless profession of love.

"I brought salads because you probably haven't had a vegetable in a week," he said on his way to my kitchen.

I followed with Nana. "It's not that I have anything against vegetables. I just forget they exist, and then they rot in my fridge. Have you ever had to clean rotted romaine soup out of your vegetable crisper? Of course you haven't. You probably use your lettuce before the expiration date."

"You have to keep your perishables on the main shelves and put all your condiments in the drawers. You won't forget that ranch dressing exists, but you'll be reminded that broccoli does every time you open the fridge door," he said, finding two large bowls and a pair of forks. He began to transfer the admittedly decent-looking salads from plastic containers to the bowls.

My stomach growled, and I was suddenly ravenous.

I opened the fridge and grabbed a beer for him and a sparkling water for me. "That's actually a helpful tip. How did you pull that out of your well-toned ass?"

"Declan was annoying me with the lightsaber choreography from *Star Wars* before court, so I tasked him with some ADHD life hack research. Figured it would keep him and his swordplay out of my hair and benefit you."

I cracked open the sparkling water and poured it over ice into a wineglass. "That's…eerily thoughtful of you. You really have no idea how this one-night stand thing works, do you?"

His lopsided grin was adorable…and tired. "Might need a refresher. Starting with the one-night part."

I laughed and made a move to pick up one of the salads. "Come on. We're eating on the couch."

"People with broken wrists are only allowed to carry items equal to or less than the weight of a beverage," he said and carried his beer and both salads into the living room.

I followed with my drink, and we collapsed against the cushions. Nana threw herself on her back and began a dramatic improvisational dance on the rug.

"So. How was your day?" I drawled. The dressing passed my taste test, so I dumped the whole container over the salad.

"It was mostly a disaster."

"My specialty. What can you tell me?" I asked, juggling my fork to my left hand and awkwardly attempting to stab some salad.

"Not a whole lot with attorney-client privilege."

"Annoying but understandable."

"I can, however, tell you about my parents showing up at the courthouse, thinking they were going to show support and discovering that their daughter and son had sided with the defendant," he said, stabbing a piece of lettuce.

"How did that go over?" I asked through a mouthful of vegetables and chicken.

Gage winced. "I pretty much let Laura handle them while

I let the DA yell at me. And then after the hearing, I'm only slightly ashamed to admit that I faked a lawyer emergency to get out of talking to them."

"Gage!" I said on a laugh.

Nana lifted her head to stare at us, tongue lolling out of the side of her mouth.

"What?"

"You're all Mr. Do the Right Thing, and then one whiff of disappointing your parents and you run for the hills."

"I didn't *run* for the hills. I drove the speed limit to Wawa, got salads, yelled at the dog for blowing the horn and scaring an elderly couple, and then I came here. It's completely different," he insisted.

It was nice to see that he wasn't so perfect. Nicer still to know that after a bad day, he'd come here. To me. Besides Hazel, I'd never been anyone's person before. Not that I wanted to be Gage's person, of course. That would be stupid. I immediately stopped enjoying the moment.

"So how mad are your parents? And why was the DA yelling at you?"

"I don't know yet, and because I put pressure on her and the investigators to bring charges."

"Ah. And there you are in court, defending the person you wanted punished," I filled in.

"Pretty much. Right about now, Mom and Dad are telling Cam and Levi. Which makes you and Declan the only people in my life who aren't pissed off at me."

I pointed my fork at him. "Give it time."

"How was your day? How did the meds go?" he asked.

The man had just pissed off three-fifths of his family, gone to court to represent the woman who had killed his brother-in-law, and he'd remembered I'd started a new prescription this morning. "Oh. Uh. It was fine."

Gage's head met the back of the couch. "*Fine?* I come over here. I bring vegetables to keep you alive. I bare my soul. And it's *fine?*"

"You're going to make some adorable children feel very guilty someday, just like a good dad would," I predicted.

"Yeah, I'm awesome. Disco."

"My day was a roller coaster. I showed up at Hazel's crying my entire face off because for the first time in maybe ever, I felt 'normal.' Which was great but also a huge slap in the face for all the years I've been unwittingly 'not normal.'"

Nana gave up on her floor acrobatics and wedged herself onto the couch next to me. I patted her on the head.

"I sat in on Hazel's big interview, which she killed. The magazine is sending an entire department to Story Lake to cover her launch and Reader Weekend and booked the rest of the rooms the lodge had available. Then I went to the high school and met with an interesting menagerie of teenagers, including your niece, and we conspired on ways to put Story Lake on the map. Two teenage boys asked for my Snapchat. Then I got so tired I felt like I was slipping into a coma, so I hit up the general store and ate a few handfuls of children's breakfast cereal straight from the box. And when that didn't work, I went to the café and chugged a triple espresso, which in hindsight was stupid and I won't be able to sleep ever again. I think it was the meds wearing off and my brain reverting to default brokenness."

"Your brain isn't broken. It just operates differently. Also, according to Declan's research, you're supposed to eat regular meals with protein to help keep your energy levels even."

"Ugh. Why does life take so much planning? Remember being in school and you'd walk into the cafeteria and nice adults would just hand you a tray of food that they prepared? I want that again."

"There are some benefits to being an adult," he pointed out.

"Like what?"

"After today, I'm having trouble thinking of any. But if we have sex again, I think I'll be able to remember," he promised me.

"You're adorable when you're sad and horny."

"You're beautiful even when you're not having sex with me."

"I'm still weighing my options on that front," I told him.

"The fact that you're on my couch and brought me dinner leads me to believe you've accidentally fallen in love with me already."

"Or I just want to have sex with you again and I'm being gentlemanly about it."

"Gentlemanly or manipulative?" I pointed out, enjoying this bantery side of Gage.

"I'd be happy to give a presentation on the difference, but I'm afraid I do my best lecturing without pants."

"Good to know. So, wanna talk about how you feel about the things you can't tell me because of attorney-client privilege?"

He shrugged. "It's just more of the same from this weekend. I feel like the rug got pulled out from under me and everything I was so sure was fact now feels like a question."

"Maybe you're having a midlife crisis. Have you been having fantasies about sports cars and women who weren't born when you graduated high school?"

"That's an offensive stereotype. Lots of midlife crises also involve golf."

"How's your short game?" I quipped. "Just a warning, if you go for the low-hanging fruit and say something about 'finding the hole,' I'm not sharing the ice cream I have in my freezer."

"This all hinges on what kind of ice cream we're talking about."

I picked a piece of lettuce off my shirt. "I forget. But I do remember being excited about it when I bought it."

He smirked and let out a sigh. "I kind of don't hate this."

"This what?"

"Your place," he said, gesturing around the room at the cushions, the knickknacks, the suncatchers. "It feels…happy… and a little chaotic."

"That's me."

"After today, I could use some chaotic happiness—"

A brisk knock at my door cut him off.

"Are you expecting someone?" he asked over Nana's rabid barking fit.

"No. But in the name of disco, I probably wouldn't remember even if I was."

"Gage Preston Bishop, I know you're in there. Open this door right now, young man," his mother shouted from the other side of the door.

"Why do I feel like we just got caught mostly naked in your parents' living room when they weren't supposed to be home for hours yet?" I hissed.

"Guilt is her superpower," Gage said dryly. "Stay here. It's safer." He put his bowl and beer on the coffee table and crossed the room to open the door. "Hello, Mother."

"Don't you 'Mother' me," Pep said. She bent at the waist to lavish the delirious Nana with pets. "Hello, sweetheart. Gram's not mad at you. No, she could never be mad at your adorable face. Just your daddy's."

"How did you find me?" Gage demanded.

She held up her phone. "I tracked you."

"Remind me to kick Levi's ass for showing you how to do that," he said.

"Remind him yourself. Family meeting. Let's go."

Gage hooked his thumb over his shoulder at me. "Actually, I'm kinda busy here."

"Zoey's attendance is required too," Pep announced with the kind of confidence only a mother doling out punishment can muster.

"Uh…it is?" Gauging the distance to the back door in the kitchen, I got to my feet.

Gage frowned at his mother. "She's not relevant to these proceedings."

Pep put her hands on her hips. "Don't you get all lawyer lingo-y on me. Not only did I help you study for the bar, I am judge, jury, and ass kicker of this family."

"I'm super irrelevant," I insisted. "I really don't need to crash your family meeting."

Seriously, who invited veritable strangers to their family meetings? Also, who actually had family meetings? Were the

Bishops some sort of throwback family sitcom with a live studio audience?

"Well, kiddo, he came straight to you after one hell of a rough day. If that doesn't make you family, I don't know what does," she said. "Now get your asses in the car."

"Yes, ma'am," I whispered meekly. "Can I at least change my—"

"No."

We walked into Pep and Frank's kitchen and into the middle of a standoff.

Pep had at least allowed us the dignity of driving ourselves out to the farm. Gage had been unhelpful on the ride over when I quizzed him on what to expect from a Bishop family meeting. He answered my questions with monosyllabic responses and grunts.

"You told me not to come to court," Cam yelled, presumably at Laura, who was sitting next to the wine fridge, arms stubbornly crossed. Bentley and Melvin were sitting under the table, keeping watchful eyes on the proceedings.

"*Us*," Levi corrected. "You told *us* not to come."

"Because I didn't want you two throwing a temper tantrum, burning down the courthouse, and ruining Valerie's shot at a fair trial," Laura shot back.

"This is insane. You know what she did, what she took from all of us, and you're more worried about her feelings than ours," Cam complained.

Hazel rubbed his back and shot me a nervous look. Neither of us grew up in the kind of family that tackled problems so head-on…or so loudly. Hazel's mother just divorced her problems. My family's favorite weapon was sly insults and the silent treatment. We were both out of our depth here.

I was heartened to see the still-seething Cam gently pull Hazel into his side. Even fuming mad, Cam treated her like she was precious.

"Damn right I am," Laura shot back. "Because we have each other. She has no one."

Cam bared his teeth. "Maybe she should have thought of that before she got behind the wheel and—"

"Enough!" One sharp word from Frank, and everyone shut up.

Pep strolled over and gave her husband a peck on the cheek before grabbing a bottle of wine out of the fridge. "Your sister stupidly and selfishly decided to handle this on her own. But what's done is done. The bottom line is if this is what brings Laura peace, this is what we want for her. Even if she went behind our backs and used manipulation to rope Gage into it, and he didn't think to remember any sense of family loyalty to give anyone a heads-up."

All eyes swiveled to Gage. He took a deliberate step in front of me. An impenetrable wall of sexy, beleaguered hero. The guy definitely had no clue how one-night stands worked.

"Nice, Mom," he said, stuffing his hands in his pockets.

She shrugged and filled her wineglass to the rim. She raised her eyebrows in question at me and Hazel. We both nodded aggressively.

"I'm gonna kick your ass," Cam announced to Gage.

"And this time, we're not pulling the carpet tacks out of it," Levi added.

"Wow, you guys are hardcore," I noted.

I waited for someone to realize I had no business being here, but no one seemed to notice how ridiculous my presence was.

"Look," Gage said. "None of this was my idea. But Laura asked me to do it, and she also asked me not to tell anyone. So that's what I did."

"If she asked you to jump off the water tower naked, would you?" Levi asked.

"Why does everyone keep asking me that? Yes, if I thought it would take one second of suffering away from her, then yeah, I would," Gage said. "And so would you."

"Still should have told us," Cam said, inching closer.

Levi was doing the same thing. I brought my hands to Gage's back as a warning and found the muscles there already tense.

"What would you have done if she'd asked you?" Gage demanded.

"Whatever she asked," Cam snarled, hands striking out to grip Gage's shirt in a lightning-quick move.

"What would you do if she'd asked us and not you?" Levi said, stepping to give Gage a shove.

"I'd be fucking pissed," Gage said, shoving them both back a step.

I raised my hand over his shoulder. "Quick question. If you all would have done exactly what Gage did, why are you still fighting?"

"If you boys break another dining chair, I'm going to invite Aunt Marie to spend Christmas with us this year," Pep warned, handing Hazel and then me glasses of wine.

"Where's mine?" Laura pouted.

"Gee, I'm sorry," Pep drawled at her daughter. "I thought you preferred to do everything on your own."

Frank rolled his eyes heavenward.

"Brutal," Hazel whispered with enthusiasm, whipping a notebook out of her purse.

"So we're all just going to be assholes about everything? Great. That's awesome," Laura said, wheeling over to the wine fridge.

"You started it," Cam reminded her as he, Gage, and Levi engaged in a three-way shoving match.

"This is exactly why I didn't tell any of you assholes," she complained.

The game of push and shove sent Levi's broad-shouldered frame into the antique china cabinet. Dishes and glasses rattled threateningly on the shelves.

"That's it. Corners!" Pep barked.

"We're adults, Mom," Gage argued, looking up from the headlock he had Cam in.

"Not from where I stand. Corners! Now!"

Hazel and I watched in fascination as four grown adults slunk off to separate corners of the kitchen.

"Now use your words and talk this out while your father and I throw the burgers and dogs on the grill," Pep said, pointing a finger at each of her children in turn. The dogs happily followed Pep, Frank, and the tray of meat out the kitchen door.

I tiptoed over to Hazel. "This is going in the book, right?" I whispered over my wine.

"Oh, absolutely."

"I didn't tell you two assfaces because I didn't want to put everyone in an uncomfortable, unfair position," Laura said.

"Oh, just me then? I'm honored," Gage said dryly.

"You were already pissed at me for this. You don't get to revisit it."

"Well, we're freshly pissed at you, and we get to wallow," Cam announced.

"That's fair. But I need you to know, Val isn't a bad person. She's just a person who made a mistake. It could be argued that I was just as much to blame—"

"Oh, bullshit!" all three brothers erupted at once.

"At least they all agree on that," Hazel noted.

"I'm just saying. She's got two little girls. She's a nurse. She lost her marriage. She lost her job. She lost friends."

"We all lost too," Levi said quietly.

"But the difference is we have each other," Laura reminded them. "I'm just asking for you to be open to *eventually* maybe having a little grace. Valerie has been there for me when I needed support the most. Gage can attest to the fact that she takes full responsibility for what happened. She's never once asked me for anything, not even forgiveness. She made a mistake. A catastrophic one."

"Don't fucking cry," Cam said stonily from his corner.

"I'll cry if I want to cry, and you'll deal with it," Laura said, hastily wiping away a tear. "I need you to eventually be good with this. But in the meantime, I'll settle for you not being assholes."

Cam and Levi locked eyes.

"Can we still kick Gage's ass?" Cam asked.

"Not over this. But he's routinely a pain in the ass, so I'm sure he'll give you another reason if you wait five minutes," Laura said.

"What now?" Levi asked. "Is she going to start showing up at family meetings too?"

I hid behind my untouched wine and tried to be as inconspicuous as possible.

"Maybe not family meetings. Possibly some family dinners. She's met the kids," Laura said.

"Those traitorous little fuckers didn't give us a heads-up?" Cam snarled.

"They're getting goose shit for Christmas," Levi decided.

"We all voted no more feces for Christmas," Gage cut in.

"Shut up," Levi said to him.

"Yeah. We're still mad at you," Cam agreed.

"Why are they still in corners?" I asked Hazel.

"I was wondering the same thing," she mused.

"Because Pep Bishop is terrifying when she's pissed off," Gage explained.

"Zoey?" Cam said, his voice low and vaguely threatening.

"Uh, yeah?"

"Why are you here?"

"I'm not actually sure. Your mom is scary. I didn't ask questions. I just got in the car."

"Whose car?" Cam demanded.

Gage was starting to inch his way out of his corner.

"Ummm…" I hedged.

An earsplitting hee-haw from outside cut off any conversation.

The back door banged open, and Pep entered with the dogs. "Zoey, your donkey wants to see you."

"I would be happy to leave this room and visit a donkey," I announced, heading for the door.

"Whose car, Zoey?" Cam repeated.

I winced.

"My car," Gage said, crossing his arms and staring his brother down. "Mom found me at Zoey's apartment and verbally berated us until we agreed to come here and fight with you. Happy now?"

"You better have been fixing something landlord-y, and not in the porno way," Cam said.

"Not this again," Levi muttered.

"What's happening?" Laura demanded.

"For Pete's sake. Can you pains in the ass stop keeping secrets from each other? Gage and Zoey are having sex," Pep announced.

I groaned. "Uh, thanks, Pep. Can you say that a little louder? I don't think Garland heard you in town."

"Oh, relax, honey. Adults have been having casual sex since the beginning of time."

"Huh. Good for you two," Laura said. "Wait. You didn't break your wrist doing a weird sex thing, did you?"

"Oh my God. Did you?" Hazel asked gleefully.

"Don't ever answer that," Levi begged.

"I'm going to kick. Your. Ass," Cam seethed at Gage. He stormed out of his corner.

"Mom! Cam moved!" the other three siblings shouted, pointing at their brother.

"The only ass kicking happening tonight is whatever ass kicking I dole out. Got it?" Pep said, stepping between Cam and Gage.

"It's like this kitchen turns them all back to ten-year-olds," I observed to Hazel.

"Fascinating," she whispered, writing furiously.

"Since when does Cam care who has sex?" Laura asked.

"Since he thinks we're going to implode and blow up his wedding," Gage explained.

"I'm just going to go see a donkey about a…something," I said and left through the back door. The dogs followed me, bouncing off each other like furry pinballs with tongues.

"They about done in there?" Frank asked, wielding tongs over the grill next to the house as I trotted down the ramp. Pepe stamped impatiently at the gate.

Raised voices from inside had me grimacing. "I think they're getting wound up again. It's probably safer out here for a while."

"Let's have a hot dog," Frank suggested.

I thought of my handful of cereal and my interrupted salad. "That sounds amazing," I admitted.

He arranged two on buns and handed me one. "The condiments are inside, so we'll have to eat 'em naked or go back in."

I took a gigantic bite. "Naked's good."

He cut up another hot dog into thirds and tossed the pieces to our drooling canine audience. "Come on. Let's take these on a walk before the donkey decides to run through another gate," he suggested.

We took our dogs—both hot and four-legged versions—across the drive to the pasture where Pepe stamped his tiny hooves in excitement.

"Hi, buddy," I said, giving his nose a scratch with my good hand. He leaned his big hairy head into me and let out a donkey sigh.

"He likes you," Frank observed as I paused to take another bite of hot dog. "So Pep tells me you and Gage are having sex."

I choked, then coughed, sending a piece of not-quite-chewed hot dog in an arc. Bentley beat Melvin and Nana to it, snarfing it up a split second after it hit the dirt.

"Oh my God. That's gross," I rasped. "Also, have you guys heard of being too open with each other?"

"If it were up to me, the only conversations we'd have would be farm, town, and weather related. But since I've got a wife with strong opinions, we have to talk about all this shit. I only bring it up because I think you're good for him."

"You do?" I said, taken aback. On what planet was the disheveled party girl good for the responsible, small-town hero?

"Kid's always been serious, driven. School counselor called it being 'goal-oriented.' But there's a hell of a lot more to life than just accomplishing goals. His brothers and sister had to fight to get him to have fun," Frank said, absently patting the donkey as he stared toward the horizon. "But he smiles easier with you."

"He does? I mean, we're not... We're just... I don't know what we are."

"Maybe that's part of the fun. Sounds like the yelling stopped," he observed, nodding in the direction of the house. "Wanna chance it?"

The back door opened, and Gage ambled out, looking unscathed.

I turned back to Frank and stroked Pepe's neck. "Hey, listen. I met with the high school marketing club today, and one of the things we talked about was them teaching a social media class for local businesses. I figured you might want to give it a shot."

He nodded slowly, and the donkey nudged me with his big face. "I could do that."

"And since Isla is in the club, I found a couple of online tutorials you can watch before the class so you know all the basics."

Relief washed over Frank's face. "Appreciate that. You're a good kid, Zoey."

"Thanks, Frank."

"It's safe to come inside," Gage called out to us.

"That was fast," Frank said.

"Mom got out the wooden spoon, so that shut everyone up pretty fast."

"I'll go get everything off the grill. See you inside."

I alternated my pets between the needy donkey and the swarm of attention-seeking dogs.

"So I'm guessing inviting a one-night stand to a family meeting isn't what you're used to," Gage said, reaching over to scratch Pepe's ears.

"It is not. Your family has a *lot* of feelings. Loud ones."

"That we do. You know, we were interrupted back at your place before you could decide to revisit the whole one-night-stand thing with me. I was thinking we should give it another try since everyone knows now. Maybe I'll get it right this time."

I tried to hide my smile by staring at the donkey. "I'm still weighing my options."

"I'll be waiting."

"So is Cam going to kick my ass if I go back inside?" I asked. "Because I kinda want a burger."

"If he tries, I'll take him down before he can get to you."

"My hero."

26

Ten percent off Bikini Night at the Beaver Dam

Zoey

"Sometimes I look at my life and wonder how the hell I got here," I said.

"It's great, right?" Harry said.

I wasn't sure if the enthusiasm was for the spectacle unfolding before us or the jumbo-sized bag of popcorn he was plowing through. He'd been giving me a rundown of his top ADHD tips for the last twenty minutes.

It was Tuesday afternoon at the lake, and the weather had gone from a balmy seventy degrees this morning to the mid-forties after a lunchtime rainstorm blew through, leaving behind icy winds. Classic Pennsylvania delivering all four seasons in one day.

Neighbors were huddled together on the bleachers and in lawn chairs facing the sports courts, all layered up to survive the chilly wind coming off the lake. I was bundled up in two sweatshirts, a winter coat, and mittens while suffering serious regrets that I'd sold my super cute Helly Hansen ski jacket online.

Skiing had been one of my spontaneously adopted and quickly discarded hobbies. I'd made a total of two runs down a bunny slope four years ago before giving it up in favor of French lessons. Now instead of snowplowing downhill or flirting with Pierre in French, I was manning the informational table for upcoming town events during Story Lake's ultimate bingo draft.

"But why is the pig here?" I asked. Emilie and Amos Rump's usually free-range pig was parading around the sports court with a floral garland that doubled as a leash.

"Rump Roast chooses the team captains. It's tradition. We tried it with Boris Banneroff's sheep one year, but Erleen Dabner's border collie herded them into the dining room at Angelo's. They had to rip out every inch of carpet. Anyway, that's why we use Rump Roast, even if his owner is currently everyone's least favorite Story Laker," Harry explained.

"I still don't understand what farm animals have to do with bingo or why there's a draft at all."

The town had taken the untaxing game of bingo and turned it into an aggressively enthusiastic sport. As a casual spectator, I had only managed to pick up on about 20 percent of the insanely specific rules, but I had to admit it was a hell of a lot of fun to watch.

"We like to do things differently around here," he said with pride. "Hey, Mrs. Jang! How's your social media game?" He waggled the social media class sign-up clipboard in the coffee shop owner's direction with a charming smile that reminded me an awful lot of his uncle.

Jennifer approached. She was wearing a backpack with an actual cat in it. "I'm pretty good at the ol' Instagram. But what else you got? Wow. This is a lot of events," she observed, taking in the half dozen clipboards we had arranged on the table.

"There's something for everyone," I said. "Since you're already in the bookstore's book club, can I interest you in Lakercise in the Park? Or how about the Expert Accessibility for Your Business panel?" I awkwardly tried to pick up one of the clipboards with my good hand and managed to shove it off the table into Jennifer's shins. This broken wrist thing was making me even more clumsy than usual.

"Ouch, and you had me at accessibility. Who are your experts?" she asked, rescuing the sign-up sheet from the ground.

"This guy's mom on the topic of wheelchair and mobility access," I said, pointing to Harry, who cheesed it up in a pose like I'd singled him out for an award. "Then we've got an adorable couple from the Haven who will be teaching some basic sign language. And Quaid will be presenting on how to better serve individuals and families with autism."

"Quaid? Bodybuilder who also looks like a surfer? That Quaid?" she clarified, eyebrows winging up.

"That's the one. His little brother is on the spectrum, and Quaid volunteers with an organization that takes his brother's peer group on field trips," I explained.

"Well, isn't that awesome? Count me in. I'll drag the hubs along. Is Hazel here? I don't want to interrogate her about her new release or anything. I'm lying. I absolutely want to interrogate her," Jennifer said, scrawling her name on the sign-up form.

"I think she's somewhere over there by the pig," I said, flapping my unbraced hand toward the sports court.

Jennifer shook her head. "God, I love this town."

"See?" Harry said pointedly when Jennifer left.

"See what?"

"Story Lake is a great place to live. You should stay here and date me when I turn eighteen."

"First of all, there hasn't been a man invented yet who can handle all this," I said, waving my brace to encompass most of myself. "Second, you sound like Hazel, trying to emotionally blackmail me into staying with you weirdos."

"But we're *entertaining* weirdos. Look how we all come together." He gestured around the park. The kid had a point. It looked as if half the town had turned out for whatever this bizarre ritual was.

"Are you forgetting how the last time you all came together, it was to try to run me and Hazel out of Story Lake?"

Harry waved away my reminder. "That was, like, a lifetime ago."

"Yeah, well, I've been trying to get everyone on board with Reader Weekend, and all I'm getting from the businesses in town is 'I'll think about it. Send me some info,'" I complained.

"You just have to give them a reason to care," Harry insisted.

"Zoey!" Sunita jogged up. The British boutique owner was looking stylish as always in flared jeans and a faux leather motorcycle jacket that I coveted almost as much as her posh accent. "I've been looking everywhere for you. I was thinking about offering up coupons for the store during Reader Weekend."

"Love the idea and that jacket."

"Of course you do. They're both brilliant. Anyway, I've got some book-themed inventory on order and was sourcing a printer for the coupons when I thought *who wants to deal with printed coupons?*"

"No one?" I guessed.

"Exactly. So I think you should gather all the special Reader Weekend deals and promotions and put them on the event website."

The panic was rising. How did I end up in charge of all this? "That's a...great idea. Thanks, Sunita," I said.

"You look extra beautiful today," Harry told Sunita.

She pinned him with an imperious gaze. "Call me when you're thirty, have a six-figure brokerage account, and send your mother flowers at least twice a year."

Harry swallowed hard. "I'll do that," he promised fervently.

"Wonderful. Zoey, do you want me to just tell you the discount details, or should I email you?"

"Email is good," I said with what I hoped was a believable amount of enthusiasm.

"Perfect. I'm going to go get a good spot for the draft," she said and headed off in the direction of the bleachers.

"I thought I was your unrequited crush," I said.

"You don't have a website, do you?" Harry guessed.

"Shut up."

He patted me awkwardly on the back. "Don't be so hard on yourself for how your brain works."

"Or doesn't work," I said into my palms. Well, one palm and one brace.

"Just because we suck at organization and details doesn't mean we're useless. We're big-picture people," Harry insisted.

"Well, this big picture is about to shatter into a thousand sucky pieces," I groaned.

"Didn't I tell you to stop making women cry, Harry?"

I peeked up over my hands to find Gage standing there looking unfairly handsome and annoyingly wholesome. He was wearing a plaid flannel under a fleece vest like a sexy cross between a lumberjack and a finance guy. New fantasy unlocked.

"Harry is just comforting me for forgetting about a gigantic essential piece of Reader Weekend," I told him.

"She needs a website…and probably someone to organize the details," Harry said.

"Talk to Felicity," Gage suggested.

I frowned. "Hazel's neighbor?" More specifically, Hazel's blue-haired, tattooed, video game–designing neighbor who rarely left her house but somehow always had her fingers on the pulse of town gossip.

Gage nodded. "Yeah. She used to design websites before she got into the gaming thing. Plus she's detail-oriented and she knows everything there is to know about this place."

There was something so *responsible* about him. For the life of me, I couldn't figure out why I found it so attractive.

I grasped the metaphorical lifeline with both hands. "Do you think she'd do it?"

The crowd around the sports court let out a raucous cheer, and we turned to watch the action. I wasn't sure what was happening, but Emilie Rump's husband, Amos, was parading Rump Roast around the court on a leash in some ceremonial sort of fashion. Someone should have been recording this for social media.

"Only one way to find out. Ask her," Gage said.

"Do you have her contact info?"

He produced his phone from his vest pocket.

I'd send her a text tonight, I decided. Or maybe I should get her email so I could explain the situation fully. It would give me more time to figure out how to entice her to say yes. I'd probably have to pay her. Which meant sharing my sliver of salary from the town, which was already earmarked for rent and other expenses. How much did a website cost? *Ugh.* I'd probably have to sell the McQueen asymmetrical midi dress I'd been holding on to for the aspirational fantasy of wearing it in New York after Hazel hit the bestseller list and sold the movie rights to her book.

Investing in my future sure was a pain in the ass to my present.

"Hey, Felicity. I'm at the bingo draft, and Zoey Moody has a question for you," Gage said.

He handed me his phone, and I blinked at it. Usually there was a standard amount of preparation I needed before making an actual phone call. I couldn't just jump into a conversation with no warning.

Gage nudged me. "Go on. She won't bite."

I put the phone to my ear and got to my feet. "Hi, Felicity. This is Zoey."

"What's up, girl?" came the chipper reply. "How's the draft going?"

I wandered a few feet away from the table so Gage and Harry wouldn't hear me flounder on the phone. "Well, Rump Roast is now off leash and roaming among the people, so I have no idea."

"He's picking the team captains."

"How does a pig—never mind. I wanted to talk to you because I don't know if you've heard about Hazel's Reader Weekend next month."

"Of course I have. Angelo's is going to give away free breadstick orders all weekend."

Had I known that and forgotten? *Shit.*

"Yeah. Great. The thing is I need a website. A place where we can list all the discounts and sales and specials for visitors as well as a schedule. Gage suggested I talk to you about it. I'm trying to come up with some pros, but it seems like mostly cons. You'd be working with me. The pay is terrible. And we need something, like, yesterday."

Speaking of Gage, I watched him casually approach Laura, who was deep in conversation with half of the Warblers. He slid his hand into his pocket and, smooth as a magician, dropped something shiny into the hood of her sweatshirt before moving on. Probably some sort of sibling prank. My sister Carla and I had a big enough age gap to ensure we never shared inside jokes. Just another symptom of my little dysfunctional family.

"Oooh. Sorry, girl," Felicity said. "I'm pushing hard on a deadline for *Cozy Core Cottage 3*. I'm basically living and breathing dopamine decor code. I wouldn't have the time to squeeze in another project unless I gave up sleep."

Rejected. This was why I didn't make spontaneous phone calls. "I totally get it. Thanks for your time," I managed to choke out over my downward spiral. Now I had to figure out how to create a website on my own in addition to everything else going on.

"No problem. Maybe next time," she offered.

"Yeah, maybe next time," I repeated and disconnected the call. I returned to Gage, trying not to let my disappointment show. Lots of people could figure out how to make a website…and fill it with content…all while continuing to be productive human adults and do things like cook dinner and change the oil in the car and pay taxes. Oh my God. Taxes. What time of year was it again?

"How'd it go?" he asked as I handed him his phone.

"Felicity's a no. But it's fine. Everything is f—"

Something solid ran into me at the knees. Gage steadied me as I looked down in surprise.

"What the hell?"

Rump Roast had his snout smushed against my leg.

"Why is his nose painted pink, and why is he putting his pink pig nose on my *very expensive jeans*?" I demanded shrilly.

The crowd around us was whistling and cheering like I'd just announced that drinks at the Fish Hook were on me. Gage was grinning down at me.

"What the hell is happening right now?" I demanded.

"Congratulations, Zoey. You're a team captain," Harry said, clapping me enthusiastically on the shoulder.

"*B-I-N-G-O*," the Story Lake Warblers sang as the audience clapped along.

If I shook my head any harder, I was going to give myself vertigo. "No no. Nope. No thank you," I said over the singing and the clapping. "I can't be a team captain. The pig is going to have to pick someone else."

"It's kind of an honor," Gage said in my ear. "You can't actually turn it down."

"An honor to have my jeans ruined by pig snout? I don't know anything about ultimate bingo! I don't have time to learn about ultimate bingo. I don't have time to do all the things I have to do now! I *hate* games. And seriously, is this water-based paint, or do I have to murder someone?"

"It's washable finger paint," Gage assured me, still looking too amused for my liking. "And being a team captain is less about knowing all the rules and more about bringing people together and leading them."

"I can't do that either! You're a lawyer. Get me out of this," I demanded.

He shrugged. "You're pretty much stuck with this."

"Congratulations, Zoey," Emilie Rump said with a noted lack of enthusiasm. "Rump Roast has never gone outside the circle of candidates to pick a captain before. It's a once-in-a-lifetime honor."

"Couldn't he honor someone else?"

Emilie's frown deepened. "Only if you enact article forty-seven of the Ultimate Bingo Rule Book."

"Let's do that. Article forty-seven me."

"Article forty-seven states that anyone can challenge the choice of ultimate bingo team captain by putting down the animal in question and substituting another."

"It's a statute from the 1930s," Gage added.

"*Putting down* like *insulting*?" I asked hopefully. Rump Roast oinked good naturedly at me. I could probably come up with a good pig insult if I had some time to think. Maybe something about his cute, floppy ears or his unfortunate moniker?

"*Putting down* like murdering my pig with your bare hands," Emilie said, narrowing her eyes to dangerous slits. "I realize that I haven't been the best neighbor recently, but the fact that you would even consider—"

"I'm not considering! No one's considering! Who came up with these rules?" I demanded shrilly.

"Dickie Dalrymple," sang the Warblers, who had gathered around me in a half circle.

"The founder of ultimate bingo. It started in the 1930s when people were more comfortable with public butchering," Gage explained.

A shadow fell over us, and I looked up to find Goose lazily circling the park.

"Is everything all right?" Darius asked, approaching with a nervous mayoral smile. He was wearing a top hat with bingo balls glued to it.

"I suggest you not enact article forty-seven," Emilie said in a steely tone.

"Uh, agreed. But I don't even know what a team captain does! I don't have time to learn." Learning the rules of a new game ranked right up there with an eight-hour plane ride next to a wet cougher for me.

"We'll be happy to teach you, Zoey," Harry said, slinging his arm around my shoulder.

Goose landed on a branch in the nearest tree and stared beady eagle eyes at us.

Gage rolled his eyes at his nephew's eagerness. "Nice try, desperado. *I'll* teach her," he said, turning to me. "Don't worry. There's a few weeks before the season officially starts. I'll have you up to speed in no time."

But Gage didn't understand that when it came to retention, I was as impossible to teach as a puppy in the middle of a parade.

"All good here?" Darius asked hopefully.

"No one is article forty-sevening my pig," Emilie insisted. She glared at me as if daring me to contradict her.

"We're goodish," I said.

Darius made a flourish with both arms like he was conducting an invisible orchestra. Goose mimicked the movement with his wings. I couldn't be sure, but it definitely looked like the bird was doing an impression of the mayor.

"Look what's happened! We have a new captain!" the Warblers cheered in harmony. The crowd roared.

Hazel came running and threw her arms around me. "Congratulations, captain!"

"No. No congratulations. I don't want to be captain," I insisted even as they guided me toward center court.

"You'll be great at this," Hazel promised, beaming like I'd won a Nobel Prize or snagged a pair of Jimmy Choos on sale.

"You need to go stand with the other team captains for the ceremony," Gage said, pointing at center court, where five other people were already standing. Each wore some kind of sash like they were in a pageant.

I was just about to protest again when the roar of an engine and screaming rock music cut me off.

Even the Warblers stopped singing, and we watched in collective shock as a convertible school bus screeched to a halt at the curb. Its original yellow paint was buried under layers of professional graffiti that spelled out DOMINION PARTY BUS. It was plastered with sponsor ads, including one for an erectile dysfunction supplement called Hardpeen.

The half door opened with a pneumatic whoosh, and a gorgeous blond in platform boots sauntered off the bus, followed by four topless men who looked as if they were all trying out for the same modeling gig of "outdoorsy hot guy." They were all shivering and trying not to look like it.

"Hello, Story Lake," she purred, peering at us over the top of sexy mirrored sunglasses.

Boos and actual hisses rolled through the gathered crowd.

Nina Vampic was a platinum blond with killer fashion sense, gorgeous skin, and the soul of the devil himself. As evil mayor of Dominion, she'd recently failed at an attempt to make Story Lake cease to exist by absorbing it into her town's border under the threat of bankruptcy. In a satisfying show of town patriotism, Hazel had shoved her ass right off the dock last summer and coined the insult *shit waffle*.

"What can I do for you, Ms. Vampic?" Darius asked, trying to sound stern.

"Shit waffle," I coughed into my hand.

"Do not antagonize her," Gage warned me.

Nina strutted over and patted Darius on his cheek. "Dear, sweet, inexperienced Darius, I just wanted you to be the first to know about our exciting new event."

"Dominion Boozetag!" barked the trying-not-to-shiver shirtless men in what I assumed were fake German accents.

"Congratulations. You can leave now, Nina," Gage said coolly.

"Why, Gage, I expected more excitement from you." She pouted prettily and slid her hands into her fur vest. It was probably real fur from adorable woodland creatures that she murdered for breakfast.

"I can't imagine why," he said.

"Nobody likes you," someone shouted from the sports court.

Rump Roast grunted in agreement. I patted the pig on the head in support of his opinion.

"You're all invited to our first ever Dominion Boozetag," she said grandly. "Competitors will construct lightweight flying vehicles and drive them off a thirty-foot platform into the lake below for a large cash prize."

"Hang on," I interrupted. "Isn't that a direct rip-off of Red Bull Flugtag?"

Her expression changed from flawless smugness to snarly defensiveness. "It's not trademark infringement if you change the name. And our Flugtag will have what, boys?" She turned to her shirtless companions.

"Booze!" they shouted.

"You want boos? We'll give you boos," someone yelled. The crowd began to boo again. I joined in with enthusiasm.

"That doesn't sound catastrophic to your insurance policy at all," Gage said dryly.

Nina sidled up to him, invading his personal space with her expensive, cloying perfume.

Oh my God. I'd forgotten that Gage had actually dated the blond villain. She sure as hell looked interested in revisiting that history. If I knew what hackles were and had them, mine would have been standing up as she laid a hand on his crossed arms.

"Okay, Cruella, let's back the hell off before I have to slap you in the face with an oversize bingo card," I said, making a move toward her.

Hazel caught me by the hood of one of my sweatshirts and dragged me back a step.

Nina gave me a frosty look. "And just who do you think you are?"

"I'm Story Lake's publicist, and your presence is bringing down the property value," I rasped, still fighting Hazel's hold on my sweatshirt as it choked me.

Nina snorted indelicately. "I wouldn't expect a backwater hovel full of uneducated hicks to know fun even if it showed up with a free Fireball fountain."

The boos intensified, and Hazel managed to pull me back a few steps.

"She's literally the worst, right? I'm not just imagining it?" I asked.

"The worst," Hazel agreed.

"She's so hot. But also just straight up evil, so that lowers the hotness factor," Harry agreed. "It's like I hate her, but I can't stop looking at her."

"You really need to get a girlfriend your own age," I told him.

"We'll look forward to you patronizing us for Dominion Boozetag. We're building an entire festival around it. No one will want to miss it." Nina's smile was feline as one of her shirtless minions unrolled a poster.

Gasps rose up from the crowd.

"You absolute shit waffle," I hissed as I read the date on the poster.

"That's Reader Weekend," Hazel hissed.

My blood boiled. Nina Vampic was threatening *my client's* book launch and terrorizing *my town*. This meant war.

"Nina, I think you should leave," Darius said.

"Nina, I think you should leave," she mimicked. "Give them their prizes, boys."

Her half-naked minions produced a T-shirt cannon and a money gun.

"I am politely requesting that you don't—" Darius's request was cut off by the first boom of the cannon.

They fired shirts and hundreds of little slips of paper into the crowd. A T-shirt bounced off Gator Johnson's grizzled face. Another one hit Junior Wallpeter in the chest. Neither of them tried to catch them. I snatched a paper off the ground. It was a coupon for discounted whiskey shots at one of Dominion's seedier bars. On the other side was a coupon for 10 percent off Bikini Night at the Beaver Dam. There was an asterisk that led to a disclaimer that the coupons were only good when the establishments were open to the public after they passed their follow-up health inspections.

"Why do these smell like beer?" I wondered out loud.

"We use special paper recycled from brewery menus because, unlike you, we're geniuses at marketing," Nina said snottily.

I wanted to take a fistful of coupons and stuff them down her throat. But that would be impulsive and probably result in a lawsuit or criminal charges. Instead, I would plot my revenge and unleash it in her dumb face when she least expected it.

"Oh, I can't wait," I said.

"To come to Boozetag when your little festival fails?" Nina asked.

"Nope." I crumpled the coupon in my fist. "To kick. Your. Ass."

Gage stepped in front of me, blocking my path to Nina's punchable face with his body. "Easy there, Disaster," he warned me.

"You go ahead and host your trademark-infringing festival," Darius said. "Story Lake's Reader Weekend *will* happen, and it *will* be a success."

I joined the aggressive applause at his statement, wishing it was Nina's stupid gorgeous face between my palms.

"We'll see about that. Who's going to care about some silly little book in some pathetic little town full of losers?"

"That's it. I'm punching the teeth out of her face," I said.

Hazel yanked my hood back as Gage blocked any forward progress.

"Just…let me…punch…face."

"God, you're cute when you're violently impulsive," Gage said, holding me back.

"You're just saying that because you want to have sex with me again."

"Much as I love the banter, let's focus on the immediate threat," Hazel suggested.

"Leave Story Lake alone, Nina," Emilie said, stepping up to join us on the front lines.

A murmur rose up around us, and I quit struggling against my captors.

"Ugh. I expected more from you, Emilie," Nina said with a roll of her eyes.

"I love this town. I thought working with you was the only way to save Story Lake. But I was wrong. I forgot just how resilient we are. We never did anything to you. You're the one who keeps going on the offensive. One of these days, it's going to *bite you in the ass*," Emilie snarled.

Rump Roast roused himself as if he'd been activated by a command and trotted menacingly toward Nina. Well, as menacing as an animal with bouncy ears and a curly tail could be.

"Oooh," crooned the crowd.

Nina ducked behind her wall of bare-chested minions. "You can't sic your farm animals on me! I'll personally sue each and every one of you into bankruptcy."

Levi Bishop materialized out of the crowd, looking annoyed. "And I'll personally fine you for every single coupon you just littered all over our lakefront. Three hundred dollars per incident, and I'm seein' at least five hundred incidents."

"Actually, it was a thousand," the minion with the money gun said.

"Shut up, Kevin," snapped Nina.

"I suggest you leave now before I cite you," Levi said.

"Fine. We're going. But you haven't seen the last of us," Nina said, turning on her heel and stalking back to the bus, her nose in the air.

"I can't believe you dated her," I said to Gage.

"Give me a break. I was nineteen and a moron. My taste has obviously improved since then."

"Can I let go of your hood to write that down, or are you still feeling punchy?" Hazel asked me.

"I will live to punch another day," I vowed as Nina and her battalion of hotties climbed back on the bus.

She locked eyes with me and raised both middle fingers defiantly.

"Someone give me a potato. Now!" I barked.

Eleven people within close proximity held up baked potatoes.

I snatched the potato out of Dr. Ace's hand. "Hey, Nina! Stay out of our town!"

"Your wr—" Gage's warning was cut off by the velocity of the potato I hurled with all my might. It landed with a wet thump against the Beaver Dam's Bikini Night bus ad, just below Nina's face. It wasn't a direct hit, but chunks of baked vegetable splattered satisfyingly over her face and fur vest.

"Ow! Worth it!" I doubled over, holding my arm to my chest.

"You forgot you broke your wrist, didn't you?" Gage asked smugly.

I punched him lightly in the leg with my good hand. "No," I lied.

"That was an excellent throw, Zoey. But medically, you really shouldn't be throwing with that hand," Dr. Ace pointed out.

Just then, Goose opened his wings and vacated the branch he was on. He swooped dramatically low over the crowd, making a beeline for the bus.

Nina screeched as the eagle sailed right for her. She threw

herself to the bus floor as he skimmed over the bus less than a foot above the seat backs. The crowd broke into applause as the bus peeled away from the curb.

"Come on, slugger. I'll get you some ice," Gage offered, slinging his arm around me and leading me toward the concession stand.

"I don't want ice. I want ice *cream*," I said stubbornly.

"I'll get you some of both. By the way, you said 'our.'"

"What?"

His grin was pure cocky confidence. "You told her to get out of 'our town.'"

Crap. "So?"

"Since you got here, it's been 'you' and 'yours.' Now it's 'ours.' I think we're growing on you," he said lightly.

"It was an us-against-them, heat-of-the-moment thing," I insisted. "I'm not about to form an allegiance to a town that allows pigs to desecrate designer jeans."

He shook his head. "I dunno, Disaster. You defended our honor with a potato. I think you like us."

"I do not," I said sullenly.

Gage's phone rang, and he answered the call. "Hey. Yeah. She's right here." He handed me the phone.

"Hello?"

"Zoey, it's Felicity. I heard what those Dominion assholes did. I'm in."

"How did you—never mind. Are you sure? The pay is really low. Like you could make more babysitting," I warned her.

"Oh, I'm doing this for free."

IntrepidReporterGuy: Story Lake citizen breaks arm potatoing Dominion mayor in public brawl over tourism.

27

Koi daddy
Gage

Audrey: Gerald is officially out of the house! Levi stopped by and made sure everything went smoothly. Thank you for everything! I think I'm starting to finally get excited about this new start.
Me: Congratulations! I told you everything was going to work out. Beers and milkshakes are on me. And remember, if he does anything that makes you uncomfortable, I want to know. I know you have concerns about a restraining order, but they exist for a reason.

"I can't believe she talked you into this," Levi grumbled as we dragged the second cooler out of the back of the truck and placed it on the ground next to the first one.

"Who?" I asked, only half listening. It was Friday, and the sun was dipping low in my backyard, signaling the end to another busy week. Nana was wriggling in the grass on her back, grunting in ecstasy. Meetcute was barking at a butterfly. Usually I'd feel a sense of satisfaction in my accomplishments, but today I was left feeling restless. And I placed the blame squarely on Zoey Moody's shoulders. For an impulsive woman, she was taking a hell of a long time to decide to let me back in her bed.

"Who?" Levi repeated. "Hell."

"What now?" Cam demanded from where he was muscling a boulder into place next to the pond skimmer.

The backyard pond I hadn't really wanted was officially in operation. According to the small frog I'd found in it this morning, it appeared to be hospitable. I'd worked on it every night after work until I was too tired to think about a certain curly-haired siren who'd cast her spell on me.

"Gigi's spaced out again," Levi complained.

Cam took his dirt-streaked shirt off and mopped his face. "It's the sex. It turns our brains against us."

I dragged off my hat and swiped a forearm over my brow. "Well, since you brought it up. Can sex be so good you change your mind about everything you want in life?"

Levi looked like I'd just asked if the Easter Bunny was real. "No."

"Yes," Cam said at the same time before punching Levi in the arm. "Then you're not doing it right."

"I do it just fine," Levi insisted before turning back to me. "What exactly did this so-called good sex make you change your mind about?"

"I'd rather have more great sex with Zoey than find the future Mrs. Bishop," I admitted.

Cam shook his head. "I told you not to fuck around. Now you're finding out."

"You're telling me that one night with her and you're ready to give up on the whole marriage-kid thing?" Levi demanded, opening the second cooler and handing out beers.

I popped the top on the bottle. "I didn't say I want to give it up. It just doesn't seem as…interesting right this second."

Cam sprawled out in the grass. "Must have been some damn good sex that I don't want to hear about," he said. "Still pissed about that, by the way. I'm your older brother. You should take my advice."

"It's hard to take a man obsessed with a raccoon seriously," I pointed out, taking a seat on a boulder next to the pond.

He raised a middle finger lazily in my direction. "Speaking of the raccoon that I'm not obsessed with, I have a new plan. I'm gonna set up a perimeter of motion detection cameras all around the house. That way, I can figure out where she's getting in."

"Sounds better than your 'all night stakeout in the garage' idea."

"That's plan B," he said.

"I'd like to clarify that I'm good at sex," Levi broke in, plopping down on the other cooler.

"Yeah, right," Cam snorted.

"Sure you are, buddy."

"Fuck you both," Levi said.

"Hey, how'd it go with Audrey and her ex?" I asked him, changing the subject.

"Fine."

"But?" I prompted.

He shrugged one shoulder. "Don't like the guy. Came in all pissed off and smelling like booze. But pulled it together when he realized I was there."

"And?"

Levi took a leisurely sip of his beer. "There were holes in the drywall in a couple of rooms. All about the same height."

"You think he was taking swings?" Cam asked.

"I asked her when he left. She insisted he'd never been violent but…"

"You don't believe her?" I pressed. I didn't like the idea that Audrey might not have felt safe enough to tell me the full truth.

"Just got a bad feeling is all," Levi said.

"I told her we could file a restraining order, but she said she wanted to keep the split as friendly as possible."

"Said the same thing to me. But nothing about that guy seems friendly," Levi said.

"We could preemptively kick his ass," Cam suggested.

"And then I'd get disbarred and Livvy would have to arrest himself," I pointed out. "I'll talk to her again about legal protection. Maybe she'll open up now that he's out of the house."

"Maybe," Levi said grimly.

We sat in silence, listening to the trickle of the waterfall and the calls of birds. My thoughts inevitably returned to their new North Star. Zoey Moody. The breeze ruffled the grass in the field, making me think of her hair. My brain was wearing ruts in itself with her being its new favorite destination. I wondered what she was doing right now and if she was thinking about me.

"Look at his stupid face," Levi said, pointing at me. "He's doing it again."

"Jesus, you're not already in love with her, are you?" Cam demanded.

I snorted. "Of course not. I only think about her as often as you think about Bertha the raccoon."

Cam couldn't rise to the bait on that one, and I congratulated myself.

Nana trotted over and nudged me with her nose, demanding attention. I ruffled her silky ears, and she gifted me with a hearty burp in the face. "Ugh. Thanks, Nan. Very ladylike."

She looked at me with love in her big dumb eyes before romping off to demand pats from Levi.

I hadn't asked my brothers to show up tonight. They just had. Because that was what our family did when there was work to be done. Trucks pulling into the driveway, unloading the beer cooler and shovels as if we hadn't already spent the better part of the day together. Two more of the Haven cottages were closing in a week, which meant we were racing the clock to finish. One of the wives had already snuck her signed Hazel Hart collection onto the bookshelf in their study. I'd taken a picture of it and sent it to Zoey. We'd been texting a lot this week. Texting and little else. I'd spent more time than I cared to admit sitting in my office, just listening to her moving around above me.

"Hazel still willing to marry you?" I asked Cam, breaking the silence.

"Long as I stay on my best behavior until the marriage license is signed," he joked.

Levi smirked. "Good luck with that."

It was a good life we'd built, I thought as I scanned the horizon. Fence lines rolled out, demarcating fields from pastures. The cows congregated on the sunny hilltop between my place and my parents'. The dogs basked in the sunshine in my backyard that, thanks to last fall's reseeding, was finally looking more like a yard and less like a dirt pit.

I was surrounded by family here. I knew my neighbors by name. The town was coming back to life like it had just finished a long, interminable winter. I wanted to build on that, to leave my mark as my parents had left theirs. I wanted to grow our family. It was something I'd always wanted. Something that I'd taken for granted would happen.

Now there was Zoey. She didn't make sense. She didn't fit neatly into the space I'd left intentionally blank. Neither did my feelings for her. Neither did the fact that I was sitting here wondering if I wanted her more than the things I had always wanted. She represented fun and flavor, light and chaos. I'd spent my life chasing security and the next logical step.

Now I couldn't stop thinking about just enjoying myself for a beat. If it was a mistake like Cam insisted, I'd at least have fun making it.

"You gonna name them?" Levi asked, nudging the other cooler with his foot.

I popped the lid and stared at the contents. Four fat koi were barely discernible in the murky green water of the sludge-infested pond they'd been rescued from. "Dunno. Do fish have personalities?"

Cam peered into the cooler. "Sure. Slimy. Disgusting. And Swampy."

"That's only three," Levi noted.

"Well, who could forget Ed?" Cam joked.

"You're worse than the kids at naming things," I observed.

"Don't listen to him, Disgusting. Gigi's just jealous that you have a fish girlfriend and he doesn't," Cam said.

"I'm not jealous of a fish. Let's get them in their new home." I put my beer down out of Nana's tail's reach and signaled for Levi to take the other handle. Together we walked the cooler to the edge of the pond. "Welcome home, guys."

We unceremoniously dumped the contents into the water.

There was a mighty splash and several flashes of color as the koi entered the water. Nana and Meetcute gathered with us and barked at the disturbance.

"You guys ever wonder why we let Mom talk us into this stuff?" I asked as we watched the fish dart around the bottom of the pond. The bright red one kept my attention as it explored the rocks and grasses with frenetic energy.

"For the same reason Hazel has me wearing ear protection when I mow the lawn and the same reason you took that fucking case when Laura asked you to. Because we love them. And love makes men do stupid, annoying things," Cam said.

"Like dig out a six-hundred-gallon pond in their backyard so you can rescue four koi from an abandoned property," Levi pointed out.

"Or represent the woman responsible for your brother-in-law's death and not tell your brothers, which I'm also still pissed about," Cam said.

"Yeah, that," Levi added.

"I'm sorry, okay? I didn't want to take it on, and I sure as hell didn't want to do it without telling you assholes. But…"

"Laura," Levi said simply.

"Yeah."

"I get it. I understand. I'm still mad," Cam said.

"I get it. I understand. I would be too," I admitted.

"How's the case you shouldn't have taken without consulting us going?" Levi asked.

Declan and I had spent most of this week wading through case law and precedents. Getting the charges dismissed was the longest of long shots at this point. But it was my job to keep Valerie out of the very place I'd hoped to put her. "Trial is set for next month. You probably know as much as I do, Chief."

"How can you do it?" Cam asked. "How can you look at her and not just see the woman who killed Miller?"

I had to stop myself from correcting him by adding *allegedly*. Instead, I watched the red koi dart under the rock ledge I'd built out near the foot of the waterfall. "I don't know. I'm just trying to remind myself she's human. She's a mom. A daughter. She's Larry's friend. She's a fucking nurse who saved lives. One minute, she was taking extra shifts to save up for a house. Now she's living in a tiny run-down two-bedroom town house, going through a divorce, and facing the possibility of missing out on the next three years of her daughters' lives. We lost more, but she lost too."

"Did she lose enough?" Levi asked, staring into the deep end of the pond.

"If Laura says so, it's good enough for me." And it was, I realized. Maybe I didn't have the warm fuzzies for Valerie, but I couldn't help but recognize her humanity now.

"Larry wants us to meet her," Cam said. "Me and Hazel."

"Me too," Levi said.

"Just try not to be dicks, okay?" I suggested. "It'll just piss off Laura."

They both grunted.

"So is Mom done punishing you for your fake chicken roost stunt?" I asked Levi. Last summer, his attempt to block our mother from saddling him with any more foster animals had come to an abrupt end when we'd discovered the coop he'd built on the back of his lakefront cabin was full of fictional chickens.

He kicked at the mound of stone I had yet to spread around the perimeter of the pond. "She's got it in her head that she wants to find the perfect retired K-9 for me."

"She always finds something worth saving," Cam said.

"Like us," I said. "Maybe we should do something nice for Mother's Day."

Levi frowned. "What do we usually do?"

I shook my head. "I order a huge bouquet of her favorite flowers and say they're from all of us."

"That's nice of us," Cam mused.

The dogs both perked up a second before erupting into barks and tearing around the back of the garage. They reappeared, jogging on either side of the UTV.

Wes and Harry came to a stop next to my truck. "Hey, uncles," Wes greeted from behind the wheel.

"Get the fish in yet?" Harry asked, sliding out to get a closer look at the pond.

Wes was the more athletic of the two. Harry had the whole curly-haired songwriter vibe going for him. Yet both somehow managed to remind me of their dad. Miller would have loved watching them grow up. I hated that he was missing out on everything that made me so fucking happy.

"Just dumped them," I said.

"What do you guys do for your mom on Mother's Day?" Cam asked.

"We take her out for breakfast at that place she likes with the gross health food and we don't complain. Then we do a family workout at the gym. And then we make her lunch, and we each present a gift to her," Wes said.

"Last year, I got her those sticky grip gloves to make pull-ups easier," Harry said.

"Why? What do you guys do for Gram?" Wes asked.

"Flowers," we mumbled.

"Flowers are…cool. What else?" Harry asked.

"Well, they're *nice* flowers," Cam said. He looked my way. "Right?"

"Yeah. They're expensive," I said, feeling defensive.

"Didn't Gram adopt all three of you together when you were split up in foster care?" Wes asked innocently.

"And didn't she miss out on her big birthday trip when you all came down with the stomach bug at the same time?" Harry pressed.

"What's your point, you little assholes?" Cam grumbled.

Harry slapped him on the shoulder. "You guys need to step up your game."

Wes nodded in agreement. "Yeah, and don't try some 'homemade card with hug coupon' bullshit either."

"Next they're going to be giving us dating advice," Levi complained.

"Speaking of dating, how did you land Zoey, Uncle Gage?" Harry asked.

"How the hell did you hear about that?" I demanded. "And why do you sound surprised? I'm awesome."

Harry and Wes shared a twin look and shrug. "I mean, you gotta admit. She's all cool and fun and you're…" Harry trailed off, looking like he'd been about to say something insulting.

"Responsible," Wes filled in quickly.

"Yeah. She just seems like she'd be into a guy with tattoos and a motorcycle and a few priors," Harry said.

"We're not dating," I said.

"So she's still single?" Harry asked with a little too much enthusiasm. "Do you think she'd be into younger guys?"

"I've been thinking about getting a tattoo," Wes said, stroking his still mostly invisible chin hair.

Levi opened his mouth, but I held up a hand.

"Neither one of you is dating Zoey. If anyone in this family is going to date her, it's gonna be me."

"Then what the hell are you doing spending your Friday night with a bunch of fish?" Harry demanded.

Cam slung his arm around me. "You see, kid. Zoey thinks your uncle is a big mistake. Just like I told him he was. But did he listen to me? No. Now he's stuck spending his Friday night with us and a bunch of fish. So the moral of the story is always listen to your uncle Cam, because I'm wise and shit."

I gave my brother a shove.

"Uncle Gage, if a woman like Zoey thought I was a mistake, I'd be out there doing every damn thing to convince her to give me another shot," Harry said earnestly.

"Yeah," Wes agreed.

Levi cleared his throat and gave them both a pointed look.

"While respecting boundaries and getting clear consent," Wes said quickly.

Harry pointed at his brother. "Yeah. That."

I blinked. Levi had had *the talk* with the boys? Levi, the brother who looked like he was in physical pain stringing together more than ten or fifteen words at a time. I glanced at Cam, who appeared to be having the same epiphany. I guessed that was how the Bishop family worked. We each played to our strengths. Cam had moved in with Laura immediately after the accident and been a stand-in father for months during her recovery. Levi modeled how to be a good man for the boys. And I started 529 plans, dealt with homework, and did impossible things when their mom asked.

We all fit. We all worked. And for a shiny spring moment, I felt just how lucky I was.

"I think we need to coach Uncle Gage on his game," Wes decided.

"*You* want to teach *me*?" I repeated.

"Yeah, man. Zoey's different from the women you usually date. You gotta surprise her, you know?" Harry said.

"Yeah, but also, like, take care of her without being all 'I'm taking care of you, little lady,'" Wes interjected with what I could only assume was his impression of toxic masculinity.

"How do you propose he do that?" Cam asked, fully amused.

"I don't know. Do something for her that she doesn't want to do for herself. Like wash her car," Harry suggested.

I'd taken her trash and recycling bins to the curb on trash day because I knew she'd forget. Did that count? Though it was less romantic and more trying to avoid a pile of garbage at my office.

"Make her realize you're not just a hot koi daddy," Wes said, gesturing at the pond.

"Hot koi daddy?" Levi repeated incredulously. He sounded like he was trying not to choke.

"Is that a real thing?" Cam asked, reaching for his phone. "I'm texting Hazel."

"Jesus," I muttered, relieved when my own phone buzzed in my pocket. I was more than relieved when I read the text. "Well, well, well. Look who Zoey just invited over tonight. You guys can clean up after yourselves. It looks like I have a date."

I strolled toward the back door to their applause.

Zoey: Help! My sink is leaking!

28

A sexy warlock

Zoey

I adjusted my robe, gave my hair one last fluff, and threw open the front door.

Gage was standing there holding a bottle of wine in one hand and a tool tote in the other. He looked me up and down, gaze lingering in all the right lingerie-clad places.

"I'm begging you. Please tell me there's no leak," he said finally.

I felt really, really good about popping on the black lace corset set I'd found on clearance at Sunita's boutique. "I may have just forgotten to turn the faucet all the way off," I purred, tracing my fingers up his chest. "I thought that maybe you'd want to…talk."

Gage walked right into me, backing me up a few steps. He dropped the wine and the tote on the rug and kicked the door shut. "Disco. Admit this is a booty call."

I twirled a curl around my finger. "We're too old to use that phrase."

"You're stalling," he said, spinning us around and backing me against the door.

"What makes you think I called you over here to have sex?" I asked, all innocence.

"The fact that you're doing yoga in lingerie," he said, tilting his head to the yoga mat I had rolled out in the living room.

"I've developed a debilitating fear of sports bras."

He reached out, his callused hand skimming over my stomach, thumb under my breast. My nipples immediately and proudly announced their excitement through the barely existent fabric.

His hum of approval had my breasts going heavy and kick-started an empty throb deep in my core.

It wasn't fair. I'd always felt in charge when it came to sex. But Gage Bishop made me feel like my best and only option was to submit to him and hang on tight.

"I think we'll get started right here," he said.

"Here?" I pouted prettily for him. "You don't want to maybe check for leaks in the bedroom?"

"I'd hate to interrupt your workout." He pulled me off the door and walked me backward, fingers barely skimming my hips, until I was standing on my exercise mat.

"Okay fine. I called you here for sex," I announced.

His mouth quirked, and he rewarded me by cupping my achy breasts in those magical hands. His thumbs brushed over my nipples, and I went weak in the knees.

"Thank God," he murmured as his mouth moved over mine.

The kiss took my breath away, and several brain cells went with it. It was hot, hard, and entirely possessive.

He pulled back ever so slightly as I clung to him. "If it weren't incredibly inappropriate, I'd send my nephews a victory text right now."

"What do your nephews have to do with this?"

"They both want to date you. They literally just asked if you were into younger guys. I told them to keep their grubby, hormonal hands to themselves, and then they tried to give me a lesson on how to be more attractive to you."

My hand found his erection behind his zipper, and I gave

it a squeeze. "I find you attractive enough without you having to work for it."

"What made you change your mind?" he asked, slipping my robe from my shoulders.

"I didn't. I wanted to jump right back into bed with you from the second I left. I just wanted to make sure."

"Took you long enough," he said.

"Wait." I stopped him when he moved in for the kill.

"What? Is there actually a leak?"

"No. There's just something you need to know. Well, you don't need to know, given our agreement. But I feel like you should know."

"Baby, you better tell me now while I still have some blood flow to the brain," he suggested.

The man was fully hard, yet he was willing to hit pause and have a conversation with me. I appreciated that.

"Let's sit," I suggested, leading him to the couch.

"What's going on?" he asked when we were settled.

"This is just sex."

"Actually, this is just talking. I'll let you know when it's sex," he countered.

I hit him with a pink, furry pillow. "I mean, just because I've decided to extend our one-night stand into a multiple-night stand, I don't want you to be getting any ideas or feelings."

He reached out and tugged on a curl. "You're adorable when you're trying to protect me."

I batted his hand away. "I'm serious. You can't start to catch feelings or whatever for me, because I can't give you what you want. I don't want you to get hypnotized by orgasms and start to have these romantic fantasies about wifing me up."

"Zoey, I'm an adult man. You don't need to manage my expectations for me. Tell me."

"I can't have kids."

I blurted out the announcement and let it hang in the air between us like an ill-timed fart. Gage was still. Too still. I launched myself off the couch and paced the length of the rug.

"So it's not a big deal. I found out in college. It's basically a structural problem. I'm fine with it. Totally fine," I insisted. "I mean, it's better to know ahead of time before I meet someone, fall in love, and get my hopes up or their hopes up. Right? Which is why I'm telling you. Not that we were going to fall in love or whatever, because we already agreed not to do something stupid like that. But I just thought it was something that you should know. You know?"

I sucked in a breath and willed myself to shut the fuck up. The silence hung heavily between us.

"Okay. Please say something. Maybe compliment my boobs? Or at least tell me if I ruined the booty call."

His fingers drummed out a beat on his thighs. "Just give me a minute. I'm processing."

I gave him nearly ten whole seconds. "Have you processed yet?" I'd been here before, and I'd survived it. I could do it again, I reminded myself.

"How about you tell me the whole story?" he suggested.

"Really? I kinda felt like the bottom line was enough."

He snagged my good hand and tugged me into his lap. I sat rigidly like a reluctant kid on a department store Santa's knee. "Disco," he said.

"Ugh. Fine. I was in college. I thought I was in love." I toyed with one of the closures on my wrist brace.

"Sam," Gage prompted.

I was surprised he'd remembered the name of the guy who had broken my heart. "Yes. Sam. I don't come from a very affectionate or attentive family, and when I met Sam, it was like he was everything I'd been missing out on. We got serious fast, and things were good…until I forgot to take a few birth control pills. I didn't even notice my period was late until the pain started. Long story short, I had an ovarian torsion caused by a cyst rupturing."

"That sounds…painful," he said.

"It was pretty horrible. I had to have surgery and a bunch of tests. That's when I found out. Honestly, I hadn't even thought about having kids. I was twenty years old. I was just trying to pass my business classes. Sam, however, had his whole life mapped out in front of him. And that life included kids and a wife who was responsible enough to notice when her period was late. We broke up. And I made peace with the fact that I wasn't going to have everyone else's happily ever after."

"I'm sorry that you had that choice taken away from you," Gage said, gently stroking my back.

"It's really not a big deal. I mean, can you imagine me being responsible for other human beings?" I joked.

Sure, maybe at first, the young me had grieved the loss of something I hadn't even thought about wanting yet. And maybe that "deficiency" had added to the shame I'd already felt for never being good enough. But I'd made peace with it. I'd built a life that brought me joy in other ways. And now that I knew most of my mistakes had an explanation, a reason, that had nothing to do with laziness or stupidity, I'd been feeling pretty damn good about my life.

"Yes. I can. And you'd be great," he said.

"Ha. Right."

"I'm serious, Zoey. Kids don't just need vegetables and pick-ups and drop-offs. They need champions. They need creativity and confidence. They need someone who'll be in their corner no matter what. That's you. So I'm sorry you didn't get the choice, because you'd be fucking great at it."

"Thanks," I said quietly.

Gage gave me an affectionate squeeze. "Thank you for telling me…even though it was because you were afraid I was too stupid to listen to you when you said you didn't want anything serious."

"To be fair, I didn't think you were *stupid*. I was concerned you were falling under the spell of my vagina."

"It's a pretty irresistible spell."

I looped my arms around his neck, managing to remove only one layer of his skin with the Velcro on my brace. "So now that you know that I definitely can't be the woman to give you the future you want, still wanna fix my leak?"

"I'm going to need you to state for the record that there is in fact no leak," Gage said, standing up with me still in his arms. The show of strength had the predicted effect on my arousal.

"No leak. Promise," I said breathlessly as he lowered us to the floor.

"Thank fucking God." Gage arranged me over him so I was straddling his hips. He was already hard and I was already wet, a heady combination.

"We should go slow," he said, lifting his head and sucking one nipple through the lace of my flimsy top.

"Nope."

He growled in response. "Hold it for me."

Now *this* was an order I didn't mind following. I cupped my breast awkwardly with my braced hand, hoping it at least looked sexy, and offered it up eagerly like a sacrifice.

The rumble in his chest sounded like approval to me. He used his mouth on me, saturating the material with his tongue while he pressed me closer with one hand at my back. His other hand toyed with my as-yet-ungreeted nipple.

Moaning in delight, I gave a testing thrust of my hips, which brought my thong-clad clit in contact with Gage's erection.

We both groaned. He shifted his attention to my other nipple, repeating the hard, wet pulls through the fabric. Every tug at the tender peak was echoed deep in my center.

"You're gonna ride me, sweetheart, and then I'm gonna ride you." His voice was a gravelly rasp.

"Good plan," I said as a delicious shiver worked its way up my spine.

Gage went back to my breast while his fingers busied themselves at my thong. In no time at all, he'd pulled the fabric covering my crotch to the side and freed his cock. "Condom?"

The two wet spots against my nipples were driving me crazy. And my vagina was straight up begging now. I could barely think straight.

"I have some in the bedroom. But I have a clean bill of health, and I can't get pregnant. Sooo…"

His eyes glittered beneath his lashes. "Say it."

I bit my lip. Why was it so scary to admit? "I don't want anything between us. I want to feel it all. But I'll understand if it's too irresponsible," I added quickly.

I definitely wasn't thinking. I wasn't even breathing. Not with the crown of his erection leaking precome an inch from my bare sex.

"If you're sure, I'm sure," he said.

"Really?"

He kissed me then. Long and deep. Each thrust of his tongue a promise. "Really," he said finally.

"Oh thank God. Fuck me, Gage."

I didn't have to ask him twice. With one arm wrapped around my waist, he guided me down onto his cock so slowly it felt like the sweetest of tortures as he penetrated me.

"Gah!" I gasped. If our first time had been heaven, this time was the apocalypse. I wasn't going to survive, and I didn't give a damn.

"Fuck," he murmured roughly as my wet channel took him deeper.

My brain ceased to function. I was only a body with one goal: orgasm before I died from pleasure. I made a move to rise onto my knees, but he gripped my hips.

"Slow," he ordered.

I scoffed. "Pfft. Yeah okay." I had no intention of following that command and he knew it, but I'd at least let us both pretend for a second or two. When I got to his tip, I hovered there for a moment before gliding back down, taking more of him this time. My core was already pulsing hungrily around him. I lifted again, loving the slick slide of his shaft.

I was in love with the feeling of taking Gage Bishop as deep as he could go.

His control unraveled as my inner walls gripped his cock. He yanked down the neck of my top, exposing one breast and closing his mouth around the nipple to feast. He sucked hard, and the sensation on my already sensitive flesh unleashed my need for more. I slammed down on him, impaling myself until I could feel that blunt heat meet the end of me.

"Goddammit, Zoey. Slow the fuck down."

But I was already lost, riding him like I was charging into battle. Hard and violent. He wrapped his arms around me and adjusted the angle, thrusting his hips to meet me.

"Oh God, Gage. You feel so fucking good," I murmured. Every drive had him nudging some sweet spot inside me, and I was afraid it was going to make me come apart. But it was too late to stop. I'd lit the fuse, and now the only thing I could do was hold on for dear life.

"Ride me like a good girl. Harder."

I followed his cues and let biology take over. I slammed down on him over and over again, each time getting that magnetic nudge deep inside me. "It's too much," I whispered.

"Finish what you start," he said, cupping the back of my neck and holding me to him.

His arm tightened at my back, urging me down harder and harder, everything inside me coiling tighter and tighter until it broke. I came…or detonated. I'm not sure which. Each wave shook me to my core as pleasure electrified me.

Gage let out a guttural groan, and I wondered if it was possible that my vagina's stranglehold was hurting him. But I was too busy coming to apologize. The tremors were still racking my body when Gage flipped me over on my hands and knees. More gently, he grasped my elbow above my wrist brace and stretched my arm onto the couch cushion.

"Don't put weight on this," he said while stripping me of my thong and freeing my breasts.

He angled me ever so slightly to the right.

When I looked up, I caught sight of us in the mirror I had propped up in the corner. Gage was behind me, yanking his shirt over his head, me with my thong down my thighs, breasts out, eager to be fucked. He'd done it on purpose, I realized when his eyes met mine in the reflection. There was a deliciously wicked gleam in those green eyes when he lined himself up with my entrance.

I'd just had the orgasm of a lifetime, and I couldn't wait for him to be inside me again. What weird good-guy spell did he have me under? How had I ever thought I could survive this fling? I'd underestimated him…and his spectacular penis.

He slid a hand up my back and gripped my shoulder.

I pressed back into him, telling him with my body that I was ready.

"Tell me to stop if I hurt you," he said on a rasp, and then he rammed himself into me to the hilt.

I cried out, needing to release the sound to make room for his invasion.

"Too much?" he asked through clenched teeth.

I met his eyes in the mirror. "Again," I demanded.

I watched him fuck me from behind. Abs rippling, biceps bulging. His sweat-soaked skin sliding over mine. His thrusts were merciless. My breasts bounced every time he bottomed out in me. And he didn't miss a second of the tableau we made, keeping his gaze riveted on our reflection.

I bowed my back and began meeting his thrusts. He powered into me again, and my arms gave out. I dropped to my forearms, angling to accommodate his mad drives. One hand left my hips, and I watched him draw it back and let it fly, landing a stinging swat to my rear end.

I let out a breathy little moan of delight. Gage Bishop was full of naughty surprises.

His hands were on the move again. One found my breast and tugged rhythmically on my tender peak. The other slipped between my legs to find the swollen nerve that controlled my existence. His thrusts were punishing, but the pads of his fingers exerted the perfect amount of pressure in exactly the right direction. His heavy sack slapped the backs of my thighs every time he slammed into me.

I sobbed out his name and felt his cock swell impossibly bigger inside me.

"Come for me, Zoey. Milk my cock with those tight little squeezes."

I was about to inform him that women didn't just spontaneously orgasm when ordered to, but I was interrupted by a surprise shattering release. I pitched forward, collapsing against the couch as I convulsed in catastrophic pleasure.

Behind me, Gage gave a triumphant shout, and I felt the first hot spurt of his release in my very depths. I quivered around him, my orgasm becoming his, the clenching ripples from my core forcing his climax to go on and on as he branded me from the inside.

Neither one of us took our eyes off our reflection.

"Well, that was…something," I mused several minutes later when I managed to peel my face off my yoga mat where we'd collapsed.

Gage grunted. He was still behind me, still inside me, still half-hard, because the man was obviously inhuman. We were a sweaty, sated tangle of limbs on the floor.

"Are you a sexy warlock?" I wondered.

His laugh was hot breath on my skin. "I think you're going to have to back up a few steps so I can follow you."

"Oh. Yeah. Forgot to take you with me. I was thinking you were obviously inhuman because you're still hard."

"Obviously," he teased dryly.

"So that means you're paranormal. I couldn't decide between vampire or warlock. Vampires are sexy, but they're cold, and you're clearly an inferno. And I'm definitely under your spell. So warlock it is."

"Your mind is a wonder," he said. On a reluctant sigh, he pulled out of me and then rearranged us so I was wrapped in his arms, my head on his chest. "If you freak out about cuddling and try to run away, I'm going to be pissed."

"Too exhausted from orgasms to run away," I murmured against his very nice pectoral.

"So that's the secret? Just tire you out?"

I shrugged. "You still have to deal with me when I wake

up. Are you hungry?" I asked, circling his nipple with my index finger.

He covered my hand with his own. "Starving. I want to eat on the floor and watch TV until I have control over my body again."

"I have no food or cable."

He groaned, then shifted me off him.

"Where are you going?"

"*We're* going to my house. Nana needs her dinner. And I have actual human food in the fridge. Bring your laundry. I assume you have a mountain of it. Might as well get it done."

"And just like that, you got even sexier. You're so bad at this one-night-stand thing."

"We'll just have to keep trying until I get it right."

29

You ridiculously practical sex god

Gage

"Jesus, Disaster. When's the last time you did laundry?" I asked, wrestling the overflowing basket out of the back seat.

Zoey shrugged from the other side of the SUV and grabbed her overnight bag. "Hey, it could be worse. I've sold, like, half my wardrobe online since moving here."

"Guess you didn't need that big closet," I said, leading the way through the garage's side door out into the driveway.

"Don't you dare touch my closet space. I fully plan to become successful enough to eventually start buying clothes again."

Nana was doing her "Where have you been? I'm hungry" bark inside the mudroom. There was a soft thump, and her blond head and front paws appeared in the glass.

"You know, for a dog, she's pretty cute," Zoey said as we trudged up the porch steps.

"Less conversation, more paying attention so you don't fall and break another wrist," I reminded her as I opened the side door.

Nana greeted us as if we'd been lost at sea for a decade, wiggling and whimpering, whipping our legs with her tail.

"Yes, hello, pretty girl," Zoey said, giving the dog a resounding chest thump with her good hand.

"You can feed her while I get started on Mount Laundry here. One scoop in that bowl, and make sure she's got fresh water," I said, gesturing at Nana's dishes in the open cabinet I'd designed specifically for feeding a sloppy dog.

Zoey put her overnight bag on the island and toed off her shoes. "Come on, you big silly hair ball. You must be starving."

Nana pranced over and helpfully picked up her food dish in her mouth. Clearly worried about subtlety, the dog bashed the metal dish into Zoey's shins.

"Ow," Zoey responded dryly. "Give me that."

I let them wrestle their way through dog dinner while I started the first load of laundry, tossing in a few pieces of my own.

My phone vibrated on the counter, and I saw a text from Mom.

> **Mom:** Can you do me a teeny tiny favor because I never ask anything from you?
> **Me:** The record reflects otherwise. What do you need?
> **Mom:** Can you put the animals in the barn and feed them? We've been invited to Laura's for dessert...to officially meet Valerie.
> **Me:** Zoey's with me. But since I'm your favorite son and overflowing with magnanimity, I will grant you this favor.
> **Mom:** Interesting. Do you youths have a term for a two-night stand?
> **Me:** It's called Nunyabizness.
> **Mom:** Just don't let her break any more bones.
> **Me:** Don't commit any crimes at Laura's. I have enough cases on my plate right now.

I put the phone back on the counter and found Zoey trying to mop up Nana's water bowl flood.

"Let's go, ladies. We have some chores to do before dinner."

Zoey gasped and paused her dramatic toweling of Nana's face. "Did you lure me out here under the false pretense of free laundry to put me to work?"

"And for more sex."

"Thank God."

"Fart Blaster 2000, you have to stop leaning on the gate," Zoey complained. She was wearing an old pair of my mother's field boots and one of my most ancient sweatshirts. Her curls were exploding out of the knot she'd pulled them into on top of her head.

"She'll stop leaning if you stop scratching her ears," I said, shooing the rest of the cows across the drive and into the barn's paddock.

"Gage says I have to stop petting you," she said in a stage whisper made all the more comical by the miniature donkey with his head shoved under her arm.

Pepe was usually a pain in the ass to put in the barn at night, but with his human girlfriend here, I had a feeling we were going to be able to march him right into his stall.

"All the feed in the right bins?" I called to her. I'd had her do the feed while I closed the chickens back into their coop and tempted the alpacas into the barn while doing my best not to get spit on.

Fart Blaster heaved a sigh and clomped across the drive, through the paddock, and directly into the pen inside the barn.

"Okay, bring your boyfriend," I said, manning the paddock gate.

Zoey strolled over with the donkey at her heels.

"Put him in that last stall on the right," I said as I swung the gate closed. I managed to get a quick picture of woman and donkey from behind as they entered the barn together and shook my head at the irony of a woman afraid of animals turning out to be Dr. Dolittle.

Inside, I found Zoey and Nana outside Pepe's stall, wishing him a good night. All around me, animals who had come from vastly different circumstances bellied up to tubs and troughs in their secure stalls.

"Please tell me you're going to feed me now," she said, turning to face me. "I'm starving after all that…'yoga.'"

I crooked my finger, and she sauntered my way with Nana shadowing her every move. "For someone who doesn't like animals, you're pretty comfortable in a barn full of them."

"I blame this town for desensitizing me. Everywhere I turn, there's a sheep or a raccoon or a pig just roaming around like a tax-paying homeowner with kids on the honor roll."

"I'm proud of you for adapting." I slung my arm around her shoulders and led her back out into the spring evening.

"I mean, it's not *that* different from facing down small armies of pigeons and rats," she joked.

We drove back to my house in the dark on the bumpy farm lane that connected my property with my parents'. Nana fell asleep with her head on the center console and her feet on the floor of the back seat. Dog radar woke her with a start when my headlights caught the house.

"What's for dinner?" Zoey asked, holding the mudroom door for Nana, who catapulted herself past us.

"How do you feel about appropriately portioned chicken parm or steak tips with peppers and onions?" I asked, making quick work of switching the first load of laundry to the dryer and adding the second to the washer.

"I knew it! You're definitely inhuman."

"Because I have food?" I flicked on the lights in the kitchen, and she followed me in. Zoey let out a groan when she spotted my meal prep fixings on the counter.

"You don't have food. You have groceries. First the perma erection, now the meal prepping. Real humans don't do that. Influencers pretend to meal prep to get sponsors. No one has time to cook one meal, let alone a week's worth," Zoey explained.

"This whole thing could have been avoided if you had food at your place," I reminded her.

"Note to self. Stock up on frozen pizza."

I patted her on the head as she plopped morosely onto a barstool and poked at a bag of rice. "Would wine and a snack make you feel better?" I offered.

She perked back up. "You have my attention, sir."

I poured her a glass of rosé and uncovered a small cheese and meat tray from the fridge.

"You knew I was going to end up back here this weekend, didn't you?" she said, pointing at me with an accusatory slice of ring bologna as I opened a box of crackers.

"I hoped you'd come back. So I planned ahead."

She peered at me over a thin slice of cheddar. "What other plans will I find if I poke around?"

"Besides the wine you're drinking?" I asked, washing my hands at the sink. "Guess you'll just have to wait and see. Now get over here so we can get dinner started."

She turned on "cooking music," which seemed to trend heavily toward bubbly pop hits from the last twenty years. Nana trotted into the kitchen, favorite stuffed alligator in her mouth, to settle under the dining room table. We worked in tandem with me supervising Zoey's kitchen deficiencies. While I seared the steaks, she breaded the chicken breasts. I refused to let her near anything sharper than a butter knife, so she was in charge of making the rice while I sliced all the veggies. Together we topped the breaded chicken with sauce and mozzarella.

"I wonder if I could do this for some kind of breakfast," Zoey wondered as she tossed all the salad ingredients into a bowl. "I'm supposed to start my days with protein to keep my brain from imploding or whatever the medicine says."

"What do you usually eat for breakfast? Everything has a high-protein version."

She wrinkled her nose and gave the salad a violent toss that had broccoli and lettuce flying everywhere. "I don't really do breakfast. Only when I'm with Hazel, so then it's usually exploded microwave oatmeal," she explained, scraping up the escapees and dumping them back in the bowl.

I skirted around her, hand skimming her lower back as I reached into a cabinet for another dish. I liked having her here in my space. While I usually enjoyed the quiet of my house, having a bit of her color and chaos was a nice change of pace.

"You don't eat breakfast. You forget lunch. So you snack on dry cereal in the middle of the afternoon. What do you do for dinner?" I asked.

"Go out or order to-go stuff when I realize I'm dying of starvation," she said cheerfully as she shook her ass to the beat of Outkast's "Hey Ya!" playing on the wireless speaker.

I made a mental note to double all my meal prep recipes for the foreseeable future.

"I can hear you judging me over there," she teased as I ran the knife through the last steak. I felt her hands at my waist as she peered around me, then snatched the dish towel from the counter next to me.

"I'll try to judge quieter next time. Chicken or steak?" I asked, holding up a container of each.

"Mmm, steak. That 'yoga' earlier made me hungry for red meat," she said, making grabby hands at me.

"Favorite condiments?" I asked.

"I can already feel your judgment, but I'll tell you anyway. Ranch dressing and A.1."

"More wine?" I offered as I pulled a beer from the fridge.

She looked up from the pool of steak sauce she was drowning her meat in. "I'm good."

Normally, I would have cleaned the kitchen, put away all the prepped food, then eaten. But Zoey looked like she was about to start chewing on her own arm.

I poured her a glass of water and handed it over. "Dining room table or here at the island?"

Zoey pursed her lips in thought. "Couch."

I didn't eat on my couch. Not that there was anything wrong with that. But wasn't that why tables had been invented? When

I was in a hurry, I'd eat standing up over the sink. But I didn't take entrées with fucking marinara sauce into the living room where who the hell knows what might happen. At least I hadn't until tonight.

"Couch and TV," she said, giving my arm a tug and bouncing on her toes. "Come on!"

I paused to grab utensils and an entire roll of paper towels, then followed her past my perfectly good dining table and into the living room. Nana joined us and body-slammed herself onto the dog bed in front of the coffee table.

It felt like a dance back and forth between the intimacy we'd created through sex and actually getting to know each other. I was working backward with Zoey. Usually I knew things like what a woman's goals were and what her favorite dessert was before we had sex.

"What's your middle name?" I asked as we settled into spots on the couch.

"Berniece. After an aunt nobody liked." She tucked her feet up under her and wriggled back against the cushions. "You need food pillows," she observed with a frown.

"What the hell is a food pillow?"

"It's a small pillow that fits in your lap. You put your plate on it." She demonstrated with a beige cushion. "But it should be a dark color so the food stains don't show." I stared at her dumbly, and she grinned. "I am really breaking your brain right now, aren't I?"

"I'm trying to open myself to new experiences," I said evenly as I watched her Pyrex container list dangerously to the side.

"Well, you're doing it wrong. First of all, you need to put your feet up." Zoey deposited her dinner on the coffee table with only a few splatters escaping onto the wood. "Here."

She grabbed one of the denser pillows and put it on top of the coffee table. Then she dragged it closer to the couch.

"Put your feet up here," she said, patting the pillow.

I rolled my eyes but did as she instructed.

"Good. Now we just need to build you a little nest," she said, stuffing pillows up against both of my sides and adding another one to my lap. "See? It's like you're being hugged by your couch."

She wasn't wrong. Had I been sitting on furniture incorrectly all this time? What else could this woman teach me?

She took a step back and observed before nodding her approval. "You need more throw pillows for this to work. And some blankets. I need a blanket for TV time."

"If you're cold, I can turn the heat up," I offered as she handed me my dinner.

"Gage, Gage, Gage, you ridiculously practical sex god. Blankets aren't about being cold. They're about being *cozy*."

"How silly of me."

She returned to her corner of the couch and angled herself so that her legs stretched out in my direction. "That's better. Now, how do we fight it out for remote control domination?"

"You're the guest. You get control," I said, handing her the remote.

"I was pretty sure you were going to say that, so we're definitely watching *New Girl* reruns."

"'Reruns' as in you've already watched it?"

"I can't watch new TV when I eat. I need to focus on my food," she said as if it were the most logical statement to make.

"Of course you do."

She expertly scrolled through my TV apps and my lists. "Hmm, a lot of documentaries in here," she noted. "What do you watch for fun?"

I gestured at the TV. "Documentaries."

She swiveled her head in my direction and let out a heavy sigh. "We have so much work to do here. You can't unwind after a long, emotional week with *Greed Stricken: The Story of How an American Billionaire Destroyed Thousands*."

"It's educational, okay?"

She gave me a thumbs-down and made a fart noise with her mouth that had the dog's head poking up over the coffee table. "I'm starting to think you need me for more than just kick-ass sex."

I was starting to think the same. But it was the weekend, and I would worry about that later.

We ate and watched her show, which was admittedly more entertaining than the docuseries on European pirates that had been my evening entertainment for the week. Then she handed the remote back and demanded we watch something I liked to watch, so we sat through a new upload from a farm I followed on YouTube. Zoey, to her credit, survived the twenty-eight minutes on tractor repair without complaint.

"Tell me something about you," I said when the video ended.

She tapped her chin theatrically. "Well, I really enjoy your penis."

I hit her in the chest with my food pillow. "Tell me something I don't know."

"What do you want me to say? You already know a lot. You know what I do for a living, who my best friend is, what my favorite wine is, why I'm afraid of dogs. And you're one of, like, three people in the entire world who knows I'm on a new prescription that gives me hope for the first time in my life but also makes me feel like some kind of amateur drug dealer from a made-for-TV movie when I try to fill it. What more do you want?"

I searched my brain. "When do you fill your gas tank? And please don't say after you run out."

She laughed and kicked my thigh with her bare foot. I captured it with my hand and pressed my thumb into the arch. Her laugh turned to a purr.

"You're not going to believe this, but I panic fill it when it hits three-quarters of a tank. I went on this summer road trip with a few friends in college. At the time, I was the only one with a driver's license. I ran out of gas *three* times because I kept forgetting to check the gauge. By the time we made it to the Outer Banks, no one but Hazel was speaking to me. I was scarred for life."

"Are all your stories so damn sad?" I asked.

She wriggled her toes in my grip. "They used to make me sad too. But now I know there was a reason for most of it, and that helps a lot. And no. They're not *all* sad. I once broke onto the Rockefeller Center ice rink at three o'clock in the morning and drank champagne straight from the bottle while skating."

"You can ice-skate?"

"Not well. But I was fast enough to evade the security guard. My turn to ask you something. You're a lawyer and a contractor. You could work anywhere in either of those professions. Did you ever want to move away from here, have your own life?"

"I wish I could say yes, because that would be more interesting. But I loved this place from the first moment I saw it. I was pretty young when I came here. But one thing I do remember is pulling up to Bishop Farm on a spring evening with the sun setting over the fields. There was a bright red tractor sitting in front of the barn, and I asked the social worker if this was heaven."

"Jeez, Gage," she choked, fanning her hands in front of her misty eyes. "Now who's the one with the emotional stories?"

I squeezed her foot and grinned. "I've loved Story Lake from the first second I saw it. It's like I recognized it. One look, and I just knew it was home."

"As you know, I had a very different first impression. Have you ever felt that way about anything else? Like you just see it and you know it's meant for you?" she asked.

I thought back to that day, that roof, all those copper curls.

"Not sure," I evaded. "What's your favorite color?"

She screwed up her face in thought. "It would have to be purple. Like an amethyst. You?"

"Green."

"Yeah but what kind of green? Puke green? Slime green? Mold green?"

"What shade of green would you say your eyes are?" I asked.

Those emerald eyes heated with fire, and then she was sliding her foot from my grasp and crawling across the couch to me.

"That was very, very smooth." She said it like an accusation as she straddled my lap.

My hands found her hips as if they had a mind of their own. "We should probably…talk."

She linked her hands behind my neck. "What do you want to talk about?"

"Sex. I mean, us. Having sex. More sex." She was short-circuiting my brain, and I liked it.

"I'm happy to talk about us having sex."

"What else are we doing? Besides sex, I mean."

"Having dinner?" she offered. "Doing laundry?"

"I know you don't want to date, Zo. And I respect that. But I also don't want either of us to be doing this with other people right now."

"Hmm, monogamous casual sex," she mused wickedly. "I guess that would be convenient."

She was shifting her hips, rocking against me in a slow, logic-destroying rhythm. "I'm all about convenience," I said through gritted teeth.

She ceased her motions and grinned. "No, you're not. You're about plans, calculations, next steps. You have concerns. What are they?"

"How long are we doing this? Do we go out in public? Or do we sneak around? What do we tell people when they ask about us? Will you spend the night, or are you going to be sneaking out and breaking bones every time the sun comes up?"

"Have you ever once played anything by ear?" she teased.

Thinking with the warm, willing Zoey in my lap was nearly impossible. "Last week, I didn't feel like eating the turkey burger I'd planned on so I made up an excuse to stop by my parents' at dinnertime so they'd have to feed me," I confessed.

"You're adorable."

I frowned as I tucked a loose curl behind her ear. "I don't think that's generally considered a compliment for men, Berniece."

Her grin went through me like warm honey.

"I bet you'll take great care of a wife someday," she whispered.

"I'll take great care of you right now," I promised. And then her mouth was on mine, and every concern I had went right out of my mind.

30

Skunk stank
Zoey

I woke up to hot, horrible breath on my face. "Jesus, Gage. Don't you own a toothbrush?" I groaned, burying my head under the pillow.

"It's not me," he grumbled from behind me. His face was in my hair, one of his arms heavy around my waist, pinning me in place.

The hot breath tunneled under my protective, downy helmet, and then a cold wet nose found my face.

"Damn it, Nana."

She gave a yip of delight at her name and slithered the rest of the way onto the bed until she was lying completely on top of me.

"This is why I don't have a dog. Pillows can't try to murder you in the middle of the night."

Gage yawned. "It's not the middle of the night. It's six in the morning."

"Like I said. The middle of the night."

"She just wants out and her breakfast."

A tongue slurped up the side of my face on the word *breakfast*.

"If we give in to her demands, will she let us go back to bed?"

"She'll pass out for an hour at least," he promised.

"Ugh. Fine. I'll let her out. You make her breakfast." I found Gage's discarded T-shirt neatly folded on the chair next to his dresser and pulled it over my head. "Come on, you furry terrorist."

Nana vaulted off the bed and nearly knocked me on my ass on her way to the door.

Muttering several uncomplimentary things under my breath, I shuffled through the house into the mudroom where I dragged on Gage's boots and then clomped out the door. "Go pee," I ordered sternly.

Nana pranced down the stairs like the star of a commercial for spring-scented laundry detergent.

There was a chill to the air, but the sunrise was annoyingly spectacular as it kissed the horizon with oranges and pinks. Mourning doves cooed their greetings as Nana charged over the dew-speckled grass. I followed her around the back of the house and admired the new koi pond while the dog did her business. I didn't know if Gage cleaned up after her like dog owners in the city did but decided that was a future him problem.

A black-and-white fish swam a steady path around the pond's perimeter while a more energetic red koi dashed in and out around it. Far above, a small airplane cut a path through the sky.

It was beautiful here. I had to give Story Lake that.

Nana gave a distant, happy bark. It sounded suspiciously like her "hello, new friend" bark, and I whirled around to spot her disappearing around the back of the garage after something black-and-white and waddly. A cat, I guessed.

"Nana!" I yelled, clapping my hands. "Leave the kitty alone."

I started to cut across the lawn when Nana's startled yelp rang out. It was blotted out by the ear-ringing hee-haw of Pepe, who charged over the pasture hill, racing in our direction.

Did cats attack dogs? I'd assumed that all Pep and Frank's animals were friendly. How much damage could a cat do? I was already running as fast as Gage's oversize boots would allow when the side door flew open and a barefoot, shirtless Gage sprinted out.

"Don't fall and break anything," I yelled over my shoulder at him as he took the stairs in a single leap. His long legs ate up the distance between us, and he was in front of me before I even made it to the garage. I turned the corner and rammed into his stationary back. I accidentally braced myself with my bad arm and let out a yelp of my own when pain seared through my wrist.

"Fuck my life," Gage seethed.

"What's wrong? Did the cat hurt her?" I asked, trying to peer around his wall of muscle.

"That's not a cat," Gage said as the seemingly unscathed Nana ran up to us.

I bent down to check her for cat-related injuries when Gage stopped me.

"You're not gonna want to touch that."

"Why n—oh my holy rotten garbage. What is that smell?" I demanded, clamping a hand over my nose and mouth.

"Skunk."

"You have *got* to be kidding me," I said, then gagged when the smell made its way into my mouth. My only life experience with skunks came from the adorable, flirtatious cartoon versions. The thing that made this smell was something sulfuric and straight out of hell.

Nana threw herself against my legs, and I gagged again.

"Her fur is wet."

"So much for lazy morning sex," Gage said, hooking his fingers under Nana's collar. "How do you feel about dish soap and hydrogen peroxide?"

"That sounds like the worst breakfast cocktail in the world," I complained as he dragged Nana toward the house.

The skunk menacingly waddled a few steps closer in my direction, and my eyes went wide in abject horror. How could something so cute be so disgusting? Pepe brayed excitedly from the fence, his dainty hooves pawing at the ground. The skunk took another step toward me, and I decided I wasn't going to stick around to see what happened next.

I turned and sprinted after Gage and Nana, gagging as I went.

"Why is she so happy about this?" I asked, wincing as Nana's wet tail thwacked me in the face again.

"Dogs love things that smell like Satan shit them out in a garbage dump," Gage said. "Hold her head still."

We were crowded around the sink/doggie bathtub in his mudroom stark naked. Our skunkified clothes were in a pile on the porch outside. I thanked my lucky stars I hadn't put on my favorite sweater to take the dog out. We'd hosed Nana off outside first, but now we were performing some ritualistic doggy car wash with a solution of hydrogen peroxide, dish soap, and baking soda.

"I feel like the smell is in my brain," I complained. I wanted to bathe in perfume and shove entire vials of essential oils up my nostrils. "Can you have your scent receptors removed? Is that an elective surgery?"

"Get her belly, will you?" Gage said, handing me the anti-skunking solution bowl.

I did as I was told, trying to keep the dry heaving to a minimum. As unsexy as the situation was, I couldn't help but admire Gage's naked body. I made a mental note to definitely tell Hazel about this. If anyone could make skunk butt juice hilarious and sexy, it was Hazel Freaking Hart.

My fingers were pruny, and we were standing in a puddle the size of the Mississippi by the time Gage deemed us done. "That's as good as it's going to get," he said, hefting Nana out of the sink. I threw a towel over her, and the two of us rubbed her down as best we could while she flailed in delight.

We watched her shake it off as she galloped around the room.

"Breakfast?" Gage asked.

"Anything that will get the smell and taste of skunk ass out of my face," I agreed.

"Next time, we're spending the night at your place. Your mornings here are cursed," Gage said fifteen minutes later as he covered the bacon with a towel and added the coffee carafe to the tray.

We were freshly showered, and I was dressed in yet another one of Gage's sweatshirts, which came down to my knees. He'd changed into low-riding sweatpants and a tight, soft T-shirt that I already knew was going to end up in my bag when I went home.

Nana and I tailed him hungrily to the deck door.

"Not you," he said sternly to the dog. "You've lost your free-range privileges."

"Sorry," I whispered to Nana as I closed the door softly in her face. I could hear her pathetic whimper through the glass as I followed Gage to the table.

It looked as though Pepe had given up on us and trotted off on a miniature donkey adventure. I admired the donkey-less view from the railing by the wheelchair ramp. Hazel and Cam had a similar ramp at their place, as did Pep and Frank.

"The fact that your entire family made your homes accessible to your sister really speaks volumes about how amazing Laura is," I observed. My own family could barely inconvenience themselves to visit once a year.

"Eh, she's okay. Really it says more about us being awesome," Gage said, unveiling the scrambled eggs, yogurt and berries, and bacon.

I pounced on the food, shoveling it onto my plate as if I hadn't eaten in days. "What? Fighting skunk stank makes me hungry," I said when I caught him watching me with amusement.

Another wail of devastation came from inside, and I guiltily glanced at the window where Nana had her nose and upper lip pressed against the glass.

"It's best not to look directly at her," Gage said. "She only looks like she's being tortured."

"But that face…those eyes."

His hand reached out and squeezed mine. "Stay strong," he said solemnly. "I really don't want to give her another bath before bacon."

"You're right. My curls can't take another shower with your utilitarian boy shampoo."

He grinned and we dug into our food, pointedly ignoring Nana's pathetic pleas.

"So what are your plans this weekend?" he asked as I attacked my eggs.

"Mmm." I held up a finger and dug my phone out of the pocket of the hoodie. "It looks like I will be hiring a high schooler to retype or magically convert Opal's first two manuscripts to digital documents. And attending a mandatory planning meeting for Reader Weekend at Felicity's tomorrow afternoon. Thank you for the idea, by the way. She's been a godsend. A scary, organized godsend."

"Always happy to help."

I continued to scroll through my calendar. "Then I have to convince Opal to sit in on a Zoom call with an acquiring editor scheduled for Monday, which I already know is going to go over like a fart in yoga. And of course there's the accessibility panel tomorrow night, which I forgot to order snacks for. Shit." I typed out a reminder, sent it to my email, and then texted it to myself. "What about you?"

"Oh, you know. The usual. Just go against everything I've ever stood for to mount the best defense possible for a new client."

"Hmm. It sounds like you need one of my famous verbal ass kickings," I teased.

"Maybe I do," he said, topping off my coffee.

"I'd give you one, but I don't think you can handle it. You're probably too fragile."

He smirked. "Please. I can handle anything you dish out. Anything," he repeated.

"That's what they all say," I said airily.

"Give me your best shot."

"Well, if you insist." I made myself comfortable in my chair and interlaced my fingers on the table. "You spend all your time and energy trying to fit everything that happens into nice, neat, labeled boxes so you can make sense of the world. But sometimes it just doesn't make sense. So you waste even more time and energy trying to make it make sense instead of just accepting that some things suck or are weird or make no sense."

I paused to reinflate my lungs.

"Your job is to provide your clients with the best legal whosiewhatsits possible. You told your sister you would do it. You took Valerie on as a client. Yet here you are, wasting this stunningly beautiful spring morning thinking about how you wish you could make sense of how you ended up here rather than just accepting it and doing your damn job."

"Whosiewhatsits? How do you even spell that?" he asked.

I tossed a hunk of bacon at him, which had Nana leaping against the back door and yelping like she was in pain. "Oh, for Pete's sake," I muttered.

I got up and dragged the two empty chairs over to the top of the ramp and blocked it. Then I opened the door. "You will stay here on the deck and act like a nice, well-behaved dog, or you will continue to be grounded from outside. Do you understand me?"

Nana sneezed affirmatively and pranced out onto the deck like she hadn't seen the sun in months. After receiving pets from her father, she put her chin on the table next to my plate and let out a pathetic sigh.

"You're the worst," I told the dog.

Nana let out a burp of agreement.

"You make sense…sometimes," Gage mused.

"This time I do," I said loftily, moving to the railing to stare down at the pond. "Stop fighting what is and just focus on doing what needs to be done. Every time you worry about what should have been or what's to come, you're taking energy away from what you need to do in the present. To paraphrase Nike, just do the damn thing."

He joined me with his coffee. Not wanting to be left out, Nana shoved her face between us and panted happily.

"Maybe I should keep you around for a while so you can remind me," he said.

"Are you talking to me or the dog?"

"I'm talking to the one who didn't actively get sprayed by a skunk this morning."

Hazel: Where are you? I'm at your place. Your car is here, but you're MIA. Did you fall in the lake?
Hazel: Okay. It's 10 a.m. and you're still not here. You didn't take up jogging did you?
Hazel: Did you decide to give up and move back to the city to join your cousin's topless catering company?
Hazel: I'm officially worried. Have you been kidnapped by Dominion?? Text once for yes, twice for no.
Hazel: You better be having hot sex that you're going to graphically detail for me later.

31

A common enemy

Zoey

"How did you get so many people to show up on a Sunday? Blackmail?" I asked Felicity as I dragged an orange, furry beanbag in front of the eighty-five-inch screen mounted on her living room wall. I knew the exact measurement because every man who'd walked through the front door had asked admiringly.

The living room, dining room, hallway, and kitchen of Felicity's tiny ranch house were filled with Story Lakers making themselves comfortable on a variety of seating options. Many of them were business owners who had refused to commit to any participation in Reader Weekend when I'd asked.

"I very casually reminded everyone that Dominion was trying to screw us over again and told them that we were fighting back this time and voilà."

"Few things are as motivating as a common enemy," I observed.

"And you potatoed that common enemy, so now everyone is on board," Felicity said, waving her arm to encompass the chatty crowd. She was a petite, young Black woman with turquoise hair and several interesting tattoos visible under her short-sleeved orange sweater. She and her house were both epically hip, and I hoped this was just the beginning of a beautiful friendship.

I pulled a partially shredded envelope out of my pocket and held it up. "I made a list of urgencies. Do you want to go over it before we start?"

"This is a war room strategy session. Let's get everyone's thoughts all at once."

This was exactly the kind of statement designed to make me want to collapse in the fetal position. I couldn't handle logistics. Certainly not dozens of logistics shotgunned at me from an eager crowd. I liked having the ideas, not executing them. But I would find a way to pull this together even if it meant not sleeping between now and Reader Weekend.

"Let's get this show on the road. I gotta get back for the dinner rush," barked Jessie, Angelo's ancient hostess, who was perched on one of the wingback thrones we'd carted up from Felicity's basement Dungeons and Dragons lounge.

"Okay, people. Who's ready to kick Dominion's ass for once?" Felicity said.

A resounding cheer rose up that could probably be heard inside Hazel's house next door.

"That's what I thought," Felicity said smugly. "Now you all know Zoey. She's in charge of Reader Weekend and its festivities."

I waved awkwardly, knowing this was the last moment I'd have the respect of those gathered.

"I'm her number two," Felicity continued. "I'm the event's organizational officer."

A hand shot up from the papasan chair in the dining room. "I nominate myself as number three, communications officer," Scooter of the Story Lake Warblers announced. "I'll handle all group communications and avail the Warblers to public announcements."

"Seconded," someone in the hallway shouted.

"Oh, wow. Thanks, Scooter," I said. I glanced down at my

list, then crossed off *Need Whatever a Phone Tree Is Called These Days and Someone to Be in Charge of It.*

"Great," Felicity said. "Next item of business."

Over the next half an hour, my anxiety turned to awe as Story Lake residents systematically tackled each problem and provided solutions. I'd never known a community organization to be so ruthlessly single-minded. My building's tenants' association had once spent four months arguing over trash bins.

"I appreciate your very generous Reader Weekend oil change discount, Gator," I said to the grizzled mechanic. "We'll be sure to add it to the list of promotions. One thing I'd like to focus on is how to keep track of what sales and discounts are happening as well as what special events are being hosted. We don't want visitors to have to decide between ultimate bingo in the park and the bonfire at the lodge," I said.

"Got you covered." Harriet Oglethorpe, mother to town mayor Darius and an extremely organized woman, held up her phone. "I created a shared spreadsheet with tabs for sales and events. Everyone can add their offerings, and we can hash out the scheduling details before we put the official listings on the website. I texted the link to Scooter."

"Oh, wow. Um, that's great. Thank you," I said.

Phones started dinging and vibrating from all corners of the house. "And I just added a contact info tab and forwarded it to everyone here," Scooter announced.

I blinked at my own phone. "Uh. Awesome. You guys sure are efficient."

Another message appeared on-screen.

"And now we have a message group for real-time questions and answers," Scooter added.

Feeling like I'd been given a sneak peek into the life of an organized person, I gleefully crossed off two more items on my list. No wonder some people liked the whole "being part of a team." With the right team, the right motivation, shit got done.

Felicity pointed her fairy princess laser wand at the TV. "Great stuff, people. Now let me walk you through this project management website. I've taken the liberty of creating user accounts for each one of you. You'll find your logins in the email I sent last night titled 'Don't Lose This Important Crap.'"

I was impressed. I knew Felicity struggled with anxiety, but here she was working around it and playing to her strengths. She gave me hope for me.

"I will be assigning you tasks in this program. You can make notes, ask questions, and check off to-do items when you've completed them. You can also assign tasks to others. For example, Garland has already requested each business take a photo of the exterior of their property so he can write up brief profiles for the Neighborly app and share them in neighboring...uh... neighborhoods to attract more visitors."

"That's too many uses of the word *neighbor*. It's now lost all meaning," complained Lacresha, the funeral home director, who was chowing down on one of the mini ramen bowls Felicity had prepared. I'd already eaten two.

"My apologies," Felicity said with a grin. "Moving on, to further our campaign to kick Dominion's ass"—she paused for the chorus of mandatory woos—"we will be focusing on what we have that those diesel-fueled shit waffles don't. Zoey hired the high school marketing club to craft a social media marketing plan targeting older audiences."

"Marketing! Club!" barked the two teenage representatives present.

"Go Vampires," someone called from Felicity's kitchen.

Everyone covered their lower faces with their arms and hissed.

Felicity poked me. "You're a Vampire now. You need to act like it."

"Oh. Uh. Yes, of course." My hiss sounded more like a cat asking a question, but it was my first attempt.

Terrance, our Story Lake Haven representative, raised his prosthetic hand.

"Yes, Terrance?" Felicity said.

He stood and removed his cowboy hat. "Story Lake Haven wants in on this. One of our first outings was to Dominion's downtown, and we had a shitty—pardon my French—experience. If you're over the age of forty, they treat you like you should be coffin shopping. We had an idea to boost attendance."

"What's that?" I asked.

"We've decided to host the Haven's first Family Day during Reader Weekend," he announced. "Invitations have already gone out from residents to their extended families. The guilt trip template received a real high RSVP rate, so shout-out to the marketing club for coming up with it." He pointed a finger gun in the direction of the teens, who fist-bumped. "We'd like to incorporate family-friendly events on campus and downtown to make sure there's crossover."

"I could kiss you, Terrance," I said.

"Get in line," Darius told me, enthusiastically shaking Terrance's hand.

Terrance tugged at his cowboy hat in embarrassment. "There's enough of ol' Terr Bear to go around."

"Thank you, Terr Bear, for that amazing contribution. We'll look for your suggestions on the spreadsheet," Felicity continued. "Now, in my spare time, I contacted the Fish Hook and Angelo's to discuss weekend specials that up their game and don't overlap. If the weather is good, Angelo's will offer to-go picnic baskets for lunch, available for preorder online. The Fish Hook will host a special late afternoon happy hour on their deck. Both will have dinner specials on Friday and Saturday nights. Now, Hana, why don't you tell us what the lodge has planned?"

Hana got to her feet. She wore stylish jeans, what she referred to as "lesbian boots" when I'd asked her, and a *Kiss the Chef* muscle shirt.

"Thanks, Felicity. So we've got the bonfire and s'mores scheduled for Friday night, book-themed cocktails all weekend, and then we're bringing in a special brunch menu for Sunday morning."

By the time Hana was done describing her menus, I was contemplating a third mini ramen, and my beanbag was flat.

Next up, Chevy filled us in on his plans for Hazel's signing.

"Saturday morning, we'll be assigning a number to each ticket holder, and they will be called to the store in groups for their designated time window. Which means they'll all have a chance to wander around downtown," he said, using Felicity's laser pointer wand to encompass several blocks of Story Lake's lakefront and town square.

"We'll set up a pop-up coffee stand outside the bookstore for readers waiting in line," Jennifer volunteered.

"And Leafy Greens and my shop will be doing sidewalk sales during the event," Sunita added.

"One more thing," Chevy added. "I talked to the high school art teacher over breakfast this morning—since we're married—and he offered extra credit to a group of students for helping businesses with their signage and window displays that weekend."

An approving murmur rolled through the gathering.

"I just added an artwork sign-up to the master spreadsheet," Harriet announced.

"This. Is. Awesome," I whispered to Felicity.

"Welcome to Story Lake, where we'll work together tirelessly to destroy you," she said cheerfully.

"I was afraid all the details were going to fall on my shoulders and therefore be immediately forgotten and Reader Weekend ruined," I confessed. "I'm not great with organization."

"Girl, with the rest of us, you don't need to be. We need your big ideas and your ability to put out fires when the chaos hits. You did great during Summer Fest when the heatstroke hit and the boat sank."

I had, hadn't I? I gave myself a mental pat on the back.

"Besides, we need you to figure out how to ruin Dominion's stupid Boozetag," she continued.

"Oh, I have a few ideas," I admitted.

"Tell me after everyone leaves for plausible deniability purposes."

I grinned. "You got it." Not only did I have a team of people executing all the details that scared me, I now had a partner in crime. Maybe there really was something to be said for small-town life.

"All right, folks. I think we've done some great work here," Felicity announced. "You all have your assignments. So let's get out there, complete all our tasks, and be productive as hell!"

Garland's hand shot in the air from the gamer's chair he had positioned in the kitchen. "Obviously I won't be reporting on any of our preparations because it could give Dominion an unfair advantage."

"We appreciate that," I said dryly.

"However, I would like to volunteer as community journalist turned spy. I can spend some time in the enemy's camp and report back on what they're planning, giving *us* the unfair advantage."

"You're hired," I said. "And by *hired*, I mean we have no money to pay you, so I'm approving your volunteerism."

"I'll need a daily report with the intel you've gathered," Felicity said. "See if you can get your hands on a schedule of events, information about party rentals, restaurant specials, that kind of thing."

"And I'd like to see some pictures of their Boozetag platform construction," I added.

Garland saluted. "You can count on me."

Felicity looked my way. "Okay, boss. Send them off with a few words of wisdom?"

Public speaking. Yet another thing I didn't really like at all. I rolled out of the beanbag and gracelessly worked my way from hands and knees to standing. "Uh, thank you, everyone, for your participation. I have one more thing on my list. We need to designate an ultimate bingo commissioner to oversee the game on Sunday, and I think Emilie Rump should do it."

I braced for any flying potatoes but only got some frowns and grumbling.

"I know that she played a role in our last battle with Dominion. She made a mistake, but she did eventually stand up to Nina. And she knows the rules of the game better than anyone. It could be a trial redemption," I offered.

There were more frowns and grumbling.

"Look, it's for one weekend. One second chance. If she screws us over again, then I will personally potato her entire house with you until it looks like a mountain of mashed potatoes."

"Fine. But if she sabotages us in any way, you're getting potatoed too," Chevy said. There were several nods of agreement.

"Great," I said with a feigned smile. "Also, our accessibility panel starts at Pushing Up Daisies tonight at seven. We still have a few spaces left. I'll put the registration link in the message group. Now let's go kick Dominion's ass!"

The cheers were so loud they rattled Felicity's windows.

I was in the middle of rearranging Felicity's white fur chairs around her dining room table with my good arm when Frank Bishop tapped me on the shoulder.

"Hey, Frank. Thanks for being here. I think planning an open house at the farm during Reader Weekend is a great idea as long as you can keep it skunk-free."

He chuckled. "Gage told us about Nana's new friend."

"How do you even get rid of a skunk?" I asked. "You know what? Never mind. My brain is full, and I don't want skunk removal knowledge rewriting any of the things I need to take care of for Reader Weekend."

"Wise choice. I just wanted to say thank you."

I blinked. "For what?" The only thing I could think of that was Bishop related was the sex I was having with Gage, and I *really* hoped that wasn't what Frank was grateful for.

"For the social media tutorial things you sent me. I studied up on 'em and got to impress my granddaughter at her workshop by already knowing most of the answers. Even got to help out some of the other old fogies like me," he said proudly. "She asked me if I'd help teach the next one."

I slapped his arm affectionately. "Frank, that's great."

"You're doing good work here, Zoey. Don't you forget that."

"I'll try not to," I promised. I would also try not to fuck it all up.

Frank filed out with the rest of the attendees, and Felicity joined me in the dining room. "I just wanted to thank you for letting us have the meeting here. I know I don't make it easy, but it means a lot when I can be included," she said.

"This worked out great for everyone," I assured her. I watched her return the Lego flower arrangements to the center of the table. "Do you mind if I ask why you don't…?"

"Like to leave my house to the point that it's weird?" she asked.

"Well, yeah. But feel free to tell me to mind my own business. This town's rubbing off on me and making me nosy."

"It started in college. Looking back, I was probably stressing about finals and drinking too many energy drinks. I wasn't sleeping well. My anxiety was so high. I had a full-blown panic attack in the middle of my Game Balancing class. I was terrified and then beyond embarrassed. The panic attacks kept on happening for a few months, and I just kept making my world smaller. Home became my safe space."

"It's a great safe space," I said, sweeping my arm to encompass Felicity's cozy living area.

She perched on one of her dining chairs. "Yeah, but it's also awful. I get really mad at myself. I mean, everyone else can do it. Why can't I?"

"I can empathize. I too have spent a long time wishing I could be like everyone else."

"What's your safe space?" Felicity asked.

"Uh, I don't know." I thought about the college-age me fresh out of surgery, getting dumped. Of my parents' persistent reminders that I was hard to love. "I guess I try to make sure no one expects too much from me or is so inconvenienced by me that they abandon me."

"You're not doing a very good job of that first part. Aren't you in charge of a huge community-wide event that dovetails with your best friend and client's comeback?" she teased.

"Yeah. Can I throw up on these Lego flowerpots?" I joked.

"Definitely not. Maybe you're just growing your safe space?"

I thought of Gage cutting up my waffles. Gage confiding in me. Gage wrapping his arms around me.

"Maybe," I hedged. "It's terrifying, but maybe…"

"Worth it?" she guessed.

"Maybe."

"Well, from one messed-up girl to another, I'm cheering for you."

"Thanks, Felicity. For what it's worth, I'm cheering for you too."

32

Boxed wine

Zoey

Me: Besides your above-average number of free-range animals and lack of delivery options, Story Lake is kind of okay.
Gage: I told you we'd grow on you. Still on for your crash course in ultimate bingo tonight after the accessibility panel?
Me: Can't I just read the rule book? Is there a rule book? YouTube tutorial? Way to gracefully resign as team captain?
Gage: I'll buy you dinner.
Me: Dinner like "date"? Because I don't think that was part of our "monogamous casual sex" discussion.
Gage: Dinner as in "I plan to be hungry around the dinner hour and will require food." Not "let's get married and plan a future together" dinner.
Me: Ugh. Fine. Since you're obviously so obsessed with me. By the way, I can't find Opal. We were supposed to have a meeting. How does the

small-town gossip network work so I can hunt her down?

Gage: I got this.

Gage: Has anyone seen Opal Mallory?
Cam: Why is the group name different? What happened to the Buttholes?
Levi: It's a new group, stupid.
Gage: The Bishop Buttholes continues on. This is a less-specific group of buttholes that includes Zoey and Hazel and Mom and Dad.
Cam: I don't like it.
Gage: What a coincidence since that's how we all feel about you.
Zoey: Sorry to interrupt the buttholing, but Gage is helping me look for Opal. She's the crabby lady in Hazel's writing class who's about to become my second client whether she wants to or not. She gets around with a walker when the nursing staff is watching. Most likely to be found yelling at birds or people who annoy her.
Hazel: Hi bestie! Welcome to the family chat!
Zoey: Shouldn't you be writing?
Hazel: I would be if you'd give me anything to work with. How would you describe your sex life with Gage? A. Dizzyingly orgasmic? B. Moderately pleasant? C. Hilariously disappointing?
Levi: How do I leave a message group?
Gage: A. Obviously. Also, I'd like to remind everyone that Mom and Dad are in this group.
Cam: Sounds like a C to me.
Pep: Don't mind my family, Zoey. They were raised in a barn. I saw Opal getting coffee and petting cats this morning at the coffee shop.

Frank: You went to Perked Up and you didn't bring me back a butterscotch latte?
Pep: Shit. Who added your father to this chat?
Gage: What part of "Mom and Dad are in this group" did you not understand?
Frank: What chats aren't I a part of?
Levi: Formally requesting to be removed from all group chats.
Pep: Nice try, son. That paintball stunt of yours ensures forced membership and participation in all family group chats forever and ever.
Levi: I DIDN'T PAINTBALL THE BARN.
Hazel: This is a family mystery I'm interested in solving.
Cam: There's no mystery. Livvy did it.
Levi: I DIDN'T DO IT!!!
Frank: I WANT A LATTE!!!
Zoey: Hazel, I hope you're being inspired right now.
Hazel: I basically just copied and pasted this entire conversation into my manuscript. I'll change the names later.
Laura: Not to break up the butthole party but Opal just walked into the general store and is filling a cart with snacks.

I burst through the general store's front door and nearly collapsed with relief—and lack of cardiovascular capability—when I spotted Opal browsing the selection of mouthwashes on the endcap. Melvin, Laura's gigantic dog, was standing by in his general store saddlebags, waiting to be helpful.

As soon as I got done yelling at Opal, I needed to snap a picture of the dog and send it to Isla so she could post it on Story Lake's official social media accounts.

"Hey!" I wheezed accusingly.

Melvin gave a cheerful bark.

Opal startled, sending a bottle of antifreeze-colored mouthwash flying. "Christ, kid. When's the last time you did cardio? Exercise is good for the brain shit you got."

"You break it, you bought it," Laura called from behind the counter.

"You were supposed to meet me…at your place…an hour ago."

"You got an inhaler or something? 'Cause you might want to use it."

"No, I don't have an inhaler because I don't have asthma. I just have no cardiovascular capacity! Now, we are having this meeting, and we're having it right now."

Opal looked to Laura for help. "I don't suppose you'd help an old lady out?"

"Sorry, Opal. You told me my jelly selection 'sucks ass.' I'm Team Zoey."

"I didn't tell you that. I muttered it under my breath like a lady," Opal insisted.

"Then you need to get your ears checked," Laura suggested.

"Back to you avoiding me," I insisted, stepping in front of Opal's cart.

She rolled her eyes. "Yeah, let's get back to me avoiding you."

"Opal."

"Ugh. I didn't feel like listening to you yammer on about how my stories aren't publishable." She pushed the cart into my thighs, but I stood my ground.

"Did you drink straight whiskey for breakfast?" I asked sweetly.

"Not today."

"Oh, then you're just stubborn and spiraling," I surmised.

"I'm a retired psychologist. I don't spiral."

"Right, because it makes so much more sense for me to set a meeting with you to explain your books are garbage instead of me telling you we need to pick an hour tomorrow afternoon to have a call with an acquisitions editor who *wants to make an offer on your series*, you insufferable, pain-in-the-ass genius," I snapped.

"Well, shit. You coulda told me that."

I shoved my hands into my hair. "That's what I was going to tell you at *the meeting you skipped*! Oh my God. Is this what it's like having kids? Because I feel like I'm losing my mind."

"Yeah, that's exactly what it's like," Laura called.

"Humph. I guess I'm free between two and three tomorrow," Opal grumbled.

"Thank. You," I said between clenched teeth, then took a deep breath. "I probably could have found a gentler way to say that. But I used up all my nuanced peopling already today, and I still have an entire event to get through tonight before I can hide on the floor in a hoodie. Also I'm hangry and shit shit shit! I still need snacks for the workshop tonight."

"Well, you came to the right place," Laura said. "Me, Melvin, and Opal will be happy to help."

"Not me. I stopped helping people at sixty. I'm outta here." Opal threw a twenty-dollar bill on the counter and left with her bag of chips and carton of French onion dip.

"I'll see you at two tomorrow," I called after her.

The door closed behind her, and I collapsed against the toilet paper display. Melvin meandered up and bumped me in the hip with his massive fluffy head.

"I'm too exhausted to reach for my phone. Can you take a picture of Melvin and send it to your daughter so she can post it on Story Lake's Instagram?"

Laura acquiesced and snapped the photo. "You really need to work on your cardio if you're going to be chasing clients all over town."

"I should have just driven, but my car roof latch is stuck again. The right side won't stay closed, so it claps up and down when I drive. Also there's this rattle in the door that's driving me insane," I explained.

Laura wheeled out from behind the counter. "I'm sure I have a brother who could fix that if you mention it to him."

"Who? Gage? I'm just using him for sex. I don't think our agreement covers car maintenance."

"If the guy isn't willing to do you a favor or two outside the bedroom, you're not doing the sex right."

"I'm doing the sex just fine," I promised. Besides, the ask was too far outside my comfort zone. It was too much. Orgasms, yes. They were mutually beneficial. But car maintenance? No. I wasn't about to start inconveniencing my casual monogamous sex partner with relationship-like demands.

"Suit yourself." She hefted a box of wine in each hand and held them out to me. "You'll need these for tonight. Story Lake doesn't gather without snacks and alcohol."

"Damn, girl. Where'd you get those biceps?" I asked, admiring her fitness magazine–worthy guns.

"Started working out with a trainer instead of just my dumb brothers," she said.

"Ah, the gym. I have heard rumors of such a place. So how much wine will it take for everyone to learn something but still enjoy themselves tonight?"

"Better grab a third box just to be safe," Laura suggested.

33

Man parts jiggling

Gage

I walked into Pushing Up Daisies and took a seat in the back of the Garden Gathering Room, pleasantly surprised to find the space almost full. I could just pick out Zoey's standout curls in the front row. The crowd appeared to be riveted by the presentation that was happening in front of Lacresha's coffin display.

Quaid stood in front of a high-end pewter coffin, looking like he'd just hopped off a surfboard in floral shorts and a sweatshirt. He had his arm around the small boy with glasses who was leaning into him and peering down at a tablet. Next to them, a young woman with a floral sleeve tattoo was leading the discussion in a brisk, no-nonsense voice.

All around the room, pens scratched on paper and fingers tapped on keyboards as my friends, neighbors, and family—of course my parents were there—took notes.

"It was this lack of public education, my own personal experience, and meeting other individuals with autism like Benjamin here that motivated me to become a community autism educator," the woman explained. "As I said before, I am considered to have high-functioning autism, which means I enjoy an above-average intelligence but I still struggle with things like social cues and interactions. I might not make eye contact with you while I bombard you with interesting facts about meteorology. For instance, did you know that lightning often follows a volcanic eruption?"

The crowd chuckled appreciatively.

"Now for individuals like Quaid's brother Benjamin, autism can present differently. Benjamin expresses himself through his speech tablet and sign language."

She paused, and Quaid nudged Benjamin, who keyed something into his tablet.

"Hello," said the tablet.

The crowd waved back at him.

"We both exhibit repetitive behaviors and share a preference for routines. But Benjamin's tolerance for overstimulation is lower than mine or yours. Loud noises, bright lights, tags on his clothing can all lead to an overstimulated brain. A neurotypical brain can take in these kinds of stimuli and choose to ignore or at least dial them down. A brain with autism cannot do that. So it's helpful to know how to minimize triggers or provide access to safe, quiet spaces. In a survey of parents of children with autism, these are the top three ways they said we can best support them in public places."

She gestured behind her at the screen on the wall. "Creating inclusive spaces with sensory considerations where individuals can take breaks from external stimulation. Having a sensory tool kit on hand with items like weighted blankets, fidget toys, or noise-canceling headphones. And finally, just providing positive reinforcement to the families when you recognize autistic behavior goes a long way in making everyone feel safe and welcome.

"It looks as though our time is up. Thank you for your time, your attention, and your willingness to learn about me and Benjamin and the best ways to support people like us."

"Thank you so much, Maria," Zoey said, popping up from the front row.

She turned to face the crowd, and I couldn't help but smile. Damn, she was pretty.

"And since Maria's taught us that loud noises can be a trigger, may I suggest that we thank her, Benjamin, and Quaid in sign language like we learned tonight from Mr. and Mrs. Blumenthal."

I watched, impressed, as every person in the audience signed *thank you*.

Maria took a little bow, and Benjamin said, "You're welcome," via his tablet.

"Thank you so much for coming out and spending the evening with us. I hope we can all find ways to implement what we've learned here tonight. Please take any leftover snacks, sodas, and wine with you," Zoey said.

Pride warmed my chest like a sip of bourbon as I watched everyone perform the ASL sign for applause for her. She was beaming right back at the crowd.

"Stop it. You'll make a girl blush," she teased.

I worked my way through the gathered crowd to find her in conversation with Darius and Kitty Suarez.

I wanted to pull her into me and kiss her but realized any kind of physical contact witnessed by this percentage of the town would be a mistake. The gossip would have us dating by midnight and planning a wedding by eight a.m. Instead, I stuck my hands in my pockets and tried to keep the lust off my face.

"Hey, great turnout," I said.

Zoey's face lit up, and her smile hit me like a tractor trailer to the sternum. *Shit.* I was in serious trouble with this woman.

"Thank God you're here. You were right. I'm starving. Feed me," she begged, sagging into my side.

I had no choice but to slide an arm around her waist, or at least that was what I told myself as Kitty's eyebrows arched upward in interest. Darius at least remained blissfully unaware of the gossip unfolding before him.

"Thanks again for organizing this, Zoey," he said. "This was amazing. I've never seen a turnout like this before. Now, if you'll excuse me, I need to get home and finish my chem homework."

"Sooo I heard you two are…" Kitty wagged her finger back and forth between us.

"Having casual sex?" Zoey supplied cheerfully. "Yep. Lots of it."

"Good for you guys. The world would be a better place if we all had more sex. Well, I've got some knitting to do, and that true crime docuseries isn't going to watch itself. Have a good night," she said with a wink.

"Well, that's gonna be all over town by morning," I said.

"We're two consenting adults. We don't need to pretend we're dating or running a book club. Besides, I don't have the energy to keep up a facade. I'm exhausted."

"I can take the heat," I promised her.

We were interrupted by funeral director Lacresha, Dahlia from Angelo's, and Junior Wallpeter. They were all wearing matching shirts that said *KDA*. "Zoey! We have something for you," Dahlia said, thrusting a thick envelope into her hands.

"What's this?" she asked, opening it. Her eyes went wide. "Why are you handing me an envelope stuffed with cash? And where can I get one of those shirts?"

"It's for the Kick Dominion's Ass committee," Junior announced, pointing proudly at his shirt.

Zoey looked at me. "I'm afraid to ask."

"What's the Kick Dominion's Ass committee?" I asked.

"We are," Lacresha announced. "Our goal is to kick Dominion's ass in all things."

"The high school marketing club made the shirts, and we sold two dozen of them tonight," Dahlia explained.

"It's so you don't have to keep paying for things out of your own pocket, seein' how you're broke and selling all your expensive underwear online," Junior added.

"To be clear, I'm not selling my underwear. It's just my regular clothes," Zoey said.

"Maybe you should think about selling underwear. My cousin Frances makes five figures a month selling hers," he suggested.

"Selling them where?" Zoey asked.

I pulled her into my side and stared down Junior.

"Uh, I forget?" he said, shooting me a nervous look.

"Well, thank you for the spontaneous fundraising and the overinvolvement in my personal business," Zoey said, waving the envelope.

"You're welcome," they all said together.

"Dinner?" I said when the Kick Dominion's Ass committee dispersed.

Zoey's face fell. "I know I said yes already, and I am starving. But I've spent the entire day peopling. I don't think I can deal with a restaurant full of nosy neighbors."

"I had a feeling you might feel that way and planned accordingly."

"Really? No more peopling?" Her face was hopeful.

"None," I promised. "Come on."

"How very you of you," she said as we made our way outside.

"Are you trying to offend me or compliment me?"

"Probably both. You identified the potential for a problem and planned around that potential. God, I wish I could be inside your brain for a day. It sounds so orderly and organized in there."

"I'm not sure I'd survive in yours," I admitted, opening the passenger door of my SUV for her and holding Nana back.

"It's not for the faint of heart," Zoey said, greeting my dog with an enthusiastic squish of her face. "Hi, baby."

Nana's tail thumped against the seat as Zoey managed to dodge her tongue.

"Back seat, Nan," I ordered.

The dog grumbled but complied.

I slid in behind the wheel and started the engine. Zoey released a long, slow breath and closed her eyes as I pulled out of the parking spot. No questions about where we were going, what we were eating. She trusted me, I realized, sneaking a look at her profile in the streetlights. She probably didn't even realize it.

I took us north on Lake Drive, leaving the town in the rearview mirror.

She opened her eyes when I turned off the road and gravel crunched under the tires. Nana poked her head between the seats, recognizing our destination with a cheerful yip.

"Where are we? Wait. Is this Levi's place?" she asked as the headlights hit the cedar shake cabin among the trees.

"It is. He's not home tonight. He had some weekend law enforcement training. I figured you wouldn't mind a quiet, lakefront dinner," I said, cutting the engine.

"This feels date-y," Zoey mused with suspicion.

"Maybe. But I bet you're hungry enough you're willing to look past any unintentional romance."

She rolled her eyes. "Stop being right all the time. It's annoying."

"Watch your step," I warned when we got out. Nana jogged off to sniff and pee. I grabbed the blanket, cooler, and flashlight out of the back seat and met her around the hood.

The evening air had a hint of warmth to it. Tree frogs sang out in the canopy above us, one of the hallmarks of spring for as long as I could remember. The lake glittered in the moonlight beyond the cabin.

Zoey followed me to Levi's back door and waited while I found the spare key on the hook.

"Your brother leaves a key hanging next to the door? Haven't you people ever heard of security? You're too trusting," Zoey complained.

"One of the perks of living in Story Lake. The only breaking and entering is usually done by bears, and they don't need a key."

"Bears?" she whispered as if she was afraid of conjuring one.

I pushed the door open and held it for her. "They're more afraid of you than you are of them."

"I doubt that," she said dryly as we entered Levi's cabin with Nana rocketing past us. The dog led the way through the kitchen into the living room, and we followed, turning lights on as we went. It was small and in dire need of updating. Cam and I razzed him regularly for being the contractor with the shitty house. But Levi didn't seem to be in any hurry to turn the shack into anything nicer.

"Your brother has interesting taste in…everything," Zoey observed, eyeing the ancient flintlock rifle mounted above an old writing desk where his laptop sat next to a pile of crumpled notebook pages.

Nana got a running start and hurled herself onto Levi's ancient plaid couch. It was ugly as sin but comfortable enough no one could stay awake on it for long.

"He bought this place when it went up for auction a few years ago. Said he appreciated the hermit-like quality," I explained. Levi wasn't subtle about his desire to be left alone as often as possible. He tolerated the loud, messy family get-togethers, but he was most comfortable here, alone.

The property had one thing going for it. I found the touch screen mounted inside the front slider door and punched a few buttons. Zoey let out a delighted squeal.

"Let's go," I said, forcing the slider open on its wobbly track. Nana opened one eye to look at me, then closed it again, too exhausted from her many skunk baths to join us.

Levi's yard rolled down a gentle slope to the lake. There was a fire ring with exactly one Adirondack chair next to it facing the water. Above us, running from cabin to fire pit, was a series of amber-colored string lights that glowed in the night.

I handed most of our haul to Zoey and set the rest on the deck. "Set up by the fire pit. I'll get the firewood."

"This is…really nice, Gage. Thank you," she said.

"Maybe hold off on thanking me until you try the egg roll in a bowl," I joked.

"Okay. You can officially add that recipe to your regular repertoire," Zoey said, putting her empty bowl on the lip of the fire ring. She sighed happily and wiggled back on the chair. I eased forward in the flimsy lawn chair I'd found on the deck and stacked my bowl on top of hers. The fire crackled, casting its warm glow over us.

"Glad you liked it. I've got extras in the cooler for you this week."

"If only we were each other's type," she said on a satisfied sigh. "I could get used to this."

"You need a me," I said.

"I know. Though I don't know how well you'd cook in a Manhattan apartment with eighteen inches of counter space. But what would a you get out of the experience with me?"

I gave her a lazy grin.

"Besides the obvious," she added, waving a hand down the front of her body.

"Well, a you sure makes things more interesting."

She fluffed her curls and winked. "I do, don't I?"

"I wouldn't break into my brother's house for just anyone," I told her.

"Will he be mad?"

"That all depends on if he finds out," I quipped.

"It's his own fault, really. I mean, what chief of police doesn't have a security system?"

"The victim not having a security system doesn't usually hold up too well in court as a defense," I pointed out.

"Well, then let's keep this out of court. I appreciate you doing something vaguely illegal for me. Maybe we're good influences on each other?" she mused. "You feed me and keep me from overpeopling, and I introduce you to the joys of questionably legal spontaneity."

"An interesting argument," I said, taking her hand in mine.

A cloud slid away from the moon, making light dance on the water. We both stared out over the sparkling vista in silence. I caught the faint wheeze of Nana's snore drifting out the door. For a weekend that had started out with a pissed-off skunk, I was pretty happy with how it was ending.

"When's the last time you went skinny-dipping?" Zoey asked abruptly.

"How can we both be sitting here looking at the same view and thinking completely different things?"

"It's called 'opposites attract,' and we're the definition of it. You didn't answer my question."

"It's April. The water is cold in July. You'd have to be extremely drunk and confused to jump in now."

"So never then?" she prompted.

I opened my mouth to defend myself, but she cut me off.

"Me neither. I've always wanted to. But growing up in Manhattan doesn't give you a ton of great opportunities to get naked in public and not get arrested."

She stood up, pulling her hand from mine, her fingers finding the button on her jeans.

"You can't make me do this," I insisted.

"Come on, Gage." She pouted prettily as she worked the denim down her legs. "Think of it as a naked polar plunge. Refreshingly naughty."

Shit. I was already screwed, and she barely had her shoes off.

I stood up but crossed my arms over my chest. "What's the goal here? Maybe we could accomplish it in a less hypothermia-inducing way."

"There's no goal. This is just fun," she insisted, kicking off her pants to reveal that once again, she wasn't wearing underwear.

"That water is probably sixty degrees. That's not fun. It's masochistic."

Her shirt hit the ground, and my mouth went dry as the purple bra with the sequined band went next.

"Come on, Gage. You fed me. Let me entertain you."

"I hate every single thing about this," I complained as I toed off my shoes.

"Yay!" Her exclamation was cut off by a gasp as she jogged into the water. "Oh, that's *brisk*."

"Fuck my fucking life, this is fucking cold," I said through clenched teeth. I slogged up to my chest after her. Zoey was in almost over her head.

This was officially the stupidest thing I'd ever done to impress a woman. My balls were in my fucking throat.

"Yeah, it's totally horrible. But look up," she said. At least that was what I thought she said. It was hard to tell with her teeth chattering.

I glanced up and spotted the moon, full and bright, blotting out clouds behind it.

"Yeah. Fucking great, Disaster. Now let's get back to the fire before your tits turn blue."

"So crass when you're freezing to death. I like it." She launched herself at me, her slippery body sliding over mine beneath the frigid water. Our lips met and tangled. A strange, heady combination of ice and heat made me temporarily forget that I hated this. My arms were full of her, her flavor, her scent surrounding me like the water. I'd never felt more alive.

I loved the way she wrapped her legs around me and held on for dear life. I felt like an anchor, a safe harbor. She trusted me to keep her safe, and I wasn't going to let her down…and in this moment, it meant not having sex in lake water when I didn't know the current bacteria levels.

"We should go back to the fire," I said against her mouth.

"And not put our clothes on?" she asked hopefully.

"Our clothes will remain off," I promised.

"Yay! Hurry up before my labia get hypothermia." And with that, she slipped off me and swam toward shore.

We exited the water together, laughing and shivering when headlights cut through the night, briefly landing on us and lighting up our world. I shoved Zoey behind my back.

"Oh my God," she squeaked, teeth chattering even harder now.

"Fuck," I muttered.

The headlights were in Levi's driveway, pulling in next to my SUV.

"Stay low," I ordered as I dragged her to shore, sticking to the tree line and skirting the edge of Levi's property. There was another cabin next door, a dilapidated wreck of a place that hadn't been lived in for years, so I pulled Zoey into its overgrown yard.

Through the trees, a backlit figure appeared on Levi's deck, staring down toward the fire.

"Is it the cops?" Zoey hissed.

"Yeah. It's the goddamn chief of police."

She prodded my naked ass with a frozen finger. "You said he was out of town this weekend."

"Sweetheart, now is not the time to get into an argument about who was right and who was wrong."

"You're just saying that because I was right," she complained.

"We're fucking naked, and Levi has been dying to get revenge on anyone who played a role in him being nominated for chief. I don't know about you, but I'm not going to jail tonight."

"Fine. What's the plan, Mr. Goose Bumps on His Ass?"

"Follow me and make as little noise as possible. My keys are in the truck. If we can swing around while he's still out front, we can make a run for it."

Zoey yelped as a branch caught her in the side. "He's gonna know it was us."

"I'd rather it be a Future Clothes-Wearing Me problem than a Now Naked Me problem," I insisted. I was one thousand percent certain my brother wouldn't hesitate to haul my naked ass to jail.

We scurried through the overgrown grass down the property's nearly invisible drive and managed to cut across to Levi's yard.

My SUV loomed in front of us next to Levi's truck. I opened the driver's side door as quietly as possible and shoved Zoey in and over the console. Given how wet we both were, she slid into the passenger seat like a seal.

I climbed in behind her and had the engine turning over before I'd even shut the door.

I floored it in reverse, backing down the driveway to the road with a roar.

Zoey squealed and held on for dear life as I whipped the front end of the SUV around. I shook my head ruefully. The woman was actually enjoying this.

Levi jogged around the corner of his house just as I shifted into drive and sped away.

"Oh my God!" Zoey said, clamping a hand to her naked chest. "Now *that* was a memorable night."

I blasted the heat through the vents and turned on our seat warmers. "I feel like you should be a little more concerned with the situation."

"Are you kidding? Some skinny-dipping, an adrenaline

rush, and now a naked getaway? This is awesome. You know, you're still sexy even when you're all hunched over running with your man parts jiggling," she observed.

"That's the weirdest compliment I've ever received."

"You're welcome," she said grandly, hugging her knees to her chest. "Can we go to your house? I need to defrost in your mega shower."

I shook my head, a reluctant smile tugging at my lips. Zoey Moody was the most fun I'd had in my life. "Sure."

My phone rang from the center console, and I pushed the button on the dashboard touch screen.

"Livvy," I said with feigned innocence. "How's your weekend training?"

"Hey, asshole. It was Friday to Saturday. Not Saturday to Sunday. What the hell were you doing at my house?"

I glanced at Zoey, who had a hand clamped over her mouth, trying to stifle her laughter.

"I don't know what you're talking about. I'm at my place with Zoey. It must have been someone else."

"You left your dog here."

Fuck.

> **Levi:** I'm holding this dog for questioning until the two naked people who broke into my house and left her here confess.
> **Mom:** Hi Nana!
> **Laura:** Nice one, Gigi. 🐶🐾
> **Cam:** You better have been with Zoey or I'll kick your naked ass.
> **Levi:** Doesn't anyone care that my property was violated by nonconsensual nudity?
> **Laura:** Nope.
> **Cam:** No.
> **Dad:** Hi Nana!

34

Literally under the sea
Zoey

"I'm coming!" My voice echoed off the bathroom tiles as I charged out to answer the insistent knock on my apartment door. If it was Gage, he was ridiculously early for our mystery date, and I was going to give him hell for interrupting my get-ready time.

We'd spent the last two weeks most often together, and some of the time, we weren't even naked. We weren't dating. But there were burgers at the Fish Hook after vigorous backyard sex or an evening stroll through the fields with Nana. His shower now had my brand of shampoo and conditioner in it, and my fridge had his favorite beer.

Did I mention the sex? Lots and *lots* of glorious sex.

My God, could Gage Bishop fuck.

Between all the orgasms, doing everything in my power to make sure Hazel had the best book launch of her life, and knowing that nearly every single personality flaw I'd dealt with had a biological reason behind it, I was feeling really freaking good.

Good enough to agree to a mystery "dress nice" evening out with Gage.

It was probably a mistake. But I didn't really care. I was having too much fun…and too many orgasms.

I was still tying my bathrobe closed when I threw open the door and discovered that the aggressive knocker was not my date for the evening.

Opal bustled past me, her cane thunking on the wood floor.

"Uh, come on in, Opal. I thought our meeting was scheduled for Monday." *Damn it.* If I'd screwed up another calendar appointment, I was going to throw myself out a window.

"Relax," she said, flopping down on the couch. "You didn't get it wrong. I just figured since I was in town…"

"You live in town," I pointed out, perching on the arm of the chair. "Wait a minute. You're excited and you want to know if there's any news now, don't you?"

She harrumphed and poked the pink crystal ball on the end table with the rubber tip of her cane. "I'm not excited. I'm… curious. That's all. Stop looking so smug."

"I can't help the smug face. I want you to be excited about this. Because it *is* exciting."

"Most folks my age get excited about a new hip or a discount on perms at the salon."

"That's stereotyping and you know it. You have lots of interesting, adventurous neighbors over there at Story Lake Haven. But I can guarantee none of them have an offer from a New York publisher, let alone *three*."

Opal pretended I hadn't just delivered the most exciting news ever. "You got a lot of disco balls in here. What are you? Thirteen?"

"Unlike certain unnamed people in this room, I *like* fun."

She harrumphed again.

"For a reasonably intelligent woman from a demanding field, I would have expected you to be less committed to the whole crotchety-old-lady vibe. You're in your seventies, and you wrote the better part of a pretty good epic fantasy series that has three major publishers frothing at the mouth. But if you want to wander around yelling at 'youngins' to get off your lawn, be my guest."

Opal scoffed. "'Pretty good'? Is that how you're selling my books?"

I examined my fingernails, which I'd actually remembered to manicure in time for my mystery evening. "Actually, the editor said 'brilliant,' but I didn't want it to go to your head."

Opal slumped against the cushions. "Fine. You might as well tell me since it's practically exploding out of you."

"Bettis Books made an offer. A good one. Which brings us to three publishers in the running."

"You gonna tell me what the offer is?"

"I will once all three best and finals are submitted to me Monday morning."

"We've already got one publishing house buffaloed into an offer. Shouldn't we just go with them? It's not like I have a lot of years left in me."

"First of all, I can tell just by your stubborn attitude that you're going to be around for your one hundred and tenth birthday. Second, I like Bettis, and I like the editor. But I think we can get a better offer. Going to auction, which is what happens when multiple publishers make you an offer and try to beat each other in the process, means you get to take your pick of their best offers."

"What if the highest bidder is a shitty publisher with a shitty editor?"

"Then we go with a lower bid from a better company."

"You think my story is worth all that?"

"Yes. And you should start thinking that way too. You've spent how many years of your life writing these books?"

"Five million."

"You look good for your prehistoric age. These manuscripts deserve more than an eternity in a drawer. And *you* deserve more than to lock yourself away in an empty, monotonous retirement."

"I wasn't supposed to be doing it alone," she said, studying the toes of her sneakers.

I waited, knowing there was more to come.

"I was married," she said finally. "We met in the eighties.

Alice was a biologist. We had forty good years together. Some couples build their family together, but we built our careers. No regrets. But now she's gone and I'm retired, and I don't even know how to go through the motions. Except for Hazel's damn class, I haven't written a word since she went into the hospital. That was four years ago."

"Opal, I'm so sorry. That sucks."

"It really fucking sucks," she agreed. "I wrote them for her. After her eyesight started to fail, I'd go home and read what I'd written out loud to her every night. They might just be stories, but they mean something to me. They remind me of her."

"And you haven't written without her."

"What's the point?" She looked at me. "No, I'm literally asking you. What is the goddamn point of anything?"

I took a breath and let it out. Her pain radiated off her like a halo. "You know what the point is. I just don't know if you can handle me saying it."

She snorted. "You think you can say anything that's gonna damage me?"

"Uh, yeah, my fragile little flower. So I want credit for saying this as gently as I can. I didn't know Alice, but I bet she was really damn proud of you, and I bet she loved the stories you wrote for her."

"So?" Opal's tone was surly.

"So I'm wondering what Alice would say to you if she were here right now."

Opal heaved a sigh that spoke volumes of grief, regret, and annoyance. "She'd say I should quit trying to fill the void with work and let old age take me."

I tossed a heart-shaped throw pillow at her. "Bullshit."

She hurled it back at me. "Can't an old lady wallow in self-pity?"

"Nope. Somewhere deep down beyond all the layers of stubborn, I think you know Alice would love that you were sharing your stories with the world. And she would definitely tell you to quit wallowing and get back to writing so she can find out what happens next."

Opal's shrug was dismissive.

"Tell me I'm wrong," I said.

"I need a drink."

"Close enough. I'm going to drag you kicking and screaming into real life. Starting with that damn exercise class at the lake this weekend."

"The fuck we are."

"Save the witty banter for the page. You and I are getting our asses down to the lake for whatever workout torture they can dish out. We're going to smile and be nice to people. And then we're going to go to lunch and talk about your work in progress."

"There's no damn progress, woman. Get your ears cleaned."

"If it's not finished, it's still in progress. Just like us."

"I see your medication is working," she observed grumpily.

"Every day until about four. Then I'm exhausted and cranky just like you. We could be mistaken for sisters."

"I'm five foot ten, Black, and three decades older than you."

"You can fight this all you want, but I'm not giving up on you. You're going to pull your head out of your ass and come back to life. Then we're going to finish your book. Then we're going to start your next one. And in the meantime, we're going to sell your series for an embarrassing amount of money."

"What's with all this 'we' crap?"

I rolled my eyes. "Yeah. I know. Stick around Story Lake long enough, and it just happens. Now, unless you're good at ladyscaping and makeup, I suggest you go home so I can get ready for some mystery evening that had better end in a lot of sex."

Opal scrambled to her feet.

"Heard you and that lawyer with the tool belt were fooling around," she said as I walked her to my door.

"Having a damn good time doing it," I said cheerfully.

"You know you could give the real thing a shot."

"What? Like a relationship?"

"Don't look so appalled. Even I managed to make one work," she said.

"Yeah, well, you've got more going for you than an executive function deficiency and a nearly empty bank account. Now get out so I can get ready to put out."

"Remind me to discuss professionalism with you."

"Oh, we're way beyond that," I assured her with a grin.

"This feels date-y," I accused when I opened my door for the second time. Gage grinned over a bouquet of spring flowers.

"Deal with it. The plant shop had a sidewalk sale, and these made me think of you," he said, looking me over from head to toe. I'd gone with red, sparkly, and sexy. "Wow," he said.

I took the wild, colorful flowers and buried my face in them to hide the pleasure of his compliment. "You know I'm a sure thing, right? I mean, every single night of the last two weeks except for the second skunk incident that we agreed never to discuss again proves that."

"They're pretty. You're pretty. Let's not overthink this," he said, taking the flowers from me and heading into my kitchen.

"Pretty?" I struck a dramatic pose, highlighting the sequins I'd stuck to the Velcro of my wrist brace.

He put the flowers down on the counter and gave me his full attention again. "Did I say pretty? I meant beautiful, sexy, 'knock the breath out of a man' gorgeous."

"Much better," I said, crossing to him and looping my arms around his neck.

He kissed me, softly at first. With a kind of delicious familiarity that made me nervous. Then he took it to the next level of heat, making my knees weak and my blood thrum.

"This is why I didn't put my lipstick on yet," I told him when we broke apart.

"Good planning," he said, running his thumb gently over my chin before returning to his task at hand.

It had been two weeks of casual, orgasmic bliss. And I wasn't hating it. I got sex, clean laundry, and meals out of the deal. While Gage got...well...sex. And whatever entertainment I provided.

"Where's Nana?" I asked, watching him fill a vase with water and arrange the flowers in it.

"She's spending her evening indoors at my parents' with strict instructions not to let her off leash."

"You know who rarely gets sprayed by skunks?" I teased. "New Yorkers. You should come visit someday."

He turned to face me, a man in a suit and tie, holding a vase of flowers that made him think of me, and something invisible punched me right in the sternum. I didn't know what it was, but it felt similar to a serious case of heartburn.

I hated it.

"You look beautiful. What the hell are you doing?" Gage asked.

"Making sure I can feel my left arm. Am I smiling on both sides of my mouth?"

"Are you having some kind of medical emergency?"

"That's what I'm trying to figure out."

He looked at his watch. "I need to know if we're going to see Dr. Ace or to the prom in the next two minutes so I can make arrangements."

"Did you say the *prom*?"

"I did. We're chaperoning."

"I don't know if I'm qualified for that. But we're definitely taking my car. A convertible is required for prom."

"I hate your car. It's falling apart, the door rattles like it's going to fall off, and every light on the dashboard is on," Gage complained.

"That's only because every time I get out of the car, I forget it and its check engine light exist. I'll schedule an appointment... eventually," I promised airily.

"This is a really weird prom," I said, taking in Story Lake High School's gymnasium, which was decked out with cardboard waves and seaweed cutouts.

"The theme is Literally Under the Sea," Gage explained.

Darius, dressed in a tuxedo, a scuba mask, and flippers, duckwalked past us, flashing an enthusiastic thumbs-up.

"Uh-huh. Um, why?" I asked.

"Student vote."

"The democracy here gets pretty creative," I said, dodging the bow of a Styrofoam *Titanic*.

"Speaking of pretty creative, wait until you see the kids," he said, guiding me toward the other chaperones, who were congregating around the refreshment table.

Bookstore Chevy and his husband, Art—the high school art teacher—were deep in discussion with the Blumenthals. Chevy was wearing an Evanescence T-shirt under a suit jacket while Art was in a handsomely tailored suit and glittery loafers. I signed hello to Mr. Blumenthal.

"What are you two doing here?" I asked them.

"The senior class has been sending students as tech support to the Haven, and we got along so well they invited us to chaperone," Mrs. Blumenthal said, waving her hand over her exquisite cocktail dress. "We can't wait to show off our ballroom dance skills."

Mr. Blumenthal gave her a dramatic twirl.

"I told you we should have practiced," Art said to Chevy.

"I see we've got some competition," Gage observed, popping a pretzel into his mouth.

"You better bring your A game on the dance floor," I said, drilling my finger into his ribs.

"Are you sure you can handle my A game?" he teased.

I was barely surviving our world-rocking sex life. I didn't know if I could survive his best anywhere but the bedroom.

"Oh good. You're all here," Principal Destiny Sprout said, rubbing her hands together as she approached. She was a woman in her late fifties with the enthusiasm of a twenty-year-old on a steady diet of energy drinks. "Your main job is to float around and make sure everyone is having a good time…but not too good a time. They're good kids. I'm not anticipating any 1980s movie moments, but check the restrooms regularly. Prom is prime heartbreaking season," she explained. "If you see anything like drugs, alcohol, or making out that's too enthusiastic, flag me down. Any questions?"

"We're good to go, Destiny," Gage promised like the responsible adult he was.

I joined the rest of the chaperones, nodding my agreement. It was ironic that I was here, chaperoning, when at my own prom, I'd snuck in a bottle of peppermint schnapps from my parents' liquor cabinet. I'd sold enough shots in the restroom to cover the cost of my graduation outfit.

"I bet you were a hall monitor in school," I whispered to him.

Gage responded with a friendly pinch on my butt.

"Great," Destiny said. "We've got two minutes before they open the doors. I'm going to go do a final sweep and be completely distracted by a brief conversation with the DJ."

"That was weird, right?" I said as Destiny headed off toward the makeshift stage in her glittering suit separates.

When I turned back, Chevy and Art had produced a flask from God knows where.

I laughed.

"Shh," Chevy cautioned as Art poured whatever was in the flask into small paper cups.

"We're not supposed to have alcohol on school grounds," Art explained. "But Destiny knows chaperoning is a pain in the ass, so she goes the route of plausible deniability."

"I had no idea being a chaperone was so cool," I said, accepting a cup.

Forty minutes into the prom and I was supremely grateful not to be a teenager anymore. As an adult, there was no one to monitor the appropriateness of my outfit. No one to tell me to quit making out with a cute boy in a dark corner. My friends were reasonably responsible adults who weren't still trying to find that delicate balance between fitting in and standing out.

While Gage handed out punch for the Blumenthals, who were cutting a rug on the dance floor to Sia's "Chandelier," I ducked into the restroom to check my lipstick…and pretend to look for nefarious teenage activity.

I was just redrawing the line of my lower lip when a wet sniffle from one of the stalls caught my attention.

"You okay in there?" I asked, recapping my lip liner.

"No," the voice sniffled.

"You wanna come out and talk about it?"

"Maybe."

"I'm willing to share half of the candy bar I have in my clutch with you if you come out and talk about it," I offered.

A moment later, a girl in yellow chiffon under a deflated life jacket exited the stall. Her eyes were red and puffy. A skilled stylist had wrestled her curly brown hair into a severe French twist that looked like it had so much hair spray it could double as a helmet.

Wordlessly, I handed her half of the dark chocolate bar.

"Thanks," she said with a wobbly voice. "You're really pretty."

"I was just thinking the same about you."

She grimaced in the mirror, her hand rising to poke at the brunette shellac situation on her head. "I look like a member of the school board. I wanted to look grown-up, not ancient." Her eyes darted to me. "No offense."

"Only a medium amount taken. What happened?"

She crammed the chocolate into her mouth. "I asked Gregory Prine to go to prom with me, and he said he wasn't going. But he's here with all his dumb friends, acting like he didn't lie straight to my face because he didn't want to go with me."

"Gregory sounds like a dick," I observed.

That got a wobbly smile out of her. "You're not the usual chaperone type."

"It's part of my charm. So what's the plan? Are you going to let Gregory Prick ruin your prom?"

She shrugged and ate more chocolate. "Probably."

"Sorry. I can't allow that to happen. I'm in charge here," I said, turning her to face the mirror. "There's only one course of action allowable here."

"Call an Uber, leave in shame, and switch to cyber school for the rest of my senior year?" she asked hopefully.

"Nope. We're going to fix your hair, then we're going back out there, and while I tell the DJ to change his playlist, you're going to get all your friends on the dance floor, and you are going to forget that Gregory Prick ever existed, because the best revenge is to have a better time than your nemesis."

"I don't mean to be a doubter, but how the hell are you going to fix this mess?" she asked, poking her hair.

"Trust me. I'm an adult, and I've known a million Gregory Pricks and a billion bad hair days."

The girl wiped her fingers under both eyes. "I'm Ruby."

"It's nice to meet you, Ruby. I'm Zoey."

"You're kind of cool for an adult."

"I know."

Ten minutes and one full head of wet hair later, Ruby and I exited the restroom.

Gage caught me by the elbow. "Everything okay? I was getting worried." He shot a concerned look at Ruby as she adjusted her life preserver.

"Everything's about to be great," I promised him. I turned back to Ruby. "Go get your girls. I'll see you on the dance floor."

"This sounds like trouble," Gage grumbled under his breath.

I patted him on the cheek. "Only if your name is Gregory."

"Gregory Prine? I hate that kid."

My mouth fell open, and I temporarily forgot my quest. "You don't hate anyone. You're too good for that."

"He made my niece cry on the playground in elementary school, *and* Dad caught him stealing MoonPies from the store when he was fourteen. Get the little bastard, Disaster."

"With pleasure." I planted a kiss on his cheek and headed for the DJ.

"Mind if I cut in?"

Gage appeared through the seaweed streamers hanging above the dance floor and tapped Wes on the shoulder.

"I do mind, Uncle Gage," Wes said cheerfully. The kid was in a burgundy tux with one of the legs jaggedly torn off and shark teeth glued to the remaining fabric.

"She's *my* date. Between you, Harry, and the rest of the literal children, I haven't danced with her all night," Gage complained, giving his nephew a good-natured shoulder check out of the way and sweeping me into his arms.

"Well, if you didn't date the hottest girl in town, we wouldn't try to steal her away," Wes complained.

"Remind me to work on compliments with you," Gage said, whirling me away from the teen.

"You are significantly less sweaty than my last several dance partners," I noted as we swayed past a drenched couple in full prom regalia.

"At least I have that going for me. Having fun?" he asked.

"I kinda feel like the belle of the ball," I admitted.

"You should. You've been asked to dance by forty percent of the male population of this school."

"And two percent of the female population. That Janice can really move. This is way better than my actual prom."

"Really? What happened?"

"My hair was up, and the stylist must have used nine hundred hairpins. It felt like I was being stabbed in the scalp every time I breathed. My date got mono from Gwendolyn Fucking Murphy and didn't show up. But the night was saved when Hazel and I convinced the DJ to play three Spice Girls songs in a row and we got every girl out on the dance floor."

"Just like you did for Ruby tonight."

"Technically it was 'I Believe in a Thing Called Love' by the Darkness," I corrected with a grin.

"My ears are still ringing from the entire junior and senior classes scream-singing. I saw you also managed to dump an entire container of coleslaw on the little shit. Where did you even find coleslaw?"

I gave him a diabolical eyebrow wiggle. "The less you know, the better."

"You always make the best of everything, don't you?" he asked.

"I just always look for the sparkle."

"You're beautiful, Zoey. And exciting. And creative. And so smart I can't believe sometimes you don't see it."

My feet fumbled the steps, and I lost my train of thought. "Gage," I whispered.

"I'm serious, Zo. You're something special. For the first time in my life, I'm not worried about tomorrow because I'm having a hell of a good time today."

"Well, damn. You sure know how to sweep a girl off her feet in the middle of the sea."

"And you sure know how to show a man what he's been missing."

Our eyes locked and held as we swayed to the music. The heartburn was back. But it was even worse now.

"Do you have any antacids?" I asked.

His grin nearly took my breath away. "You never say what I expect you to. I like that about you."

"Yeah, that's nice. But I'm serious about the antacids."

Still grinning, Gage led me off the dance floor. He got a lead on antacids in the nurse's office from the principal and followed Destiny out of the gym.

"That boy is head over heels for you," Mrs. Blumenthal observed.

"We're just having a good time," I said, rubbing a hand over my weird, glowy chest. Why did I want her words to come true? What was happening to me? What was in that damn flask?

"I had a good time once too," she said, nodding at Mr. Blumenthal, who was distributing cups of soda to a group of kids dressed as varieties of fish.

The couple at the front of the line signed, "Thank you," to him, and the glow in my chest got warmer. Jesus, was I actively dying?

"We met at a Fleetwood Mac concert," she continued. "His sister was there signing the lyrics to him. I took one look at him and fell head over heels. I didn't know how to sign a single word. He lived two states away. And I was in the middle of an engineering degree. But we made it work."

"It couldn't have been easy. I mean not with those obstacles."

"Nothing good is ever easy, dear. Relationships shouldn't be easy, because people aren't easy. But for the right person, all the hard is worth it."

"I've never been the right person before," I admitted.

She gave my hand a squeeze. "Or maybe you've always been the right person and you've only met the wrong ones so far."

"Did you believe in the whole happily ever after, 'the one' thing when you met Mr. Blumenthal?" I asked.

"I don't know if I believed it, but I sure hoped for it. Sometimes that's all you need. To be brave enough to hope. I just knew that no one else gave me that warm, glowy feeling in my chest like he did."

"Shit," I muttered.

Hazel: I can't believe Gage took you to prom! Send pics! Also, I'm suddenly thirsty for peppermint schnapps.

35

Dimes

Zoey

"How did we get talked into this again?" I demanded through gritted teeth as I lunge-walked my way across Story Lake's gym. It was smaller and significantly less bougie than any of the Manhattan gyms I had ever stepped foot in, but it turned out that the physical torture was the same.

"I think it might have been my fault. I said something to Laura about wishing I had her arms for my wedding, and here we are," Hazel panted as she lunged next to me.

"I would hate you if you weren't such a great person," I said. My legs were trembling, and my vision was impaired by an infinite waterfall of sweat. And I was sore from yesterday's sneaky, harder-than-it-looked Lakercise class with Opal.

"To be fair, you said something along the lines of 'Exercise is good for my brain. I will join you.'"

"I know you can go lower than that, ladies," Laura's personal trainer barked behind us.

Manuel "Manny" de la Cruz was buff and bronze with the

kind of smile that could light up entire stadium-size venues. However, that affable charm disappeared the second the workout started.

"He was so nice when we got here," I whined.

"At least the whole 'unnaturally handsome' thing didn't go away. We'll have a nice view for the last few minutes of our lives," Hazel pointed out.

"Who carries around weighted vests 'just in case' anyway?" I complained.

Hazel managed a smirk and a wheeze. "You're just mad because you thought you'd get out of weighted walking lunges with a broken wrist. When can you take the brace off?"

"Not until after Reader Weekend despite my best attempts at bribing Dr. Ace. I'm officially adding Manny to my People I Hate list."

"How many are you up to now?" Hazel asked.

"Gwendolyn Murphy. Jim, of course."

"Of course," she agreed.

"Nina Evil Pants from Dominion."

"She's the worst."

"And now Manny the Meanie."

"Moody, you're not doing yourself any favors half-assing these lunges. Either shape up or you both do another set," Manny announced to the entire gym from where he was spotting Laura's chest presses, which she was rocking from a sporty low-backed wheelchair.

"Please shape up. I don't want to die before my wedding," Hazel begged.

"I'm officially deducting handsome points," I hissed.

We made it to the opposite end of the gym and collapsed against the wall.

"Take thirty," Manny said, reracking Laura's weights.

"Minutes?" Hazel asked hopefully.

"Years?" I added.

"Seconds," Manny corrected.

We groaned and sagged against each other in a sweaty heap.

"I can't believe we paid money to have someone murder us," I said.

"You two are whining worse than my brothers," Laura said as she wheeled herself toward the squat rack, looking energetic and dewy. "I thought for sure you'd be less annoying than them."

"There's probably significantly less farting, so that's a point in our favor," I reminded her weakly as I mustered the strength to line up my water bottle with my face.

"Gloves," Manny said.

With one hand, Laura snatched the fingerless workout gloves he tossed her out of the air.

"Show-off," he teased.

She snorted and slipped on the gloves while he set up the bar above her. "Please. You're the one practically blowing kisses to yourself in the mirror."

Manny chuckled. "Sounds to me like you're checking out my form."

"You wish," Laura shot back.

He ruffled her blond hair with one massive hand.

"What did I tell you about messing up my hair, you bald barbarian?" Laura snarled.

Hazel made a humming noise. "Is it my dehydrated imagination or are they—"

"Flirting?" I filled in for her.

"Show me what you got today, Guns," Manny said to Laura as she gripped the bar overhead with both hands.

"That's definitely a cutesy nickname," Hazel observed.

"I love this for h—oh my God!" I squeaked as Laura executed a pull-up in her wheelchair.

Hazel shoved her bangs out of her eyes in disbelief. "Did she just do a *pull-up*?"

"And now she's doing another. And another one." We watched as Laura pumped out five in a row.

"Come on, Laur. Give me one more. I got your back," Manny encouraged, spotting her from behind.

Her jaw was tight as her sweat-slicked muscles strained to pull her up. With a grunt, her chin crested the bar again.

"That's what I'm talkin' about," Manny barked as she lowered back down.

"One. More," Laura rasped, still gripping the bar.

"I don't know if that's a good idea," I began. "What if she gets hurt?"

"Only if you're a hundred percent sure," Manny said. "You sure you got one more in you?"

"Fuck yes," she growled, adjusting her hold.

"Then let's do this. I got your back. Pull, baby. Pull!" Manny's voice echoed through the place. Every gym goer in the building had stopped to watch.

Hazel and I managed to climb back to our feet as Laura fought against gravity, against the weight of her chair, and pulled with all her might.

"Come on, Laura," I yelled, grabbing Hazel's arm.

Every muscle in her back was shaking with the effort, her arms seemingly stuck at ninety degrees.

"Pull, girl!" a woman on the treadmill behind us called.

"You fuckin' got this, Upcraft," Quaid bellowed from a nearby weight rack.

Laura let out what sounded like a battle cry and dragged herself the last four inches to the bar. To victory.

The gym erupted in cheers. Towels were tossed, water squirted, and for a moment, pandemonium reigned. And in the middle of it all, Laura rolled her eyes and gave the beaming Manny a celebratory fist bump.

"Badass, baby," he said.

"Oh, he *definitely* wants to kiss her," Hazel whispered.

As if his personal trainer radar had been activated, Manny glanced in our direction. His dimples disappeared.

"Uh-oh," I said.

"You done whining, ladies?"

Hazel nodded vigorously. "Yes, sir."

"I will never whine again," I promised fervently.

"So that was pretty awesome," I said as I huffed and puffed on the treadmill.

"Yeah. I'm aiming for ten by the end of the summer," Laura said nonchalantly from the adaptive rower next to me.

From the rower next to Laura, Hazel gave me a thumbs-up. We were supposed to be finishing off our torturous workout with fifteen minutes of Manny-prescribed cardio.

"You and Meanie Manny…" I began as I reduced the speed on my treadmill.

"Ha. He'll love that," Laura puffed out.

Hazel sent me a look that roughly translated to "you ask her because we're about to be family and I don't want to piss off the woman who just did seven pull-ups with the added weight of her wheelchair."

"He's obviously into you."

Laura fumbled her next pull and nearly dropped the handle. "Excuse me?" she said in a terrifying voice.

"You're joking," I said. "Oh my God. You're not joking. You had no idea."

Laura's head swiveled around to Hazel, who winced and nodded. "I mean, it's super obvious," she said.

Laura resumed rowing…and scowling. "No," she announced. "No! I mean…no!" She stopped again.

I took it as an invitation to slow the treadmill to a crawl. "He calls you Guns *and* baby. He looks at you like you're some sexy goddess of war. And if you didn't have an audience watching your athletic prowess, I am a thousand percent sure he would have kissed you in the heat of the moment."

"No," Laura said again.

"You were flirting back," I pointed out.

"No! I wasn't! Was I? I don't even know how to flirt."

"Trust me, Laura. I'm a literal expert at chemistry, and you two have an explosion on your hands," Hazel said.

Laura shook her head so hard her blond pompadour flipped to the opposite side. "No. He's just training me. I'm not in any headspace for…anything."

"Not to completely overstep but I'm totally going to anyway. Are you in any 'body space' for anything?" I asked.

"She's asking if you want to have sex with him," Hazel translated.

"I know what she's—no. I mean…well. No. I haven't been with anyone since Miller. I wouldn't even know how to date another man, let alone…"

"Boink his brains out?" I offered helpfully.

Laura shoved her hair back to the correct side. "I guess he is objectively hot."

"So hot," Hazel and I said in unison.

"God. I never thought I'd be in this fucking position," Laura said, taking a swig from her water bottle. "Me and Miller. It was supposed to be forever. I loved him since I was a kid. I don't know how to not be with him."

"How did you know Miller was the one?" Hazel asked.

Laura studied her water bottle. "I guess there were a million reasons. He was stupidly gorgeous."

"I've seen the pictures. I can confirm," I agreed.

"He was an exceptional athlete. So damn strong. He was always nice to his parents, even when he was a teenager. He was so serious and responsible, but he also had the best sense of humor."

Miller sounded a lot like Gage to me.

"And that confidence." Laura let out a rough laugh. "We met when he came in the general store and I was running the register. I gave him his change, and he flipped a dime back to me with this ridiculous wink. He told me to keep it as a reminder of the perfect ten he just met. Every time we came across a dime, he would toss it to me and wink. To this day, every dime reminds me of him."

Holy shit.

The pieces fell into place. Gage hiding something on the floor at Laura's house. Him sneaking something into the hood of her sweatshirt at the lake. The literal bowls of dimes he kept in his house. Gage Bishop was reminding his sister that she wasn't alone in the smallest, most heartbreaking way.

As the realization bloomed in my chest like acid reflux, I lost control of my body and tripped on the treadmill. My tailbone and hip took the brunt of the unceremonious landing as the belt continued to revolve without me.

"You okay there?" Laura asked.

"Ugh. No," I whimpered.

I was in love. And it was officially the worst thing ever.

36

Penis-to-the-eye meet-cute

Zoey

The knock at my bedroom door woke me from a dead sleep. Gage was already halfway to it, completely naked, before I reached for my phone.

The clock numbers wavered blearily in front of my eyes: 12:00 a.m.

"Shit. Wait, it's not a murderer," I called a split second too late as Gage threw open the door.

"Happy b—whoa! I see there's a strong Bishop family resemblance," Hazel said, admiring my sex partner's below-the-belt region.

"We're lucky girls," I said on a yawn as I felt around for my discarded sweatshirt and shorts.

Gage jumped back, using his hands to cover as much of his impressive nakedness as possible. "Hazel, what the hell are you doing breaking into Zoey's apartment at midnight? I could have hurt you."

"Yeah. Good thing I wear glasses. Otherwise, I could have

lost an eye." Hazel grinned. Then her expression changed, and she got that faraway look in her eyes.

"Now you did it," I said, handing Gage the bedsheet and giving him a sleepy kiss on the cheek. "Your penis gave her a meet-cute idea."

"What's going on? Why is she in pajamas, holding a cupcake?" he asked me, wrapping the sheet around his waist.

"It's nothing. Just a little tradition. Go back to sleep."

Back from her imaginary penis-to-the-eye meet-cute, Hazel whipped out a lighter and lit the candle atop her cupcake. "As I was saying. Happy birth—"

"Let's take this out into the living room," I said, pushing her through the doorway.

"It's your birthday? And you didn't think to tell me about it?" Gage said, his voice raspy from sleep and annoyance.

I didn't want Good Guy Gage—who I'd accidentally fallen in love with—to feel obligated to make my birthday less sucky than it always was. There was no need to involve him in the mess I'd made. "It's a long story. Don't worry about it," I said.

"She hates her birthday because her parents are terrible," Hazel filled in. "I can't believe you didn't tell him."

I rolled my eyes. "Thank you, Megaphone Mouth. Give me a minute." I shoved her the rest of the way into the hall and shut the bedroom door in her face. "I swear to you I'm not putting you through some kind of 'will he remember my birthday' test. I don't celebrate it. It's actually a day of torture that I prefer not to acknowledge. Hazel knows this, and every year, she shows up at midnight and we have our own little pajama party before things go to hell."

"I'm gonna need a hell of a lot more information," Gage said grumpily.

"Yeah, well, it'll have to wait until breakfast. Please go back to bed."

"Can I have a cupcake first?"

I sighed and opened the bedroom door.

"Cupcake me," I said. Hazel handed me one, which I delivered to Gage. "There. Happy?"

"Still confused but also happy," he said before giving me a kiss on the top of the head, ruffling Hazel's hair, and closing the bedroom door.

"The resemblance is uncanny," Hazel said. "I wonder if Levi is the same in the penis region?"

"Let's go break into his house to find out," I suggested. "We could be in jail before my parents even get here."

"You're not going to my brother's house to look at his dick," Gage grumbled through the door.

"Party pooper," Hazel called back.

We headed for the privacy of the living room.

"Sorry about crashing your postsex sleep," she said. "I thought you two were keeping things casual. I wasn't expecting to find him naked in your bed."

"That's the nice thing about casual sex. It's very energetic, and we just keep falling asleep after it," I said. "Okay. I'm ready now."

Hazel grinned and retrieved the cupcake with the candle from the bakery box. She lit it again and cleared her throat. "Happy birthday to you. Happy birthday to you. Happy birthday, dear Zoey. Happy birthday to you!"

I leaned in, closed my eyes, and blew out the candle.

Hazel handed me the cupcake and took one for herself. We settled ourselves on the living room floor with the traditional bottle of champagne. "I'm so glad you're here," she said, taking a swig directly from the bottle.

"Where else would I be?" I shoved the cupcake into my mouth.

"I mean, I know you want to go back to New York. I just…I can't imagine not getting to be there for your birthday. I can't imagine not having our lake lunches or laundry days. I just love you so much."

I frowned. "Are you PMS-ing?"

"No. I'm just stupidly happy," Hazel said with a sniffle.

"If you start crying right now, I'm gonna be pissed," I said through a mouthful of cupcake.

"You're my best friend. And right now I feel like I have it all. I have you, I have Cam, this town. I'm just scared thinking about how things can change. What am I going to do when you leave? What happens if this book flops? What happens if your parents finally push you over the edge and you murder them and go to prison and we only get to hang out during visitations?"

I stole the champagne from her and put my arm around her shoulders. "I'm the one who needs you, not the other way around, remember?"

She shook her head. "I don't want to make your birthday all about me, but I see everything you're doing to support me and this town that I fell in love with. Nobody is going to champion me the way you do, and I feel like I owe all this to you. I'm so happy and so fucking scared that it's all just going to go away again."

"You're so pretty when you're being an idiot."

Hazel looked down at my pajama shorts. "Hmm, those don't look like your mean pants, yet here we are."

"It's my birthday. I'll be mean if I want to."

"Why does having it all scare the hell out of us?" she asked, reaching for another cupcake.

"You're a real downer on my birthday."

"Yeah, well, I'm sorry for not syncing up my creative crisis with Arbor Day instead."

I heaved a sigh. "You're scared because you've also lost it all before. You know what that rock bottom feels like, and it sucks. But you have to remember, you've already climbed back out once. You've already been lonely and blocked and wounded. You made it through, and you managed to find an even better kind of happy than before. If something changes, you'll just do it again. Just like you've already proved you can."

"You're my best friend, Zoey."

"Duh. You really should expand your horizons."

"I'm serious. I need you to know how amazing I think you are. Even when you're wearing your mean pants."

"The birthday ass-kissing is appreciated but not required."

"I wouldn't be here without you. I wouldn't have any of this, and I just want you to find your happily ever after."

"Haze, you're my best friend. I'd do anything to make you happy, including letting you drag me away from my entire life so you could find your inspiration. But not everyone gets an HEA." I couldn't take that chance again, be that burden again.

"You deserve one. A good one. And I know this sounds crazy, but I think it's here. I think we're both happier here. I just worry what would happen to both of us if you move back to New York."

I dropped my head back on the couch cushion and groaned. "You're the worst. 'Hey, Zoey, here's a birthday cupcake and a side of emotional blackmail.'"

"Just because I personally benefit from you staying doesn't mean that I'm being completely selfish. I see how you're fitting in. I see what you're accomplishing here. And I think you're enjoying it. Admit it." She drilled a finger into my ribs.

I slapped her hand away and stole her half-eaten cupcake. "Fine. As per the midnight birthday honesty clause, I haven't been hating my time here as much as I thought I would."

"I bet that naked hunk of Bishop in your bed wouldn't mind if you stuck around."

"The man lives in a barn, Hazel. A *barn*. I know opposites attract works out in your books, but we both know I'm not going to trade Sephora for skunk baths."

"All I'm asking is that you promise you'll *consider* the possibility of staying."

"Ugh. Fine. I will add *slowly rot into old age with no access to a local Sephora* to my list of options."

"Great! Now, what's a skunk bath?"

"Let me give you some advice. If Meetcute ever runs after a black-and-white cat, don't follow him."

I filled her in on Nana's antics and Pepe's ridiculous crush while she took six pages of notes. I thought about the prom, the home-cooked meals, the dimes, the vagina-defining sex. Maybe

I *was* living the life of a romance heroine right now. But things never stayed good for me for long relationship-wise. There was always a point where I got to be too much for the beleaguered hero.

"How did you know Cam was worth the risk?" I asked her.

She got that dreamy look on her face that was usually reserved for her fictional couples. "He showed up for me like you always have. Different but the same. If I know one thing, it's that no matter what happens, you and Cam will always be in my corner."

"Damn right we will."

"And I'll always be in yours," she promised me. "Because you're more amazing than you know."

"People keep saying that. I'm starting to get suspicious."

"Maybe you'll start believing it."

"Yeah. Sure. When bald eagles bring my bra back."

37

Little Theo stands next to a boy who has a solo

Zoey

"Dad? You're early...and not alone."

I was still sweaty from my two emergency grocery trips and my anxiety-ridden cooking marathon and hadn't changed out of my shorts and sauce-splattered sweatshirt yet.

"I wanted to get a better parking space than your mother. Say hello to Brinsley," my dad gruffly ordered, pointing to the young woman behind him, who appeared to be glued to her phone. She had long blond hair swept back into a flawless ponytail and the dewy face of a woman who had never once skipped her skin-care routine.

"Hey," she said, popping her gum without looking up from her phone.

"Uh, hey?"

So far, the birthday fiasco was right on schedule.

"Brinsley's the assistant manager at the Banana Republic," Dad said proudly.

That explained his rumpled linen shirt and leather flip-flops.

This was the first time in my adult life that I remembered seeing my father's toes.

"Brinsley's also an influencer," he announced, brushing past me into my apartment.

"Are you wearing sunless tanner?" I asked him. There was a distinct orange ring around his collar.

"Maybe. I dunno what the hell she put on me. Where's the john?" He didn't wait for a response and went in search of the bathroom.

Brinsley floated across the threshold, still typing on her phone. She was wearing a gauzy button-down stylishly tucked into a pair of cropped khakis.

"So nice to meet you. I'm Zoey, the younger, screwup daughter with the inconvenient birthday," I said to her retreating back.

I should have pretended to be in Europe for my birthday. Next year, I was going to officially reclaim the day and put an end to this madness.

"I can't believe you made me drive all the way here for your birthday and you couldn't even bother changing out of your pajamas," a flat, familiar voice groused from the open door. "But whatever Zoey wants, Zoey gets."

My mother entered, carrying a crushed baker's box with blue icing smeared on the lid. She was wearing a beige sweater two times too big for her frame over a pair of saggy, dirt-brown leggings. Her hair, even more silver than last time I'd seen her, was pulled back in a lumpy no-effort bun.

"Nice to see you too, Mom," I said, going in for a hug. The offered affection startled her enough to make her back into the doorframe like I was a growling dog. I patted her awkwardly on the shoulder instead.

"Your cake fell off the back seat, so you're just going to have to make do," she said, recovering from the near hug and shoving the box at me.

"I told you we didn't have to get together this year," I said, staring down at the smooshed confection.

My mother scoffed. "Oh, I wouldn't *dream* of committing the crime of not celebrating your birthday again."

We were off to a stellar, if predictable, start.

"Make yourself at home," I said, gesturing toward the living room with my food-laden arms.

"You're out of air freshener, and you need a new plunger," Dad announced from the bathroom doorway.

"I see you brought a child with you, Richie," Mom announced by way of a greeting to my father. She looked at Brinsley like she was covered in fire ants.

"Oh look. It's my ex-wife. Did hell give you a half day today, Adrienne?"

I was in the process of shutting the door and trying to remember what cabinet I'd put the emergency whiskey in when an enormous bouquet of lilacs appeared in the doorway.

"Happy birthday, Zo," the flowers said with a surprisingly masculine voice.

"Oh my God. *Gage*? What are you doing here?" I hissed, pushing him back into the hallway and following.

He lowered the flowers. "It's your birthday. I want to spend it with you and yell at you for trying to sneak it past me."

"I wasn't trying to hide my birthday from you. I was trying to save you from this. You *really* don't want to be a part of this," I said desperately over the raised voices coming from my living room.

"Oh, but I *do*."

Gage was a Bishop. The Bishops were a tight-knit family that actually enjoyed spending time together. The idea of Gage witnessing a meal with the Moodys was terrifying.

"You're very handsome and thoughtful, and you'll totally get points for the flowers. But I'm serious. My parents are…kind of weird and maybe a little mean? It's a lot if you're not used to it."

"Tough shit. I'm celebrating with you," he insisted.

I crossed my arms in frustration. "Hazel told you about this, didn't she?"

"I plead the Fifth. Let's just say there's no way I'm letting you deal with them alone on your birthday."

I shook my head. "I only have enough energy to fight with my family today, so I'll let you have this little win. I mean, it's a brave move. Brave and stupid. And I will be here to tell you I told you so in the end."

He grinned, and my stomach took a pleasant nosedive for my toes. "Deal."

"Oh please, Richie. Like you even know how to work a microwave," my mom bellowed behind me. Two minutes in, and they were already fighting. Impressive but not a record.

"Stop distracting me with your hot cardigan," I warned Gage. "I need to get back in there before one of them brings up Atlantic City 2001."

"It was 2001, the kids were on spring break, and *you* insisted on dragging the whole family to Atlantic City," Dad began.

Too late.

"We already have dinner plans tonight. No one's seen you yet. Why don't you go back to contracting or lawyering and I'll see you later?" I offered. Then, because it was my birthday, gosh darn it, I grabbed him by his shirt and hauled him down for a fast, hard kiss.

He didn't fight me, didn't try to pull back and deliver a chaste peck. No, the man dove in and assumed control of the kiss, leaving me a quivery mass of lust on my own doorstep. Gage Bishop was dangerous.

"Who the hell is this?"

"Wow," I managed to murmur dazedly.

Gage winked.

"Zoey, care to explain why you have your tongue down that man's throat?" Mom demanded from the open doorway.

Gage and I broke apart to discover both my parents standing there looking like they were about to ground me. Brinsley was too busy taking a no-look selfie behind them to notice what was going on.

"This is Gage. He's my…flower delivery guy."

"I'm Zoey's boyfriend," Gage corrected.

"Oh, you are going to regret that," I sang under my breath.

"Boyfriend?" Dad barked. He gave Gage a once-over, then shot a worried glance at Brinsley.

Great. My dad was concerned his girlfriend was going to leave him for my boyfriend…er…semi-regular sex partner. It was another birthday for the books.

"When did you get a boyfriend?" Mom asked, sounding like I'd just announced that I'd been nominated for a Nobel Prize.

"Uh, it's new. We're mostly just having sex. Shall we get this over with?" I asked, gesturing toward the table I'd decorated for myself in the living room.

"You're joining us, aren't you?" Mom said to Gage.

"He can't," I said almost as quickly as Dad growled, "No."

"Of course he's staying," Mom announced and stepped back inside the apartment.

Dad pointed at Gage. "No funny business," he said before joining my mother inside.

"Quick sidebar," I told Gage, "in case Hazel didn't give you the whole story. When I was fourteen, my parents forgot my birthday for the third year in a row, and I threw a fit. With a great deal of teenage angst and a mouthful of braces, I accused them of not caring about me. They asked me what I wanted them to do about it, and I told them I wanted them to *want* to celebrate my birthday every year."

"A reasonable request."

"Reasonable for adults who don't survive on passive aggression. Every year since, my parents' version of 'celebrating' is showing up to remind me that I'm totally selfish for tearing them away from their lives for the day. So I passive-aggressively do my best to make it a terrible experience for us all. It's *super* fun. And I'm hesitant to expose you to it because I don't think you'll want to have sex with me after experiencing it. And I really want birthday sex."

"Hi, I'm Brinsley."

I jumped back from Gage and stared at the woman's outstretched hand. Her face was no longer obscured by her phone, and she was even prettier than I'd realized. I thought she was introducing herself to Gage, but it was me she was looking at.

"Uh, hi, Brinsley. I'm Zoey, and this is Gage," I said cautiously.

She smiled in a way that showed no teeth or fine lines. "You have amazing skin," she said to me.

"Thanks. Um, it's been dry. From winter. And being in my thirties." I was babbling, and Gage was smirking.

"Oh, I've got some great serum recommendations if you're open to it," she offered.

"Are you and my dad…dating?" I gagged just a little on the last word.

"If your mom asks, we are. But I feel safe telling you I'm actually just spearheading his midlife makeover."

"Midlife makeover?" I repeated.

She showed me her phone. Her Instagram account was full of befores and afters of people going from frump to fantastic. She gave a humble little shrug, "It's no big deal. Just half a million followers. I have a podcast too. Anyway, give me your number, and I'll text you some of my recs."

Rattled, I gave her my number, which put her attention back on her phone.

Gage put his hand on my arm. "Do you smell something burning?"

"Shit! The lasagna!"

I ran for the kitchen even though I knew it was already too late. I pushed my parents aside and threw open the oven door. Gage nudged me out of the way and pulled out the blackened lasagna.

"Damn it," I muttered. I'd followed the recipe to a T, but I'd forgotten to set the mother freaking timer.

"Classic Zoey," Dad snorted. "Makes us drive all the way out here, then tries to get out of feeding us."

"I see some things never change," Mom observed as I flapped a dish towel in front of the oven while Gage opened the back door to let the fresh air in. "You know, your sister made the most incredible salt-baked red snapper when I was out there last month. Her talents know no bounds."

"Unlike Zoey, who knows no talent." Dad guffawed at his own joke.

Gage took a threatening step in his direction before I jumped in front of him and held the dish towel in front of his face like it was laced with chloroform. "How about we go to Angelo's for lunch instead?" I suggested brightly.

———

"So where's *Kirk*?" Dad said my stepfather's name like it tasted like a cat hair ball smoothie before shoving half a breadstick into his mouth.

Mom didn't even look up from the chicken parm she was carving into minuscule pieces. Brinsley was too busy taking pictures of her Italian salad to participate in the conversation.

Jessie had seated us in the middle of Angelo's dining room with Wes as our server. On our left were the Story Lake Warblers. On our right was the entire high school cross-country team, including Darius.

"Kirk is at our grandson's spring choral concert. Little Theo stands next to a boy who has a solo. The first two shows were wonderful. I hated to miss it today, but we can't have Zoey feeling left out again," Mom said pointedly.

"You wanted to go to a repeat of a first-grade chorus concert?" I asked, certain I'd heard her wrong.

"Of course. I love showing my support for my family."

"You left in the middle of my volleyball quarterfinals because you said the gymnasium ventilation was drying out your eyes," I pointed out. "You told another mom to tell me to take the subway home. I sprained my knee, and my coach had to take me to a walk-in clinic."

"Oh, don't be so dramatic. You were fine after a few weeks," Mom said, waving a hand in my direction.

"Yeah, Mopey," Dad said through a mouthful of pizza.

"Here she goes again, Gage," Mom said with an exasperated

eye roll. "I don't know how you put up with her. Everything's always a competition. Theo's seven years old, Zoey. You don't *always* have to be the center of attention."

Gage put down his beer. And I could tell just by the clink of glass on the table that he was about to say something.

I reached under the table and grabbed his thigh. "The important thing to remember here is they're just people. They honestly don't know any better," I whispered to him.

"They're about to," he promised darkly before turning to my mother. "Let me get this straight, Adrienne. You're here to celebrate your beautiful, accomplished daughter's birthday, to see her new home and meet some of the people who are important to her. But you want her to know you'd rather be in an auditorium listening to a bunch of tone-deaf kids sing 'Itsy Bitsy Spider'?" His voice was deceptively friendly, and no one but me seemed to notice just how dangerous that was.

"Actually, it's a religious school so they mostly stick to Jesus loving them," Mom said, missing the entire point. "Now if you want to talk accomplished, you should meet our daughter Carla."

"She's a biochemist, you know. And she can cook a hell of a lasagna," Dad explained, lifting his beer in a mock toast. "Not like this one. She just came out wrong."

Gage's thigh muscles tensed under my hand, and I squeezed harder.

"Carla's never forced us to put our lives on pause to celebrate her. Zoey on the other hand..." Mom was on her third glass of wine, which made her twice as loud as usual. One more, and the entire restaurant would know everything she was thinking.

"Oof," Dad agreed.

The only time my parents were in sync was when it came to discussing what a burden I'd been on them.

"This kid never stopped crying as a baby. For the first four months, nothing but screaming at the top of her lungs like she was on fire or something," Dad said.

"I believe it's called colic," I explained to Gage.

"Okay. This is a joke, right?" Gage asked, draping his arm over the back of my chair and dragging it and me closer.

"The joke is on us. We used to have to leave her alone in her room crying for *hours* because none of us could take the noise," Mom remembered on a laugh. "You were just *so needy*."

"That's me," I said lightly. I'd gotten used to the barbs and complaints. They were easier to deal with than the idea that none of us were capable of a real relationship.

"Remember how she couldn't get herself out of bed in the mornings?" Dad said, slapping the table.

Mom rolled her eyes. "Ugh. We got so tired of making sure she was ready for school, we just stopped waking her up."

"Sounds like you were just tired of parenting," Gage said.

"Please don't," I begged him.

"What's that?" Dad barked.

"No more breadsticks," Brinsley said, slapping my father's hand away from the basket.

"Remember that time she got lost at the museum and had an absolute friggin' meltdown?" Dad said to Mom.

Mom groaned. "My God. You could hear her sobbing all the way from the African mammal exhibit."

"'Where's my mommy? Where's my daddy?'" Dad mimicked in a near shout. He and my mother burst into raucous laughter, drawing the attention of everyone in a twenty-foot radius.

"I was four," I said. "Needless to say, by six, I could read a subway map and find my way home."

"And don't even get us started on the teenage years. It's not too late to run, Gage. No one would blame you," Mom teased.

I was getting sympathetic looks from the cross-country team.

Gage pushed his chair back from the table and gave my shoulder a squeeze. "Excuse me for a minute."

My heart sank. I wanted to dissolve into the carpet.

"Oh boy. He's already on the run," Dad said, nudging

Brinsley, who dropped her phone on her salad. "She chased that one off fast."

"You know what? I think it's time we give up this little birthday tradition," I suggested.

"Oh ho!" Dad chuckled.

"Nice try, Mopey. We wouldn't dream of it. Not after the guilt trip you laid on us. No, ma'am. We're stuck with you, so you're stuck with us," Mom said.

"'You're bad parents,'" Dad said in another over-the-top whiny impression.

"'Parents who love their kids don't forget their birthdays every year,'" Mom mimicked. "Meanwhile, who was the one who never remembered her homework or her class schedule or her locker combination?"

Everyone in the restaurant was staring at us, at me. I felt like I was experiencing one of my "naked in public" nightmares in real life. Only instead of everyone knowing I forgot to wear pants, they all knew I was unlovable.

"There was actually a reason for that. All of it," I said, picking up my water glass.

Dad snorted. "Shyeah. It's called laziness."

Brinsley put down her phone and blinked like she'd just woken from a long nap. "I'm not comfortable with you talking to your daughter that way. That's the way a before talks, not an after," she said.

"Sorry, Brinsley," Dad said, immediately contrite.

She looked at me and gestured for me to go ahead.

I cleared my throat. "Actually, there's something I wanted to tell you."

"Oh boy, here we go again. What did we do wrong this time, Zoey?" Dad asked.

"Besides drop my cake, forget my presents, and blame me for your divorce?" I quipped.

Brinsley, confident that I was going to stand up for myself, picked up her phone again.

"I didn't forget your present. Your cake is your present," Mom insisted.

"And I'm *going* to get you a gift card to a gas station. It'll be in your email tonight. Or maybe Monday," Dad said.

I laughed. "Oh my God! Guys, can we please call time of death on this thing? None of us wants to be here. I'm sorry for being fourteen and thinking I'd want to celebrate my birthday with you. I don't want to do this anymore. In fact, I don't think it's healthy for us to be around each other. And the reason I was 'so difficult' is called ADHD, and if I'd had a diagnosis earlier, my entire life could have been easier. Maybe yours too."

But they weren't listening to me. They never were.

"Honestly, if it weren't for all the stress you caused us, I think we might have lasted a few more years. Don't you, Richie?" Mom said.

They'd taken me out to my sister's favorite restaurant the day after she left for college and told me they were getting a divorce.

"You shouldn't talk about that in front of my girlfriend," Dad said, gesturing toward Brinsley like she was the Stanley Cup.

Gage returned, stowing his phone in the pocket of his sweater. "Okay. Here's what's going to happen. You three are going to leave. Now. I paid the bill. Consider it a parting gift. On your way out, either you're going to apologize to Zoey for being the most comically selfish parents in the history of modern parenting or you're going to promise not to contact her again until you can at least pretend to behave like supportive parents."

"Who the hell do you think you are, telling me what to do?" my father blustered.

"I'm Gage Fucking Bishop, and this woman you spent the day being a narcissistic asshole to is someone very special to me. She should be someone very special to you too. But since you're incapable of the bare minimum of human decency, I'm not allowing you to ruin her day for a second longer. Now get the fuck out of here."

I would have said something, but I'd temporarily lost the

power of speech. My mouth hung open like a puppet with its strings cut.

"But what about my food?" Mom demanded, holding up her plate.

"Take it to go," Gage said through clenched teeth.

Wes reappeared at that moment with three takeout containers. He tossed them down in the middle of the table. "I'd tell you to have a nice day, but I really hope it sucks," he said to them.

I clamped a hand over my gaping mouth. If my family had punished me for this long for something I'd said at fourteen, I'd be paying for this for the rest of my life.

"You can't just tell us to get out. You don't own this town," my father insisted as Brinsley neatly boxed up her salad.

Chairs around the restaurant pushed back from tables.

"I don't need to own this town. I belong to this town. So does Zoey. You'd see that if you thought of anyone but yourself. It hasn't once occurred to you that it's pathetic to pay a stylist to pretend to be your girlfriend?" Gage said, going toe-to-toe with my father. My dad had significantly more belly mass on him, but Gage had height and muscle in his favor.

"I knew it! I *knew* she wasn't your girlfriend," Mom said triumphantly as she shoved her leftovers and a shaker of parmesan into the box.

"And *you*," Gage said, turning his ire to her. "What the hell kind of mother feels the need to put down her daughter every sentence?"

"You don't understand how difficult she was," Mom said, digging her heels in like she always did whenever someone told her she was wrong.

"Maybe you don't understand that what she needed was support, not criticism. Maybe you look at her and you see how beautiful and vivacious and interesting she is, and a small mean part of you envies that," Gage said coolly. "It doesn't really matter, because no one here wants to spend another minute with you."

My mother gasped. "I am a *delight*. It's not my fault that

she's so sensitive. No one could give her all the attention she needed. It's not my fault."

"You're, like, a really bad mom," Wes said, standing next to Gage. "Like so bad I wanna go home and hug my mom."

The cross-country team nodded as they formed a line behind them.

"We have something to say," Scooter announced from behind me before blowing his pitch pipe. The Warblers hummed in harmony and then broke into an a cappella version of Rodgers and Hammerstein's "So Long, Farewell" with the creative twist of replacing *night* and *bye* with well-timed mouth fart noises.

My parents huffily made their way toward the door as they were sung out of the restaurant by the Warblers and a dozen other restaurant patrons.

Brinsley lingered behind.

"Okay, so I DMed you my top three recs on serums for dry skin," she said, sliding her phone into her bag. "I also included two of my favorite moisturizers and an eye shadow palette that would look amazing on you. And I threw in the contact info for my therapist. She does virtual appointments, and she can undo a lot of this." Brinsley waved a manicured hand in the direction of my parents. "Thanks for a lovely afternoon. Follow me on Insta!"

And with that, she was gone.

I put my head on the table and prayed for invisibility. Gage sat down next to me and put his hand on my back.

"Zoey, that was...really shitty."

"I'm so embarrassed," I groaned to the tabletop. "Like I don't even know which part is the worst. My parents being my parents. The entire town witnessing it. You picking a fight with them. Gage, they are going to make me pay for that for the rest of my life."

He pulled me up, his green eyes searching mine. "I'm sorry."

"No, you're not!"

"Fine. I wish I was sorry. But, Zoey, they were horrible. Every time I think about you dealing with *that* on your birthday alone every year, I wanna punch someone."

"They're not that bad. I still had a roof over my head and food on the table," I insisted.

What kind of person am I if my own parents couldn't love me? It was the question I'd asked myself for as long as I could remember. I'd often wondered if there was some inherent flaw in my DNA. That maybe it was for the best that I couldn't have kids because there was a possibility that I wouldn't be able to love them. At least the feelings of inflicted inadequacy would end with me.

"Sweetheart, that's a low fucking bar. Providing the bare minimum for survival doesn't make them good parents. And you needing more than the bare minimum doesn't make you a burden. You were never too much. They just weren't enough."

His words tickled a spot deep inside me that I thought I'd healed a long time ago.

"You're going to be a really good dad someday," I said quietly.

"I'm more focused on being a good partner right now."

I blinked and locked in on his face. This was a man who collected dimes just so he could hide them for his sister because he knew they gave her comfort. A man who showed up uninvited to my birthday lunch because he wanted to share the day with me. A man who not only willingly waded into my family drama but told off my parents for their shitty behavior.

A good partner.

Before I could ask him to clarify in explicit detail exactly what he meant, our moment was interrupted by the arrival of the entire waitstaff—including grumpy Jessie—and a cannoli flattened under the weight of an excessive number of candles.

"Just because your parents suck doesn't mean your day has to," Wes said, placing the plate in front of me.

"'Happy Birthday' on three, people," Scooter announced before pulling out his pitch pipe again.

While a restaurant full of my neighbors sang to me, the man who had witnessed my darkest parts smiled at me like I was something special.

38

But my shorts fell off
Gage

"I don't know if you've already forgotten the lunch debacle from a few hours ago—which would be medically concerning—but my birthday isn't exactly fun for me. So when you say 'birthday surprise,' I kinda want to throw up," Zoey told me as I took her by the hand and led her through the lodge's front door.

I was still pissed off about the mess with Zoey's parents. The idea of her enduring that kind of treatment for her entire life enraged me.

I opened my mouth to respond, but she cut me off. "And don't say, 'Trust me. You'll like this surprise.' You should trust *me*, because I won't, and I'm already emotionally scarred enough for the day that I won't be able to pretend to be excited just to protect your feelings."

"I would hope that our disco clause prevents either of us from having to pretend in order to protect each other's feelings." I tossed a salute in the direction of the front desk.

"Hi, guys! Everything's all set up outside," Billie said, jogging around the desk so she could hold the patio door open for us.

"What exactly is 'everything'?" Zoey asked.

"You'll see," I told her.

"It's awesome," Billie promised.

"Why can't we just hide in my apartment and have sex?" Zoey demanded.

"Jesus, Zoey," I muttered.

Billie grinned at us. "I'm sure that will be an option after the surprise. Happy birthday, and I'm sorry your parents are the worst."

Zoey gave an embarrassed chuckle. "News sure travels fast."

Billie gave her shoulder a squeeze. "We gossip because we care. I grew up in a similar situation. I was supposed to go into the family accounting business. Instead, I became a lesbian innkeeper. But you know what? Hana's family more than made up for the disappointments of mine."

I made a mental note to take my parents out to dinner in the coming week as a thank-you for not sucking. Hell, I'd fucked up by not telling them I was representing Valerie, and they'd just complained for a while before telling me they trusted my judgment.

"I'm sorry you had to deal with that," Zoey told her.

Billie waved it away. "Honestly, I think coming from difficult parents makes us cooler people in the long run. Something about overcoming early adversity and whatever. Now, in better news, the lodge is completely booked for Reader Weekend! The magazine people took the last rooms."

Zoey brightened. "Really?"

"*And* I checked with Chevy this morning, and he said the signing is officially sold out. Reader Weekend is going to be a certified hit," Billie predicted.

Zoey grinned up at me, all complaints about the surprise forgotten. "Okay. Fine. This is officially my best birthday ever!"

The fact that it took so little to make her happy pissed me off all over again.

"Anyway, have fun," Billie said, ushering us out the door.

"Come on," I said, coaxing Zoey out onto the patio overlooking the lake.

"You're not taking me to feed a bald eagle, are you? Because I can't afford to lose another bra," she said, dragging her feet.

"I wouldn't do that to you. I promise this is something you'll actually enjoy."

"Surprise!"

Zoey assumed a defensive stance as Hazel and my entire family waved from the lodge's dock. The *Tiki Barge*, Story Lake's newly repaired party pontoon boat, bobbed in the water, decorated for the occasion.

"What is this?"

"Your family sucks, so I thought I'd lend you mine," I explained. I'd given Zoey her space after lunch and had Declan reschedule all my afternoon appointments to make this happen. She deserved more than she'd gotten. More than she'd ever ask for.

"Gage…" Her voice quivered.

"It's a cake cruise. The Hernandezes are going to start offering group rentals this weekend. We're the maiden voyage, and they're going to use pictures on their social media, so you're contractually obligated to say yes."

She looked back at the boat. "This is really sweet, but it's not necessary."

"Yeah, well, whatever escape plan you're hatching, you're not backing out now," I told her, towing her toward the lake.

"Oh my God. Are those—"

"Disco balls? Yeah," I confirmed as the globes hanging from the canopy glittered in the sunshine. "My mom made a special trip to the party store. Now you definitely can't say no."

"Now I don't want to say no," she admitted.

"Get your butts down here so we can pop this champagne," my mother yelled through cupped hands.

"This was the best birthday I've had in…ever," Zoey admitted as we walked toward my office building hand in hand.

The cake cruise was over, and seeing as how the boat hadn't capsized this time and no one had been shit on by Goose, it was considered a rousing success by all. Especially when Laura and Hazel had teamed up to push Cam in the water while we docked at the Fish Hook to pick up tropical drinks and pizzas.

"You're getting worse and worse at this one-night-stand thing," she teased.

I chuckled and slung my arm around her shoulder. Evening had fallen, and everyone, tired from all the laughter and sunshine, had peeled off and gone their separate ways.

"Told you it could be salvaged."

She wrinkled her nose. "Maybe next time, I'll learn to listen to you," she teased.

"Now who's bad at one-night stands?"

She slipped her arm around my waist. "Your family is pretty great. I'm so happy that Hazel gets to be a part of it. She deserves you guys."

I wanted to ask her what she thought she deserved, wanted to argue her into reaching the correct conclusion, to present the evidence that would make her change her mind, make her realize just how very much she deserved. I wanted to fix everything that was broken and make it into something new and solid for her.

We paused on the sidewalk in front of the entrance to my building. "Before we go in, I got you something," I said.

She let out an exasperated laugh. "Gage, you've already done enough today."

"Yeah, well, don't get too excited. It's nothing sparkly or fun. Just practical," I warned, leading her around the side of the building.

"Oh! Let me guess. Did you sanitize my trash bins?"

"No, but I did put them away for you."

"Thank you for that. Did you paint my parking space like a high school senior's?"

"I did not."

"Ooh! I know! Do you have a children's choir waiting to serenade me with a medley of songs from the year I was born?"

I steered her into the small parking lot behind the building and walked her over to her ridiculous convertible. "No, but I did steal your car today."

"Obviously, you're not very good at stealing cars since you brought it back. I'm adding it to the list of your flaws. Terrible at one-night stands and stealing cars. Wait. Why is it so shiny? And how did you get the roof up?"

"I took it to Gator's garage this afternoon when you were recovering from the lunchtime shit show. He changed the oil, fixed the roof latch, rotated the tires, and washed it for you. I also had him inspect it so you're good to go for a while…at least until something falls off. Gator didn't have enough time to figure out what was causing the rattle in the door, but he said if you bring it back, he'll pull the panel off and fix it for free."

Her mouth fell open as she stared at the beat-up little car.

"I told you it wasn't anything fun or exciting," I said.

"This is better than a children's choir. This is thoughtful and helpful and…" She turned to me, her face a masterpiece in the streetlights. "Do you have any idea how much time and frustration you just saved me?"

"I'm glad you like—" The wind was nearly knocked out of me when she threw herself in my arms, her body colliding with mine.

"Thank you for making my birthday not suck," she said a split second before her mouth claimed mine.

This woman could kiss the life right out of a man. Or maybe she was breathing life into me. I couldn't be sure, and in the moment, I didn't fucking care. I gripped her ass, holding her against me. "Let's take this inside."

She murmured her agreement against my neck before sinking her teeth into my skin. Somehow I managed to unlock the back door to my office and kick it open. Inside, I pressed her against the wall and let myself feast on her.

A primitive need thrummed in my blood as our hands frantically explored.

"Office," she said between violent kisses.

"Your nice, comfortable bed is right upstairs," I pointed out.

She slid out of my grip.

"A compelling argument, but my shorts fell off down here," she said, sliding them down her legs and kicking them free.

I groaned. "God, I love that you hate underwear."

"You pulled off a miracle today," she said, leading me by the dick to my office.

"I did?" Hypnotized, I helped her out of her shirt and bra. There she stood, naked and smiling, her hair wild, cheeks flushed. She was so full of life, of energy, of chaos.

My nice, orderly office was for nice, orderly work. How the hell was I going to concentrate on anything ever again if I fucked Zoey Moody on my desk? I could already barely think about anything else when I could hear her walking around dropping things on the second floor.

"You gave me a birthday with good memories. The least I can do is return the favor."

"Sweetheart, you're already unforgettable."

She sank to her knees in front of me.

"Oh fuck." Her fingers were on my zipper. I forgot about all the reasons we'd be more comfortable upstairs. I forgot about worrying about someone seeing us through the window. I forgot about everything but Zoey freeing my cock from my jeans.

"Watch your wrist," I ordered as she gripped me with both hands.

"Watch my mouth," she shot back just before she slanted it over the crown of my cock.

I held the edge of my desk in a death grip as she took me to the back of her throat.

"Goddammit, Zoey." I gritted out the words.

She was playing with me, taunting me, torturing me. And I loved every fucking second of it. I pushed one hand into her curls and gripped so I could guide her speed.

But she didn't need guidance. Her mouth was a weapon, and she deployed it against me. Something on my left toppled off the desk and hit the floor, but it barely registered as Zoey slicked her mouth over me again and again.

My blood sang as the need to come lit and sizzled like a fast-burning fuse.

"Fuck," I growled, forcing her off my cock.

She muttered uncomplimentary things including "BJ police" and "birthday cocktease" as I lifted her off the floor, but all complaints stopped when I swept the contents of my desk onto the carpet and dropped her on top.

Those green eyes lit with an irresistible seductive fire. I slid her closer to the edge of the desk as she yanked my shirt over my head. "Isn't this better than a bed?" she whispered as I lined up the swollen head of my erection with her entrance.

This woman took me places so far beyond my comfort zone, I was never sure I'd survive.

I answered her question with an unforgiving thrust.

She gasped and I steadied her with a light grip on her throat. She looked delighted, and I would have laughed if I had the oxygen to spare. Without breaking eye contact, Zoey braced her heels on the edge of the desk, inviting me deeper.

"Happy birthday to me," she purred as I pulled out slowly before driving home again.

It took over as it always did with Zoey. The clawing need to pleasure and take pleasure. Everything else faded into the background of my mind until the only thing I was conscious of was her body and mine working in tandem.

She hooked me around the neck, dragging me down to her as I took us both to the edge. A loud crack preceded the desk shifting, but still I didn't slow. I kept thrusting, kept filling her as we breathed the same air, chased the same release.

"Gage?" Her voice was breathy.

"Yeah, baby?" I grunted as her inner walls clasped me tighter.

"I love…this."

She came, shattering in my arms, around me, dragging me over the edge with her. My orgasm scorched its way out of me and into her, an intimacy I'd never imagined and now feared I couldn't live without.

We came together, holding each other as our bodies shook,

our muscles tensed until finally we were limp and exhausted, draped over the desk.

"When I'm not completely broke, I'll buy you a new desk," she panted under me.

A chuckle rumbled in my chest. Only Zoey could take me to places of excruciating pleasure and then make me laugh.

Declan: Your office appears to have been ransacked. Should I call the police?

39

Moving to Bolivia with my corneas

Gage

"Zo? What the hell are you doing? It's three a.m.," I complained from the doorway to Zoey's office/dining room.

She was naked except for a pair of fluffy slippers, and she was sitting on the floor, pawing through multiple stacks of paperwork. Nana was sprawled on her back against her, snoring like a chainsaw.

"Nothing. Go back to bed," Zoey said without looking up.

"This isn't nothing. You look like you're gonna start ripping the drywall from the studs."

"I'm just looking for something. It's not a big deal."

The panic in her tone told me it was a very big deal.

On a sigh, I joined her on the floor and picked up a stack of mail. "Tell me what we're looking for."

She shook her head, manically paging through a folder. "It's just an envelope. It's nothing."

"What kind of envelope?"

"The kind of envelope with all the cash the Kick Dominion's Ass committee stupidly entrusted me with. I thought I put it in my Don't Lose This pile, but it's not there, and it wasn't in my Upcoming Stuff I Need pile. It was almost four hundred dollars that I was supposed to use to pay for the live band during Reader Weekend, and now I can't find it. And I don't have four hundred dollars in my account to spare, and I can't sell any of my clothes fast enough to make up the difference. And why didn't I tell them I couldn't be trusted with something like that?"

I ran the calendar calculations in my head and kept the obvious answer to myself. "Here's what we're gonna do. We'll look together. And if we don't find it tonight, I'll pay the band this weekend, and we'll look again after it's all over."

"This is my mess to clean up. I'm responsible for losing the money," Zoey said.

"I hate to break it to you, but your messes are my messes." That didn't have her looking any less panicked, so I tried again. "If I was worried about something that you could help with, you'd want to help, wouldn't you?"

"Not at three a.m."

"I guaran-damn-tee if it were Hazel or me with a problem at three o'clock in the damn morning, you'd be there."

She shrugged a shoulder. "Maybe."

"Definitely. Now go put on a robe. I've been distracted since I walked out here and haven't looked at a damn piece of paper yet."

With the faintest smile on her lips, she leaned over and kissed me on the cheek. "Thank you."

"For what?"

"For not making me feel worse."

"Nobody gets to be an asshole to my girl. Not even you."

Zoey groaned from her prone position on the floor twenty minutes later. "I must have thrown it out. I went on a cleaning spree a couple days ago and threw out a bunch of things." She had her head on Nana's belly. "Who does that? Who grabs an envelope full of cash and thinks *this is clearly garbage*?"

"You'd be amazed at the dumb shit we all do. It's just no one goes on social media to tell everyone about it," I said, replacing the mouse pad and blotter on her desk.

"Here. You can check my purse. I went through it twice, but that doesn't mean it's not in there," she said, dropping her bag on the desk in front of me.

"You sure?"

"Oh my God, Gage. It's not like there's a bear trap in there. There's nothing but tampons, receipts, and candy wrappers."

"Speaking of tampons, how much trouble am I going to get into if I point out that you're getting close to your period and maybe the end-of-the-world sense of doom is related to a hormonal shift?" I asked as I gamely dug into the purse.

She leveled a dangerous look at me. Invisible fire blazed out of her eyes in my direction. In that moment, I knew two things for sure.

1. I was in danger.

2. I was absolutely, beyond a shadow of a doubt in love with Zoey.

It wasn't a slow, steady knowing like I had always imagined. It was a sucker punch to the face. Of all the women in the world, it had to be this one. The one who couldn't use a calendar to save her life. The one who made me go skinny-dipping in the freezing cold. The one who knocked me off a roof with just one glance.

"Shit," she muttered.

I silently concurred.

"I didn't realize it was coming up. How did you?" she asked.

"I keep track of things." Except apparently what my fucking heart was doing.

"Of course you do," she grumbled, climbing off her dog pillow and returning to a pile of contracts.

I decided to keep my inconvenient romantic epiphany to myself for now and tried to focus on the task at hand.

"Did you know you're missing your driver's license?" I asked after I went through her wallet a second time.

"Are you serious? Fuck my life!" Her face was stricken.

I immediately regretted mentioning it. "Let's focus on one crisis at a time."

The interior of Zoey's purse gave me a glimpse into her inner world. Her wallet was open, spewing cash and cards everywhere. Half of the paper I pulled out from the depths was crumpled-up to-do lists. I neatly flattened each one and lined them up on her desk in case there was anything on them that was still relevant. Tasks included things like *Talk to Felicity about Reader Weekend live updates* and *Follow up with Cosmo on Hazel's excerpt* and *Send that guy's kid a gift card for birthday. Also look up kid and guy's name.*

There was an expense report with handwritten notes all over it paper-clipped to an accounting firm invoice, one pair of pantyhose, three of Hazel's signing pens, and two planners—one of which had never been used. Loose on the bottom, I found a health insurance card, three pizza coupons, and nine business cards for plumbers, publishing professionals, influencers, a massage therapist, and a veterinarian specializing in birds.

I spread them out on the desk next to the to-do lists.

I was going to buy this woman a digital scanner, and then I was going to send Declan up here for an afternoon to organize her life for her.

"Tell me about the piles," I said when she started muttering under her breath.

"Huh?" She looked up, eyes still wide with fear.

"You organize in piles. How does that work?"

"Obviously, it doesn't. I just need to keep important things out in the open where I can see them or…"

"Or what?" I asked, sliding her cards back into her wallet one by one.

"Or I forget they exist. You've heard of 'Out of sight, out of mind'? Well, my brain takes it literally. If I don't leave it out where I'll see it every day, I'll forget about it completely until I wake up in the middle of the night weeks later in a panic." She waved her arm out to encompass our current situation.

"Makes sense," I said, already mentally redesigning her pile space.

"It must be amazing to have a brain that functions the way it should," she said, then sighed.

"It does make things easier," I admitted as I returned the last now-neat stack of papers to the credenza on the wall. When I set them down, I noticed a gap between the table and the wall.

"I bet you've never thrown away four hundred dollars," she said.

I dropped to my hands and knees and peered under the table. "Gimme your phone."

"Why? So you can memorialize the moment you realized I was too much of a disaster to have sex with anymore?"

"No. So I can use the flashlight."

"Did you find something?" she asked, perking up. Nana lifted her head too, tongue lolling out of her mouth.

I gestured for the phone, and Zoey slid it across the rug to me.

"I found two somethings," I announced, reaching under to pull out both items. "I found your driver's license in a photocopy of your driver's license and an envelope of cash."

Zoey tackled me while I was still on the floor and rained kisses over my face and neck. Nana joined in on the celebration by licking us both.

Feeling like a hero, I laughed and righted us.

"Thank you thank you thank you!" Zoey said, wrapping her arms around me when I sat up. "I don't know how to make this up to you, but I'm going to figure it out. Do you want your own disco ball? Of course you don't. Maybe a fancy power tool?"

Maybe it was the fact that she made me feel like a hero. Maybe it was the sleep deprivation or the sex we'd had before falling asleep in each other's arms. Whatever it was, I decided to be spontaneous. "Can we talk?" I asked.

"How about we go back to bed and sleep for a hundred hours and then you tell me you don't want to have sex with me anymore?"

"Zoey, there's something I want to talk to you about."

She looked like she was trying to decide which door to run out of.

"It's nothing that would put that look on your face. But we don't have to talk about it now," I promised.

She wrinkled her nose. "Yeah. Here's the thing. If we don't talk about it now, I'm going to be thinking about whatever it is nonstop until I've blown it up into something catastrophic, like your illegal gambling ring is about to get busted by the FBI and you're going to steal some of my internal organs to fund your life on the run in Bolivia. Are you moving to Bolivia with my corneas, Gage?"

"I think we have a shot."

"A shot at what? Running from the FBI?"

"I think you and I have a shot. At being together."

Her mouth dropped open, and I held up my hands to hold off whatever verbal barrage she was preparing.

"I know it's early. I know we're new. I know we both agreed we weren't going to go down this road. But, Zoey, I love being with you. I can see us having a future. I want to know if you can see it too."

She shook herself out of her freeze. "Huh? What?"

"You aren't breathing," I observed.

"Oh, right. Yeah. Oxygen. That's kinda necessary," she said on a strangled laugh before taking a shaky inhale.

"I freaked you out."

"No. What? No! Not in the least. Not at all," she squeaked.

"You don't have to answer right now. I just…need to know sometime."

"Gage, you know I can't have kids. It's medically impossible. Would you really want to throw that goal away just for me?"

"You've given me more in the past few weeks than any goal I've ever accomplished. To me, that's worth pursuing. I'm falling for you, Zoey. Stop shaking your head."

"I'm not," she insisted, still shaking her head. "You want a family *here*. I want…I'm not sure what I want anymore."

"There's more than one way to have a family, but that's a conversation for another day when it's not almost four o'clock in the fucking morning. Right now, I just want to know, do you have feelings for me? Do you think we could have a future together?"

She sucked in a shaky breath. "I...I don't know if I can give you what you want."

I drew her into my arms. "It's more important that you tell me what you want, not what you think you can give me."

"Ugh. Why are you so smart and logical in the middle of the night?" she complained to my neck.

"Tell me what you want, Zoey."

"You know what I want," she scoffed, clearly buying time. "I want to make Hazel's book a huge success. I want to land Opal a deal that will knock her compression socks off. And I want to rub my victory in the faces of everyone who doubted me."

"All admirable goals," I agreed. "But what about after literary agent domination?"

"Please don't take this the wrong way, but I'm scared that you can't handle me. Not all of me," she confessed. "This is pretty mild. But my life is... It's like life is soup and I'm a fork. Wait until I screw up something big like a mortgage payment or I forget about someone's father dying and then I'm all like 'Hey, how's your dad doing?' even though I went to the funeral and sent flowers. That's my life. I don't know how to settle down and not be a disaster."

"Okay," I said. "And I don't know how to breathe life into every room I enter. I don't know how to make every person I meet feel important. I have no fucking clue how to make a memory out of the most mundane day. That's *why* we work. We bring different things to the table."

"And then we have sex on it." She clapped a hand to her forehead. "Do you see what you'd be dealing with? Things just fly out of my mouth sometimes. Like the fact that I want so badly to be good enough to deserve you. But, Gage, I'm a fucking mess. You can't trust me to be a good partner. I'll let you down. I'll disappoint you. I'll need you too much and won't be able to give enough back. You deserve more. You deserve better than me."

"There is no better than you."

"Oh please," she harrumphed, then softened against me. "You deserve what your parents have."

"Zoey, honey, my parents have a partnership that plays to both their strengths. That's all I'm asking for here."

"I am freaking the fuck out right now," she admitted.

"Yeah, but you haven't kicked me out yet, so I'm feeling pretty confident I'm going to get what I want."

"Shut up," she huffed.

"What are you afraid of?" I pressed.

She sat up and looked me in the eye. "That I'll go all in with you and show you my whole hot mess of a self, and you'll try to hang in there because you're a good guy, but I'll disappoint you and inconvenience you over and over again until you have no choice but to leave me because I'm too much or not enough and it would all be so much easier with someone else. Which will destroy me, because I'll have finally let myself believe that I could be loved. Which means I'll have no secret hope left that somewhere out there is a man who could actually really love me for me. And I don't know how to live without that secret hope."

"There's only one way through this," I told her.

"I should leave Story Lake under the cover of night, never to return?" she suggested.

I laughed. "No. Show me."

"Show you what?"

"Show me what I'm getting into," I insisted. "Drop the masks. Stop editing what you're thinking and feeling. Stop hiding your mistakes and trying to fix them alone. Show me everything you're so sure will scare me off."

She snorted. "Yeah. Right. You say that now, but you're expecting the reveal to be like when the librarian takes off her glasses and lets her hair down and she's ten times hotter. I'm just ten times more dumpster fiery."

"Show. Me. Let me handle you."

"Gage! Yesterday, I showed up two days early for a Zoom call that I put in my calendar app wrong. I ate crackers and old cheese that I had to scrape the mold off for dinner *two* nights *in a row* because I forgot to get groceries again. I walked everywhere yesterday and told everyone it was because I wanted to 'enjoy the spring weather' but really it was because I lost my keys and didn't find them until this morning on top of the aforementioned moldy cheese in the refrigerator, which I *still* haven't thrown out. There's no sexy librarian waiting to be revealed here. There's just profound disaster."

"Well, that's a start."

She snorted. "That's not even scratching the surface."

"Zoey, partners aren't two people who are good at the same things. Real partners are two people who bring their own strengths and weaknesses to a common goal."

"Yeah, well, my goal every morning is to not completely fail at adulting. Spoiler alert: I go to bed every time thinking about all the ways I failed. You don't want me. You want someone with loftier goals than 'finally schedule overdue gynecologist appointment.'"

"You about done with the chickenshit excuses?"

"Moldy cheese, Gage," she emphasized.

I shook my head. "Not falling for the adorable charming distraction. I want a chance to make this thing real. You have a way of connecting with people that makes them feel really seen. You're fiercely loyal. You're a shark in negotiations. You're funny as hell. You're the steadiest shoulder to lean on in a crisis. You pay such close attention to the people around you that you can predict what they're going to do next. And when I'm lucky enough to get this close to you, you make me feel like I'm some kind of goddamn hero. I don't give a fuck if you don't know where the car keys are or if you forgot your cousin's kid's birthday, because you make the time we're together so fucking magical that the mundane shit doesn't matter."

"But the mundane shit is actual life. It's paying bills and going to meetings and deciding what's for dinner every stupid night of the week. I don't wanna decide every night for the rest of my life."

I stroked a hand down her back. "I know I'm asking for a lot. I know it's scary as hell. But let me show you how much I want this. How much I want *you*."

She covered her face with her hands. "This is gonna end so badly, Gage."

I pulled her back into me. "You keep saying that, and I just keep falling harder for you."

She groaned. "I really hate how much I love your cardigans."

"Look. It's late. Reader Weekend is this week. All I'm asking is that you think about it. Okay?"

She took a deep breath. "Fine. But just remember. You asked for this," she said grumpily.

I cupped her face gently. "And while you're doing your thinking, just remember that I could spend the rest of my life with your 'too much' and it still wouldn't be enough."

"Stop being so good at words."

40

Shenanigans

Zoey

Me: Stop panicking.
Hazel: How did you know I was panicking?
Me: Because it's release day. You always panic on release day.
Hazel: I hate being so predictable.
Me: We can't both bring unpredictable chaos to the table. Remember, we only have our careers and the future of this town riding on how well this weekend goes. No pressure AT ALL!
Hazel: Har har.
Zoey: I'll pick you up later. Don't dress like shit.

"This is Curly Calamity to Little Mule. What's the status at the farm?" I said into my walkie-talkie. Story Lake had graduated from last summer's selection of donated children's radios to the cheapest ones the general store could order, and honestly, it felt like a win.

Opal snorted next to me at the welcome booth. It was nine in the morning, and we were set up in a shady spot near the lake's parking lot.

"Hey, laugh all you want. I still got you out here volunteering for the early shift."

"I believe it was more emotional blackmail than volunteering," she said, fanning out the coupon packets across the table.

"This is Little Mule for Curly Calamity." Isla's voice crackled over the radio. "We've got a full barnyard. Repeat, a full barnyard. Opening up the lower pasture for more parking now."

"Excellent. Call me if you need anything. Curly Calamity out," I said. I crossed off the half hour check-in with Bishop Farms from my minute-by-minute checklist Felicity had developed and turned my attention back to the picnic tent that was going up next to the lake. If I dropped the ball on something this weekend, it wouldn't be for lack of trying. That was for damn sure.

I hit the button on my radio again. "Logistics Lover, this is Curly Calamity requesting a weather check. I want to leave the tent walls off if possible."

"Logistics Lover reporting for duty." But Felicity's voice wasn't coming from my radio. It was coming from behind me. I whirled around on my metal chair to see Felicity standing behind us in her *Story Lake Reader Weekend* T-shirt.

"What are you doing here? You know we were fine with you handling the communications from home," I said, jumping up to greet her.

Her eyes darted from side to side, and her arms were crossed. "I know. But this is important. And for once, I wanted to be there to witness it in person. Besides, I baked a dozen potatoes in case Dominion shows up today," she said, pointing at her backpack.

"That is very brave and generous of you, and that's all I'm going to say about it. Why don't you take over here with my friend Opal so I can go check in at the bookstore?"

Opal harrumphed at Felicity. "We're not friends. She blackmailed me to be here."

"I did not. And stop saying that before someone tries to investigate me for elder abuse," I warned.

"I'm actually here for the revenge plot against Dominion," Felicity said.

"Excuse me."

I looked up and found a woman with a nose ring and a smile looking at me. "Are you Zoey?"

"That depends on how much trouble I'm in."

"I'm Audrey. Gage's friend-slash-client. I'm here to volunteer."

"Here's a shirt," Opal said, throwing a staff T-shirt at her.

"Please excuse my crabby acquaintance," I apologized. "Thank you so much for being here. We could use some extra hands in the bingo tent."

"Perfect," she said.

"I'll walk you over as long as you two promise not to scare anyone off," I said to Opal and Felicity.

"Can't promise anything," Opal harrumphed.

"So you're dating Gage," Audrey said as we headed for the tent.

"Oh, well, I wouldn't say *dating*."

"Well, whatever you're doing, it's putting a smile on his face, and I love to see it. He's one of the good guys," she said.

"He really is," I agreed on a sigh. He was *my* good guy. For better or worse.

"I can't wait to find one of my own someday," Audrey admitted. "Divorce," she explained, holding up her ringless left hand.

"Congratulations," I said. "There's nothing like a fresh start, is there?"

Audrey grinned. "That's what this weekend smells like. Fresh starts."

She wasn't wrong. I deposited her at the bingo tent and decided to check in on the businesses on Lake Drive to see how they were holding up to the increased traffic.

The whole town was putting its best foot forward. Storefronts sported fresh paint, pretty greenery, and hand-lettered signs. I could see the coffee shop was already doing a brisk business thanks to a few dozen readers all sporting their Reader Weekend totes. And Garland was on the scene at the lodge, reporting that another gaggle of readers was having breakfast and exclaiming over how cute the town was.

I was just passing Gage's office and looking up to make sure I'd closed my living room windows when I ran into a wall of man. I'd have known him by his scent or at least the feel of his cardigan without even opening my eyes.

"Well, this is a pleasant run-in," Gage said, rubbing my arms. His green eyes were warm and affectionate this morning. It made me feel like I had a belly full of honey and a heart full of burn.

Damn it.

I, Zoey Moody, had gone ahead and fallen in love with a cardigan-wearing, dog-dadding, law-abiding, blue-collar hottie. I kept hoping the feelings would just go away. That I'd wake up and everything would be back to normal. But nooo. Every day, I just got sucked in deeper and deeper.

This was going to mess up everything.

"Hi." I managed to get the word out without choking on it.

"You left early today," he said, plucking a piece of lint off my Reader Weekend Committee shirt. "I thought I'd have time to wish you luck."

I'd been avoiding having any non-naked, non-unconscious time with Gage until after this weekend while I sorted out our most recent potentially life-altering conversation. But a girl could only pretend to fall asleep after sex so many times before the guy got suspicious.

"I had a lot of things. To do," I added hastily in case it wasn't clear. Oh God. I was turning into a blathering idiot. And I was going to stay here in this town and marry a man who made me say stupid things because his hot niceness threw me off. "So you're looking handsome and stuff."

Way to save it, me. Way. To. Save. It.

Thankfully further embarrassment was temporarily delayed by the walkie-talkie on my hip. "Come in, Curly Calamity. This is Marvel Mayor. We have a situation at the lake."

"I'm on my way," I said.

"I'll come with you," Gage volunteered.

"Um, thanks?"

"I'm only doing it because you think I'm 'handsome and stuff.'"

"Come on," I said with an eye roll and the pitter-patter of panic in my chest as we made a U-turn for the lake.

Situation didn't even begin to cover what we saw when we crossed the road into the lake parking lot.

Nina Vampic, looking evilly beautiful as always, was watching four people in *Dominion Dominates* T-shirts unload several animal crates and carriers from two vans.

"Why does she have different minions every time?" I wondered.

"Probably because no one can stand her for longer than a day at a time," Gage guessed.

It was the only acceptable answer.

"What the hell is this?" I demanded, pretending to consult my clipboard. "I don't have 'Arrival of Queen Assface' on the schedule."

Darius held up his hands. "Mayor Vampic was just explaining—"

"You mean lying to our faces," Felicity cut in helpfully. I didn't see her backpack, but I knew her potato stash couldn't be far.

"The mayor said there was a water main break at the shelter, and she needs us to take in all their strays for the weekend," Darius said.

Nina flashed one of those viciously fake smiles that made me want to punch her in the boob. "I figured you do-gooders would have plenty of time on your hands after your silly little book reading event bombs."

"Why are you so unlikable?" I asked. "I mean seriously.

You're so pretty. All you'd have to do is just not open your mouth, and you could have all the friends you want."

"I don't know why you think you can speak to me that way. But I do know you've got fourteen cats and dogs to deal with. Good luck with that, publicist." She gave a loud fake cough.

No one moved.

Nina cleared her throat, then pointedly coughed again.

"Did you swallow a bug?" Darius asked.

"Damn it, Gary," Nina said. "Do the thing!"

One of the minions, with glasses and a beanie, looked up. "Oh right. Sorry. Oops. I fell over and accidentally unlatched this cage," he announced as he slowly lowered himself to the ground. With an exaggerated flail of his arm, he reached for the door of the closest crate and, after some fumbling, managed to pry it open.

Whatever was inside didn't move a muscle, but it did let out a pathetic whimper.

"Damn it, Gary! I told you to open the Jack Russell's crate. That little son of a bitch can run like the wind."

"Sorry, Nina."

"Okay," Gage said, taking a preemptive step in front of me. "You have to have another option. We all know you're just doing this to wreak havoc and distract us."

She gave a dainty shrug. "I don't know what you're talking about. Of course, if you can't handle them, you're welcome to take them to the next-closest shelter. It's high-kill," she said with a creepy smile.

"You're, like, a legit monster, you know that? We're going to make stuffed versions of you to put up in our gardens to scare away the pests," I said, peering around Gage's shoulder.

"Easy there, Disaster," he said quietly.

Darius stepped forward. "We'll be happy to help you out. For one hundred dollars per animal per day."

Nina's smile faltered for a moment. Then she smirked. "Whatever. Send me a bill." She whistled shrilly. "Let's get back to Boozetag, Dominionites!"

"Hmm, sounds forced. Why not Domineers?" Felicity suggested.

"I like Dominoes better because we get to knock. Them. Down," I said, baring my teeth.

"Nobody asked you, Curly Sue," Nina snapped.

"All trash talking aside, this feels like a real half-assed attempt at messing with us," Gage interjected.

"He's right. Summer Fest involved actual sabotage. But this seems like a plot that second graders came up with," I observed.

One of the Dominionites eased closer. "We were going to 'accidentally' launch fireworks into your town square, but we set our own fire department on fire during the practice run, and then we broke the fire hydrant, and that's what flooded the animal shelter. So now you just get a bunch of displaced pets."

"Ah," Gage said. "Makes sense."

"Amateurs," I muttered.

Nina flipped her icy-blond hair over her shoulder. "Oh, and by the way, most of the animals are really old and need medicine around the clock. So have fun with that." She slapped a garbage bag full of pill bottles to Darius's chest. "Ta-ta, losers," she said before strutting back to the vans.

"I'd like to potato her entire town," I muttered.

"What are we going to do with fourteen dogs and cats with special medical needs?" Felicity said.

I crossed to the open crate and peered inside. A skinny silver pit bull in a pink collar shivered pathetically in the corner. She was curled into a ball, the tip of her tail covering her little heart-shaped nose. Her brown eyes locked on me, and I again felt that strange warm glow in my chest.

"It's gonna be okay, little girl," I promised.

The tail tapped hesitantly against the crate's plastic floor.

I straightened and faced the crowd. "Okay, people. We can handle this. A couple of cute animals is better than illicit fireworks exploding in town square."

"You know who's good at taking medicine all the damn time?" Opal said as she limped toward us.

I grinned. "I do, and that gives me an idea."

"I had it first," Opal insisted.

"Fine. Let's go."

Forty minutes later, I was sitting in the passenger seat of Gage's truck with the little pit bull on my lap, my phone glued to my ear.

"Yeah, we're going to need play yards, baby pack-and-play things, whatever we can use as a bunch of doggy and cat jails. But, like, friendly doggy and cat jails," I said into the phone. "I need this to look like an adoption fair, not a police operation. Oh, and something the cats can't climb out of."

The dog that I had quietly nicknamed Buttercup after *The Princess Bride* wriggled in my lap and bathed my chin with kisses. I was absolutely not falling in love. Again. No. Nope. No way. I was staying focused on the task at hand, which was…something important.

"Look at you," Gage said when I hung up.

"What?"

"You're holding a dog in your lap while organizing a last-second adoption fair. You've come a long way from running out in front of my truck, screaming about eagles and snakes."

"And you've gotten to see my boobs since then," I reminded him.

"It's been a good couple of months for us both," he agreed, giving me a pointed look.

"Yeah, yeah. I'm still thinking," I fibbed.

I was done thinking. This was what I wanted. A chaotic Saturday spent with a good dog and a good man. There was no amount of temporary professional success that was going to make me feel as happy and satisfied as this moment. I wanted more, and I wanted it with Gage Bishop.

I just needed to figure out the perfect grand gesture to tell him, because I was nothing if not dramatic.

"Can you hurry it the hell up?" Opal demanded from the

back seat, where she was wrestling a bonded pair of cats back into their crate.

"I told you not to open it," I said smugly.

"What was I supposed to do? They were meowing their little faces off. Maybe someone with a cold, shriveled heart can ignore that, but I can't," she complained.

She's going to adopt them, I mouthed to Gage, who grinned and turned into the Haven's entrance. Behind us, Levi's truck did the same.

"Okay, people. Let's make this work…somehow," I said.

41

Gosh darn delight

Zoey

"Are you sure that's not the line for the coffee shop?" Hazel asked for the third time.

I was covered in dog hair and still out of breath from racing to the bookstore from Story Lake Haven's last-minute pet adoption fair, where Gage and Levi were constructing temporary enclosures to introduce the senior humans to the senior animals. Opal had already wrangled a half dozen residents and staff to volunteer at the event, which had left me free to hurry back to the bookstore in time to get ready for the signing.

So far, I hadn't let anybody down. Yet.

I pushed Hazel down in her chair, patted her head, and laid out the pens in front of her. "Pretty sure that's the line for your signing."

Chevy and Cam paced in front of the door, each pausing to shoot worried glances through the glass.

I spotted the woman from Thrive's social media team jogging down the line with a handheld camera, capturing the joyful chaos. I felt giddy, energized, a little bit ready to vomit...but like in a good way.

"It's a mob scene. The store can't hold this many people. What were we thinking?" Chevy said to me, wringing his hands.

Cam swiped a hand over his face. "That's too many people. What if some of them try to kidnap Hazel? I can probably take on five or six, but if it's a whole team of kidnappers... I mean, you guys saw *Misery*, right? Maybe I should call Livvy?"

"What if I spell my name wrong? What if I just start writing *Hazmat* on people's books?" Hazel wondered.

I clapped my hands, startling everyone. "Relax. Okay? Despite what your nervous systems are telling you, this is not a dangerous situation. This is a celebration. Those are romance readers outside. They are the nicest of all humans, and they are here to tell Hazel what a good job she did. Then they're going to spend a whole bunch of money in your shop, Chevy, and then they're going to spread their joy and money all over the rest of this town."

"They're waving at me," Cam said, ducking behind a revolving book display.

"Then pretend you're a human being and wave back," I suggested.

Hazel hid her laugh behind a cough.

"You two have one job today," I said, pointing at Cam and Chevy. "Be charming. There will be no panicked bookstore owner, no Cactus Cam. You will be a gosh darn delight to every single person who walks in here."

"Gosh darn delight. Got it." Chevy nodded aggressively.

"Have you fucking met me?" Cam demanded.

"I have, and I know as prickly as you are on the outside, nothing is more important to you than Hazel's happiness. And what's going to make Hazel happy today is you being with her to experience the most magical of events. A romance novel book signing. Got it?"

"Make Hazel happy. Got it. What are you going to do?" he asked.

"Everything else."

"Yeah, that sounds fair," Cam said.

"I'm good with that," Chevy agreed.

"Great. Now I need you two to go into the back room and recount the boxes of stock before we open the doors," I said.

They practically raced each other through the doorway.

"What was that about?" Hazel asked. "You recounted the boxes twice today and four times yesterday."

"I just needed a minute with you."

"Aww! That's sweet. Did you get me a present?"

"Yeah. Kind of." I took a shaky breath. "Okay. Here goes. I'm staying."

"You're staying."

I nodded.

"Here? In Story Lake?"

I nodded again.

"For how long?" Hazel asked with an appropriate amount of suspicion.

"For as long as Gage still wants a future with me."

"Oh my God!" Hazel shrieked. She stood up so fast she knocked her chair over behind her.

Cam sprinted out of the back room. "What's wrong? Where's the kidnapper?"

"There's no kidnapper," I assured him.

"Go back to your boxes," Hazel shouted, then winced. "I'm sorry. That was aggressive. I love you. Please go back to your boxes."

Cam narrowed his eyes. "Why are you both being weird?"

"Publishing stuff," I lied.

"Social media," Hazel said.

We both smiled with feigned innocence.

He pointed at us. "For the record, I don't believe either one of you. But I also don't see any kidnappers. So I'll go back to the boxes."

"Thank you! Love you," Hazel called after him. As soon as he disappeared, she grabbed my arms and shook me back and forth. "Tell me you're serious and that you're also not just doing this because I guilted you into it."

"I'm serious and I'm only partially doing it for the guilt. The rest of it was Gage asking me to stay. Which he did after seeing me at my middle-of-the-night worst *and* after meeting my parents. *And* after knowing that I can't have kids."

We were jumping up and down in celebration now. Hazel, my best friend and soul sister, had been there for me through it all, from pregnancy scare to unanticipated diagnosis to mourning something I hadn't even known if I'd want. Her eyes welled with tears. "Oh, Zo! I'm so freaking happy for you!"

"I'm happy for me too! But don't say anything. I haven't told him yet. I'm going to wait until tonight."

"I love that. Now tell me everything. How did he ask you to stay? I need all the details."

"I promise I'll spare nothing, but first you have something more important to do."

She blinked and stopped jumping. "What?"

"Wow, I need to do more cardio," I wheezed. "First you need to sign books for a few hundred excited readers, because you just released your first book in years, and it's gonna be huge."

"Oh right. That. Yay me!"

She started jumping again.

"Yeah, no. I'm just gonna stand still for this celebration."

"Can we come out yet?" Cam yelled from the back room.

"Let's do this," I said, guiding Hazel back to the table and picking up my walkie-talkie.

"We're gonna need more books," Chevy called from the register, a tinge of hysteria in his voice.

We were an hour into Hazel's signing, and the crowd was buying books like it was Christmas Eve in Iceland.

"I'm on it," I yelled back. I signaled for Cam to take over flapping for Hazel. He looked a little shell-shocked, having already peopled so intensely. "You've got this. You're just turning pages," I told him as I abdicated my seat to him.

I weaved my way through shoppers, smiling and

commenting on their selections until I made it to the back room. I closed the door behind me and sagged against it. The signing was already a success, and I could only hope that it was indicative of how the rest of the world was receiving Hazel's new book baby.

Nerves performed Olympic-level gymnastics floor routines in my belly. I wanted this so badly for her. For me. I could see our futures. More books. More events like this. Maybe even some for Opal, who would surely hate every minute of it. Ultimate bingo and lake cruises on the weekends. Gage in his sexy cardigans when the leaves started to change. A sky-high Christmas tree in his living room. A stocking for me on the mantel. He definitely needed a chandelier or some kind of fixture to add the requisite Zoey "wow" factor.

"Get a hold of yourself, Moody. Focus on the books. Books, books, books," I repeated to myself as I scoured the boxes on Chevy's ancient metal shelves. I had just snagged an open box cutter from the desk when two things happened at the same time. A raucous burst of laughter erupted in the store, and I misjudged the distance between my body and the nearest shelf.

I smacked into the corner, bobbling the box cutter. I watched in horror as it flew through the air as if possessed by a murder demon.

I didn't even feel it at first, but as soon as the blood began to soak through the denim, I knew I was in trouble. "Fuck."

> **Me:** I need you, a first aid kit, and a pair of pants at the back door of Stories ASAP.
> **Gage:** I'd ask questions, but this sounds like there's blood. Be there in four minutes.
> **Me:** Thankyouthankyouthankyou.
> **Gage:** There's blood, isn't there?
> **Me:** It looks like I was attacked by the Fighting Vampires.
> **Gage:** Damn it, Zoey!
> **Me:** Yell at me later! It looks like a crime scene in here!

Three and a half minutes later, the back door flew open, and Gage rushed inside, looking grim.

"Wow. That was fast."

"I was in my office when you texted. Are you okay?" he demanded as he cracked open a professional-looking first aid kit.

I waved with my handful of bloody paper towels. "I'm fine. My jeans kept it from cutting too deep. I just didn't want to go back out there and bleed all over everybody."

We both looked down at the neat slice through the blood-soaked denim.

"Jesus. I can't leave you alone for a minute," Gage said, kneeling in front of me and unceremoniously ripping my ruined pant leg up to the knee.

"Okay, that was hot," I noted.

"Zoey," he said in his "you should be taking this more seriously" tone. "You need to see a doctor."

"Because I'm going to pass out from the sexiness of my boyfriend ripping my jeans off?"

"Boyfriend, huh? Little sting," he said, not taking his attention off the cut on my leg.

"Little sting? Is that what you want me to call you? Because as a nickname it—ahh! Ouch!"

Fire seared up my leg. Gage smirked up at me, holding an alcohol pad to my wound.

"There was nothing little about that sting," I said accusingly.

"This is what happens when you're careless," he lectured.

"I wasn't being careless. I was distracted." I wasn't about to tell him this wasn't the first time I'd rumbled with a box cutter and lost. But at least this time, I'd kept the blood spray away from the books.

"Anything that makes you temporarily forget things like personal safety falls into the careless category." His voice was gruff, but his hands were gentle on my leg as he bandaged the cut.

Goose bumps cropped up on my skin from his touch. Would it always be like this? Would the connection always feel so real, so tangible?

There was a cheer from the crowd in the store, followed by laughter.

"How's it going out there?" Gage asked as he secured the last piece of tape. He pressed a kiss to my shin, and I fell in love with him all over again. Damn, this guy was good.

"Good enough that I have my fingers crossed for a spot on all the bestseller lists. The readers are loving it here, and it's the best thing in the world to see Hazel being adored."

"You know, she credits Story Lake with her comeback," Gage said conversationally as he packed up the first aid supplies.

I had to roll my lips together to keep from smiling. "Is that so?"

"Just sayin'. Good things happen here. I'd hate for you to miss out on anything by moving back to New York."

"I'll take that under advisement. Now where are my pants?"

"Not knowing the extent of the injury situation, I brought you three pairs to choose from and a couple of shirts in case there was any collateral clothing damage," he said, tossing me a grocery bag of clothes.

I sighed and looked down at my neatly bandaged leg. "My hero."

He ruffled my hair and finally delivered the smile I'd been waiting for. "Don't you forget it. Now, if you're done being careless, I'm going to go check on the adoption fair at the Haven and see how things are going at the farm."

I tossed him a salute. "I will do my best to keep all injuries to a minimum for the rest of the day."

"That doesn't make me feel any better," he said.

"Hey, have you ever thought about putting a cool chandelier in your living room?" I asked.

He blinked, then chuckled. "Someday I'll learn to keep up with you."

"Oh, I doubt that," I teased.

The signing lasted three and a half hours. By the time the last reader left with her freshly inked copy of *Story Love* and the six other novels she picked up while in line, Chevy was on the floor behind the register. Cam was massaging Hazel's shoulders while barking a to-go food order into his phone at Levi. "I don't fucking care. Bring me all the onion rings they have," he snapped before hanging up. "I'm so fucking proud of you, Trouble."

"That was a lot of people," Hazel said, looking dreamily shell-shocked.

"That was a lot of *books*," I said, massaging my face. It hurt from smiling.

Hazel leaned over and punched me weakly in the shoulder. "We're back, baby."

I gave her a grin that might have been closer to a grimace. "Damn right we are."

She blinked at me. "When did you change clothes?"

"About an hour in when I got into it with a box cutter in the back room."

"Again? Didn't you learn your lesson last time?"

"Apparently not, but at least this time, I didn't geyser blood all over your books."

"I have a first aid kit in my bag. Why didn't you tell me?" she demanded, groaning as Cam moved to massage her hand and wrist.

I shrugged. "You were in the groove. I texted Gage, and he came over and played doctor and wardrobe specialist."

"Speaking of Gage, when are you going to tell him about that thing?" Hazel asked.

"What thing?" Cam asked gruffly.

"Can I tell him, please please *please*?" Hazel pleaded. "You know he hates to talk to people. He won't tell anyone."

"Ugh. Fine." I was too tired and too happy to worry.

"Gage asked Zoey to stay, and Zoey is going to say yes! She's going to stay here in Story Lake, and we're going to get married, and they're going to get married, and everyone is going to live happily ever after!" Hazel announced.

"Whoa whoa whoa. Hold your free-range horses there. First

of all, I'm only agreeing to stay. No one has said anything about getting married."

Hazel shook her head. "I refuse to let you take this fantasy away from me."

"Writing brilliant books makes her a little loopy," I told Cam.

"I like loopy. And you and Gage better not fuck this up," Cam said gruffly.

"He means *congratulations*," Hazel said, leveling him with a look.

"Yeah. Sure. That. Also, don't fuck this up. Because if you make my wife sad, I'll make you regret it."

Hazel and I looked at each other. "My wife," we growled before breaking into hysterical giggles.

42

The shit show
Gage

> **Zoey:** I have some big news. Well, two big news... newses? Newsi? Whatever, come find me at the bonfire, and I'll give you all the newsuals.
> **Me:** You know texts like this terrify me.
> **Zoey:** Why do you think I keep sending them? See you at the lodge!

The lodge was busier than I'd ever seen it on a Saturday night. Story Lakers old and new mingled on the patio and shoreline with visiting readers. There was also a small surprising contingency of Dominion neighbors and tourists.

The crickets and tree frogs were drowned out by the beats of Darius's little sister deejaying on the far side of the patio. Billie and Hana had set up two pop-up bars outside to keep up with the overflow from the lobby, where Opal was holding court with Darius, my parents, and some of the Haven residents.

By all accounts, Reader Weekend was a hit. Hazel's signing was a sold-out success. My parents' farm sanctuary was off to a great start, earning more than $5,000 in donations for the day. Town businesses were reporting record sales. And all fourteen displaced animals had been adopted in mere hours, mostly by the retirees at Story Lake Haven.

All thanks to Zoey.

I didn't know if she knew it yet, but today had proved just how well she fit here. And I was going to find a way to convince her to stay.

Something sharp poked me in the side. "Weenie?"

My sister had wheeled up next to me and was brandishing a roasting stick.

"Ow, Larry. What the fuck?" I said, rubbing my ribs.

"It's for the bonfire. I thought you'd want to impress Zoey with a weenie," she said, all innocence.

"For the record, I've already impressed her with my weenie."

"Ew."

"You started it," I reminded her.

"Yeah. Yeah. I really like her, Gigi."

"So do I."

"And not just because she ruined Dominion's Boozetag," Laura added.

"She did what?"

"It seems Dominion's event couldn't pass the surprise safety inspection today. And now it sounds like their insurance carrier might be dropping the town," Laura said smugly.

"And what did Zoey have to do with that?"

Laura snorted. "I'm not telling you if you're going to prosecute her for it."

"I'm always Team Zoey," I assured her.

"Inspectors mysteriously received an anonymous tip about the event and the shoddy construction of the platform. The whole thing was shut down before it even started," she explained.

"How did she even have time…? You know what? Never mind. That woman never ceases to amaze me," I said.

"So you gonna wife her up or what?" Laura asked.

"If I can convince her to stop wreaking havoc long enough to fall in love with me."

"Good luck with that." My sister pointed across the crowd to the bonfire on the beach, where my client Audrey was laughing with her kids as they attempted to roast marshmallows. She looked more carefree than she had in years. "By the way, nice job getting Audrey away from that prick Gerald. I hear she and the kids are moving to be closer to her parents."

"That should help," I predicted.

"It helped me. Did you know today is the anniversary of the first time Miller and Levi left on deployment after I had the boys?"

The memories hit me like a flash.

I need you to watch out for them, Gage. Take care of my family when I'm not here.

"I was scared shitless," Laura continued. "I still felt like a kid myself, and there I was with two babies. But I had Mom and Dad. And I could always count on you, Mr. Dependable."

She was teasing, but my ears were ringing. Maybe I'd been there for diaper changes and day care drop-offs. But when it counted most, on the side of that road, I hadn't been there. I hadn't protected her or the kids from a loss that would never heal.

When Miller had tasked me with protecting his family, I'd been a twenty-year-old kid. His faith in me, the fact that he trusted me with the most important things in his life, had meant everything to me. That responsibility, that trust, had made me feel like a man.

Grief was thousands of different moments over the course of a lifetime. It was thousands of ways to miss someone.

"That's what family is for," I said gruffly.

"I'm glad you're my family."

"You're not wearing your wedding ring," I noted. My voice sounded strained to my own ears.

Laura reached under the collar of her *Reader Weekend* T-shirt and pulled out a chain with two wedding bands on it. "It felt like it was time. But I still wanted to keep it close for a while."

"I love you, Larry."

"Love you too, weirdo. Now if you'll excuse me, I have to go instruct my children to make me and Val the perfect s'mores."

"And I have a redheaded maniac to sweep off her feet."

Laura paused and took a deep breath. "Miller would have loved all this."

"Yeah, he would have," I agreed, feeling the loss like a boulder in my throat.

"I like to think he's still around. Still looking out for us. I found a dime on my floor mat this morning."

"They just seem to find you," I said.

"Thank you, Gigi."

"For what?" I asked uneasily.

Her smile was soft and sad. "For being you."

"I don't know what you're talking about," I lied.

"Yeah. Right." She sent me a knowing wink and wheeled off into the crowd.

I watched her as she made her way to a table on the far side of the patio. Hazel, looking happy but exhausted, was seated next to Cam, who looked just plain exhausted. And there was Zoey standing behind them, her unmistakable laugh carrying on the night air.

My feet were already carrying me toward her like she had a gravitational pull when the crowd parted and I saw the pink leash in her hand. Buttercup was perched in the chair next to Hazel, looking adoringly at Zoey.

Zoey Moody had willingly adopted a dog. That was definitely big news. It was a sign. I was going to marry that woman, and we were going to spend the rest of our lives driving each other crazy.

I couldn't fucking wait.

My parents and Levi joined the happy crowd at the table. Everyone I cared most about was right here within fifty feet of me.

Everyone except Miller.

I was halfway across the terrace when Valerie walked up to the table with two glasses of wine. She put one down in front of Laura and took the empty chair next to her.

The grief that had been tiptoeing around the edges of my consciousness hit me like a sledgehammer.

I still couldn't believe it was Valerie and not Miller bringing Laura a drink and joking with Cam and Hazel. He should have been here to watch his kids grow up, to enjoy his retirement from the military, to take Laura on all the vacations she'd always dreamed about, to lend a hand on the farm. To still be the one I called for advice on life.

But he was gone, erased from our lives forever, and now the woman who'd taken him from us was sitting in his place.

For a second, I felt the tenuousness of life. Of how one moment, everything could be fine, and the next, it could all be taken away.

We'd survived it. We were making the best of it. But would I survive the next bad thing? Would I be ready for it? Could I stop it before it happened?

Zoey leaned over and said something to my sister that had Laura throwing her head back and laughing. Zoey's hair seemed to glow red under the torchlight. She was ethereal and real and beautiful and messy, and my heart ached to be closer to her.

I was in love with her. I wanted her to stay, to be part of my life, my family. But could I survive if the next bad thing happened to her? Could she survive it if it happened to me?

If I hadn't been watching her so closely, I would have missed it. Zoey's brows pinched as something along the shoreline caught her attention. She was already handing the leash to Laura and on the move before the first startled cry rang out over the music and everything stopped.

I was running before I even knew why. But in a second as I dodged my way around people still having fun, it became clear. Zoey was running toward Audrey, who was on the beachfront with her kids. But she was leaning back at a funny angle, a look of terror on her face. And then I saw why.

Gerald, her soon-to-be ex-husband, stood behind her, arm tight around her neck. Audrey's eyes glittered with fear that I could see from yards away. Her kids stood rigid, still holding roasting sticks.

"Zoey! No!" I shouted as she barreled through the crowd toward them.

Adrenaline slowed time, and I saw the face of each bystander as they went from surprise to shock to horror as they cataloged what Zoey had seen before any of us.

I was too far away. I was going to be too late. I wasn't going to be able to save her.

"Cam! Levi! Miller!" I barked, praying that one of them was closer than me.

I saw Laura pushing back from the table and Valerie putting herself in front of my sister, blocking her.

And then Zoey let out a chilling scream. My heart stopped even as my body continued to move. Everything registered to my senses in fractured pieces. The surprise in Gerald's bloodshot eyes. The fear in Audrey's. A cry from Hazel as she grabbed for Audrey's kids, pulling them to safety as Cam raced forward.

They went down in a heap, and I lost sight of her for a split second.

Everyone was finally moving now, tightening a circle around the disturbance rather than running away. Because that was what Story Lake did when one of our own was in trouble. Levi and Cam waded into the mess, one step behind me.

Gator picked up a folding chair and wielded it like a pro wrestler. "Lemme at him!" On my left, Erleen Dabner from the town council led a pack of furious readers armed with wine bottles off the patio into the sand.

"Zoey!" I called, pushing through the crowd.

Audrey was on her hands and knees, sobbing and crawling toward her children.

Zoey was rolling on the sand with Gerald. He was on top of her, pulling his arm back as he wound up to hit *my woman*.

But Zoey got him first. "You goddamn son of fucking fuck!" she gritted out as she slammed her palm into his face.

My vision went red as my body moved of its own accord, watching his fist fly in slow motion. Spurred by a combination of rage, grief, and adrenaline that I could taste, I grabbed the man from behind and threw him off her. I didn't remember following him to the ground, but I did memorize every sensation of that first punch. I could smell the liquor on his breath. I could feel the cartilage in his nose break under my knuckles. I hit him two more times before Cam and Gator dragged me off him.

Chaos erupted as Levi flipped the bruised and bleeding Gerald onto his stomach to cuff him. Audrey and her shaking kids were led away by my parents and Dr. Ace.

"Nice punching, good guy," Zoey wheezed cheerfully from the ground. She had blood on her forehead, on her face, and her cheek was already starting to bruise.

I pulled her to her feet. "He could have had a fucking weapon," I said coldly.

"He did," Levi said. His voice was coldly furious as he held up a small fixed-blade knife.

Zoey examined the bloody cut on her left forearm while she cradled her braced wrist to her chest. "That explains this."

"Jesus fucking Christ," I breathed. I was so enraged I could barely see straight.

"Damn, kid. Where did you learn to hit like that?" Cam asked her as half a dozen people offered cocktail napkins to Zoey.

Because she was bleeding. Because she'd run at an armed and dangerous man without thinking about the consequences. She'd literally thrown herself at danger.

I couldn't breathe. Couldn't think. Couldn't do anything but stare at the blood and the blade.

She could have died. He could have killed her.

I could have *lost* her because I couldn't get to her. Because I couldn't count on her to prioritize her own safety. "That was the stupidest fucking thing you could have done, Zoey," I snapped.

My tone had Cam and Levi pausing to give me "what the fuck" looks.

"Whoa there, Gage. I get that you're upset. That was pretty intense. But that guy was dragging her away, and no one was doing anything," she said. "Can someone get me a glass of wine or, like, a vat of margaritas?"

"So you decided rather than call for help, you were going to be the fucking hero," I pressed.

"Man, don't do this," Levi said under his breath, but I ignored him.

Hazel raced up with an open bottle of champagne. "Zo, are you okay?"

"I got hit in the face, stabbed in the arm, and my wrist hurts again, but I'll be fine after that bottle," she joked.

I still couldn't move. Couldn't breathe. This was what life with her would be like. One disaster after the next until she took a risk she couldn't come back from.

"You could have been killed," I said.

Hazel slowly began to put herself between me and Zoey. "He's upset," Zoey said.

I stepped around my brother's fiancée and pointed at Zoey. "I knew you were impulsive, but that was just stupid and selfish. You didn't ask anyone for help. You just threw yourself into a dangerous situation without thinking about anything or anyone else."

"She called for help, man," Cam said.

"She yelled for you," Levi said.

I shook my head, trying to clear it, trying to remember. But all I could see was her running away from me. Toward danger.

Zoey was suddenly in front of me, hands on my chest. "I called for you and then Levi because I knew he was nearby and could handcuff the guy," she said calmly.

But I couldn't listen to her, couldn't look at her. Fear was a living beast trying to claw its way out of my chest.

"Hey, your heart's beating really fast," she whispered.

"Maybe it's because I can't believe you'd be so stupid," I said icily.

Her hands slid from my chest. And Hazel stepped in again, looking like she was ready to murder me.

Zoey took a breath. "I get that you're having some big feelings right now, but you don't get to talk—"

"You tried to warn me. Said it would be a mistake. You weren't kidding," I said on a humorless chuckle. My heart couldn't stop pounding. Everything was a jumble in my head. Zoey lying on the ground. Laura lying in a hospital bed. "I can't be with someone who would be that careless, that reckless. I can't deal with this. With you. I'm done."

I felt like there wasn't enough oxygen. I'd almost lost her. I couldn't protect her. I couldn't protect anyone. Audrey had been in danger because I hadn't insisted on the restraining order, and Zoey had almost paid the price for it.

"Hey!" Hazel snarled, stepping between us once more. But Cam cut in front of her and shoved me back a step.

"You're gonna wanna shut the fuck up now." Cam's voice was low, and I heard the warning in it. But it didn't matter. Nothing mattered.

"No, it's fine," Zoey said flatly. "We're definitely done here."

There was a finality in her tone that cut through the surface layer of rage and fear.

I opened my mouth to say something, anything. But nothing came out. Nothing but the bitter taste of fear.

Audrey reappeared, gauze visible through a small bloody hole in her shirt. "Oh my God, Zoey! Are you okay?"

"I'm one thousand percent fine, Audrey. I swear. Are *you* okay?" Zoey asked, forgetting all about me and opening her arms.

Audrey fell into them, and the two embraced. "I'm so sorry. So sorry."

Zoey pulled back and put her arm around Audrey. "It's not your fault."

Audrey shook her head and blinked back tears. "Things had been… escalating. I should have said something, should have anticipated. I'm so sorry."

Levi and I shared a heated glance. My brother had been right. There was more going on than Audrey had let on to either of us. I'd missed it and Zoey had almost paid the price. Voluntarily. It was too much to unpack. Too many failures to dissect.

"You're not responsible for anything he did. But boy, am I extra glad about your divorce now," Zoey said. "Let's go get a drink and maybe some more hugs."

"That sounds good," Audrey said shakily.

Zoey looked over her shoulder at me, and I saw nothing but emptiness in those gorgeous green eyes. Hazel followed after them, shooting eye daggers at me as she went. Together they returned to the patio, where my parents and the better part of Story Lake converged on them.

"Jesus, how the hell are you supposed to drive attempted murderers around in your fucking pickup?" Cam complained as we loaded Gerald into the back seat of Levi's truck.

"Maybe you should've thought of that before you forced me to be chief," Levi snapped.

"Do we even have a jail?" I asked wearily. I felt like I'd lived a decade in the last thirty minutes.

"You called for Miller," Cam said to me.

"What? No, I didn't."

"Yeah, you did," Levi said.

"Whatever. Is she okay?" I asked, unwilling to say Zoey's name out loud.

"Who? Audrey?" Levi asked.

"No," I said stubbornly.

"Zoey's fine," he said, taking pity on me.

"But what the fuck is wrong with you?" Cam demanded.

"Nothing. I'm fine."

Levi slammed the door on Gerald's drunken pleas. "That was really fucking stupid back there."

"I know. She never thinks before she acts," I agreed.

"Not Zoey. You, dumbass," Cam cut in. "You better hope she's as forgiving as Hazel was when I was a complete dickwad and almost ruined our relationship for the rest of my miserable life."

"I really enjoyed handcuffing you that night," Levi mused.

"I know you did, asshole. Gigi, you fucked up. You better find a way to fix it," Cam told me.

I scraped my hands over my face. "You sure she's okay?"

Levi leveled me with a look. "Why don't you go check for yourself."

I shook my head. "I can't. I need to go."

I was on my third glass of bourbon still not fixing a damn thing from my couch when I heard someone let themselves into my house. Moments later, Nana, the world's worst guard dog, escorted my mother into the living room.

Mom flipped on the lights, sat down next to me, and propped her feet up on the coffee table. Nana hopped up on the cushion next to her grandmother.

"It's eleven o'clock at night. What are you doing here?" I demanded through the pleasant numbing haze of alcohol.

"Came to see if you're all right."

"Why wouldn't I be?"

"Because your sex partner got hurt defending one of your clients from the man you were helping her divorce, and you yelled for your deceased brother-in-law's help. Then you said some really stupid things and came home alone."

"I had a long day, Mom. I appreciate the concern, but I'm fine and fucking dandy." The bourbon made it hard to pronounce all the words.

She heaved a sigh and patted me on the leg. "Sometimes you're so good at being almost perfect, I forget to worry about you too."

"There's nothing to worry about."

"Ha. Right. Listen, kid. We all went through one hell of a trauma. We're all going to handle it differently. We all have our go-to coping mechanisms. Some of them are healthy, some of them not so much."

I took a loud slurp of bourbon.

"When you and your brothers were finally reunited, I put you to bed that first night, and I stood outside your room and listened to you say your prayers. You wanted to know that if you were a good enough boy, would that mean nothing bad would happen ever again."

"Mom, I was barely four fucking years old."

"And you spent the next thirty-plus years doing your best to be perfect to make sure nothing bad ever happened again."

"Yeah, well, obviously I wasn't perfect enough."

"You were the sweetest little boy. For six months after your brothers came to live with us, you would get up in the middle of the night and go into their room just to check on them."

"I probably wanted to make sure they weren't doing anything to make you regret bringing us home."

"You were a little boy then," she said again. "But you're a man now. And you know that no matter how good you are, you can't protect everyone you love from all the bad things out there. You also know you can't just stop loving us."

I grunted. "A fucking inconvenience if you ask me."

She took the glass from me and downed the rest of the liquor.

"Hey, get your own," I complained.

"You fucked up a little tonight, kiddo. You weren't perfect. But you *are* good enough. And I have a feeling that after a good night's sleep, you're probably going to see things more clearly in the morning."

She patted my leg again.

"Thanks, Mom."

"Want me to tuck you in?" Mom offered.

I cracked a sort-of smile. "I think I can find my way."

"Okay. We'll see you at the lodge for brunch tomorrow. Do some celebrating. This was a big thing Hazel and Zoey pulled off for all of us."

"Yeah. Sure."

She got up. "I'm gonna go home and fight your dad for the last of the Chubby Hubby."

"Text me when you get home."

"My sweet boy." Her smile was soft, and then it sharpened. "You're going to feel like shit tomorrow, and you'll deserve it, but remember I love you."

43

Shithead McCrapFace
Zoey

I woke up to a growl, a hiss, and a strange weight on my feet. On a grumble, I shoved my eye mask up and blinked to clear the blurriness. Then I blinked some more because there was no way what I was seeing at the foot of Hazel's bed was actually there.

But the more I blinked, the clearer it became that I was sharing a bed with a dog, a fat cat, and a disgruntled raccoon. Buttercup let out a squeaky growl that ended in a whimper like she wasn't sure how big a threat the visitors were.

"Ugh. Bertha, seriously? You're a woodland animal. Go back to the woodland!" I grumbled. All three animals looked at me for guidance, but I was in no shape to be the adult in this situation. "Hazel!"

I heard bare feet in the hallway, and then the door flew open. Hazel, in a pair of her favorite "I'm on a deadline" pajama pants and a *Bishop Brothers Construction* T-shirt, padded inside. Her glasses were on crooked, and her bangs looked as if they'd been involved in a leaf blowing accident. She had a Wild Cherry Pepsi in her hand. "Well, shit. I leave you alone for five minutes, and you Dr. Dolittle my bed."

"Only one of these animals is supposed to be here," I complained, patting the mattress.

Buttercup abandoned her new fur acquaintances and belly crawled up to me. DeWalt the cat and Bertha the raccoon seemed to think the gesture was meant for them as well and tried to follow suit.

"No! All cats and raccoons must vacate this room immediately," Hazel said, pointing to the hallway.

Miraculously, both cat and raccoon complied. Though it probably had more to do with the smell of bacon wafting up from downstairs than Hazel's verbal instructions.

When the intruders left, she shut the door and climbed back into bed. "How are you feeling?"

My face hurt, my arm and leg stung, my wrist throbbed, and the rest of my body ached like I had a mutant case of the flu. But it was my heart that hurt the most.

"Like my heart has a hangover."

Buttercup gave my armpit a generous lick.

"What the fuck? Bertha!" Cam's bellow from downstairs rattled the crystal light fixture over the bed.

Hazel stacked her hands under her head and stared up at the ceiling. "I'm going to kill him," she announced.

"Who? Cam?"

"No, Gage."

His name was like a barbed arrow to the chest. "Can we not use his name for a decade or two?"

"That's a good idea. We'll call him...Shithead McCrapFace," she decided.

Hazel was much better with insults on the page than off. "I like it. Really paints a picture."

She perked up. "Hey! Maybe this isn't a real ending. Maybe this is your third-act breakup?"

"This is not a third-act breakup. He showed me who he is. And who he is is someone who enthusiastically reopens every one of my emotional scars. I need to face facts. I'm the girl eagles throw other, grosser animals at. Not the girl who gets the guy."

"No. You're the girl who gets to be the heroine of her own story."

"Then this heroine is going to live off takeout with her shy pit bull for the rest of her life and never date again."

Hazel drew in a long breath and then blew it out slowly. "I've given it a lot of thought, and I think I'm going to squash him with the prize-winning pumpkin at the Fall Festival."

"We don't have a pumpkin contest at the Fall Festival," I pointed out. Except there was no *we* anymore. I wasn't really a part of Story Lake. I'd been a *we* by association. But this was *his* town. These were *his* neighbors. They weren't mine. God, how had I gotten so caught up in this disaster? For a disillusioned, hard-hearted realist, I'd fallen headfirst into a vat of toxic hope. And I was pissed as hell about it.

"I meant on the page. I'm going to murder him on the page. But I'm open to discussing a real-life homicide. We'll need a tarp."

"If anyone's doing any murdering, it's gonna be me," Cam announced from the doorway. He was holding a tray with a plate of bacon and a cup of coffee. Meetcute was on his heels, sniffing the air.

"Did you just bring me breakfast in bed?" I asked.

"It's not a full breakfast because we're out of eggs. So here's your meat and caffeine. Figured you wouldn't want to go to Reader Weekend brunch with your face looking like that."

"Cam!" Hazel chastised.

"What? I'm not being an asshole. She looks like she got punched in the face."

"I did get punched in the face *and* the heart," I said, prodding my cheek with my fingers. Yep. Still hurt.

"If only some older, wiser, too-handsome-for-real-life genius had warned you," Cam said, dropping the tray unceremoniously on my lap.

"You were right," I sighed.

"No shit," Cam said, pausing to ruffle Buttercup's ears. "Maybe someday your mommy and your aunt will learn to listen to wise Uncle Cam."

The dog dissolved into delirium every time someone was nice to her, and it just kept breaking my stupid broken heart over and over again. I would make it my life's mission to make sure that no one was ever mean to Buttercup again.

"Maybe," I agreed.

"But probably not," Hazel teased.

He pointed at me. "You, eat your breakfast meat. I'm going to feed your dog and let her out in hopes she'll chase that goddamn raccoon off the picnic table. And *you* need to get ready to go," he said, pointing to Hazel.

She pouted. "Fine. But if your brother Shithead McCrapFace is there, I get to throw a drink in his face."

"Before or after I punch him?"

"Let's play it by ear," Hazel mused.

"Deal." Cam looked at me. "He'll get his head out of his ass and apologize."

"He dumped me in front of the entire town. There's no apologizing for that."

"He didn't dump you. He was a stupid asshole and picked a dumb fight. There's a big difference."

"I said maybe it was a third-act breakup too," Hazel said chipperly.

"I know neither of you is telling me to stay with a man who calls me stupid and selfish and yells at me in front of half of Story Lake's population," I said coolly.

Cam and Hazel shared a look.

"Come on, Buttercup. Let's go fight a raccoon." With that, Hazel's hero hightailed it out of the room with my dog.

I sighed and poked at a piece of bacon. "Besides his misreading of the situation, Cam is awesome. I can't believe he slept in the guest room so we could shit talk his own brother and cry over *Pride and Prejudice* last night."

"He's the best. Which means his brother should have been at

least half as good for DNA reasons. I mean, they basically have the same penis, you know?"

"Hazel, I'm not talking about the man's penis ever again." This was why I didn't date. There were fewer memories to erase after a one-night stand.

She sighed. "I just can't believe he'd end things for no reason like that."

"It wasn't for no reason. It was because once again, I was too much."

Hazel rolled to her side and propped herself up on one elbow. "That's bullshit."

"That's my life."

"What are we going to do with that pile of Shithead McCrapFace's clothing?" Hazel asked, jerking her chin toward the small mountain on the floor. Before I'd shown up at her front door with my second stab wound of the day and all the pieces of my broken heart, I'd swung by my apartment and grabbed every article of clothing I'd liberated from Gage's wardrobe.

"I was thinking fire, but I'm open to suggestions," I said.

"I like fire. Or maybe we can put them in the pigpen on the farm?" Hazel suggested.

The farm. I felt another pinch in my chest. Frank and Pep were going to get their farm sanctuary up and running. Frank was going to grow their social media. And Pepe the donkey would find a new love. They'd all forget about me. They'd all move on as if I'd never been here.

"This whole thing was one huge mistake. You know the worst part? He stood there yelling insults at me last night, and I didn't defend myself. I didn't say a damn thing back. My brain was just frozen."

"Ugh," Hazel groaned. "I hate that! The nice thing about being an author is I can at least put all the belated insults I come up with to use on the page. But regular people just spend their lives walking around with a list of comebacks they should have said bouncing around in their brains."

"Yeah. Maybe I should have said something like 'You think

you're Mr. Perfect? You wouldn't know a good time if it slapped you in the face with its tits.'"

She nodded thoughtfully. "Yeah, that's pretty good. You definitely should have said that. Maybe you can put it in a note? Or we can print posters and hang them outside his office?"

"The New and Improved Medicated Zoey says I should probably just take the high road."

Hazel blew a raspberry.

"Ugh. The only silver lining is I didn't tell him I was planning to stay," I said.

"Why are you saying that in past tense?"

I looked pityingly at my friend. "Haze, you know there's no way I could stay now. It's going to be bad enough seeing him on the holidays you invite me to. I can't handle running into him and his perfect future wife at the general store or on the lake with his six perfect children."

Everything sucked and hurt and was awful. Hope was the worst, most dastardly thing in the world. And I blamed Gage Bishop for making me believe the impossible.

"I'm going to actually for real kill him," Hazel announced, throwing the covers off and stomping out of the room.

"Aren't you going to change for brunch?" I called after her.

"I don't want to get blood and internal organs on a nice brunch outfit," she yelled back as she thundered down the stairs.

I waited until I heard the door downstairs close and the rumble of Cam's truck as it left the driveway before rolling over to check my phone. Not that I'd been expecting a groveling text or voice mail, but it still felt like another volley of pointy arrows when I saw Gage hadn't tried to contact me since last night.

That didn't happen in real life. This entire thing had been a mistake, and I'd known better.

And now he'd get away with it because I was too mature to make him pay. This whole "being less impulsive" thing was stupid.

I heard the tip-tap of dog nails on the hardwood and felt the mattress dip as Buttercup rejoined me.

"Looks like it's just us two from now on, Buttercup."

Her skinny, whiplike tail thumped lightly on the duvet as she sprawled out next to me.

My phone vibrated in my hand. It was a text from Hazel's editor.

> **Editor Susan:** First day sales were astronomical. We're thrilled! Are you sure we can't convince Hazel to do an event or five?

44

Puke in the petunias
Gage

Laura: Don't forget we have a brunch reservation for 10 a.m.
Cam: Haze and I are on our way. I vote we disinvite Gigi. He sucks.
Hazel: I hope he chokes on his toothbrush.
Pep: Oh dear. I was afraid of this.
Frank: Has anyone seen my going out jeans?
Levi: Gonna be late. Still trying to remand the prisoner to the county jail. I hate you all.
Laura: Is this about Gigi being an embarrassment to the family name by losing his shit last night?
Cam: Yep. Stupid jackass.
Levi: He's the worst.
Hazel: I'm going to crush him with a pumpkin in my next book.
Mom: Everybody calm the hell down.
Dad: Seriously. Where are my jeans?

My hangover was bad enough I seriously considered (A) throwing up in the shower and (B) not showing up to brunch. But after Mom's late-night visit, I knew I'd only end up with a bunch of Bishops on my doorstep if I didn't show my face. So it was with great amounts of determination and ibuprofen that I managed to get dressed, feed Nana, and get out the door.

The morning sunshine mocked my bloodshot eyes, making my head pound even harder as I steered toward town. I dialed Zoey's number, knowing an apology was in order. I'd been an ass at the bonfire, and then I'd just abandoned her there like an emotional little asshole.

My call went straight to voice mail. I winced.

Flowers. I'd stop at the plant shop and get her flowers. A *lot* of flowers. I pulled over at the curb and got as far as the front door before realizing I'd left my wallet at home.

Shielding my eyes from the sun with one arm, I sent Zoey a one-handed text.

Me: Sorry about last night. See you at brunch?

When I arrived at the lodge, I found the parking lot packed. Just what my hangover needed. A loud restaurant with a lot of weird smells. But I deserved the discomfort.

I kept my sunglasses on as I navigated my way through the lobby and bar area, barely noticing that my friends and neighbors were all avoiding eye contact with me.

I spotted my family at a long table along the windows overlooking the lake, too close to the smells of the buffet for comfort.

"Hey," I rasped, taking one of the three remaining seats.

"Sunglasses indoors. Seriously?" Laura asked with a smirk.

"Rough night," I said, reaching for the coffee carafe.

Cam glowered at me from across the table.

"What's your problem?" I demanded.

Hazel scoffed and crossed her arms. "As if you didn't know."

I rubbed my temples. "Look. I'd appreciate it if everyone would just let me suffer through this hangover without adding any other bullshit to it."

"Yeah, you'd like that, wouldn't you?" Cam said.

"Yes. I would."

"Where's Zoey?" Dad asked, looking up from the buffet menu.

"Yeah, Shithead McCrapFace. Where's Zoey?" Hazel said, crossing her arms.

"What?" I asked, not sure if she was talking to me.

Hazel just glared at me like I was something of the feces variety tracked inside on the bottom of a shoe.

"Looked like she took a pretty good shot to the face last night," Laura said. "How's her arm? I can't believe she took a knife for a woman she barely knew."

I squeezed the bridge of my nose. Forget a bouquet. I was going to need to plant a field of flowers.

"She's fine. Except for her heart, you shit waffle," Hazel announced. She dramatically pushed her chair back, jumped to her feet, and threw her goblet of orange juice in my face.

"What the f—"

I didn't even finish spitting the juice out of my mouth before Cam came around the table and hauled me to my feet.

"What is your fucking problem?" I demanded.

"You're my fucking problem," he said.

"Did I miss the ass kicking?" Levi asked, appearing next to the table.

"Okay. Take it outside, boys," Mom said as she calmly poured herself a cup of coffee.

Cam's fists gripped me by my citrus-soaked shirt and dragged me out onto the patio. He spun us around and pushed me into a flower bed. "Why the fuck don't you ever listen to me?"

"What the hell are you talking about?" I rasped.

"Did I not tell you not to fuck around with Zoey?" he demanded.

"Can confirm. He did tell you," Levi chimed in, holding a cup of coffee.

I kicked Cam in his shin and shoved him backward. "Why are you being such an asshole?"

"Because I had to put two angry women to bed last night and then go sleep in a guest room with the damn dog and cat," he complained.

"Maybe you should try not pissing Hazel off so much before the wedding," I suggested, straightening my shirt.

"She's not mad at me, dipshit. She's pissed at *you* for dumping Zoey. And *I'm* pissed at you because I told you not to date her in the first fucking place. But you never fucking listen to me."

"He did tell you. I remember," Levi added.

"For fuck's sake! I didn't break up with Zoey," I insisted. "I may have said some stupid shit…" I winced at the memory. "Okay, a lot of stupid shit."

"According to Zoey, you broke up with her after she knocked herself out to make this weekend a success. Not just for Hazel but this whole damn town. And then she single-handedly stopped your client from being kidnapped by her ex. What the fucking fuck is wrong with you?"

Levi grimaced. "That's fucking stupid, man. What were you thinking?"

"He wasn't. Because he's an emotionally stunted idiot," Cam said.

"We didn't break up," I insisted, patting my pockets for my phone. "We had a fight. I was a dick, but I didn't break the fuck up with her. I just told her that what she did was stupid and impulsive or something like that."

"Are you an absolute fucking idiot?" Cam demanded.

Apparently I was.

"Dude." Levi managed to pack a reproving punch into the monosyllable.

"What? So I'm not perfect, okay? I said something stupid, and I went home to regroup. Is that so wrong?" Of course it was fucking wrong. Even hungover me knew that had been a shitty thing to do.

"Yes," my brothers announced.

"What exactly did you say?" Levi asked.

"I don't fucking know. I was pissed and scared. Fuck." I wiped a hand over my face. "I said something like she was stupid and selfish and I was done."

My brothers both threw their hands up and turned away from me like I was a bad football call on TV.

"Christ, Gigi. What part of that doesn't sound like a breakup to you?" Levi asked incredulously.

"I fucking told you," Cam said, drilling a finger into my shoulder. "Why doesn't anyone listen to me?"

"We're not broken up. I asked her to stay. She was considering it. She just adopted a fucking dog yesterday," I said, yanking my phone from my pocket. I dialed her number again. It went straight to voice mail again.

I dialed again and got the same result.

Then I checked my texts. Not only hadn't she responded to the one I'd sent, she hadn't read it.

"No, no, no," I chanted while I started pacing. "This isn't happening."

"No offense, but this isn't some random thing that 'happened.' You did this," Levi pointed out.

"What part of that am I not supposed to be offended by? Christ. I wasn't thinking straight last night," I insisted.

"So you decided to use every weapon you had against her?" Cam cut in.

"What are you talking about?"

"Is he seriously this stupid?" Cam asked Levi.

Levi rolled his eyes. "He's hungover. His brain cells need time to recover."

"Your girl tells you she's felt stupid all her life and is afraid of being abandoned because she's 'too much,'" Cam said.

This time, I didn't give him shit about the air quotes.

"And how exactly do you know this?" I demanded.

"Because I fucking listened to the woman crying in my house because you broke her fucking heart, you walking turd."

"So you basically imploded your relationship on purpose using everything you knew would hurt her?" Levi questioned.

"No, I—" But that was exactly what I'd done. I'd panicked, and in that state, I'd lashed out, using everything she'd confided in me against her.

"I fucking hate men," Cam muttered.

"We're not all complete dickheads," Levi contended.

"Thanks, Livvy," I said gratefully.

"I wasn't talking about you. You're definitely a dickhead."

"Let me get this straight before I turn your face into ground beef," Cam said, crossing his arms. "She didn't want to be in a relationship in the first place?"

"Yeah. So?"

"Because she was scared you didn't have the staying power to handle her," Levi added.

Fuck my life.

"It gets even better. Dumbass here wore her down with his hero act. She was going to tell him last night that she was going to stay," Cam said to Levi.

"Shut the fuck up," I said.

"I swear on Gram's lemon squares. She told me after the signing. She and Haze did this bouncy, screamy victory dance and everything."

"I think I'm going to throw up."

After I finished vomiting in the flower bed, I went back inside to guzzle two cups of coffee standing up.

Was it the hangover paranoia, or was everyone looking at me?

Kitty Suarez was violently stabbing her knitting needles through what looked like a dog sweater as she stared at me. Gator glared at me over his pitcher of Bloody Marys before pointing two fingers at his eyes and then at me in a threatening "I'm watching you" gesture. The conflict-avoidant Darius was actually hiding behind a potted plant with his waffles.

Shit. News sure traveled fast.

"Everything okay?" Mom asked brightly, as if she hadn't just watched me puke in the petunias through the wall of glass.

"I'm reserving my punches for when he's sober so he'll feel them more," Cam said, returning to his seat.

"I have no regrets about the orange juice," Hazel said stubbornly.

"I thought you really liked her, Gigi," Laura said in that quiet disapproving mom voice that was a thousand times worse than when she yelled.

"I did—I do. I'll fix it."

"Did you guys try the chocolate chip pancakes with the strawberries? It's like heaven in my mouth," Dad said, shoveling in another bite of breakfast.

"Frank," Mom said, kicking him under the table.

"Ow! What?"

She pointed at me.

"Oh, right." Dad cleared his throat. "Son, sometimes we do stupid things, and when we do—"

"Save the lecture, Dad. I have some groveling to do."

"My work here is done," Dad said cheerfully.

I felt it then. The change in the air like a thunderstorm was rolling in. I'd felt it the first time I'd seen her. Me on the roof, her on the ground, wind blowing through her curls.

Zoey stormed up to the table. Every chair in the lodge screeched as their residents jockeyed for a better view. She had Buttercup on a leash in a pink spiked collar I had no idea when she'd had the time to buy. Her curls were a fiery halo around her head. She was dressed in a body-hugging bloodred dress. Makeup carefully covered most of the bruising on her beautiful face. Everything from her eyeliner to her stilettos was causing me physical pain with the realization of the damage I'd done.

She looked like an avenging heroine…which made me the villain.

"Zoey," I said, standing up so abruptly my skull felt like it was going to cave in. "There's been a misunderstanding—"

"No. You did enough talking last night. Now it's my turn."

Everyone in the entire building was holding their collective breath, including me.

"I might be selfish and impulsive, but I am not, nor have I ever been, stupid."

"You're right. I was an absolute idiot last night," I agreed.

"Shut the fuck up," Levi sang out of the corner of his mouth.

Zoey continued as if I hadn't said a word. "You wanna talk about stupid; you're so busy being worried about getting everything exactly right that you miss out on the very best things in life. Including me. If I'm too much, go find less."

Laura started applauding. It quickly caught on and spread to the tables around us.

"Zoey, honey, if you could just let me explain," I began.

"Don't you 'honey' me. There's no misunderstanding. Either you said those things and broke up with me, or I broke up with you *because* you said those things. The end result is the same."

She was so fucking beautiful, and I was so fucking stupid.

Cam handed Hazel his glass of orange juice. Hazel passed it to Zoey. I braced for it, but there was no real way to prepare for a cold glass of juice to the face…not even the second one.

She hurled the juice at me and turned on her heel.

"Zoey, you can't leave. We're in the middle of this."

Her green eyes were blazing with a heat that singed me to my bones, but her words froze the blood in my veins. "Actually, it feels like the end to me." And then she walked out.

I stood there staring after her, dripping until my father handed me a napkin.

Hazel was on her feet, leading the standing ovation.

"You tell 'em, Zoey," Gator yelled.

Even Darius peered out from behind the potted plant and

managed a frown at me while clapping. My own mother was applauding while mouthing *sorry* to me.

I stood there and took it because I deserved it. But this sure as hell wasn't going to be the end, I decided, as I mopped orange juice out of my eyes.

"Here. Maybe this will help," Cam said, tossing a glass of water in my face.

———

I tried Zoey's number three more times on my way to the parking lot and got her voice mail every time.

"Zoey, pick up. Please," I said into the phone as I left a trail of breakfast beverages behind me. "We need to talk this through. I'm coming over."

I drove back to town, barely registering the foot traffic on the sidewalks and the exercise group in the park by the lake. This level of fuckup was new to me. I'd always been so careful, so focused on doing the right thing. Now I was left wondering how I could fix this.

I parked across the street from my building and jogged up to the front door, only to find I didn't have my keys. I ran back to my truck as quickly as my hangover allowed and dug out the keys in the center console.

I stepped out to cross the street and nearly walked in front of Amos Rump's pickup truck. He leaned on the horn. "You got your head up your ass, Bishop?" Amos yelled from the driver's side window.

Emilie's curly blond head appeared over the roof on the other side of the truck. "Heard about what you did to Zoey. Not cool, man. Not cool."

I should have known from the particularly delighted spark in her eyes what was coming. But my instincts and reflexes were slower than usual thanks to the residual bourbon fog. The baked potato hit me squarely in the chest with enough heat on it to remind me that Emilie had been a fast-pitch softball pitcher in high school.

The Rumps sped away, leaving me in all my orange juice, potato, hangover glory.

I scraped as much potato off my shirt as I could and stepped off the curb again. I managed to cross the road without incident and unlocked the front door. My stomach rebelled as I took the stairs to Zoey's apartment two at a time, but my desire to make things right was stronger than my need to vomit again.

"Zoey," I said, pounding on her door. "Open up."

But there was only silence within.

"Come on, Zo," I pleaded. "I was an asshole. I owe you an apology. Several apologies. And some presents."

A cold sweat was starting to mingle with the beverages on my shirt.

"Zoey, you can't hide from me forever."

45

Howdy fucking doo, dumbass
Gage

The woman avoided me for the three longest, most potato-filled days of my life.

Every time I showed up at her apartment or Hazel and Cam's house or Opal's place, I'd just missed her. Zoey was an expert at pulling a disappearing act, and I was just the bumbling idiot dazzled by her magic. The flowers I'd sent, all four bouquets, had been returned to sender. Not that the plant shop gave me any refunds.

Wednesday, I arrived at my office after a long morning of fighting. First with suppliers, then my brothers—who were consequently barely speaking to me—and finally the eight-year-old kid who'd cut in front of me at the coffee shop and gotten the last chocolate croissant.

Even Nana hadn't wanted to come to work with me. I'd opened the door and grabbed her leash, and she'd shot me a disappointed look before slinking off to the living room. To add insult to injury, I'd been the victim of a drive-by potatoing when George rolled by on his mobility scooter outside the bungalow

I'd been working on. It appeared as though Story Lake's traditions had infiltrated the retirement community.

"You look mad," Declan observed when I stomped into the office.

"Really? Because I was having the best day ever," I snapped.

"You also sound mad."

"I'm fine," I enunciated. "I'll be in my office."

I closed the door with deliberate calm and leaned against it. At least in here I was safe from judgmental glares and flying potatoes.

The sound of something being dragged across the floor upstairs caught my attention. She was up there. I almost ran for the door but decided I needed a game plan first. The knocking and shouting apologies through doors hadn't worked so far. Maybe I could get Declan to knock on her door with some landlord business, and then I could jump out from behind him? I scrubbed my hands over my face.

God, I sucked at this. I was much better at avoiding mistakes than apologizing for them.

And a simple apology wasn't going to cut it. I needed to make a case and prove how sorry I was.

It was an obsession, ruminating about the mistake I'd made. I'd forgotten to shower two days running. I had the unintentional beginnings of a beard and had to buy deodorant from the general store between client appointments. Not only had Laura not given me the family discount, she'd charged me double.

I paced the carpet, listening to the signs of life above me. Was she rearranging furniture or working out? Maybe she'd lost something and was looking for it? Maybe I could help? If I could remind her that I was at least useful, maybe she'd agree to hear me out.

I could argue my ass off in court, sway juries, mediate tricky divorces. I just needed the opportunity to get Zoey to listen to me. She'd see where I was coming from and understand how sorry I was.

"You're pathetic," I announced out loud and threw myself down in my chair.

There was a neatly folded piece of paper sitting in the center of my desk. The word *Landlord* was scrawled across it in Zoey's haphazard handwriting. I pounced on it, unfolding it so aggressively that I tore a chunk off the top corner.

"What. The. Fuck?"

Paper in hand, I stormed out to Declan's desk. "What the hell is this?" I demanded, slapping the paper down on his desk.

Declan blinked, unimpressed. "A piece of paper."

"When did this piece of paper arrive, and why didn't you stop her?"

My paralegal took a leisurely spoon of plain yogurt. "Zoey dropped it off this morning. I didn't know I was allowed to physically detain tenants. That seems illegal."

"She thinks she can just move out because I made one mistake?" This was not how things were going to end between us. I was going to make her listen to reason.

"It was a pretty big mistake," Declan said without sympathy. "Did you even thank her for standing up for client 0347? I mean Audrey."

"Declan, I appreciate the work you do here more than I can say, but now is not the time for criticism. I am hanging on by a goddamn thread."

"Understood. I was just making sure you know that you're the responsible party."

I was mid-growl when I spotted Hazel's SUV stopped in the street for a group of slow-moving Haven residents and caught the flash of reddish-gold hair in the passenger seat.

Zoey was on the move, and I was going to put a stop to this once and for all, even if it meant kidnapping her off the street.

I snatched up her notice and ran for the street. I crashed through both doors and dodged my way around the cluster of senior citizens to jump in front of the vehicle.

Hazel's eyes narrowed at me through the windshield, and I held up my hands.

"Wait. Just wait!"

My command was drowned out by the throaty rev of the SUV's engine as it lurched forward to smack solidly into me.

I slapped my hands on the hood. "Seriously, Hazel?"

Zoey looked like she couldn't decide whether to be horrified or amused.

My future sister-in-law rolled down her window and stuck her head out. "I just want you to know that wasn't an accident. I did it on purpose, and I want credit for it!"

"You can't just play bumper cars in the street."

"And you can't just go around breaking people's hearts!"

Zoey unbuckled her seat belt. "I've got this, Haze. Just give me a minute," she said.

"Put that thing in park right now," I told Hazel.

Zoey got out of the SUV and faced off with me in front of the hood, her arms crossed. She wasn't wearing any makeup now. The bruising on her cheek had shifted from a dark, ugly purple into more green tones. I felt the anger rising up in me again.

"Is there a specific reason you're blocking traffic?" she asked flatly.

"Yes. You. I've never broken the law before in my life, but I will lie on top of Hazel's hood if you don't talk to me."

"Pretty sure I said everything I needed to say."

I reached for her, but she put her hands up and took a step back.

"Don't even think about it," she warned.

"I was an ass Saturday night. I'm sorry. Let me explain—"

"Look, I don't need an explanation or an apology. I'm not mad," she said, cutting me off. "In fact, I should be thanking you."

This felt like a trap. "Why?"

"Because you reminded me of an important lesson I'd forgotten."

I definitely didn't like where this was going. "What lesson is that?"

"That I'm the only one I can count on. Maybe I temporarily

fell for your whole 'aww shucks, I'm one of the good guys' schtick, but you reminded me that anyone can be good when things are good. It's when bad things happen that you see who a person really is. So thank you for reminding me of that before I made a gigantic mistake like moving here permanently."

"I'm going to murder you in fiction for that," Hazel yelled from her open window.

"You were going to tell me you wanted to stay…with me," I said to Zoey. "And I fucked it up. I made a huge mistake, but I can fix this."

"Look, I'm not going to be pissed at you for reminding me that I was right. We both knew this was going to be a colossal mistake. We're both responsible-ish adults. But I will say this. You might think that I'm too much, but the reality is you're just not enough."

Every apology and request for a second chance died in my throat. I stood there frozen to the spot, and she took the opportunity to climb back in the car.

This wasn't how it was going to end. One mistake wasn't going to destroy the best thing that ever happened to me.

"I'm going to make this right, Zoey," I announced.

"Good luck with that," she said, securing her seat belt.

Hazel laid on her horn. Several other horns behind her joined in.

"We got a problem here?" Levi got out of his truck across the street and sauntered up.

"Shithead McCrapFace is blocking traffic and creating a dangerous hazard, which if I'm not mistaken is against the law," Hazel yelled helpfully through her window.

"Don't you dare, Livvy," I said to my brother as he continued to advance on me.

"Been waiting to do this for a while," he admitted, reaching for a pair of handcuffs.

"I'm warning you. If you come near me with those things, I'll make sure you get reelected for the rest of your life."

He clicked one cuff on my wrist, and I knew better than to resist.

"Worth it. Smile pretty for your perp walk," he said cheerfully.

It was as he secured the second cuff that I noticed the suitcases in the back of Hazel's SUV.

> **Laura:** Junior Wallpeter just told me that Gage staged some kind of protest on Lake Drive and was arrested.
> **Cam:** Hazel called. Said she did something that I personally find hilarious but for inappropriately traumatic reasons I can't say in front of Larry.
> **Laura:** SHE HIT HIM WITH HER CAR? Wow! Nice. Golf clap hands.
> **Levi:** I can't decide if joking about this makes you the healthiest or the most mentally unstable sibling in the bunch.
> **Laura:** Did you really arrest Gigi?
> **Levi:** I detained him to assess the threat. Less paperwork. The suspect has been released on his own recognizance. Here's his unofficial mug shot.
> **Gage:** You assholes know I'm in this message group. Right?
> **Laura:** Yep.
> **Cam:** Howdy fucking doo, dumbass.
> **Levi:** Don't leave town.

"I brought whatever the hell this is and my last container of buffalo chicken dip," I announced as Nana and I entered Cam's garage.

It was nine o'clock at night, and I'd been invited to take part in a brothers-only raccoon stakeout. Nana trotted over to Meetcute and Buttercup, who was obsessively chewing on a squeaky toy hammer in a dog bed.

"Why do you have Zoey's dog?" I demanded.

"Shut the door," Cam growled at me. He was standing at the window, peering at his house through a pair of binoculars. A thermal scope rested on the windowsill next to him. The workbench beside him held a laptop and two tablets. All screens were divided into quarters with each quarter tuned to a different security camera feed of the exterior and interior of Cam's house.

Levi, my unapologetic arresting officer, was kicked back in a zero-gravity lounger with his laptop.

"What's his problem?" I asked Levi.

Cam lowered the binoculars to glare at me. "My problem? *My* problem?"

"He's gonna say it's you," Levi predicted without looking up from his screen.

"My problem is my wife is headed off to Bangor, Maine, and Beavercreek, Ohio, and some other places that aren't here thanks to you."

"Me?" I leaned down to ruffle Buttercup's ears.

"Because you fucked up, broke her best friend's heart—like I told you not to—so Zoey talked Hazel into doing a spontaneous book tour."

"Book tour?" I was simultaneously devastated and relieved. That explained the suitcases. "So she's coming back?"

"We're getting married next month. Of course she's coming back."

"I meant Zoey. She gave notice that she's breaking her lease and moving out."

"You're not dumb enough to be surprised, are you?" Levi asked.

I took the seat next to Levi's and put my head in my hands. "It was one fucking mistake. She wouldn't even let me explain."

"For fuck's sake," Cam said, turning away from the window to face us. "Explain what? The explanation is you were an asshole who lashed out at her."

"Yeah, but if I could just tell her why—"

"Dude," Levi said, finally glancing up at me. "Even *I* know that's not what a woman wants to hear."

"You're so fucking bad at this. You're not trying a case, dumbass. There's no exhibit A. No jury to impress. There's no winning," Cam insisted.

"How the hell else am I supposed to get her to forgive me?"

Cam opened his mouth, then shook his head. "You know what? No. You need to figure this out on your own. I had to figure out how to unfuck things with Hazel myself."

Levi scratched his head. "Didn't Mom and Dad give you a verbal ass kicking and some advice?"

"Yeah, but I still handled the unfucking myself."

I had to admit, Cam had made it impossible for Hazel not to forgive him. He'd finished her dream house, got her book rights back, and then threw in an engagement ring and two pets on top of that.

"Fine. I can unfuck things. If you did it with Hazel after you fucked up, it can't be that hard," I said.

"Remind me to never date anyone," Levi muttered. "I'm exhausted just listening to you two. It's like you fall for these women who hold up a mirror to show you your shittiest pieces, and then you have to unshit the pieces or be miserable and alone forever."

Cam and I shrugged.

"Yeah, that's pretty much exactly what relationships are," I agreed.

We sat quietly for a few minutes ignoring each other until the silence got to be too much for me.

"Hey, did you know women get stuck in sports bras?"

I couldn't tell who was snoring louder, Meetcute or Levi.

It was after three in the morning, and Cam was back at the window, legs braced, binoculars up. Our empty beers were lined up in a serpentine path from the door. The buffalo chicken dip was no more, and I was regretting the fact that I hadn't brought an air mattress. I let out a yawn. "This is one of your worst ideas. Why not just call animal control and relocate Bertha to a nice forest somewhere?"

"Because Hazel loves that fucking trash panda, and I love Hazel," he said. "And we do stupid shit for the people we love even when they're out of town for a week because our brother is a dumbass."

"Glad to see you're letting that go," I said dryly.

Cam put down the binoculars and returned to his camp chair. He scrubbed his hands over his eyes. "Larry tell you Felicity came into the store this week to pick up her order?"

"I heard," I said on another yawn. Felicity usually conned or blackmailed one of us into delivering her groceries. "It's good to see her getting out like that."

"Yeah. Making an effort instead of just whining about how things didn't go her way."

"I take it we're back to me and how I fucked up?" I guessed.

"It's not totally your fault. You spent tens of thousands of dollars on law school, where they drilled into your head to never admit fault and never assume responsibility. You wouldn't know how to apologize if you had cue cards," Cam joked.

"That's not accurate," I argued.

"Life isn't some court case or legal argument to win. People make fucking mistakes. Big ones. Your job as a human fucking being isn't to play judge and jury. You can't argue your way to forgiveness."

I sat back in my chair and stared up at the dark ceiling. Fuck. He was right. I spent so much of my life focused on making sure people who did bad things were punished accordingly that I'd never learned a damn thing about forgiveness. Especially how to earn it. There was a difference between justice and forgiveness, and I was just now realizing it. "I hate when you're ri—"

"Shut the fuck up, fuckface," Cam hissed.

"I'm in the middle of a breakthrough thanks to your rarely exhibited brotherly wisdom, and you want me to shut the fuck up?"

He was pointing at one of the tablets.

Motion detected.

"What the hell? Your kitchen door just opened."

"No shit."

"Is the house haunted?" I wondered.

I watched the screen while Cam tiptoed as quietly as a man his size could back to the window. A minute later, a furry blob waddled up onto the deck and headed straight for the door like it had a time clock to punch.

"That furry son of a bitch," Cam growled. "I'm putting an end to this once and for all."

He turned for the door, accidentally kicking over the first bottle, setting off an explosive chain reaction.

All three dogs lurched awake, barking like a garbage truck and a mail van had gotten into an accident in front of them.

Levi sat up abruptly. "Wha's happening? Where's the chicken dip?"

"You're not going to believe this," I told him.

"Hi," I said breathlessly two hours later when Valerie opened the door.

"Uh. Hi. It's not even seven a.m., Gage," she said. Her hair was standing up in clumps, and she had an extra-large coffee mug clamped in her hand. Behind her, I could hear the sounds of a children's TV show and giggles coming from the living room.

"I know. And I'm sorry. But I've been up all night because my brother's cat has been letting a raccoon into his house at night. They have the door lever handles instead of knobs, and the back door has the dog's potty bells hanging from the handle, so the cat pulls on the bells and—you know what? That's not important. I've had a lot of caffeine. The important thing is I screwed up big time with Zoey, and I realized how can she forgive me if I can't forgive you?"

She blinked in confusion. "I think I'm going to need a lot more coffee for this."

"Valerie," I said, grabbing for her free hand. "I forgive you."

"You…what?"

I took her by her bathrobed shoulders. "I don't think I realized it until Saturday night when you put yourself between my sister and danger. But I forgive you."

Her lower lip trembled. "Y-you don't have to do that. What I did was unforgivable."

"You made a mistake. It was just a mistake. You shouldn't have to pay for it for the rest of your life. Not when you're trying so hard to make things right."

"They'll never be right again," she said quietly.

"They'll never be the way they were before. For any of us. But knowing that you hurt like we hurt means something. You taking responsibility, not making excuses, not asking for anything in return means something. So I forgive you. I mean it."

Her face crumpled, and she fell into my arms. Her robe was sticky with something that I hoped was syrup. She had a butterfly sticker in her hair. I was hugging the woman who had ended my brother-in-law's life. I was hugging the woman who was sorry enough to be forgiven, the woman who'd taught me everything I needed to know about forgiveness.

"Thank you, Gage," she said, pulling back.

I gave her shoulders another squeeze. "I'm going to fix this. I'm going to fix everything."

46

It's not a wedding gazebo
Gage

To: Zoey
From: Gage
Subject: Disco apology

Dear Zoey,

I wake up in the middle of the night trying to catch my breath because I keep seeing your face by the bonfire that night. You did exactly the right thing before anyone else even reacted, and I panicked and stupidly blamed you for the situation. I've spent so much of my life trying to do the right thing. Yet when it came to the person who matters the most to me (you, if that wasn't clear), I self-destructed and made a colossal mistake.

I keep reliving it. The pain I caused so unnecessarily. I don't blame you for not forgiving me. What I did came from a place I didn't even know existed inside me. A wound that needs to be exorcised, according to Opal, who told me that and then hit me with an unbaked potato. Her brand of unofficial therapy is…painful.

At the bonfire that night, I was looking for you. Because I'm always looking for you. I saw you with my sister, and I was thinking about how well you fit with my family. Like you're the missing piece I'd been waiting for. Then I saw Valerie, and it made me think of our other missing piece.

Miller and I weren't as close as he was with Cam and Levi at first. I was the tagalong little brother when we were growing up. But I was the one he asked to take care of his family while he was deployed. We were both intense, cautious, responsible people who always tried to do the right thing. And now he's gone.

I wasn't able to protect Laura from that.

I wasn't able to protect Audrey from her ex.

You noticed she was in danger before anyone else did. Before me. She came to me to protect her from him. But all my legal filings and papers didn't stop him from trying to hurt her in front of their kids. The law failed her. I failed her. Doing the "right thing" wasn't good enough.

But you barely knew her, yet you ran to her rescue.

Instead of acknowledging how brave you were and how you saved Audrey's life, all I could see was you running away from me and toward danger. The most important person in my life, and I couldn't protect you. Or Audrey. Or Laura.

So I did the stupidest thing possible and used your worst fears and beliefs against you. I made you feel like you were the problem. Even though we both know it was me.

A lifetime of doing the "right thing." Of making every effort to avoid mistakes. None of it was good enough to keep the people I love safe. So I took it out on you when you did nothing wrong. Since I met you, I've learned that the world isn't as black-and-white as I always thought it was. It's not gray either. It's every color, and you're the one who showed me that. You and your damn disco ball.

I've been living my life, as my brothers would say, with a "clenched asshole," trying to be good enough to stop the bad from happening instead of accepting that the bad is inevitable and usually out of our control. I should have understood that without the bad, the good would be taken for granted.

I won't take you for granted again, Zoey. I can't promise I won't be an unevolved moron ever again, but I can promise you I will spend my life working to be the kind of man who not only deserves you but that you deserve. I will make it my life's mission to be that man for you…even if you don't forgive me.

I'm asking for a second chance even though it's well within your rights to tell me to fuck off. That doesn't stop me from hoping or trying though. Now if you'll excuse me, I'm going to go continue my groveling tour at the courthouse, because you taught me the value of vulnerability, and I think I finally know how to save Valerie.

Story Lake isn't the same without you. I miss you. I'm sorry.

Love,
Gage

Me: Cam told me not to tell you because he's afraid of you, but since he's flying out to meet you and Hazel in Houston, Buttercup is having a sleepover at my house. Please enjoy this picture of all three dogs on your side of the bed. No skunks allowed. Miss you. Love you.

Me: Today, in between dodging potatoes thrown at me by everyone who identifies as Team Zoey (the entire town), I talked to Billie and Hana. They told me the lodge is completely booked through mid-August. Their reservation system crashed twice after Reader Weekend with people trying to book the rest of the summer. They're calling it "the Zoey effect."

Me: Goddammit. Nana taught Buttercup and Meetcute how to chase skunks. I smell. They smell. Here's a picture of them all crammed in the sink together. I hate everything except you. I miss you.

Me: Buttercup misses you and so do I. See our matching sad faces?

Me: Obviously you told Cam that I told you I was watching your dog because he just kicked my ass with a piece of leftover drywall. I deserved it. He also said you met a swarthy European prince with a mustache and that you're moving to a country I've never heard of to join the royal family. I think he was lying, but just to be on the safe side, I'm willing to grow a mustache if it brings you home.

Me: That piece in Thrive on you, Hazel, and Story Lake is working its magic. Darius has three house showings next week, and Angelo's had to start a waiting list Saturday night. First time in history.

Me: I don't know if I can do this whole "life" thing without you. And not just because people keep throwing potatoes at me. The Warblers chased me out of the Fish Hook yesterday with an a cappella version of "All Too Well." The 10-minute version.

Me: Audrey's ex didn't make bail, so he'll be in jail until the assault trial. Just thought you'd like to know that Audrey and the kids are safe for the foreseeable future.

Me: It's 2 a.m. All I can think about is how much I miss Miller. How much I miss who Laura used to be. How much I miss you. The worst part is knowing I'm missing you because I broke us.

Me: Cam told me you were going to stay in Story Lake. I can't believe that I so carelessly ruined that chance at an HEA. (I've been reading some of Hazel's books and trying not to sympathize too much with the heroes during their dumbassery.)

Me: I'm risking life and limb here to tell you first, Disaster. I went to the courthouse and threw myself on the mercy of the DA. I accepted responsibility for pressuring her to press charges against Valerie in the first place, groveled for forgiveness, and admitted that I'd selfishly used my pain to inflict an unfair punishment on others. That one horrible mistake shouldn't cost another family a parent. Tarini, understandably, let me have it, then kicked me out of her office so she could think. She called me with a plea deal three minutes ago while I was meeting with Valerie at my office. Careless driving unintentional death. No fucking jail time. Valerie accepted (and told me I could tell you). Someone is cutting fucking onions in here. Even Declan has to keep pausing to blow his nose while he celebrates with *The Princess Bride* sword fight choreography. Buttercup is Inigo Montoya. DON'T TELL LAURA I TOLD YOU FIRST.

Me: I love how proud you look in the background of every picture of Hazel on social media. (Not that I'm stalking you online. I mean, I am, but in a noncreepy way.) A sold-out tour and a #1 bestseller. And you made it all happen. You're a miracle for all of us. I'm so proud of you. I wish we were celebrating together.

Me: Come home, Zoey. Nothing feels right without you.

Me: Please have dinner with me when you get back.

I pulled into Cam and Hazel's driveway to the sound of power tools. Meetcute trotted over to greet Nana and Buttercup before the three of them darted off into the flowery front yard.

"Well, if it isn't Mr. Ruins Everything by Being a Dumbass," Cam said, tossing the newly cut piece of treated lumber onto the nearby stack in front of the garage.

"You're just mad that I stole your title," I said, kicking at the leg of one of two sawhorses holding a simple craftsman-style arch. "What the hell is this? A gazebo?"

Cam yanked off his safety glasses and scowled. "It's *not* a wedding *gazebo*. It's a wedding *pergola*. I didn't chop down any fucking trees. I bought the wood from a lumber mill like a normal human. And if you say the word *gazebo* in front of Hazel, I will screw you to the top of it."

"Okay. This sounds like something I don't have enough context for. So let's start with what's a wedding gazebo?"

"It's a wedding *pergola*!" Cam snarled.

I picked up the sketch half pinned under his cooler and studied it while he fired up the circular saw again to finish the last support. According to the drawing, it would be a simple but elegant arched pergola just big enough for two people and an officiant to stand under.

When the saw cut off again, I put the drawing down and eyed my brother. "Can I ask why a wedding pergola is pissing you off so much? You lose a bet or something?"

"There was no bet. Hazel just suggested early on that I was going to get so attached to her, I'd build her a wedding gazebo."

Still not understanding the problem, I gestured at the drawing. "Well, clearly she was wrong. This is a pergola, not a gazebo."

He shrugged. "Didn't have enough room for a gazebo back here. Figured I'd make a pergola. We'll carve all our names and wedding dates in it and then hang a swing for the kids."

I blinked. "All our names?"

He shrugged. "If I'm making it, the rest of you pains in my ass might as well use it too. Make it a family tradition or some shit like that. What? No law-school-smarty comeback?"

"I'm too busy looking for obvious evidence of an alien abduction."

"Fuck you."

"Seriously, Cam, this is really…something. Mom's going to cry when she sees it."

"She better once we hang this," he said, tossing me a flat, arched board with the words Happily Ever After carved into it.

"Fuck," I said, fighting the tightness in my throat. I wanted to be there to see Cam and Hazel exchange vows and start their ever after. I wanted my own. "I need your help."

"It's about fucking time."

"You don't even know what I need," I complained.

"You wanna get Zoey back," he announced, digging through the tool tote on his tailgate.

"I love her. I fucked up. And she won't let me argue my case. She doesn't give second chances. But I need one. So how do I get one without crossing a line and making it worse?"

"You haul that over here," Cam said, jerking his chin at the pergola arch.

Grumbling, I hefted it over my shoulder and staggered after him into the yard. Peonies and azaleas swayed in the gentle breeze. Climbing vines meandered up and over the fence. "Are you just going to con free labor out of me and then tell me to get the fuck out of your face?"

"Yep. But first I might actually help you."

"Gee, thanks."

"Do you really want to be with Zoey? Or do you just feel guilty for hurting her?"

"Cam, I can't fucking sleep at night because my sheets smell like her. I'm working in the conference room because I keep remembering what we did on my desk. She made my life fun and exciting and unpredictable, and I should have hated that, but I didn't. I've been missing out on everything, just trying to stay in control, trying to make everything make sense. I fucking love her, and I hurt her, and I don't know if I'm ever going to be able to forgive myself for that."

Cam grunted. "Maybe you're not totally hopeless." He helped me lower the arch to the grass.

"What if I'm not good enough for her? What if I don't deserve a second chance?"

Cam clamped a hand on my shoulder, "Welcome to the club."

"What club?"

"The club of men who know they're not good enough for their women so we dedicate all our resources to making them forget that. By recognizing your huge and obvious inadequacies, you have made yourself slightly more worthy."

"Uh, thanks?"

"Zoey is out of your league. Like way out."

"You're not making me feel better. If I'm such a bag of shit, isn't it wrong to try to convince her to give me another chance?"

"You're asking for a chance to be a better person with her. You're asking for a chance to grow into someone who's good enough for her. You'll do better by her, right?"

"God, yes. I'll do anything. I'll build her a stable for her shoes. I'll schedule every oil change and inspection for the rest of our lives. I'll move to New York."

The shrill cry of a bird accompanied a dark shadow above us.

"Do not shit on this wedding pergola, Goose," Cam ordered.

The rebel eagle acted like he hadn't heard and swooped dramatically lower over us.

"What the hell is that?" I asked, shading my eyes against the sun as Goose released something from his talons.

The object fluttered to the ground, landing on my boot.

"If you don't know a bra when you see one, I've got my work cut out for me," Cam complained as I picked up the sparkly pink bra. Zoey's bra. A little worse for the wear with streaks of dirt and missing a few crystals, but it was unmistakably hers.

All three dogs came running, barking deliriously as the eagle completed one last lazy circle over us.

Cam cheerfully clapped me on the back. "If Goose thinks you're good enough, then you've officially earned an audience with the expert."

"The expert had better not be you."

"It's not. And it's not Levi either. But you should text him to come help with the pergola in case he ever finds a woman willing to marry a man who uses up all his words by breakfast."

Me: Cam gave me permission to reach out and grovel. I need your expertise.
Hazel: What expertise is that, Shithead McCrapFace?
Me: I'm in love with Zoey. I know you're just as mad at me as she is. I know I fucked up. But I also know she's my one. I'm hers. Please help me fix this.
Hazel: Hmm, I'll think about it.
Me: Would it help if I bribed you with some romantic inspiration?
Hazel: Hmm. I do like bribes.
Me: Here's a picture of what Goose just returned to me after I professed my love for Zoey and said I'd be willing to move to New York and build her an entire apartment-sized closet for shoes.
Hazel: Goose returned her sparkle bra???

Me: Seems like a sign, right? I'm willing to do anything for a second chance with her.
Hazel: Hold please...

Zoey: Fine. Since you can't seem to take a hint, I'll go to dinner with you. But only because Hazel says it's a good way to tell you all the reasons you're a shit waffle. I started a note on my phone so I won't forget any. Oh, and it better be a good dinner and not some high-protein, bullshit meal prep dinner.

47

Emergency poop would not be my legacy

Zoey

Dear Zoey,

Congratulations on Hazel's blockbuster hit. We'd love to have a conversation with you about both of you coming back home to Beau Monde. As you probably heard, Jim Whitehead is no longer with the agency, and we'd like to discuss you taking over his client roster. We're also extremely interested in your new client's romantasy series.

Sincerely,
Lawrence Rawley, CEO

———

"Great. Thank you. I'll be in touch as soon as Opal makes her decision," I said before disconnecting the call. Buttercup was snuggled up against my side. Her little tail hadn't stopped tapping since Cam had picked Hazel and me up at the airport. I was exhausted and hungry, and all my clothes smelled like airplanes. Hazel had killed it at five sold-out tour stops. I was so proud of her my face was frozen in a creepy, permanent smile.

I just wanted a shower and to crawl under the covers with my dog for forty-eight hours without talking to another person.

Which was what I would do as soon as I delivered the news to Opal that she was about to close one of the most lucrative deals for a debut author in the last decade.

"Good news?" Hazel asked from the front seat, where she and Cam were holding hands like it had been weeks instead of days since they'd last seen each other. Meetcute was perched on her lap, paws on the door as she stared out the window.

"I can't discuss another client's deals with you," I said in my most professional tone.

"Of course," Hazel said. "But…"

"But I will say *I'm the greatest agent in the history of literary agents!*"

Cam hunched his shoulders against our in-the-car victory dance and squealing. "You two just spent eight days on the road together. Aren't you sick of each other yet?"

"Never!" we said in unison.

Story Lake's welcome sign came into view, and my heart skipped a beat. Gage had kept up a steady stream of apology communications since I'd left town with Hazel. I'd nearly responded to him a thousand times. But I'd resisted.

He'd hurt me. Deeply. But during one of our calls while I was gone, Opal had given me a grumpy, no-nonsense explanation of why people like me were sometimes naturally more sensitive to rejection than others.

It had given me a lot to think about while I had too much quiet time in anonymous hotel rooms. I was still mad and hurt. And I sure as hell wasn't going to make a life-changing decision based on a week of nice emails and texts. But I *missed* him. And once I was back to my gorgeous, well-rested self, I would at least hear Gage Bishop out.

See? Growth…and meds…and a mean retired therapist.

Cam steered us through the town square. The storefront next to the future cheese shop no longer wore its For Sale sign. In its place was a placard announcing a dog groomer coming soon.

I'd text Gage tomorrow and schedule our dinner for later this week when I was showered and less emotionally vulnerable. In the meantime, I'd schedule a few dog-friendly apartment viewings back in New York. Because I had options.

Cam pulled into the small parking lot behind Gage's office building. My car and my trash bins were in their rightful places.

"Home sweet home," Hazel said cheerily.

Or something like that, I added internally. I really, really hoped Gage wasn't in his office. I wasn't ready to see him yet.

"I'll get your bags," Cam volunteered, practically vaulting out of the SUV.

"Thanks."

I got out with Buttercup. Hazel and Meetcute joined me. "Well, I guess this is it," I joked, going in for a hug.

"Actually, do you mind if I come up? I really have to pee…and I need a glass of water. That plane air makes my throat so dry." She demonstrated with a weak cough.

Cam appeared with my carry-on and overnight bag. "I'll carry these up," he said with a weirdly suspicious smile on his handsome face. But the guy had gone the last four days without seeing his fiancée, and love made people act like weirdos, so I went with it.

"Okay, I guess we'll all go up," I said.

Buttercup sprang up the stairs ahead of me with Hazel and Cam bringing up the rear.

"Shit," I muttered. "Hang on. Let me find my keys."

"Why don't I just kick it in?" Cam suggested five minutes later as Hazel and I pawed through my tote and suitcase.

"Aha!" I triumphantly held up the key ring I found inside one of my favorite stilettos.

Cam snatched the keys from me and opened the lock with barely restrained violence.

"Calm down, man. Do you have an emergency poop brewing or something?" I asked as he all but ripped the door off its hinges.

"Yes. Yes, he does," Hazel said quickly. "I told you not to eat that...wheel of cheese."

Cam gave Hazel a baleful look before ushering us across the threshold.

"Fine. Whatever. Just don't clog the toilet, because I'm not calling my landlord," I told him.

I left Hazel and Cam whispering suspiciously in the kitchen and headed into my bedroom. I dumped my bags on the floor and was just getting ready to face-plant on the bed when I noticed that something was different. Several somethings. Both my clean *and* dirty laundry piles were missing. And my sock drawer had somehow miraculously closed itself completely despite the fact that it had been overflowing before I left.

I opened the drawer and gasped. It was empty.

I yanked open the next drawer and the next and discovered they were empty as well. Tripping over my suitcase, I threw open my closet door and screamed.

"I've been robbed!"

"She found out fast," Cam said from my doorway.

"I told you she'd notice," Hazel said. "Zoey, honey. I know this looks weird—"

"Someone broke in here and stole all my clothes! Even my dirty laundry. What kind of a pervert steals dirty laundry?" I pushed past them and stormed into the living room. "Where are my throw pillows? And my disco ball candle holder? Someone call Levi. There's been a robbery."

Hazel approached me with her hands up and an expression usually reserved for skittish animals. "You haven't been robbed. There's a simple explanation for this."

"Okay. Explain," I said, crossing my arms.

She shot a guilty look at Cam. "Well, we can't. But we can take you to someone who can."

"You want to take me to the person who robbed me? Fine. Let's go. I just need to find my pepper spray."

"Told you she wasn't going to take it well," Cam said out of the side of his mouth.

Still grinning, Hazel patted his arm. "I'll tell you you were right later."

"What the hell's going on?" I demanded.

She beamed at me. "We can't actually tell you, but I do need you to put this on, because we have someplace important to be."

"Put what on? Handcuffs? A bag over my head?"

She nudged Cam.

"Oh right." He pulled a T-shirt from behind his back and threw it at me. It hit me in the head and draped over my face.

"I'm tired. I'm grungy. I still have recycled airplane air in my lungs. I want a shower, and I want my damn clothes!" I was embarrassingly close to stomping my foot but was saved from the indignity by sheer exhaustion.

Hazel walked over and put her hands on my shoulders. "I know you're tired. I know you've got a lot going on. But something wonderful is happening, and it's all for you. I'm not letting you miss out on it."

I closed my eyes and exhaled noisily through my nose. "Will there at least be food?"

"No," Cam said.

"There can be if you want there to be," Hazel insisted.

"There was no emergency poop, was there?" I asked Cam.

"Not today."

"So you're escorting me. Okay. Fine. This isn't weird at all," I complained, adjusting the hem of my *Story Lake Ultimate Bingo* T-shirt as Hazel and Cam marched hand in hand down the sidewalk in front of me. We were drawing quite the parade. Every person we passed smiled the same cheesy, secret smile at me and then fell into step behind us.

"Will someone please tell me what's going on?" I asked the crowd as we marched in the general direction of the lake.

"Oh, look. There's Goose," someone announced. The bald

eagle soared in a slow circle overhead above the gigantic banner. *Ultimate Bingo Kickoff Today.*

"No. No. No! Nope. I haven't had time to read the manual! I don't know the rules or the chants. I am in no condition to lead a team!" I turned around, trying to flee, but found my way blocked by a line of maniacally grinning townsfolk. "You can't kidnap someone and force them to play bingo!"

Buttercup pulled anxiously at her leash as she trotted by my side.

"You'd never kidnap me and make me participate in some weird town ritual when all I want to do is shower and sleep, would you, sweetie?" I asked my dog.

She looked up at me with utter adoration. Her cute, perky ears bounced as she trotted along next to me. The jagged pieces of my heart came together for a painful "aww." This was why people had dogs. Unconditional love and ear bouncies.

Hazel fell in step with me and took my hand as we crossed Lake Drive.

"What is happening?" I couldn't see past the wall of people in front of us.

"You'll see."

"Hazel Pain in My Ass Hart, if this is one of those over-the-top public grand gestures, I will *never* forgive you."

"I don't know what you're talking about," she said haughtily.

"Oh really? You didn't once write a hero who dressed up as Santa Claus, got stuck in the heroine's chimney, and then had to propose from a stretcher in front of the whole town after he was extracted by professionals?"

"I tell you what. If you see a Santa suit today, I give you permission to run."

"Look, I said I'd have dinner with the man so he could grovel. I didn't agree to some new public humiliation fiasco."

"Oh, this isn't Gage," Hazel said with the smugness of someone who knew what was going on. "This is Story Lake."

"I should have just stayed at the airport," I muttered under my breath as the entourage led me through the parking lot and right onto the sports court. I spotted Levi getting out of his truck and waved him down. "Hey, chief cop guy. I need to report a crime. Someone stole most of my stuff."

He shot Cam and Hazel a pointed look, then sighed as he fell into step. "We'll talk later."

"What exactly do you all know about my clothes?" I demanded a moment before running into Cam's back as he came to an abrupt stop in front of me. "Ow. What are you made of? Steel?"

Cam sidestepped out of my way to reveal a line of serious-looking Story Lakers all wearing the same T-shirt as the one I'd donned.

Darius and Scooter were at the center. Cam and Hazel joined the rest of the town council on the left. To the right were Levi, Laura, several business owners, and…the only face I *really* saw.

Gage Bishop.

He looked unfairly good in jeans and a tight-fitting *Story Lake Ultimate Bingo* shirt. His mouth was unsmiling. His chiseled jaw showed more than a day's growth of stubble. His hair was messier than usual, and he had a splatter of paint on his forearm and another on his jeans. He'd probably come straight here from some jobsite. Or maybe he'd been helping his parents on the farm. Gage's life hadn't stopped just because I'd left town. Despite his constant volley of emails, texts, and pictures, I assumed the past week had been business as usual for him.

Then I saw his gaze. That fierce green fire was fastened on me. And there was nothing disinterested about it.

I *ached* just looking at him. How could I have let myself fall so hard for him? How could I forget all the wonderful moments we'd shared? How could I ever look at him and not want him?

Buttercup sighed and leaned against my leg, offering canine comfort.

Oh no. My vision was tunneling. No, wait, Gage was getting closer. He was stalking toward me, closing the distance. I couldn't breathe. Couldn't think.

He didn't stop. He pushed one hand into my hair to cup the back of my neck and used the other hand to haul me against his body. "I love you," he said before kissing the crap out of me.

My brain scrambled faster than a dozen eggs in a frying pan. He loved me? *Gage Bishop loved me?*

His mouth was hot, hard, and so excruciatingly familiar against mine. I'd missed *this*, missed *him*.

"Aww!" Hazel crooned.

"That wasn't the plan," Cam said from somewhere that sounded far, far away.

Gage drew back, still staring at me. "Sorry. Got carried away," he said gruffly.

And then he was sliding his hands down my arms and releasing me before taking a step back. My knees nearly buckled.

"She's gonna start catching flies with that open mouth," Gator said from the crowd.

I managed to snap my jaw shut and bring myself back to reality. I was standing center court, surrounded by most of Story Lake. Darius and the Warblers strutted up to me. Scooter made a mouth trumpet noise right in my face, breaking the spell of Gage's proclamation.

Darius nodded solemnly at him. Scooter bowed and then returned to the ranks of the Warblers.

Darius unrolled an actual scroll and cleared his throat. "On this day," he bellowed, "Story Lake is proud to bestow one of our highest honors on one of our own citizens."

Was it me? Was I the citizen? Was the highest honor getting kissed by Gage? Because it was a damn good prize. *Oh crap.* What if this was some weird award ceremony for some *other* weirdo and I just assumed it was about me because of the fake emergency poop and group march to the lake?

"Zoey Moody."

Thank God.

"For your services to Story Lake in creating the wildly successful Reader Weekend, increasing our tourism, making our small businesses more profitable, and most importantly ruining Dominion's stupidly dangerous plans, do you accept this honor?"

"Uh, what honor exactly?" I asked, sending a nervous glance in Gage's direction. The man still looked like he wanted to ravage me. And I was open to the idea.

Darius put down the scroll and picked up an oversize bingo card. "The honor of the middle square."

"Ooooh!" crooned the crowd with awe as the mayor pointed to the free square. Prior to today, the free space had been home to a generic yellow star. Now in its place was a disco ball and several tiny words jammed together that I couldn't quite make out.

"The free square has officially been renamed the…" Darius gestured like an orchestra leader for the crowd to join him.

"Zoey Moody mumble mumble mumble mumble," everyone said.

I sidled a step closer to Darius. "The, uh, Zoey Moody what?"

He handed me the card and a magnifying glass. "The Zoey Moody Excellence in Public Service Free Space," he announced grandly.

"Wow. That's actually really nice," I said, studying the card.

"We'll probably have to shorten it to Zoey Moody XPSFS," he pronounced. "But it stands to remind players that, like the free space, we all benefit from public service."

"Of course. Makes sense," I agreed solemnly as if I was even remotely following the logic.

Emilie Rump stepped forward. "As the official ultimate bingo commissioner, I hereby declare that you may now choose a rhyme or action players will perform when utilizing the Zoey Moody XPSFS."

"Oh, uh, right now?" I asked.

She nodded regally.

Man, these folks really took their bingo seriously. Okay, I was absolutely not going to say "emergency poop" right now. No matter how much my impulsive self wanted to. Emergency poop would not be my legacy.

"Okay, a rhyme or an action. A rhyme or an action..." I tapped my chin and started to pace. The audience followed suit. "No, wait! I'm thinking, not choreographing."

"No, wait! I'm thinking, not choreographing," they repeated.

"Fuck."

"Fuck!"

I looked to Gage. *Help?* I mouthed.

He closed the distance between us. Every footstep that brought him closer made my heart hammer harder.

"What do you need?" he asked, his voice a rough whisper that carried memories of all those nights together.

"I don't know how to come up with something on the spot that perfectly represents me. I'm a mess."

"You're not a mess, Zoey. You're amazing."

"Stop kissing my face and ass, and start coming up with solutions."

"Okay," he said with an affectionate smile.

"This honor is giving me anxiety. What's my essence? And how do I apply that to bingo?"

"You're really hot," Harry shouted out.

Laura rolled her eyes, then gave her son a good-natured punch to the back of the knee.

"You're a hard worker," Chevy said.

"You always bus your own table on the deck at the Fish Hook," one of the servers called out.

"You didn't laugh when I farted during Lakercise," George yelled from his scooter.

"You kicked Dominion's ass," Kitty Suarez bellowed. That one earned a resounding cheer from the crowd.

"You're less annoying than I thought you'd be," Opal announced. "And you took an interest in a grumpy old lady and reminded her what it's like to maybe wanna stick around."

"You make everything sparkle," Gage said.

"Stop it," I whispered.

"It's true," Hazel said. "You do."

"*Sparkle* works," Laura agreed, wiggling her fingers in the air.

Darius looked relieved. "Thank goodness. That's a lot more family friendly than the old O69 call."

This shouldn't be so heartwarming. I shouldn't be getting emotional. But this town. This lovely, loony little town had made a space for me. Literally.

My eyes were damp. Someone was definitely chopping a large quantity of onions here in the park. "I don't know what to say besides thank you," I squeaked.

"Scooter, please present the ceremonial tissues," Darius requested.

———

"So there you have it," I said, handing the paper over to Opal. With the ultimate bingo ceremony officially over, we were sitting on a park bench at the lake's edge as the sun dipped low in the sky. Buttercup rested her head on her paws and stared out over the water like she was pondering life. "A seven-figure advance and your dream editor," I said with satisfaction.

"For *my* books," she said, squinting down at the number I'd written out for her. A life-changing number.

"For your books," I agreed.

"You're shitting me."

"I can assure you there has been no shitting today."

"Sounds like someone needs more fiber in their diet."

"Come on. Go back to admiring your shiny offer, and then tell me what a good job I did," I said, tapping the paper.

She peered at me through the tinted lenses of her glasses. "I didn't think I'd be taken seriously. I didn't think anyone would make room for me, let alone be stupid enough to offer me this kind of money."

"Yeah, well, sometimes the good guys win. And you, Opal, are a good guy. A grumpy one, but a deeply talented, grumpy good guy. So yay you! Tell me you have a bottle of champagne in your apartment."

"I got one on me," she said and pulled a mini split of sparkling wine out of her tote bag.

Gage was standing a few feet away on the dock, admiring the setting sun with his sister and Val while all five kids entertained each other.

"So what do I do?" she asked, unscrewing the top and taking a swig.

"Well, we'll chug warm purse champagne right out of the bottle, and then you'll decide if you're taking the deal."

"Of course I'm taking the damn deal. Alice didn't marry a fool," Opal announced.

I collapsed back against the bench. "Thank God. Part of me thought you were going to tell me to fuck off out of stubbornness, and I already picked out my celebration shoes."

"I'm only doing it to keep you from bankruptcy," she said, passing me the bottle.

"Liar," I said, taking a sip. "Now I want you to bask in the sparkly glory that you, Opal Mallory, a seventy-three-year-old woman, were wooed at auction by three of the top publishers in the industry. Each one salivating at the thought of getting their hands on the books you wrote."

"You're a lot less annoying when you bring me buckets of money."

I handed the bottle back to her with a wink. "I was just thinking the same about you."

That earned me a small smile. "You're a hell of a girl, Zoey."

"Stick with me, kid, and I'll make the rest of your seventies and your eighties memorable as hell."

"Who's gonna make yours memorable?" Opal asked, looking pointedly in Gage's direction.

"Me," I said firmly.

"Folks sure seem to love you around here," Opal continued. "Him included."

"Maybe," I hedged, taking the bottle back.

"Mistakes were made, kid. But you know what? As long as you learn from them and do better, you don't have to be defined by them."

"Listen, Opal. I haven't slept more than five hours a night in the past week. I haven't showered in two…" I paused and sniffed my armpit. "Make that three days. I'm tired and hungry, and someone stole all my clothes. I'm in no frame of mind to make a life-altering decision that includes the hot guy who broke my heart."

"Well, you better get yourself into the right frame of mind," she said, nudging me.

I looked up to find Gage approaching. Buttercup perked up, tail thumping against my leg. I couldn't blame her. My heart did its own thumping as he got closer. So serious. So attentive.

He loved me.

I couldn't stop thinking about his words.

He stopped in front of us, and Buttercup scrambled to her feet. I had to stop myself from doing the same. "Opal," Gage said by way of greeting as he bent to offer my delirious dog affection. I was not jealous. Nope. Definitely not.

"Don't fuck it up," Opal told him, getting up.

"I'll do my best," he promised.

"Where are you going?" I asked her as she tucked the paper with the offer into her tote bag and gripped her cane.

"I've got shit to do. Bigger champagne bottles to open. I'll see you tomorrow." Her gaze skated to Gage. "But not too early," she added.

The implication was clear as she walked away. Well, I'd show her. Zoey Moody didn't make the same mistake twice. I was a strong, independent woman with a modicum of self-esteem. I wasn't about to fall under the green-eyed, hard-mouthed spell of Gage Bishop so easily again.

"You ready for that dinner?" Gage asked me.

"Sure."

Damn it, me.

48

Stop with the grand gesturing
Zoey

I may have caved to the invitation with an appalling lack of backbone, but at least I had the wherewithal to drive myself and Buttercup to Gage's house.

My hair was still damp from the shower, but I put the top down so the breeze would take care of that. In keeping with the whole "I'm not trying" thing, I was still wearing my ultimate bingo shirt, because it was the only clean item of clothing that I currently owned, seeing as how *someone* had stolen my entire wardrobe.

I was apparently the only person in the entire town concerned about the whereabouts of my clothing.

I cranked up my music and gave the sharp wings of eyeliner an approving nod in the rearview mirror. So I may have gone a little sexy on the makeup, but that wasn't to entice Gage. It was my armor. It was my reminder that I was a strong, independent woman…who accidentally accepted a dinner invitation from a man who had temporarily dicknotized her, broken her heart, and then announced that he loved her. If the smoky eye and red lip reminded Gage that he was in fact a big dumb idiot, well, that was just a bonus.

Buttercup grumbled in the passenger seat.

"Stop judging me," I told her. "Someday when you're a grown-up doggie and you get your heart broken by a boy—or girl—doggie, you'll understand."

Buttercup was indifferent to my sharing and began an enthusiastic grooming of her nether regions.

I wondered if I should have done a more intensive grooming just in case Gage pulled off the impossible and managed to officially earn my forgiveness. No, that was ridiculous. For once in my life, I was going to be logical about something. I wasn't going to jump into a second chance without weighing every single option carefully. I owed it to myself…and my dog.

The rattle in the car door intensified, drowning out Freddie Mercury's high note. "Damn it all to hell," I snapped, whipping my car off to the side of the road. "I have had it with this stupid rattle!"

I threw open my door and violently jiggled the handle with both hands. The rattle echoed in my brain.

"Stupid, dumb, terrible rattle," I said through gritted teeth as I felt around the door panel, looking for a way in. "Aha! The speaker grille thing is loose," I said to Buttercup, who was watching me with her head cocked.

I yanked off the cage, and the speaker immediately fell out of the door, dangling by its wires. I shoved my hand in the hole the speaker left and felt around inside the door. My fingers brushed something…weird.

"What in the…"

I nearly pulled a neck muscle, but I managed to get a grip on the item and pull it out.

I blinked in disbelief at the cause of weeks of annoyance. It was an entire roll of dimes.

"You've got to be shitting me," I murmured, shaking my head.

Buttercup cocked her head to the other side, trying to understand.

I stared up at the sunset looking for some kind of answer. Buttercup looked up too and gave a little bark.

But there was no response for either of us.

I finally managed to return the speaker to its hole and pulled back onto the road.

"This is *not* a sign from someone's deceased brother-in-law that I never even met. This is just a coincidence," I insisted as I drove. I turned onto Gage's lane as dusk settled on the land. My headlights washed over the house. I was hit by a longing so intense it took my breath away. All the things that could have been. Things that I'd only dared to secretly hope for.

I stared down at the roll of dimes in my lap.

No. This was a mistake. Any kind of proximity to the man clouded my judgment. I was just about to turn the car around and find the nearest fast-food drive-thru that accepted coins when a barefoot Gage stepped out of the house with Nana as his shadow. Buttercup whimpered excitedly next to me.

"Ugh. I know. They do make a gorgeous picture, but remember, Gage is a butthead," I grumbled. I parked in front of the garage and stuffed the dimes in my bag before getting out of the car. Buttercup nimbly hopped out after me.

I pointedly ignored Gage in favor of watching the dogs get reacquainted. Nana seemed like she was happy to see me specifically as opposed to her general joy over contact with a generic human. And she also seemed to be ecstatic about Buttercup's presence.

The two of them began a series of high-speed zoomies around the car, leaving me no more excuses to avoid Gage.

"She missed you," he observed. "So did I."

"I missed her too," I said, trying desperately not to look directly at him. He wore worn jeans slung low on his hips and an ancient gray T-shirt that would have ended up in my collection had I still been stealing his clothes. Despite the physical distance between us, I could smell his shower gel.

A delicious and completely unwanted shiver rolled up my spine when I remembered what those hands were capable of in the shower.

This had been a mistake. I shouldn't have come here tonight. I should have insisted on a less sexy meal in a more public place. Breakfast in a fluorescent-lit diner with coffee stains on the table. Booths that made fart noises when you scooted across them.

"I made steaks," he said, hooking his thumb toward the deck.

"Sounds good," I said, not moving.

It's possible we would have stood there all night if it weren't for Nana hurling herself into my driver's seat through the open door and laying both front paws on the horn. Buttercup froze mid-zoomie.

"I am suing you if your dog teaches my dog that trick," I yelled over the blaring horn.

"Damn it, Nana," Gage grumbled, pulling Nana out of the car and shutting the door.

He released her, and she and Buttercup took off into the inky evening, racing across the cool grass.

Visions of skunks and other nocturnal dangers ratcheted up my anxiety. What if Buttercup ran into the woods? What if a bear mistook her for a sandwich? What if a cow stepped on her? What if she didn't come back?

"She's fine. The skunk has been relocated, and Buttercup doesn't leave Nana's side," Gage said, reading my mind.

He gestured for me to take the ramp up to the deck first. I was glad I was wearing my great-ass jeans, so I knew his view was impressive. Unfortunately, so was mine.

He'd turned the fire table on and added candles. The string lights that cast a cozy glow above us were disco balls. The table was set for romance with wineglasses and actual cloth fucking napkins. I stopped abruptly, and Gage ran into me. The feel of his front to my back was electric. The solid heat of him reincarnated a dozen clothing-optional memories.

"This is a mistake," I announced.

"It's just dinner," he said, his mouth an inch from my ear.

His hands found my hips, and he guided me forward. His touch overpowered my capability for rational thought. I just wanted more. More of this, of him, of this place.

Shit. I was going to forgive him whether I wanted to or not. Damn it. Damn it. Damn it.

"Have a seat," he said, pulling a chair out for me.

I collapsed into it like an abandoned puppet. He looked down at me, eyes smoldering, and then reached out to smooth a curl away from my face.

I refused to give in to the urge to purr. Instead, I pounced on the glass of water in front of my plate and guzzled it like I'd been lost in the desert for the last week.

Gage headed to the grill where he unveiled two mouthwatering steaks and a pair of mammoth foil-wrapped baked potatoes.

"You're not going to throw those at me, are you?" I asked with suspicion. The side dish had lost its innocence since I'd moved to Story Lake.

"If anyone deserves to get hit with potatoes, it's me," he said, returning to the table and divvying up the food between our plates. The dogs galloped back onto the deck from their romp and stuck their faces in a water bowl against the railing.

"She really likes it here," I noted as Buttercup flopped down on her side and pawed at Nana.

"She feels like a missing puzzle piece," Gage said, not taking his eyes off me. "Do you want any wine?"

I shook my head. I needed to keep a clear, level head where he was concerned. "What are we doing here?" I asked as I attacked my steak.

"We're just talking."

"What's left to say?" Damn it. The steak melted in my mouth like meat-flavored butter. Why did he have to be so stupidly good at everything?

"I love you, Zoey."

There it was again. The proclamation that had my entire

body freezing. The steak lodged itself in my throat, and after a brief coughing fit, I chugged the rest of my water. "Jesus, Gage."

"What?"

"I thought you'd start with something like 'Sorry for being an irredeemable shit waffle.'"

"Sorry for being an irredeemable shit waffle. I love you," he said, a teasing smile playing on his mouth.

I buttered my potato with violence. "Look. I forgive you or whatever. We both knew what we were getting into when we started this disaster. And we both knew it wasn't going to end well, so there's no point in being upset about it. And I was more sensitive about the rejection than I should have been. So let's just call it even. Thanks for the steak."

"Zoey, I want a second chance."

"Nope." I forked up a bite of potato, butter, and sour cream. Just because we weren't getting back together didn't mean I couldn't at least enjoy the meal.

"I was hoping you'd say that," he said.

My fork hit the plate with a clatter. "Oh, come on! You were not!"

He grinned. "It would have been too easy if you gave in. I have a case to make."

"If you start quoting precedent, I'm out of here," I warned before stuffing another bite of steak into my mouth.

"I want you more than all the things I thought I wanted before I met you. I didn't realize how much until you were gone. There are a lot of things I didn't realize. Like how much light and color you brought into my life. Everything before you was black-and-white. I had no idea how much I was missing out on. Until you."

"Uh-huh. Are you going to eat that?" I asked, pointing my fork at his untouched steak.

"Yes, I am, but there's another steak on the grill. I screwed up. I made a catastrophic mistake, and I underestimated the hurt that I caused you."

I closed my eyes and took a breath. "Gage, really, it's fine.

People get their feelings hurt all the time. People break up all the time. There's no reason why we can't still be friends."

"Yes, there is. I'm not having sex with and marrying my friends."

I choked on potato. "Jesus, man."

"Zoey, I lashed out at you when I was feeling vulnerable. In that moment, I lived up to every one of your low expectations of me. And I'm so sorry for that. But the thing I'm most sorry for is that somewhere deep down inside, you expected it. You believe you have some kind of internal failing or you don't measure up, and that's why people you love keep letting you down."

"Maybe, but I'm pretty sure I blame *you* for this," I said, pointing the knife in his direction.

"You should. But you don't. At least not completely. You've been hurt enough times by the people who are supposed to care about you to believe that you're the problem. And you're not. You never were. It's not your fault. Not me taking out my insecurities on you. Not your parents treating you like the source of all their problems. Not that idiot Sam leaving when you needed him most. It has nothing to do with you and everything to do with them. None of it is your fault."

My throat went dry and tight. "I think relationships are a two-way street. Nobody is completely innocent."

He reached out and took my hand. "Zoey, the realization that I hurt you keeps me up at night. I can't sleep. I can't think. I can't fucking breathe. Not because you won't forgive me but because I made you doubt how I really feel about you. I get how badly I hurt you, and I get why you wouldn't want to give me a second chance. But I can promise you I'll never do that again. I'll find new ways to fuck up. But I will never again make you feel like you were too much for me."

I wanted to believe him. Every piece of my heart wanted it to be true. But I owed it to myself to stay strong. Not to put myself in the position to be hurt like that again. "Gage, look, you can't be responsible for my feelings. So I'm more sensitive than the next girl. That's my thing to deal with. Not yours."

"There is no next girl. I don't fall off the roof for just anyone. You're it for me, Zoey."

"We're too different," I argued, hanging on to the last shreds of self-preservation.

"How?"

"I'm disco balls and no underwear. You're calendars and meal prep."

His grin was victorious. "I'm glad you brought that up. I have some evidence to present."

He pulled me to my feet and towed me toward the door. The dogs scrambled to get there first, pressing their wet noses against the glass before Gage slid it open. They dashed ahead into the darkened living room. I caught the faint scent of fresh paint.

The dogs scrambled past us and headed for the kitchen.

"Here," Gage said, handing me a remote control without letting go of me. It felt so right to be there, to be touched by him.

"You wanna watch TV right now? Aren't we kind of in the middle of something?"

"Just turn it on."

"Turn what on?" I grumbled, hitting the power button.

Light and color twirled to life above our heads.

"Oh. My. God," I said. There, hanging from the center beam in Gage's living room, was a disco ball silently spinning. "You didn't."

"I did. Do you like it?"

"Do I like the giant disco ball you hung from your living room ceiling? Yes, Gage. I do." I pulled away from him to turn in circles in the rainbow of light. "You did this for me?"

"Everything is for you," he said, stopping me mid-spin.

"Hey. You got throw pillows. Wait. Those are my throw pillows! That's my blanket. And my candle," I said, noticing my possessions mixed in with his.

"There's more."

"More?"

"Come with me."

I allowed myself to be dragged into the bedroom, mildly disappointed when we didn't stop at the bed. Confusion set in when we headed into the bathroom. But I was dazzled when he opened the door to the closet.

"You didn't," I breathed again.

The unfinished closet was unfinished no more. Shelves, cubbies, and clothing rods. There was an island—no, a continent—in the middle of the space with a pretty stone counter and drawers galore. Gage's clothes, his sexy suits and scruffy work clothes, still occupied their original space in the front corner, but the rest...the rest was *mine*. My clothes, my accessories, my entire wardrobe was organized by color and displayed like we were in some high-end retail space.

"So you're the one Levi has to arrest for theft," I said.

"He'll have to arrest himself since he helped me move everything. I wanted to make a grand gesture, but I didn't want to make it creepy by stealing everything you owned and moving it here. So I stuck with the biggest wow factor."

"Everything looks so nice, and you *know* how I hate packing and unpacking." I turned to face him. "This is emotional manipulation."

"Damn right it is. Is it working?"

"Maybe," I hedged.

I spotted it then. The tin of dimes tucked out of the way on a shelf in Gage's section. The evidence that no matter what, deep down, Gage Bishop was a good man.

Damn it. What was I supposed to do now? Accept his apology? Start trying on all my own clothing in the mirror? Suggest we step out of the closet and into the bedroom? I'd never been here before, at the beginning of a second chance. I wished I were one of Hazel's heroines so I'd know what to do, what to say.

"Zoey, I love you. I want a life with you. Together. It doesn't have to be here. If you want to move back to the city—"

I bit my lip. "Manhattan doesn't have closet space like this." Or men who collected dimes to hide for their grieving sister to remind her she was loved.

The dogs pranced into the doorway, noses sniffing all the newness.

"Or backyards for dogs," I pointed out. I needed a sign. Something to tell me how to do this. "Holy shit. Is that my bra?"

There, hanging by itself on a bedazzled hanger, was my three-hundred-dollar pink sequined bra.

"How did you get another one? They were discontinued six years ago."

"It's the original," Gage said. "Goose gave his blessing."

I turned to face him. "You're saying the bald eagle that stole my bra *returned* it to you?"

"When you say it like that, it sounds ridiculous. But it's true."

"This is a lot to take in," I admitted, looking around me.

"I was kind of hoping to emotionally overwhelm you and sweep you off your—where are you going?"

"Stay right there," I ordered. "I'll be back."

The dogs followed me like I had steak in my pockets. I stepped out on the deck, grabbed my purse, and stomped back to the closet. Gage was in the same spot.

"I wasn't sure if you were coming back," he admitted.

I reached in my bag and plunked the roll of dimes down on the counter. "I know about the dimes. The thing you do for Laura. I've known for a while, and it's pretty much the only reason I didn't junk punch you when you deserved it, because anyone who would do that for their sister isn't a completely terrible person."

"Uh, thanks. I think," he said, drumming his fingers nervously on his thigh.

I blew out a breath. "I just found these in the door panel of my car on my way here. Like some ridiculous, over-the-top, flashing neon sign from the universe or something."

We both stared at the roll like it was some kind of religious artifact.

"It's definitely a sign," Gage said with authority, his voice thick.

"Okay. Fine. It's a sign. Then I guess there's only one thing left to do."

"What's that?"

I launched myself at him, wrapping my legs around his waist, my arms around his neck. His mouth found mine in a frenzy as he managed to shut the door in the dogs' faces.

"I really love you, and I'm not just saying it because I'm closet drunk," I promised. "Even though the closet really helped."

"Thank fucking God," Gage murmured. "I thought you were going to kick my ass for stealing your stuff."

"Still might depending on how the night goes." I reached a hand out to steady us, but he spun me around.

"Don't touch anything. Some of the stain is still tacky. It was a photo finish," he said between breathless kisses.

"Shut up and take your pants off."

He pulled back again and looked at me. "Just so you know, I'm planning to propose."

"Yeah, okay. Great. Let's get married. Now get those pants off, mister."

"I'm not proposing tonight. This was already a lot of decisions tonight, and I don't want to pressure you into something that big."

"Makes sense. I'll panic about it later. Now, speaking of 'that big,'" I said, looking down pointedly.

"Also, I was thinking we could use the den for your new office, and I'd like your thoughts on adoption. I mean, I'm happy as long as I have you, kids or no kids. But there's options, and we can talk about them later."

My heart tripped over itself and fell into my vagina. "I would really like to talk about those options later," I admitted.

He grinned, and in a flash, I envisioned our future together. Dogs and kids and way more animals than I was comfortable with. Family. Lazy days on the lake. Books. So many books.

"I'm going to need bookshelves," I announced.

"Zoey, I'll build you an entire library."

"Okay, cool. Glad that's settled. Now stop with the grand gesturing and put your cock in me!"

"I'm all yours, Disaster," he said, unzipping his jeans and depositing me on the counter.

"Wait wait wait," I said, planting my palms on his chest just as he notched himself into place between my legs. "Are you sure about this?"

He dropped his forehead to mine. "Sweetheart, you're so easy to love, I've never been more sure of anything."

"Damn, that's a good line," I sighed. "What kind of ring are you going to get me?"

"The sparkliest one I can find."

Epilogue

Fast-forward a few months
Zoey

I can't believe I'm here…on a terrace overlooking a lake…in a bridesmaid dress that I frantically had to scrub deodorant streaks out of…watching my best friend in the world marry her soulmate…while my fiancé makes "let's get naked" eyes at me from the other side of the aisle.

Of course I'm the maid of honor. And I look fabulous in my chiffon bridesmaid dress, especially since I no longer have to accessorize with a wrist brace. Broken bones *and* hearts have healed. This place is practically medicinal.

Hazel is so beautiful I can't look at her directly without crying. And Cam is as happy as I've ever seen him, which doesn't sound like much, but *trust me*. You'd believe in happily ever afters too just looking at them.

It's my second summer here, which means I've already sweated through my misapplied deodorant. This Pennsylvania humidity is no joke.

Which is why Gage and I are getting married this fall when cooler temperatures prevail. Did I mention we'll be getting married on his parents' farm? Yes, you heard that correctly. I, Zoey Moody, am getting married on a farm.

Life sure is funny, isn't it?

I never imagined I'd get married, let alone on a *farm*, let alone wake up in an actual barn under a pile of dogs next to a small-town, blue-collar hunk. But here I am. I'm basically glowing from daily orgasms and regular high-protein meals. It would be annoying as hell if it wasn't me.

It's been a busy few months. With Hazel's book becoming a #1 *New York Times* bestseller and Opal's big fat seven-figure advance, I climbed out of the financial hole and have been *responsibly* rebuilding my wardrobe as well as my retirement savings. I work out of the den that Gage sexily converted to a home office for me. He also extended the pasture so that it comes right up to my office window so Pepe the miniature donkey can say hi every day.

I know. I know. I take donkey-petting breaks. If it weren't for the curls and constant clumsiness, I might not recognize myself in the mirror.

When he's not terrorizing the tourists in town, Goose hangs out on our garage roof and shits all over the cupola. I think it's his love language. Gage says as long as the eagle doesn't start eating koi out of the pond, he'll just deal with power washing the roof once a week.

Mr. Responsible also insisted I get a new, more reliable car with all-wheel drive, so I did the irresponsible thing and gave Isla the Miata. I am officially the favorite aunt! Suck it, Hazel! And now I have an SUV with air-conditioned seats. So it was pretty much a win-win. Gage and I both keep dimes in our cupholders for luck.

In between ultimate bingo games (my team is in second place thanks mostly to having Gage as my cocaptain), Gage's dual businesses, and me coddling my authors into writing books, we're having an ongoing conversation about kids. (Me and Gage, not me and my authors.) Should we? How? How many?

It's a lot to process after so many years of accepting it just wasn't in the cards for me. But Gage makes everything feel possible. Plus, I feel less terrified at the prospect of raising kids, knowing that Pep and Frank are just over the hill with their decades of parenting expertise.

Things with my parents are still strained but a little less so. I didn't hear from them for a month or so after my birthday. Then both parents started texting me out of the blue. Mom about seeing Hazel and her book on the morning show and Dad asking for advice about his new wardrobe. We're a long way from healthy, and I don't think we'll ever have the deep, heartfelt "I'm sorry I wasn't the person you needed me to be" conversation. But I'm okay with it.

We're all just doing the best we can.

I am still a natural disaster. I still have ADHD. But I'm learning how to manage it (and myself) with a little more grace. I carry a paper calendar with me everywhere. Opal bought me a pair of incredibly expensive noise-canceling headphones that help me focus. And Gage has been a good sport about body doubling when I need to finish important tasks. Of course, it usually ends up in strip body doubling. But no one's complaining about that (except Declan, who walked in on us after-hours once just as Gage lost his pants).

Having a partner who loves and appreciates me even with all my little "quirks" makes life so much better.

And having me around has made Gage loosen up a little. He didn't even bat an eye when I set up an air mattress and a bunch of candles in the backyard so we could have sex outside during a meteor shower.

Of course, the dogs popped the mattress, and one of the candles caught the grass on fire. But the sex was still awesome. Life is an adventure!

Speaking of adventures, Levi has hinted—through a series of monosyllabic grunts and phrases—that he might be ready to share a draft of his book with me. It's kind of cute to see Mr. Tough Silent Guy creatively terrified.

I'm excited enough to read his manuscript that I haven't

warned him about Hazel. When she gets back from their honeymoon in Turks and Caicos, she's going to be looking for inspiration for the next story. Which means her matchmaking obsession will need a new target, and who better than the handsome, single, small-town cop?

Heh. Poor guy.

I can't wait to see what happens next!

That's life in Story Lake: Birds throw snakes at you here!

Acknowledgments

Kari March Designs for another spectacular cover.

Deb Werksman, Katie Stutz, and the rest of the team at Bloom Books for their vision and effort.

Team Lucy, including Joyce, Tammy, Lona, Rachel, Heather, Dan, and Tim for literally everything. Like, seriously.

Jess and the team at LEO PR for PR-ing me.

Flavia and Meire, the best agents ever.

Every sensitivity reader for their thoughtful suggestions.

Editor Jess for her eyeballs.

Narwhals for believing in themselves even when I didn't.

Jami and Erika for the best damn retreat ever. I love you!

James, Cissy, Nathan, and Boo. We might not have a castle, but we'll always have the Tiki Bar.

Madison, Avery, and Jill for being the best accountability sprinters an author could ask for.

Author's Note

Dear Reader,

I have a few things in common with our heroine, Zoey. Much like Zoey, I didn't know until (very) recently that narwhals are real. I too needed to be saved from a sweaty sports bra once. I had to interrupt Mr. Lucy during a video poker game with his friends to be extracted.

But perhaps my biggest similarity to Zoey is that I was also diagnosed with ADHD in my late thirties.

It was eight minutes into my first session when the therapist cut to the chase and changed my life. Decades of shame and failures finally made sense, and I was finally able to stop seeing myself as "lazy" or "stupid."

I've spent the years since doing research, finding the right medication for me, and learning life hacks to help me manage the way my brain operates.

I still make mistakes. I still can't follow verbal directions. And I still can't use my calendar app to save my life. But I no longer wallow in shame spirals triggered by executive function mishaps. I also have learned how to celebrate my wins because, as anyone who loves someone with ADHD knows, it's really hard for us to finish anything, let alone an entire book!

This *why* has made all the difference in how I feel about myself. And it meant a lot to me to finally be able to explore this personal journey on the page through Zoey.

Here are a few resources on Adult ADHD that I personally found helpful:

Dr. Russell Barkley: I recommend starting with some of his talks on YouTube.

Tracy Otsuka: I found Tracy's book, *ADHD for Smart Ass Women*, entertaining and informative.

How to ADHD: This YouTube channel is full of tips for adults living with ADHD.

Thanks so much for being so supportive of me and Zoey with all our flaws!

Xoxo,
Lucy

P.S. There's more Story Lake to come! Don't miss out on Levi's story in *Just One More Chapter*.

Sign up for her newsletter by scanning the QR code below and stay up on all the latest Lucy book news. You can also follow her here:

Website: Lucyscore.net
Facebook: lucyscorewrites
Instagram: scorelucy
TikTok: @lucyferscore
Binge Books: https://bingebooks.com/author/lucy-score
Readers Group: facebook.com/groups/
    BingeReadersAnonymous
Newsletter signup:

RAISING READERS
Books Build Bright Futures

Dear Reader,

We'd love your attention for one more page to tell you about the crisis in children's reading, and what we can all do.

Studies have shown that reading for fun is the **single biggest predictor of a child's future life chances** – more than family circumstance, parents' educational background or income. It improves academic results, mental health, wealth, communication skills, ambition and happiness.[1]

The number of children reading for fun is in rapid decline. Young people have a lot of competition for their time. In 2024, 1 in 10 children and young people in the UK aged 5 to 18 did not own a single book at home.[2]

Hachette works extensively with schools, libraries and literacy charities, but here are some ways we can all raise more readers:

- Reading to children for just 10 minutes a day makes a difference
- Don't give up if children aren't regular readers – there will be books for them!
- Visit bookshops and libraries to get recommendations
- Encourage them to listen to audiobooks
- Support school libraries
- Give books as gifts

There's a lot more information about how to encourage children to read on our website: **www.RaisingReaders.co.uk**

Thank you for reading.

---

[1] OECD, '21st-Century Readers: Developing Literacy Skills in a Digital World', 2021, https://www.oecd.org/en/publications/21st-century-readers_a83d84cb-en.html

[2] National Literacy Trust, 'Book Ownership in 2024', November 2024, https://literacytrust.org.uk/research-services/research-reports/book-ownership-in-2024